BEYOND
SHAME

to Kat:
Welcome to
Sector Four!

Kit
Rocha

kit rocha

Beyond Shame

Edited by Sasha Knight

ISBN-13: 978-1479327577
ISBN-10: 1479327573

For the people who keep us sane.

1

SHE'D BEEN CAST out of Eden and straight into Hell.

Noelle had never seen anything as menacing as the Sector Four slums at twilight. Back in the city, the buildings were elegant, each carefully planned to fit the aesthetic of those around it, each maintained by silent crews of landscapers and cleaners tasked with making every inch of the city sparkle. Shining towers with crystal windows reflected the endless blue sky, and straight roads intersected at perfect angles.

Here, in the slums outside Eden, squat, ugly buildings seemed dropped with careless imprecision. The roads followed no logic she could discern. Brick and wood alike were dark with soot from generators spitting smoke into the air. Graffiti covered the walls, lewd curses and symbols she couldn't begin to decipher. Garbage littered the cracked asphalt and dirt paths, broken glass and suspicious liquids. Noelle swallowed the pain of her ridiculous high heels and picked a careful path toward the end of the street.

Walking grew more difficult with every step. The military police had thrown her out the gate at the west checkpoint with nothing but the clothes on her back. No money or credits, just a pair of earrings and a colorful party dress she'd bought on the black market, a flashy bit of fabric meant to catch a boy's eyes.

It was still catching boys' eyes. She felt the weight of their gazes as she stumbled, barely catching her balance against the frame of a vendor's stall. Bright lights strung on wires twinkled above her head. Danced. She blinked and rubbed her eyes. The lights only swam worse, each flaring like a tiny sun trapped in glass.

Her mouth tasted odd. She touched her earlobe, felt the empty hole. She'd wasted the entire morning and most of the afternoon looking for someone who would trade cash for the glitzy baubles. Finally, one man had taken pity on her and traded a sandwich and a cup of juice for the earrings, laughing as he confided that his wife wouldn't know real diamonds from fakes.

Too aware of all the eyes on her, Noelle turned. The little table where she'd devoured her meager meal was around the corner, but the man who'd owned it wasn't. He was following her. Watching her.

Laughing.

Panic surged. Noelle spun and stopped, but the world kept on whirling by. Her ankle buckled and she pitched into a solid wall, a wall that reached out and grasped her arms in a steely grip.

A man frowned down at her, his gaze sweeping her body. She registered a stern face, dark, flat eyes and a full beard. Tattoos—on his wrists and arms, the kind they taught about in school and whispered about at church socials. The sector gangs, the rough criminals who controlled the slums and waged war on virtue and life.

She'd been cast into Hell, and he was a demon.

The strange girl in the even stranger dress collapsed in his arms, barely conscious. Jasper shifted her weight to one arm and bared his teeth at the man who'd been following her. "What's she on?"

The bastard looked ready to bolt until Ace stepped forward, one hand on his gun. Faced with two men wearing O'Kane ink, the man froze and did the only smart thing—he spilled his guts. "Just drops. Nothing serious."

"It's a piss-poor way to get a date," Jasper growled. "Dallas won't like it."

The shopkeeper blanched, but he choked out a wheedling defense. "Come on, man. It's a city bitch on a walk of shame. No one gives a shit."

Jasper pushed down his anger, hiding it behind a stony facade. "*I* give a shit. It might fly in other sectors, but not this one. If you can't pay for sex, use a little charm. If you don't have any of that either, keep it in your pants. Otherwise, you might have an accident. A nasty one."

Ace slid his thumb along the butt of his pistol. "Or you could have a nasty one now and get it over with."

"Fuck." The man raised both hands in a gesture of retreat and submission as he backed away. "Never again. You got it."

Jasper rolled his eyes and turned away, back toward the compound. "He'll be up to no good before nightfall."

"We can have Flash check in on him tonight." Ace

unsnapped a pocket on his vest and slipped out a thin black scanner. "Want me to tell you what you've got there?"

Jasper didn't want to know. The girl hung limply over his arm, her skin silky and unmarked. Her hair had the sort of sheen that came from regular trips to some city salon, and her fingernails were painted some gentle shade of pink none of Dallas's women would be caught dead wearing.

Soft. Everything about her, head to toe, was just *soft.*

He sighed and held out her arm. "May as well. We can't leave her here, can we?"

Ace slid the scanner over the inside of her wrist, where thin lines of ink formed her identification bar code. The box beeped, the sound somehow both melodious and strident, and Ace whistled through his teeth. "Shit. Maybe we should."

"Why, who is she?"

"That's a Cunningham. As in Edwin Cunningham, the whackjob councilman who wants to firebomb the sectors like God raining down fire on Sodom and Gomorrah."

Terrific. "Well, when she wakes up, we can ask her what the fuck she's doing on the wrong side of the wall."

"Judging by the state of her ID, the twitchy bastard following her was right. She's flagged as a second offender, all accounts frozen." Ace frowned. "Locked records, though. Can't tell what she did to get in trouble."

"Jaywalking?" Jasper suggested sourly.

Ace snorted as he pocketed his scanner. "More likely criminally poor taste. That dress looks like the sort of shit you pawn off on rich fuckheads by telling them it's pre-Flare vintage."

As if her dress mattered a damn. Jasper hefted her over his shoulder with another sigh. "Maybe Lex will know what to do with her."

"There are easier ways to get Lex nose-deep in pussy."

"Charming, but not what I meant."

The market cleared ahead of them. The denizens of Sector Four knew when to duck for cover, and if the military police came through here in an hour, no one would admit to seeing a member of O'Kane's gang carting a city girl off over his shoulder.

No one would dare.

Ace shook his head as they turned off the main street leading out of the market. "That princess over your shoulder? Probably a prissy little virgin. If dragging a stray like her home isn't about the corruption, it's not fucking worth it."

The insinuation that he couldn't simply feel sorry for her—that maybe he had to bring home a helpless, unconscious woman to fuck—made Jasper recoil with a frown. "Lex could show her the ropes—we need a new waitress at the club, don't we?"

"Yeah, but Dallas was going to bump one of the dancers over, maybe hire one of the groupies." Ace swung in front of Jasper, his dark eyes hard as he blocked the way. "I know you've got a soft spot for damsels, brother, but this piece of ass could get you killed. Are you *sure* you want to go out on this limb just because the girl fell on you?"

"No, but we can't dump her in the gutter and hope she makes out all right." Jasper knew what that was like, being helpless but still left to fend for yourself against shitty odds. "At the very least, she needs time to sober up."

"All right." Ace stepped aside and grinned at him. "Lex is going to kick your ass. You're not getting head for a month."

"S'okay. She bites."

"Only if you ask nicely."

"I CAN'T BELIEVE you did this, you jackass."
The words pierced darkness and splintered agony behind her eyes. Noelle groaned and pressed her hand to her forehead, as if she could hold the pieces of her shattered skull together. And it *had* to be a shattered skull—nothing else would explain the pain knifing through her.

"I didn't have a choice," a gruff voice murmured. "If I'd left her out there—"

"Don't kid yourself," the woman interrupted. "You didn't do her any favors. Look at her, for Christ's sake. You should have put her on the first transport out to the communes."

Communes. The word dragged her fully out of confused darkness. The communes were horrifying places where farmers lived primitive lives of indentured servitude. No electricity or running water, only backbreaking labor from dawn to dusk and being bred until you died in childbirth. Her father had threatened her with an ex-tended stay on the farms often enough to make her heart seize now. "No," she whispered, her voice cracking. "No communes."

A feminine hand pressed against the back of her neck. "Here, sit up and drink this."

Cold water splashed her lips, but hazy memories of the last drink she'd accepted made her pause. But she was parched...and helpless. The numbness of having lost everything melted into a hollow sort of trust, and she parted her lips and drank deeply before speaking. "Thank you."

"Sure, honey."

The man huffed out a sigh. "Lex—"

"Forget it." The woman tipped the cup to Noelle's lips again. "Let Dallas sort it out. He's the man in charge, isn't he?"

"I called him already."

"Good." Lex set down the cup and snapped her fin-gers in front of Noelle's face. "How many fingers?"

Noelle blinked and focused on the woman's fingers. "I'm not injured, just confused. Where am I?"

"Sector Four. The Broken Circle."

She'd heard of it. Who hadn't? The Broken Circle— the heart of sin, the club her friends spoke about in whispers because no one was brave enough to bribe an official for a pass into the sectors. The moonshine that had gotten them all arrested had been taboo enough.

"O'Kane Liquor," she whispered, remembering the black-and-white labels affixed to the bottles. "This is where it comes from." But how had she ended up here?

"Comes from a warehouse across the compound, ac-tually, but close enough." The woman held out her hand. "I'm Lex."

"Noelle." The other woman's hand was soft but strong. She looked tough, even before Noelle struggled to sit up and caught sight of Lex's clothes—leather boots with stiletto heels and the kind of sleek, skimpy lingerie you couldn't find in Eden, not unless you bought it under the table from a black-market vendor. Noelle had never seen a person bare so much skin with so little concern, so little *shame*.

Lex lifted an eyebrow. "See what I mean, Jas? She's looking at me like I have two heads."

The man frowned—an expression that seemed habitual, if not permanent. "She's from the city."

Now that she was upright, Noelle could see him too. He filled the corner of the room with his bulk, made it seem smaller just with his presence. His clothing was as foreign as Lex's, everything cut from denim and leather and edged with silver and steel. His forearms were covered with ink, and the dark swaths snapped her disjointed memories into sharp clarity.

Being thrown from the city by a stone-faced guard.

The drugged juice and the man following her.

Stumbling into the arms of a gang member.

She forced her gaze to his. "You saved me."

His eyes widened in a flash of panic. "Uh, no. You fell on me."

But he'd caught her. He hadn't left her in the street, at the mercy of the predators prowling the sectors. He hadn't hurt her. And the panic in his gaze intrigued her—surely if he was the monster she'd been taught, he'd be eager to accept credit. To twist her gratitude into obligation, and then use that to place lurid, degrading demands on her. The kind she wasn't supposed to know about.

He hadn't done anything of the sort. He'd simply been kind, and that deserved kindness in return. "Thank you for catching me."

Lex covered her face with her hands and mumbled something under her breath.

The door slammed open hard enough to send Noelle's heart rocketing into her throat. A slightly older man stepped through, clad in a leather vest that bared tattooed arms, and pinned her rescuer with an irritated look. "Jasper, you're a pain in my ass."

He rose. "Come on, Dallas. You would've done the same damn thing."

"God willing, we'll never know." He leveled a finger at Noelle, the gesture somehow menacing *and* exasperated. "Three questions. You'll answer them honestly or I'll boot your ass back into the street."

She'd fared badly out there before, so Noelle laced her fingers together to hide their trembling. "Honest answers," she promised.

"Good." He flicked up one finger. "Is your father motherfucking Edwin Cunningham?"

Shame heated her cheeks even as pain sank claws in her chest. "Yes. Though he's probably already filing the paperwork to have me officially severed from the family."

A grunt. Dallas held up a second finger. "Your ID shows two offenses. What'd you get arrested for?"

Oh, no. She couldn't admit it in front of Lex, and certainly not in front of her rescuer. Jasper. Humiliation joined the mix of emotions churning in her middle as she stared at the floor and forced herself to answer. "Possession and consumption of alcohol and—" The word froze on her tongue. She had to whisper it. "Fornication."

Silence. Then Lex shook her head with a disgusted snort. "Bunch of dickless bastards." She turned on Dallas, her shoulders squared. "She can stay with me until she gets on her feet."

"That's the third question. Look at me, Noelle Cunningham." Compelled by his voice, she lifted her gaze to his. He had steely eyes, seductive and overpowering at once, and she had to fight to focus on his words. "Do you want me to put you on a bus out to the communes right now? If not, the best I can offer you is a week's probation under Lex. I'm not taking a poor little rich girl from Eden into this gang until I know she can handle it. So do you want a week of training, or do you want the bus?"

Two choices. Two lives. The farms would wear down her body. They had fertility drugs there, the kind that counteracted the contraceptives administered in Eden to prevent overpopulation. Resources were precious in the city—but in the communes, babies *were* resources. Fornication wasn't a sin there, but sex was only acceptable as a means of making more strong bodies to work the land and make the farm owners rich. In Eden, they called it noble work. Honorable. Toil for the body to enrich the spirit, surely deserving of eternal reward.

None of the things that might happen to her body in the sectors would enrich her spirit. The gangs outside Eden knew a thousand ways to sin, and—according to Noelle's father—ten thousand ways to secure a place in Hell.

If she were righteous, there'd be only one possible choice.

If she were righteous, she'd still be in Eden. "I don't want to go to the communes."

"Fine." Dallas pointed at Lex. "She gets full fucking disclosure. If she's not willing to tend bar, clean house, or suck dick by the end of the week, she's gone."

"Fuck you," Lex shot back pleasantly.

"Hop on my cock anytime, love." He jabbed his finger at Jasper. "You, out. There's a shipment over at the warehouse that needs your attention."

"I'm on it." Jasper hesitated. "If she needs any-thing—"

"She won't," Lex interjected. "Now get out." When the door slammed behind him, Lex dropped to a chair across from Noelle. "You hanging out for all the gritty details, Dallas? I know you get off on it."

Dallas raked his gaze over them in a way that made Noelle think perhaps he was imagining them both naked—and enjoying it. He grinned slowly as he hauled open the door. "Another time. Have Ace fill in her bar code, but no cuffs. Not until she makes it through the week."

He snapped the door shut behind him, and Noelle let out a breath and tried to meet Lex's eyes without flinching. "You must all think I'm a ridiculous, naïve fool."

"Of course you are." Lex leaned back in her chair and crossed her legs. "You're from the city. They won't let you be anything else."

No judgment, at least, and maybe even a little sympathy. "I tried to be something else. That probably makes me more of a fool."

"Only if you thought it'd work." Lex pulled a small etched silver case from her boot. "Not many rules. First one is, the group means more than anything. We survive because we stick together—no exceptions. If you join up, it won't be a free ride, but it'll be a good one."

Tend bar, clean house, or suck dick. Noelle stared down at her brightly patterned dress and traced a finger over one swirl. A dark craving dug its hooks into her as the fantasy formed, one where she wasn't responsible for the filthy things they commanded her to do. Surely it couldn't be a sin if she didn't have a choice. "I'd have to give them all sex?"

"Nope. You don't have to lay a finger on anyone, not if you don't want to. Get a job, work the club, whatever. The sex is a bonus, not an obligation."

Noelle *was* sick, twisted, because the only emotion she felt at hearing the words was vague disappointment—and crushing shame to cover it. "Oh. That's good."

Lex grimaced. "I thought you were into fornication.

What a waste. Anyway, one of the runners managed to get his hands on some fertility drugs, and now he and his woman are having a baby. She used to wait tables at the club, so there's an open job there. Ever done that sort of thing?"

"No." Her mother would have slapped her hard enough to leave marks for a week if Noelle had breathed a word about working outside the house. "I can learn, though. I've read books about pre-Flare technology, and I'm a hard worker."

"Any dance lessons?"

Finally, a question she could answer in the affirmative. "From the time I was five."

"But none of them were on a pole, right?"

She shouldn't even know what the question meant. Pornography was every bit as illegal as liquor, but it was the only place in Eden to learn about a stripper pole. "No, not exactly."

Lex just nodded. "If you don't want to wait tables, we can show you a few things about stripping. There's a ton of credits in it. Not as much as the hardcore shows, though."

Surely she didn't mean... "Isn't that illegal?"

Lex paused in the act of lighting a cigarette, her lighter sparked and waiting. "Honey, you're not in Eden anymore. The only laws here are the ones Dallas hands down."

"I'm not in Eden anymore." The words hit her in the gut, stark and real, the first thing to come close to penetrating her creeping numbness. Her breath rattled out of her lungs, and she shuddered and fought to drag it back in. "I'm not—I'm not in Eden anymore."

"Oh shit." Lex tossed the unlit cigarette aside. "Hey, it's okay."

"No, I know." Noelle clutched at her silly dress and tried to force herself to breathe normally. She wasn't in

Eden anymore, so she might as well avail herself of one of the advantages. "Can I have a drink?"

"No." Lex held up her hands. "I'm not an uptight bitch, but you were rolling pretty hard when you came in here. I don't want to accidentally kill you."

Of course. Stupid. Noelle closed her eyes. "You're right."

The other woman sighed. "Look, bottom line. No one's going to force you to do anything you don't want to do. You have to work, but you can keep all your clothes on while you do it. And don't fucking listen to Dallas—he won't set you out. Not if I ask him not to."

It was too much to process. The loss of everything Noelle had, everything she'd ever known, everything she was...and the tantalizing promise of freedom that made her want to *hope* when hope was an emotion she'd never learned how to feel. "I think I'm just overwhelmed, and maybe still fuzzy from whatever that man gave me."

"Then you need to rest." Lex crossed the room and pulled a pillow and a blanket out of the small closet by the bathroom. "Want something else to wear?"

Anything besides her fancy party dress. "A nightgown, maybe?"

"Uh, T-shirt?"

"All right." Noelle managed a smile. "No more layers and layers of modest clothing, I guess. That's a good thing, right?"

Lex handed her a folded bundle of white fabric. "It's whatever you make of it, honey. Whatever you want, it's all up to you."

What a terrifying thought. "The last time things were up to me, I got arrested."

"Then I guess it's all looking up from here, huh?"

"I hadn't thought of it that way." But maybe it was time she started.

Noelle woke in darkness, disorienting in and of itself. She blinked up at the empty space above her and tightened her fingers around the blankets as her heart tried to hammer its way out of her chest.

She wasn't in Eden, that much was certain. Her bedroom had too many sources of illumination—the glow of the display panels that controlled the brightness and temperature in her suite, the soft light from the computer screen embedded in her desk, even the moon and streetlights shining through her gauzy curtains. Her family might live in the penthouse, far above street level, but Eden was a city of light. Too many of her parents' generation remembered the years of darkness, after the solar storms had plunged the world into chaos and shadow.

Her mother had been afraid of the dark, but Noelle had never shared that anxiety. Still, she felt a twinge of it now as she wet her lips and spoke. "Lights, twenty percent?" She turned it into a question out of instinct, and her answer was more darkness.

No, no one out in the sectors would rely on computers for something pre-Flare technology could handle just fine with far less expense. Which meant she had to stumble out of bed and find a light switch. How deliciously uncivilized.

The cement floor was cool under her bare feet, and rough. No plush carpets softened the hard expanse, only a rug half hidden by the bed that had folded out of the couch. Noelle skirted the edge of the mattress with halting steps and blinked into the gloom, trying to make out the shapes around her.

She stumbled a little as she worked her way around the room, but eventually her questing fingers encountered a switch. Turning it on flooded the room with low, diffuse light, something that made everything visible enough but kept the corners shadowed and the room itself...intimate.

Or maybe it only seemed that way because of the bed. All of Lex's furniture was nice, but her bed dominated one side of the room, piled with sleek cushions and luxurious sheets that could have easily belonged in Noelle's bedroom back home. High quality, expensive—and utterly out of place surrounded by unadorned brick walls and cement floors.

There were four doors Noelle could see. One opened out into the hallway, and another she thought might be the closet. Hoping one of the remaining two led to a bathroom, she opened the one closest to her and found a treasure trove instead.

This second room was smaller and contained only a table and a pair of chairs. But the walls were covered in art—not the digital kind displayed on the enormous plasma screens currently popular in Eden, but pre-Flare masterpieces. Hypnotized, Noelle moved to stand in front of the closest painting, an Impressionist piece in a gilded frame.

This close, she could smell the slightly musty scent of the canvas and paint, could see the individual brushstrokes. She touched a faded red rose petal and marveled at the subtle ridges of the paint, three-dimensional and *vivid* in a way nothing in Eden was, not anymore.

Lex spoke sharply from the doorway. "That's probably older than anything you've ever owned. You might want to stop pawing it."

Noelle stumbled, shoving her hands behind her back, as if that would change what was already done. "I'm sorry. I've never seen anything like it outside of textbooks. I was just—" What? Snooping? No explanation was adequate.

"Having a look around. I get it." Lex dropped her black knapsack in the corner and began to peel off the high-collared jacket she wore. "It was a gift. The Renoir, I mean."

Noelle tugged at the hem of her borrowed T-shirt, self-conscious about her bare legs. "It's beautiful. Priceless. Someone must think very highly of you."

The woman snorted and turned toward a small sliding door on the far wall. "It cost money. Some people have more of that than they know what to do with."

Lex seemed to be one of them. Noelle tried not to be nosy, but the open closet door revealed tangled piles of jewelry and sculptures mixed with electronics that must have been smuggled from the city at great cost. She even saw one or two sleek weapons—guns, honest-to-God *guns*, something she'd rarely seen within the walls of Eden, and never anywhere but in the hands of the military police.

Noelle turned her attention back to the painting, back to Lex's words. People—men—with more money than they knew what to do with. Eden had its share of those. More than its share. "I'm familiar with people like that. They think they can buy anything. Or anyone." And in her experience, they usually could.

"No, not—" Lex stowed her bag and faced Noelle. "You can't buy people here with money, especially women. You buy them with security, safety, all the things that have always been true in societies where men hold the power. But we hold power, too. Remember that—there are things we have, things we can offer. Things they need."

Noelle couldn't imagine that any of the men here gave a damn about the things she'd been raised and trained to do. Organizing and managing a household, hosting elaborate dinner parties where she smiled at important city leaders and used her mother's encyclopedic knowledge of their foibles and vanities to flatter them into agreeable moods.

Noelle gripped the hem of her shirt again. "I don't have much to offer the men here. Except..." If she couldn't even choke out the word, how was she supposed to offer them sex?

"Fucking is the least of it," Lex muttered. "Everyone has a couple of holes a guy can stick his dick in. The important stuff is all above the neck."

It felt like her entire body had flushed, but Noelle fought past self-consciousness. "What's the important stuff?"

"Using your brain, baby girl. There's nothing you need to know about anyone that you can't figure out in ten seconds flat." She beckoned. "Follow me."

Lex walked into the bedroom, flicked on another lamp on the nightstand and sat on the bed, crossing her legs. "Now—how do you get under my skin? What do I like?"

During the course of their acquaintance, Lex had shouted at Jasper, whose formidable presence weakened Noelle's knees, and had snapped just as viciously at Dallas O'Kane, a figure of criminal legend. Everyone in Sector Four lived or died by Dallas's whim—Lex had admitted as much when she'd said he made the laws here.

But she'd yelled at him, and she hadn't shown fear. Noelle sank to the edge of the bed and rubbed her fingers over the expensive duvet. She thought about the priceless art, the silken sheets and the closet full of valuables hidden away like a treasure instead of displayed proudly, the way her father's friends showed off the things they bought with their vast wealth.

"You like beautiful things, but you don't need them to make you feel important." She smiled a little shyly. "Maybe you have a soft spot for things that get thrown away."

Lex laughed. "The last part's true." Her amusement faded. "Dallas gave me the paintings."

Noelle wet her lips. "Are you and Dallas—" Did people marry in the sectors? In Eden, marriage was a sacrament, but nothing sacred was likely to survive in the slums. "—together?"

"What do you think? If he had me already, would he be dropping thousands on pretty presents to catch my eye?"

"Perhaps not." She tilted her head and regarded Lex, searching for the meaning beneath the words. "Is that the only power we have? Not being caught?" The thought turned Lex's blithe freedom into its own sort of cage.

"No. It's your first lesson." Lex brushed Noelle's hair back behind her ear. "It's not like in the city. Belonging to someone isn't the endgame, the point where they're allowed to get lazy. It's a beginning, one you have to be damn sure you want."

Her skin prickled under the other woman's touch. Not sexual arousal, not exactly, but a sensual pleasure she'd only begun to crave when she'd started spending time with people who violated the social taboo forbidding unnecessary physical contact.

"Thank you," she blurted out, leaning in to Lex's touch. "For convincing Dallas to give me a chance. I'll learn anything I need to learn. I can't go to the communes—they're even worse than Eden."

"You'd go if you had to, and you'd be all right. Trust me, honey. *That* is the important thing."

To Noelle's everlasting humiliation, her eyes burned. She blinked them twice before realizing there was no stopping it, then squeezed them shut as the first tear slipped free. "I didn't really think my family would throw me away. I only wanted to feel something. I know I was privileged, that I must seem like a spoiled city brat..."

Her chest felt *tight*, as if all the weight of Eden's claustrophobic expectations were closing in on her again.

"Are you kidding me?" Lex pulled her into a hug and made soothing noises. "No offense, baby girl, but I wouldn't have had your life there for anything."

Her tears soaked Lex's shirt, but the answer was there, just beyond reach. "Why?" Noelle didn't even know what she was asking. Why wouldn't Lex want her life? Why hadn't it been enough for *her*? Why had she thrown it all away?

Lex answered them all with three words. "You weren't free," she said. "You can be here, you know. Dallas talks big about shit, but he's never forced a woman to do anything she didn't want. Remember that too, Noelle."

"I don't know what I want. I don't know *anything*."

"That's why you try things. Eventually, you stumble across the ones that make you happy." Lex kissed her cheek. "And you learn. Everything anyone tells you, file it away in that brain of yours."

She could do that. She'd always been mind-hungry, devouring everything in her parents' digital library before going so far as to learn how to circumvent tablet security to gain access to the more restricted titles, old books from a time before fear and morality had swallowed everything. "I'm good at remembering things."

Lex patted her back. "Go crawl in bed, honey. I'd let you stay in mine, but I don't think you really want to."

She rather did, and not just because the sheets would feel heavenly against her skin. Touching Lex meant having an anchor instead of being cast adrift in the darkness that would soon envelop the room.

But she'd already cried and laid her soul bare. Enough humiliation for one lifetime, let alone a single evening. She slipped from Lex's enormous bed and crawled back onto the lumpy mattress that folded out of the couch. "Can you help me find a job tomorrow?"

"We'll see, all right?"

It was as close to a promise as she was likely to get. Noelle settled her head against the pillow and closed her eyes, feeling more hopeful than she had in...forever, maybe. "Thank you, Lex."

The lamp clicked off, followed by the overhead lights. Clothing rustled in the darkness, and a light flared, illuminating the space closest to the couch. "Here," Lex murmured, setting the tiny round lamp on the end table near Noelle's head.

The glow was just enough to paint Lex's features in intriguing shadows, but not so bright that it would give Noelle trouble sleeping. "I guess you only needed ten seconds to figure me out," she said, trying to turn the words into a joke.

"Maybe a little more. Get me drunk sometime, and I'll tell you what I figured out."

How convenient it would be to have Lex explain Noelle's own secrets to her. Then she wouldn't have to bother to learn them herself. "As soon as you'll let me drink."

"Uh-huh. Good night, Noelle."

lex

S HE DIDN'T ASK Dallas for much, never had, but
she'd ask him for this.

Lex leaned against the side of the car. "She doesn't
have anyone, and she's helpless. Tossing her out on her
ass would just be *wrong.*"

Under the hood, Dallas grunted as metal clanged on
metal. "Eden spits out a dozen like her a week, love.
That's what happens when you only give reproductive
drugs to the righteous. They pop out ignorant, helpless
babies like it's a contest to see who can produce the most
useless human being."

"She has a name, you know." Lex reached out to
trace the shell of his ear. "And if she were really useless,
she'd be crying in a heap on my bedroom floor."

Dallas spared her a look, turning his head just
enough to bite the tip of her finger. "Don't tell me she's

not damn close to it."

"A couple weeks, okay? Give her a chance. She'll probably blow you once or twice and then settle down, make one of the guys very, very happy."

He snorted and focused on the old car's engine again. "That girl couldn't spit out the word fornication without turning fifteen shades of red. What the hell happened after I left? I miss a hot time?"

Not even close, but the spark was there. The hunger. Lex could practically taste it. "She wants to be a little bad. How is she going to do that on a peanut farm or whatever?"

Sighing, Dallas straightened and tossed aside the wrench. "Are you seeing what's really there, Lexie? Or what you want to see?"

As if he knew the first damn thing about what she wanted. "Easy way to find out. You throwing a party tonight?"

"I was, yeah." He wiped his hands on a rag and rubbed his thumb over her lower lip, a clear sign that his thoughts had shifted from cars to sex. "You think she could survive it?"

"One way to find out." He still tasted like motor oil and metal. Lex licked the pad of his thumb and wrapped her fingers around his belt buckle. "Are you saving your strength for later?"

"My strength doesn't need saving, love. Not with you around."

His jeans were already tightening across the hard bulge of his cock. Lex kept hold of his belt and pulled him toward the back door of the warehouse.

Inside, she reached under his shirt and traced circles over his chest while her vision adjusted to the near darkness of the back hall. Dallas leaned against the wall and watched her through narrowed eyes. "Don't think I'm not on to you, girl."

She tensed, but only for a moment, before unbuckling his belt. "What do you mean?"

He caught her wrist with one hand and her chin with the other. "Don't get on your knees for this. If you're that damn taken with the girl, she can stay. Hell, have Ace give her the full wrist cuffs if you want."

Relief warred with anger. He hadn't really figured her out, that secret part of her with all its insane desires. But the fact that he thought she'd use her body, her mouth, as currency, pissed her off plenty.

Lex still had one hand free, and she slapped him with it. "I'm not a whore. Not even for you."

She'd seen Dallas kill men for less, but he only growled and caught her other wrist. "Everyone's a whore for me *except* you. It gets goddamn tedious."

She could barely think with his fingers wrapped around her wrists, trapping her and yet careful not to squeeze tight. "Liar. You need me to keep your head on straight. Just one person you can't buy."

His laugh swept over her. "Sweet, silly bitch. The whores are the tedious ones."

Too close. Too intimate. "So let it lie, Declan," she urged, using his given name. "And apologize, for fuck's sake."

He moved fast, jerking her around to crash against the wall, her hands pinned next to her head. "Watch the sharp side of your tongue, Lex," he rumbled, voice low and dangerous. He loomed over her, his heat its own oppressive weight.

No room to move, breathe, nothing but *him*, everywhere. "Why don't *you* watch my tongue?" She started to slide down the wall. When she was halfway to her knees, he released her hands, sinking his fingers into her hair instead.

Hard didn't begin to describe him now. His erection jutted against his fly, jumping when she smoothed her palm over its length. "Do you want my mouth?"

Dallas growled and tightened his grip on her hair, skating the line between arousal and real pain. "Am I breathing?"

"Don't know." She hummed as she opened his pants and wrapped her fist around his dick. "You've got a strong pulse, though."

His head fell back as he pushed against her hand with another of those hungry, rough noises. "You going to teach your little stray how to do this? If she can get half as good as you at sucking dick, maybe she *will* get marked."

Noelle would wind up marked anyway, just as soon as she learned to let go a little. "I thought men liked the wide-eyed innocence."

"Men think they like wide-eyed innocence until someone like you swallows their cock down like she can't get enough of it." He forced her head back at a rough angle. "Or did you see something I didn't, clever girl?"

"Like Jasper showing off his protective side?" Lex teased her tongue over her lower lip. "Watch them together. You'll see."

"All the girls throw themselves on Mr. Hero. He lets them bounce on him for a little while, and then he bounces them right back off." A rock of Dallas's hips bumped the head of his cock against her mouth. "Goddamn, Lex. Fucking blow me already."

One quick lick, followed by a slower one, over and over in succession until his shaft gleamed wet enough to slide between her lips. Not too much pressure, not at first.

"Never enough," he growled, slapping one palm against the wall. His entire body shook with restrained hunger, but he didn't thrust against her mouth. Not yet.

Instead, he demanded with words. "Harder, Lex."

She complied, but only for a moment. Then she

pulled away and stroked him with her hand.

"Tease." Pressing one thumb against her lips, he smiled slowly. "I think I changed my mind. I *am* saving my strength for tonight. I want a hell of a show."

Lex took a deep breath to ease the sharp pang of disappointment. "Maybe I won't bother."

"Oh, you'll bother." He stepped away and tucked his cock back into his pants. "I'll know you're really pissed if all I get to do is watch."

"Or I won't show at all." Even as she spoke, she knew the words for a lie. She'd go, all right, just to make him watch another man spend the night face down in her lap.

"We'll see. Up, Lexie love."

She rose, hunger still twisting in her belly. "Have fun trying not to walk funny."

Dallas gripped her chin and kissed her hard and fast, nothing but growls and teeth and gone a moment later. "The girl can stay as long as you keep an eye on her. Bring her around to Rachel. See if she's waitress material."

Rachel wasn't even waitress material. She should have been the one tinkering under the hood of that car outside, because God knew she was better at it than most of the men, including Dallas. "And the party?"

His smile was positively wicked. "Let's leave that to Jasper."

Lex held his gaze as she traced her index finger over the corner of her mouth and licked her fingertip. "Yes, sir."

3

B REN SLID INTO the back seat, but he left the door open and one foot on the ground. He never shut himself into a car until they were ready to roll. "We leaving now?"

"Waiting for Flash," Jasper muttered.

"Aw, shit. Did we check to see if he had his hand in Amira's pants? 'Cause that'll take all day."

Flash jerked open the front passenger door. "That's why I have a woman and you don't."

"Something you never let anyone forget," Bren drawled.

The third man folded his immense body into the front seat and grinned, looking entirely self-satisfied. "Marking that girl was the smartest move I ever made. You think the women are hot *before* they get the ink around their throats? You have no fucking idea."

Flash's satisfaction was a tangible thing, filling the scant space left in the car. Jasper started the engine. "Where's this place supposed to be?"

The man's smugness melted away, replaced by brisk, businesslike seriousness. "Over by the border with Five, just outside the second perimeter. I think they took over an abandoned church."

"Are they stupid or desperate?"

"Probably both."

Both was dangerous. Jas pointed the car toward their destination. "Our orders from Dallas are to tear it down. Standard shit. This is their warning. If they rebuild, we tear *them* down."

"Standard shit," Bren agreed.

"Violence and mayhem." Flash grinned. "I hope someone takes a swing at me."

Jas unbent enough to smile. "And ruin that pretty face?"

"Didn't say I'd let them hit me." Flash clenched his fists. "I'm itching to deal a little damage. Property, people... Whatever gets in my way."

Bren leaned over the back of the front seat. "Save it for the cage. Pick up some extra money."

"Why, you going to climb in there with me?"

"Hell, no. But there's never any shortage of dumbasses who will."

"Chicken." Flash muttered the word, but there wasn't much heat behind it. He played for keeps in the cage and didn't relish facing off against the few men he actually liked. "So what's the deal with the new girl? Amira says she's like a baby deer in the woods."

Jas shifted gears as the car pulled free of the more congested, debris-scattered streets and gained speed. "Something like that." A woman desperate to find a place and a little bit of safety was more like it.

"I hope she takes to waiting tables. Maybe then

Amira'll quit bitching that Rachel's got too much on her shoulders. She's pissed I won't let her work, but fuck if she's gonna haul trays around when she's pregnant with my kid."

"She could do something less physically taxing," Jasper pointed out.

"I don't want her around outsiders, either."

No, Flash wouldn't rest easy having her exposed to unknown dangers. "Amira's sharp. Dallas could probably use her help with paperwork. Keeping the books."

Flash grunted and glanced at Bren. "No smartass comments from you?"

"What? He's right." Bren shrugged. "The only questionable thing the woman's ever done is place her bets on a monster like you."

"Monsters always get the girls," Flash said, his haughty arrogance returning. "We're the ones who can keep them safe."

Safe. Jas swallowed a growl. Amira wanted a damn sight more from Flash than that, and she got it—even if the man barely seemed to realize it. She always watched him with a mix of adoration and indulgence, and none of it had to do with his macho posturing.

As usual, Flash was oblivious. "Up here." He pointed to an intersection where rundown buildings sagged alongside burned-out warehouses.

Jas slowed the car and took a turn around the block. "Remember what I said, both of you. No blood."

"And if they hit first?"

"Then you do what you've got to do."

Bren checked his sidearm as Jas parked in a shadowed spot in the alley. "We've got it—no excessive force."

"No excessive force." Jasper jerked open his door.

Flash popped the car's trunk and pulled out a sledgehammer before falling in behind him as they headed for the side door of the warehouse. "Is kicking the door in excessive?"

"Come on, man." Bren stretched his neck and grinned. "Jasper's polite. He'd rather knock."

Flash tightened his grip on his makeshift weapon with an answering expression of mirth. "Good. That'll make the surprise bigger when I rip the place up. Go on, lover boy. Knock."

"You both talk too much." Jas shouldered through the door and watched as the men surrounding the copper monstrosity in the center of the room scattered. "Nice still, boys."

The leader cursed and dove for a gun, swinging it up to point at Jasper's forehead as chaos erupted behind him. "We're on the border between sectors," he snapped. "This isn't O'Kane territory."

Bren swore and reached into his jacket, but Jas held up a hand as he stared down the barrel of the gun. There had been a time when the sight had scared him, a time when that tiny little black space inside the muzzle had expanded to encompass the world, and he'd been so sure it could swallow him whole.

It still could. Jasper wondered idly where the fear had gone, then forced his thoughts back to the task at hand. "It's possible you don't understand what a non-compete clause is. I've come to explain it to you."

The gun barrel wavered. "What the fuck sort of fucking bullshit is this?"

"It's an opportunity," Jas said evenly. "A chance to start over someplace else."

The blond man hesitated, his gaze leaping to Bren and Flash and back. "We can't move our operation."

"Yes, you can." Jasper gripped the man's wrist and twisted until the barrel of the gun pointed toward the exposed steel rafters above. "Once we're done, you won't be operational anymore. Easy enough to move then."

As if to punctuate the point, Flash hefted the sledgehammer and swung it through a crate of bottles. Everything shattered, wood and glass alike, crashing to the ground.

Blondie cursed and tried to free his gun hand. "Fuck, you can't do that."

Jasper gestured Bren forward to check the tanks. "First warning's your only warning. Next time, Flash tosses that sledge through your face."

"Tanks are clear," Bren declared. "Looks like they're between batches."

Two of the men started forward when Flash lifted his weapon again. A snarl and bared teeth had them scrambling back, and Flash demolished their remaining supplies in an orgy of gratuitous destruction, the very recklessness of it its own message. O'Kane didn't need to steal supplies from competitors. O'Kane would just wipe them off the map.

Jas didn't release his grip on the leader's wrist, even when the man kept fidgeting. Instead, he spoke calmly. "You're going to let us walk out of here with no trouble and go set up shop someplace else. You're going to do it because nothing here is worth dying for. Yes?"

The leader rolled his eyes toward his men, who looked torn between rage and disgust. He could let Jasper walk away, but he wouldn't be leading anyone.

He knew it, too. Bravado and bluff filled his eyes. "There're more of us than there are of you."

"Yes, that's true."

He twisted fast, thrusting his free hand behind his back. Another gun. Jasper jerked the man's arm with a snap. "Don't."

The second gun spilled from nerveless fingers as Flash stomped across the floor, scattering splintered wood, glass shards, and cheap liquor across the cement. "Boss?"

"Back to the car. They've learned their lesson." He

squeezed a little harder, and the bones in the leader's wrist ground together. "Haven't they?"

"Yes," came the pained, shaky whisper. "We're gone."

He released him and stepped back. "Don't forget—Dallas O'Kane doesn't do second chances."

No one tried to stop them as they left. No one said a damn word.

Back in the car, Flash heaved a sigh. "So much for a fight. What a bunch of limp-dick cowards."

Cowardice or intelligence, Jasper didn't really care what had motivated them. "Would you rather fight, Flash? All it takes for someone to get the jump on you is a split second, and Amira could be raising that kid alone."

"She'll never be alone," Flash shot back, "not while she's an O'Kane." He shifted on the seat with a growl. "Are you telling me you don't miss it, even a little? Having to *fight* to protect our territory instead of showing up and watching them all piss themselves?"

"Of course I miss it," Jasper muttered. If he didn't, he wouldn't spend so much time in the brawling ring and the cage. "But this is what we were fighting for. Enough recognition and respect to not have to spend all our time cracking heads to get the point across."

Bren spoke from the back seat. "He's saying you should get your ya-yas out some other way, 'cause this is the new standard operating procedure."

"Fuckin' hell." Flash grumbled for a few minutes more before subsiding with a sigh and switching back to his favorite topic. "The cage is better anyway. Amira gets fucking wild watching. You two don't know what you're missing."

Bren kicked the seat. "But you're gonna tell us—at length, whether we want you to or not."

How would Noelle react to the violence of the cage fights? Amira knew how members of the gang blew off steam and settled scores amongst themselves. Noelle, on the other hand, was used to pacifism. Civility.

And look where it got her, a voice growled deep inside him. *Drugged and helpless, waiting to die.*

Flash was still running his mouth. "Since when do you not like the dirty details? Or am I supposed to shut up 'cause the bleeding heart over here's got his panties in a twist? Honestly, Jas, why *are* you in such a fucking foul mood?"

"Because I have to deal with you. Isn't that enough?"

"Nah, I'm a laugh a minute."

Jasper didn't fight his grin. "Your face is."

"Least it's not my dick. Poor Bren."

Bren snorted. "Amira seems to like it okay."

Flash lunged, driving his hip into Jasper's arm as he swung at Bren between the seats.

Jasper swore and jerked the wheel to correct their course, but the left front bumper clipped an already-dented garbage can. "This is one of Dallas's new cars. He just got it running the way he wants it."

"Fucker." Flash settled on his seat. "I'll punch you when we're back home."

"When we get back, we're all going to have a drink and think of a good way to break the news about the busted headlight to Dallas."

Noelle couldn't carry a tray worth a damn.

Not that it mattered much. Lex had poured her into a pair of leather pants that hugged her ass and a halter top that only precariously covered her tits. Jasper caught himself staring, watching for the inevitable moment when the slinky silver fabric would shift just a *little* too far.

"We're stuck with her," Dallas drawled next to him.

"We might as well ink your waif now. Lex went and got attached, and now she'll take my dick off if I kick the girl to the curb."

Dallas wasn't scared of Lex, not for a second, which meant something more like sentimentality—or mercy—motivated him. "She's trying. After a day, that's about all you can ask."

"Yeah, she's trying." Dallas ignored the women gyrating on stage and watched Noelle smile at two customers as she set drinks in front of them. "And she's a little lost lamb in a den of wolves."

The other waitress who'd been training her, Rachel, joined Noelle in animated conversation with the customers, and Jasper finally looked down into his glass. "Maybe Lex'll keep her."

"Unlikely." Dallas stirred his drink. "If it'll bother you when the men start fighting over her, you better get straight. Because that girl wants it, and when she gets around to admitting it, the boys are gonna give it to her."

Jasper didn't have time for a woman, much less one with big eyes who would expect *things*. "What, you don't like her?"

A shrug. "She's got a nice ass. Pretty mouth. I like the idea of Lex teaching her how to give head. But I'm not in the market for a keeper."

Jasper let his gaze stray back to Noelle. "Neither am I."

As if she could feel his gaze, she glanced up and smiled, an open expression edged with a hint of shyness. An unwitting invitation.

Dallas snorted. "That one's in the market to keep *you*."

How could she be? "She doesn't know me, and a day isn't long enough to know what it's like around here, either."

"She doesn't know shit about shit," Dallas agreed.

"But you're her bloody fucking savior, and good for you. What I don't need is you beating the other men bloody outside of the cage 'cause you're a jealous motherfucker. So hit it or quit it."

"You're a humorless bastard. When did you get so cranky?"

"Times are tough in the slums of paradise. Politics are heating up in the city."

Politics. Jasper hated them, thought about them as little as possible, and even that effort was reserved for the careful dance of power between the gangs that ruled the sectors. He never thought about the shit going down in the city. "Uh-huh."

Dallas huffed out a laugh and rose, glass in hand. "You suck at pretending to give a shit, Jas. I'm going to go find someone who'll suck at something more interesting."

Nothing went on at the Broken Circle without Dallas's approval, explicit or not. "If I kept her—and that's a big if—it wouldn't be because she has no place to go. I'd rather help her out as a friend than rope her into something she doesn't understand."

"I'm not fucking heartless. She can stay, and you and Lex can be responsible for her." Dallas hit him with a stern look. "But don't make a habit of this. I can't take in every stray the city kicks out."

True, and Jasper had seen him flat-out ignore people a lot more pathetic than Miss Cunningham. Whatever was driving him to tolerate Noelle probably had more to do with Lex than his compassion. "Yes, sir."

Dallas strode away, stopping to say something to Rachel and Noelle. Noelle looked at the stage and transferred her tray to Rachel's more competent hands.

Then she turned and wove a path through the tables, heading directly for Jasper.

He pulled out a chair and nodded to it. "Taking a

break?"

She slipped into the seat, and for a moment he thought the halter was going to lose its grip on her breasts. "Dallas told me I should watch the show with you."

"I'm sure he did."

Her cheeks colored. "You don't want me to?"

"He's testing you," Jasper explained. Testing them both was more like it, but she didn't need to know that. "He wants to see if watching makes you run and hide."

"It might make me squirm and blush," she admitted, eyeing the stage. "But if I was prone to running and hiding from sex, I wouldn't be here."

"If all sexual encounters were equally shocking, you'd be set," he murmured. "But there's shit that goes on up there that *I* never saw before I joined up."

"Really?" Her eyes widened, their blue faded to smoky gray in the dim lights. "Like what?"

"Depends on the night. This? It's just a little dancing, some making out for show." He stretched his arm across the back of her chair and motioned to the curtain behind the front half of the stage. "There's a raised section back there they use for the real action. Most nights, it's two or three of the girls getting it on."

"Oh." Still wide-eyed, but she didn't look appalled. She leaned back, and her curly, unbound hair tickled across his arm. "It's kind of hot," she whispered, watching the current dancer swivel her hips. "That's what I used to dream about. Being that free. Not having to hide."

Or maybe her fantasies were simply that. "If you want to see what that freedom's like, you'll have the perfect chance tonight. Dallas is having a party after hours."

She tore her gaze from the dancer and studied him. "The parties are like that?"

He'd have to lay it out for her. "Some people are paired off, but they're not hard to spot. They have the collars, you know, or ink. Everyone else just wants to get off. You can join in or you can watch, but that's pretty much all it is. Wall-to-wall fucking."

Her top was so slinky he saw her nipples stiffen under the fabric. "That's the sort of party we were trying to have when I got arrested. None of us were very good at it. People who are good at it don't last long in Eden."

"Yeah? Well, remember—it's optional."

She slid her hand onto his thigh, awkward instead of smooth. Her fingers dug in, and her expression was more earnest than sultry. "Are you going to be there?"

"I'd planned on it." But that wasn't what she was really asking—and it wasn't what he wanted to say, either. "You want to go with me, Noelle?"

Shivering, she swayed toward him. "Do you think I'm a harlot?"

She could *not* be serious. "No. I think maybe you're a lady who likes to fuck."

Noelle's lips twitched. A laugh bubbled up, and she jerked her hand from his leg to cover her mouth. "You say it so easily, like it's not the same thing at all."

"Because it's not. No one here is going to think you're a bad person." Seeing her mouth covered was a travesty, so he pried her fingers away and rubbed his thumb over her lower lip. "I'll show you tonight, and you'll see."

She wet her lower lip, her tongue flicking over the tip of his thumb. "I've only done it once," she admitted in a husky whisper. "They caught us the other night before I made it to the actual fornicating."

Practically the virgin everyone would assume she was, and the big guy was right. The other men would be fighting to get balls-deep in her by the end of the night. "Tonight, you can watch," he said evenly, a fucking miracle when she was already licking him.

"With you?"

Her chest heaved with every breath, and Jasper flicked the material aside just enough to catch a hint of one pink nipple. "Yeah, with me."

She gasped, and this time she licked his thumb on purpose. "But no sex?"

"No sex." If he could manage it.

A tiny frown tugged at her lips. "Why not?"

"Because first I've got to figure out how to give it to you."

She shivered again and looked down. Her hair spilled forward to hide her face, but not before he saw her blush. "Maybe I'll get some ideas tonight."

Or she'd run screaming, thinking a simple life in the communes might not be a bad idea, after all. "We'll see, sweetheart. We'll see."

4

N O ONE HERE'S going to think you're a bad person.

Noelle smoothed her fingertips over the white lace clinging to her curves. Lex's dress drew tight across her breasts, which were shamelessly on display above the plunging neckline. She was taller than Lex, too—or maybe the dress was supposed to brush her legs at mid-thigh and flash her ruffled panties if she bent forward too far.

How could anyone claim she wasn't at least a *little* bit of a bad person?

By being a gang member, of course. Bad was probably relative in the slums, where men killed without consequence. No laws but the ones Dallas made, that was what Lex had told her, so she wasn't breaking any rules by dressing in scandalous lace and waiting for Jas to bring her to a party full of fornicat—

"Sex," she whispered. Out loud, because hearing the word made it more real. Fornication was a sin, a law, a meaningless concept in a place without either.

She was going to a party full of sex. *Real* sex. Dirty, experienced sex, not the fumblings of sheltered virgins drunk on smuggled moonshine, taking their cues from descrambled vintage pornography.

"Ready?" Jasper's voice rumbled through the darkened hallway, and he slowed as he approached. "You look nice."

Dirty and experienced. That was what he looked like in his dark clothing and shining silver chains. He filled the hallway, shoulders so broad she felt small and curiously vulnerable. Curious because it wasn't frightening, because she liked imagining herself tucked against his chest, utterly at his mercy.

He'd said something, and here she was, staring at him, concocting fantasies when a reality she couldn't imagine already awaited her. "Thank you," she said as her cheeks warmed. "Lex let me borrow something to wear."

"Yeah." He smiled and gestured to the ruffled hem. "It looks better on you."

It had been one of the few things in the closet Noelle could imagine wearing in front of people without dying of embarrassment. "So it's okay for the party?"

He took her hand and nodded toward the other end of the hall, where a door led through to the stairs. "Most people's clothes end up in a pile pretty fast. We sort 'em out later."

Could he feel her tremble? "And this sort of thing happens all the time?"

"Once a week." He urged her ahead of him with a hand at the small of her back. "Sometimes more if everyone needs to blow off steam."

His fingers burned. She could feel each one pressing against her through the thin fabric, each so far apart that it emphasized the massive size of his hand. She wobbled on her borrowed heels as she climbed the steps. Sounds of the party reached her before they got to the top of the stairs. She turned to the right and saw another hallway leading to an open doorway, and through that—

Skin. The lighting was dim, but she could still make out a naked woman standing just inside, the endless expanse of pale skin interrupted only by the tattoos at her wrists and throat and the jewelry dangling from her—

Noelle wet her lips and jerked her gaze away, but it was too late. Lace scraped her sensitive nipples, and she couldn't help but imagine how much more maddening it would be to have them pinched by silver hoops as chains and jewelry swung freely, tugging with every movement.

And she thought her earrings were daring.

"Hear them already?" Jasper spoke low in her ear, and the pressure of his hand at her back increased. "Go in, Noelle. Or do you want to stand here for a minute and see if what you can imagine is filthier?"

She felt hollowed out and hungry. This was the curiosity that had led her to make friends with the wrong girls at school, the interest that had brought her to a dark room with a young man who'd pretended to know what he was doing. He'd fumbled under her dress with clumsy fingers for twenty minutes without getting her as hot as Jasper's voice tickling over her ear.

Maybe he thought she wanted to run, that she was as cowardly as she was ignorant. Stubbornness forced her forward, obeying that heavy pressure at the small of her back. "I can't imagine much, unless you're going to give me ideas."

Before he could answer, Lex stuck her head through

the doorway. "You're late, honey. I was about to start without you."

"Start?" Start *what?* She looked back at Jasper for an answer.

He raised an eyebrow. "Tonight?"

Lex grinned slowly. "Unless there's some reason she shouldn't." She reached out and grasped a flounce of lace, pulling Noelle forward. "I'll show you the secret to keeping all these bastards on their knees. Jas can watch."

He caught her dress too, his hand twisting tight in the fabric. "You don't have to do anything but watch, either. Remember that."

Noelle imagined them tugging on her dress until it ripped in two. It was oddly thrilling, being trapped between them, Jasper's hard body at her back, Lex's softness a match for her own. She could imagine kissing Lex like the girls in the movies had kissed, while Jasper's hands roved her body, fingers stroking, teasing, taking...

Torn, she looked at him again. "Do you mind?"

He leaned in and touched his tongue to the corner of her mouth. "Go. Let her show you a few tricks. You can try them out on me."

She licked the spot he had and was disappointed she couldn't taste him on her skin. *Soon.* Turning, she smiled at Lex. "What sorts of things are you going to teach me?"

"The best kind." Lex folded Noelle's arm over her shoulders and pulled her through the door, past the woman with the chains on her nipples. "This is Dallas's party room."

The walls were lined with sofas, the center of the room strewn with cushions. Between and over nearly every surface were people—some talking quietly, laughing, while others groaned and gasped as their bodies moved together. It was impossible to tell where most began or ended. Noelle only saw miles and miles of skin, and none of the shame that always hung in the air back in Eden.

They were *fucking*, all of them, and no one seemed the slightest bit ashamed.

There was no safe place to rest her gaze, and she couldn't decide what she wanted to stare at first. "Our party was...not like this."

Lex laughed and kissed her cheek. "This is more fun. Come on."

A raised platform at the far end of the room held a couch. Dallas sat—no, *sprawled* out on it, his arms stretched across the back of the sofa, his gaze burning hot as Lex led her up the stairs. "All she's missing are the pigtails. Well played, Lex."

"I'm not that devious, sweetheart. She picked it out." Lex leaned close to Noelle's ear. "See that look? He's thinking about you on your knees, with your pretty pink tongue on his cock."

Noelle thought Dallas spent more time stuck on Lex, but when the leader did turn those steel-silver eyes on her, she *wanted* to fall to her knees in deference to the unchecked power there. How Lex managed to snap at him and seem so casual, Noelle couldn't begin to imagine.

Dallas smiled, as if he could read every thought as it flickered through her mind. "What do you think, Lexie my love? Still shy or just adorably submissive?"

Lex's hand slid into Noelle's hair and tightened, jerking her head back. Noelle gasped, first because of the sharp pull, the should-have-been-pain that left her senses a jumble, and then because Lex's mouth was on her throat, the woman's tongue raspy and a little rough.

Lex eased away. "I suspect a bit of both."

With her head still wrenched back, Noelle could only whimper softly and close her eyes as she began to melt. Maybe Dallas heard that thought too, because he laughed. "Dirty girl. Put her on her knees before I decide to put you over mine. Unless that's the lesson you want to teach her first."

"Behave." Lex scratched her nails down his bare chest and knelt at his feet, then glanced expectantly up at Noelle as she tugged at his belt.

Lex seemed unashamed, which made it easier to join her. Noelle fought to ignore the press of attention, telling herself that the people at the party were already engaged in far more engrossing activities than staring at her. But when she peeked over her shoulder, plenty of men watched her with eyes that held no secrets. If Dallas was imagining her tongue, these hard men with their menacing tattoos and their slow, greedy smiles were imagining things far more vulgar.

She turned back in time to see Lex pull Dallas's belt open. Noelle lifted her gaze to his, and he nodded in acknowledgment. "They're watching us. If it makes you feel better, pet, it's not all about you. Lex has men beating each other to a pulp once a week in the cage fights, just trying to impress her enough to use her clever mouth on them. You learn some of her tricks, and the boys will crawl to give you anything you want."

Lex's purring hum was almost lost under the sound of Dallas's zipper rasping open. "Who wants a man who'll crawl?"

The dirty movies gave this a name. A blowjob. Dallas had given it a cruder one—*sucking dick*. She imagined Jasper's big hand on her head instead of the small of her back, imagined him pushing her head toward his groin while he rasped those coarse, raw words. *Suck my dick.*

Warmth pulsed between her legs. She squirmed and watched Lex's hands as the woman freed Dallas's dick and stroked it slowly with both hands.

"Beautiful." Lex reached out to catch one of Noelle's hands and pressed it to the hard length of his shaft. "Have you ever done this before, honey?"

"Once." Under a blanket in the semi-darkness, because even that small rebellion had seemed wild. It couldn't compare to this, to Dallas watching through drooping eyelids as she eased her fingers carefully up his erection. She couldn't look away from it, from the shameless jut and the way it seemed alive under her hand, especially when her fingertips brushed the flared head.

He groaned and tilted his head back. "You're a curious little kitten, aren't you? No wonder my favorite snarling cat's gotten so fucking protective of you." Dallas sank a hand into Lex's hair, tugging the same way she'd tugged at Noelle's, and her face went slack with pleasure. "Show her how you use your tongue, Lex."

She bent her head and licked over Noelle's fingers. "Watch him," she whispered. "You'll know what he likes."

She curled her tongue around the head of his cock until it gleamed, wet and slick, and Noelle could see what Lex meant. Dallas was the one with a dominating hand twisted in Lex's hair, but every swipe of her tongue made him exhale sharply, a gruff, quiet noise that grew deeper, gravelly and rough.

"He likes your tongue," Noelle whispered, her own voice husky too. If she slipped her fingers beneath her panties, she knew what she'd find. The slickness of arousal, the proof that she was dark and twisted, bound for sin. She was so far past saving that she might as well admit it. "It looks...exciting."

Dallas laughed roughly. "That's right, kitten. You're going to like it here just fine, aren't you?"

Maybe. And what did that make her?

Lex lifted her head, her breathing as jagged as Dallas's, and dragged Noelle's mouth to hers. A sure kiss, certain, gentle and rough at the same time. And Noelle could taste Dallas on the other woman's tongue, something sharp and foreign, something that made Noelle moan as she squirmed, desperate to relieve the empty ache between her thighs.

Strong, forceful fingers snagged in her hair. Dallas jerked the two of them apart, pulling both their heads back with another deep, rumbling laugh. "Jas, come get your kitten. Lex can't concentrate on blowing me properly with all this sweet virgin tongue nearby."

Lex slapped at his hand. "I can teach her just as well on Jasper's cock."

"We'll see," Dallas drawled before turning Noelle's head. Jasper was walking toward them, his brows drawn together in a frown that looked more *intense* than anything. Her heart beat wildly as she imagined fumbling open his pants and copying Lex's technique. Tongue and lips and staring up into his eyes and—oh God, everyone would be watching her, and she didn't even care.

When Jasper stopped at the foot of the stage, Dallas lifted one eyebrow. "Want to join me on the couch so blowjob lessons can continue, or have you got something else in mind?"

Jasper held his hand out to Noelle. "We're going to talk, maybe have a few drinks."

"Uh-huh." Dallas released her hair, and Noelle inched to the edge of the raised platform before slipping her hand into Jasper's in silence.

He led her down, closer to the center of the room, to one of the couches lining the wall. Instead of sitting beside her, he dropped and pulled her onto his lap, facing the room. "What did you learn, Noelle?"

No safe place to rest her gaze again, but at least most of the people weren't staring at her anymore. Noelle wiggled a little, shifting restlessly in spite of herself because she wanted something hard to rub against. "Dallas likes to watch Lex lick him. I think he likes the watching as much as the feeling."

"Close," he whispered, easing one hand between her knees. "What else?"

She edged her legs wider, too wanton to deny him—

or herself. "Dallas thinks I'm adorably submissive."

Jasper's voice dropped to a growl. "Are you?"

The growl was good. It shivered through her, pulsed between her legs, and if he didn't touch her soon, maybe she'd do it herself. "I don't know. I understand the words, but I think they mean more to you than they do to me."

"You do know." His fingers gripped her thigh. "Did you like it when she pulled your hair? When he did? When he was telling the two of you what would get him off?"

Submissive. Inclined to submit. To obey, to yield. To give control and authority over herself to another. Wasn't that at the root of her confusion? Lex had offered her sexual liberation, and Noelle had reacted with shame and disappointment. But was that because she didn't want to shoulder the burden of her sinful desires, or because it truly appealed to her?

Did it matter, in the end, if she enjoyed it? "I liked it," she admitted. "I like imagining you doing things."

"Things like this?" His hand moved higher, and his thumb brushed the thin fabric covering her sex.

The touch set off a cascade of desire that left her trembling, and yet it was so gentle. Too gentle. "Worse things." It came out as a breathless whisper. "Bad things."

"Luscious things," he countered, turning her head toward Dallas's stage. "Watch them now."

Her breath escaped on a gasp as she watched Lex take Dallas between her lips, into her mouth—*deeper.* Noelle clutched at Jasper's arm, transfixed as Lex surged down again. "She's taking him into her throat?" She couldn't decide if the thought was terrifying or so hot she might combust.

"Swallowing him whole." The pressure of Jasper's thumb increased, but only for a moment. "Does it look like she's submitting?"

She parted her lips to say *yes*, but hesitated. There was too much power in Lex's posture, too much defiance. Even when a dark-haired man covered in tattoos slid behind her and began to ease up her dress, Lex looked entirely in control of both men, as if Dallas was putty in her hands and the man behind her was there only for her pleasure.

"No," she answered finally. "She's not submitting."

"No. She's in charge. She's the one who decides." He moved his hand then, lifting it to cup Noelle's breast through her thin dress. "Just like you."

Her nipple grew tight, pushing against his hand, and she wanted to feel his broad fingers against her skin. "What if I don't want to be in charge?"

"Then you get ink. Because once you submit to a man, really *submit*, he's not gonna want to let you go."

She wet her lips, suddenly uncertain. "But how do I keep from doing that before I'm supposed to?"

"You give pleasure, not yourself." He pulled the bodice of her dress lower, baring her breast.

Across the room, a redhead with a wicked smile stared at her. No, at her chest, his gaze starved as it traced the curve of her breast, the tight nipple, and she felt the first stirrings of power. Was this how Lex felt when Dallas gazed at her with naked hunger? This certainty that she was desired, coveted, and could grant or withhold her affections at her whim?

Maybe bestowing it would be enjoyable. Lex seemed to revel in tormenting Dallas with her tongue while the dark-haired man stroked his fingers between her thighs.

Noelle turned her face enough to speak against Jasper's jaw. "Do you want me to give pleasure to other men?"

"Your desire, Noelle," he reminded her. "Do *you* want to?"

"I don't know," she lied, because she didn't want him

to encourage more fantasies. Her imagination was all too ready to conjure one involving the smiling redhead and Jasper and being held immobile as rough hands explored her body.

Jasper made a quiet noise and set her on her feet, rising behind her. "Back to the platform," he murmured.

"Why?" she asked, nerves rendering her clumsy, but he was already guiding her back to the raised platform where Dallas watched her approach with half-open eyes.

"Because you won't know if you like pleasuring other men until you do it." Jasper's voice dropped, and his lips brushed her ear. "Get your mouth on his dick this time."

An order. A command. No shame in obedience, no wondering if they'd find her dark urges repellent. The stage was low enough she could climb onto it without using the steps. It left her on her hands and knees, her dress riding up to flash her panties, and she twisted to peer at Jasper, more aware this time of the way she must look to the room. "Now?"

He reached out and slid his hand up Lex's spine. "Move over, greedy bitch."

Lex braced one arm on the couch beside Dallas and drew her tongue up the underside of his shaft. "Plenty of room." She brushed Noelle's cheek with her free hand. "You come back for another tutorial, honey?"

Pressing up to Lex also brought her closer to the tattooed stranger. He was familiar—maybe he'd been the one with Jasper in the market, had helped to rescue her.

He grinned at her and gave Lex's hip a swat that made Noelle's insides clench in envy. "Want me to knock off, Lex? Or are you so good you can teach a virgin to suck cock while you're riding my hand?"

"Ask our fearless leader here how good I am, Ace." She circled her hips slowly against the man's hand as she leaned over to lick Noelle's lower lip.

Lex made it easy to fall into. It felt good to kiss her,

open mouthed, felt better to follow her back to where Dallas's erection—*dick,* she whispered to herself, *cock*—stood thick and glistening, harder than before. Shivering, Noelle parted her lips and traced the tip of her tongue up his shaft.

Dallas sank a hand into her hair, his fingers more gentle than commanding. "Come now, kitten. Lex didn't teach you to be so prissy."

No, Lex had lapped at him like a melting ice cream cone on a hot day. The image made Noelle laugh as she opened her mouth wider and swirled her tongue around the crown of his cock.

Jasper whispered her name, and she felt the careful brush of his hands pushing her skirt higher, up over her hips to her waist. Then he curled his fingers under the back of her panties and drew them down.

The whole room could see her. Jasper's bulk might block some people's field of vision, but others would see everything. Her bare ass. Her—her *pussy.* Just thinking the word felt wrong, even with one man's cock under her tongue and another man pushing her panties down her legs.

Her cheeks burned, but the rest of her burned so much hotter that she prayed Jasper would touch her and put her out of her aching, frustrated misery.

He eased her legs apart, as far as they would go with the restraint of ruffled lace still around her knees. His touch strayed close, so close, to her throbbing clit...and vanished.

Then his palm descended on her ass with the sharp, stinging crack of flesh on flesh.

She couldn't stop herself from squealing. The cry escaped her lips, and she tried to throw her head back, but Dallas's hand tightened, holding her in place as she panted and squirmed.

Jasper's handprint was burned into her skin, but

somewhere inside her the sharp pain had twisted. *She was twisted,* a dirty, wicked girl who wanted this crude mistreatment, who craved it.

Maybe if he spanked her enough, he'd purge all the shame from her heart.

Dallas tugged at her hair, forcing her to look at him. His lazy gaze drifted over her features, and his lips twitched up in a smile. "Ah, Lexie my love. Your kitten's a bad girl. You'll have to make sure she doesn't get distracted from my cock."

"Dirty old man," she muttered, sliding her fingers into Noelle's hair. "Take him in your mouth, honey, and trust me. Yes?"

"Yes," she whispered, savoring Lex's touch. Different than the men's. Softer but more direct, as if she knew just what it took to blur pleasure into pain.

She probably did. She probably knew everything, all that Noelle wanted so badly to learn. So she parted her lips and let Lex guide her head down until Dallas's cock pushed into her mouth, hard and hot and deliciously demanding.

It was a good thing Lex was showing her what to do, because most of Noelle's attention was focused on Jasper, on waiting for him to touch her again. *Please, please spank me...*

But it was Lex's hand that drifted down her back and over her ass, her nails lightly scratching the reddened handprint Jasper had left behind. It sparked a squirming sort of pleasure, different from the fleeting pain of the slap.

Then she slipped her hand lower, over Noelle's swollen, wet pussy lips, and immediately pressed deeper. Searching.

Noelle moaned. Whimpered. Her hips shifted on their own, rocking desperately, and it was Dallas who groaned as his cock seemed to jump in her mouth. "Goddamn it, Lex," he growled. "I said keep her from getting distracted, not get her off."

"Oops." Lex moved her fingers, but only to spread Noelle's aching flesh wide. Opening her.

And then she whispered something that sounded like Jasper's name—a mere second before a beard grazed Noelle's upper thigh. A second before his tongue, warm and rough, rasped over her clit.

Her thighs trembled as he licked her, the sensation so sinful she couldn't concentrate on what she was sup-posed to be doing with her mouth. Every pulse in her body had centered on that one point, and she realized hazily that there must be more to pleasure than she'd ever known because this was what she'd always thought an orgasm felt like, but clearly, *clearly* there was more. Her body knew it. Strained for it.

Dallas hissed and jerked her head up with the hand still threaded through her hair. "Watch the teeth."

"Sorry, s-sorry—" How could the mortification make her hotter? "Let me try again, I won't—"

"Shh. Tell us the truth—have you ever come before?"

Were her cheeks as red as they felt? "I think so. Maybe."

Lex nuzzled the spot under her ear. "*Maybe* means no, honey. Definitely not."

Dallas reached down to rub his thumb over Lex's lower lip before doing the same to Noelle's. "You're gonna miss a hell of a show down there, Jas. Don't you want to see how big these eyes can get?"

Jasper locked his hands around her hips and lifted her off her knees. The world spun, and when she landed it was on her back, on the floor at Dallas's feet.

Only Jasper didn't slide down between her thighs again. Instead, he loomed over her, his gaze boring into hers. "I already know how big her eyes get."

He blocked out everything, became her entire world.

Noelle raised a shaking hand to his shoulder, barely daring to touch him as she drowned in the darkness of his eyes. "Please. Show me what it feels like. I'm dying."

"Not dying. Waking up." He kissed her, warm and firm, his beard brushing her chin and his tongue on her lips. She wanted to press them tight together so he'd lick them forever, but at her first gasp he was there, edging into her mouth, and she opened for him with a small sound that took all the air she had.

Her dress was rucked up beyond her waist, and the back of his hand grazed her stomach as he glided his tongue over hers.

More. She tried to say it, but it came out muffled against his mouth, a hungry noise that would have to be enough. No one had stopped her from touching him, so she slid her fingers down his arm until she encountered skin and edged one fingertip under his sleeve.

His muscles tensed, turning to steel under her touch, but his hand was gentle between her thighs as he explored, tracing the shape of her pussy, fold by fold, before delving deeper.

If her panties hadn't been tangled around her knees, she would have spread her legs like a true harlot, anything to encourage him. She needed it so hard she spoke, whispering her plea against his lips. "I'm so empty I ache."

He caught her lower lip between his teeth, caressing it with the tip of his tongue as he pushed one finger inside her, stretching untried muscles. Then he lifted his head with a groan. "Not empty anymore. Tight as fuck though, sweetheart."

Overwhelmed, she dropped her hands to her sides, whimpering as her fingertips scraped across the smooth wooden stage. Nothing to cling to, nothing to anchor her as he stroked over places that shouldn't feel this good, this *much*.

This had to be it. "I think I'm coming."

"Getting there." He moved his finger, twisting his hand so he could rub circles over her clit with his thumb too, and that was too much. Her back formed an arch as his touch sparked electricity, so sudden and wild she cried out and tried to pull away.

Soft hands, Lex's hands, gripped her wrists and stretched her arms over her head, holding her in place. Jasper rocked his whole body, thrusting his finger deeper—and grinding his denim-clad erection against her thigh.

Noelle's pulse expanded until her entire body was beating. A shudder welled up, shaking her as she clenched around Jasper's clever, wicked finger, and then she understood what Lex's words meant because all of that pleasure was a prelude to this. This moment where she screamed her relief because all the needing turned to hot, slick bliss.

5

NOELLE SPENT SO much of the night drifting in and out of dreams where Jasper smoothed his hands over her skin and rasped dirty words against her cheek that at first she thought the familiar rumble of his voice was just another dream.

Lex's irritated reply wasn't.

Noelle jerked upright, clutching the sheet to her chest as Lex continued grumbling. "I'm going to take her myself. Later, when normal people are awake and moving. So fuck off, Jas."

He shook his head, ignoring the fact that Lex was yelling at him *and* stark naked. "No ink yet. Dallas says she goes with me or not at all."

"Do you mean shopping?" Noelle sounded breathless, but maybe they'd attribute it to sleepiness and not the way her heart leapt into her throat at the sight of Jasper's stern face.

"The market," he confirmed. "Meet you out front?"

A whole morning with him. "I'll be right down."

Lex shut the door and wrapped an arm around her bedpost as she watched Noelle scramble off the sofa bed. "No, that's okay," she said wryly. "I can make other plans."

Noelle froze, teetering on her toes. "I'm sorry. I just thought—if you want me to go with you, or if you want to come with us..."

"With you and Jas?" Lex laughed. "I think I'd rather eat glass than watch you two make googly eyes at each other, especially after last night."

Noelle's cheeks heated again, but she hurried toward the closet. "Last night was...interesting." What a confusing understatement.

"Yeah. If you're planning to talk to him about it, you might want to sound more enthused."

"No, it was amazing. It *was*." She wiggled into her borrowed pants and hesitated. "It's just that everything was so good, and then he stopped."

Lex arched an eyebrow. "You didn't expect him to fuck you the first time, did you? And at one of Dallas's parties?"

No one else had hesitated. Every surface at Dallas's party had been covered by naked bodies writhing together in pairs and trios and some tangles with too many limbs to easily count.

"I didn't know what to expect," she admitted, tugging on a shirt. "I still don't."

"Well, how did he treat you before last night?"

It seemed like weeks or months had passed since she'd nearly collapsed at his feet, but it had only been a matter of days. "He's been kind. Careful."

"Okay. So if he treats you worse after last night, kick his ass to the curb. You don't need that shit." Lex stifled a yawn. "That's not really Jasper's style, though."

Noelle tried to imagine a world where she would be capable of kicking a man like Jasper anywhere, much less out of her life. Impossible. Then again, a week ago she wouldn't have been able to envision a world where she could take advice from a naked woman as if nudity were a casual, acceptable thing.

She settled for a noncommittal, "I'll remember that. Do I need anything else?"

"To go shopping or to deal with Jas?"

"To go shopping." She knew she wasn't ready to deal with Jasper.

Lex grinned, leaned over to dig through her nightstand, and emerged with a handful of folded bills. "Don't let him pay for anything."

"Lex, I can't—" The other woman pressed the stack of money into her hand, and Noelle hesitated for a moment, struck by the novelty of holding cash. Actual bills, the tangible paper kind that her father never would have let her touch. All banking in Eden was electronic, with accounts tied to the bar code you were given at birth. But the rich and powerful kept paper money in vaults, along with stacks of gold bars and precious jewels, all the things they swore were unnecessary in a clean, digital world.

It wasn't the only way her father was a hypocrite. Noelle closed her fingers around the bills. "I'll pay you back."

"Are you kidding? Dallas wipes his ass with that kind of money. I'll get it from him."

"Thanks." She tucked the money into her pocket and smiled. "Go back to sleep. I'm sorry he woke you."

"Mm-hmm." Lex crawled back under the covers and dragged them up almost over her head. "Just be yourself, Noelle. You'll make out all right."

She would have replied, but Lex was already asleep

by the time she slipped out the door. No one else was stirring this early in the morning—no surprise, not after last night—so Noelle navigated the twisted warren of hallways that led to the front entrance alone.

Jasper leaned against the front wall, a cigarette in one hand. "Walk or ride?"

"Is it safe to walk?"

"It is. Market's only about five blocks." He held out his hand.

She stared, caught up in the memory of him working those broad fingers into her body, stretching her as pleasure singed her from the inside out. Her nipples tightened as arousal crept through her, riding the moment when memory drifted into fantasy. In her dreams, he'd pushed his cock into her one agonizingly blissful inch at a time, making her beg for each thrust with obscene words she could only imagine saying in her own head.

Praying that he couldn't follow the path of her thoughts, she slid her palm against his, shivering as calluses scraped her skin. "Let's walk."

He folded his fingers around hers and pulled her toward the street. "Lex give you a hard time?"

"No, not at all. She's good to me."

"I know. I was teasing." A smile tilted his mouth at the very corner. "I'm bad at it."

She was gripped with the irrational urge to stroke his cheek, where a tiny dimple had almost formed. Maybe if she could coax him to smile wider, it would appear. "I need practice being teased. You should do it a lot."

"I just might."

"Maybe I'll even learn how to tease you back."

"Someone has to." Something oily and noxious had puddled on the cracked asphalt in front of them, and Jasper lifted her over it like she weighed nothing.

Even when he set her on the street again, she

gripped his arms, dizzy from his proximity and the sur-real moment of tenderness in a dirty, dark alley. "Thank you."

"Sure." He dropped his hand to the small of her back. Hard-looking men were already filling the narrow gaps between buildings, but they averted their gazes as Jasper led her past, and the few stragglers still in the street melted to either side. One or two nodded to Jasper in recognition, but even those greetings were tinged with as much fear as respect.

Aware that her safety rested entirely in Jasper's hands—or in the ink curling above them—Noelle pressed closer to his side and lowered her voice. "Do you know most of these people?"

He shook his head. "Not really. I've seen them, and they know who I am, by the tats if nothing else. Once you have yours, it'll be the same."

It sounded more *when* than *if,* and she fought a smile. "So you think Dallas is really going to let me stay?"

He eyed her with puzzlement. "Don't you?"

"He seems like a complicated man. If he's letting me stay, I think it's mostly for Lex."

Jasper squinted at her. "It matters to you, doesn't it? *Why,* I mean."

"A little." If she lifted her gaze, she could just see the shining outer wall of Eden in the distance, the barrier that supposedly kept the city pristine. Like so many things about the city, the safety of those walls was an illusion. "I know I'm naive about a lot of things, but I was raised to know my value as a councilman's daughter. To his allies *and* his enemies."

He guided her around a cart piled high with bolts of fabric. "Then...maybe, yeah. For Lex's benefit. Or for mine."

Warmth kindled in her belly. "I'd rather it be for

your benefit than because he hates my father. Not that I'd blame him. My father is easy to hate."

Jasper snorted. "I'm not saying it's impossible that he's thought of something like that, but it's not really who Dallas is. Not when you get right down to it."

"He's intimidating," she admitted. "He comes across as relaxed, easy and laid-back. But still dangerous. Even when he smiles, he makes me nervous."

Jasper drew her to a stop, grasped her shoulders, and turned her to face him. "There isn't anyone in Dallas's gang who *isn't* dangerous, sweetheart. Him, Lex, Rachel...even me."

"Rachel?" The pretty blonde waitress was no more threatening than Noelle herself.

He ignored the question. "Even you," he murmured softly. "You need it to live out here, or you die, one way or another. Dallas sees that danger in you too, or he'd have sent you packing already."

Even more ludicrous. "The only reason I'm still alive is you."

"Because you don't know how to survive out here. Once you learn, you'll do anything you have to do." He sounded certain.

It made her feel certain too. "Will you help me learn?"

"Yep." He grinned and pointed her at the cluster of carts and ramshackle booths that lined the street as it began to widen. "First lesson. Never pay anyone what they ask right away. They'll rob you blind."

The market. It looked nothing like the high-end shops she usually patronized. The area directly in front of them was devoted mostly to carts full of clothing. Bright fabrics hung from ropes strung between buildings, swaying in the early morning breeze. More items lay stacked on carts or in front of makeshift tents.

Noelle caught her reflection in a tarnished mirror

and almost laughed at her own wide, delighted eyes. Her expression matched the feeling in her chest, light and excited. "I get to barter?" It was like something out of a history text.

He chuckled. "Coming to an agreement about price is called haggling. Bartering is trading. We're paying cash."

Haggling. She made a mental note and returned his grin. "*I'm* paying cash. My own cash. That's Lex's first rule."

"Why am I not surprised?"

"You can still help me pick out something to wear to Dallas's next party." It was the closest thing to sugges-tive she could manage, and some part of her braced in anticipation of a brush-off or a quiet rejection.

He moved his hand, curling it around her hip as his smile faded into something darker. Hotter. "Too long to wait. There's a thing tomorrow night. You can come watch me fight."

She couldn't concentrate on his words when his fin-gers stretched almost to the small of her back. She felt tiny under his hands. Powerless, vulnerable—two states that were familiar, but they'd never heated her blood like this before.

She wet her lips because she liked the way his gaze followed her tongue. "What should I wear?"

He glanced around, then nodded to a booth draped with displays of leather—belts, bracers, even corsets. "Stuart does quality work."

Stuart's booth looked like Lex's closet, though Noelle had seen enough custom tailoring to know most of the other woman's outfits had been made specifically for her. None of the designs on display were familiar, but one corset drew her closer. Smooth, supple leather with laces across a neckline that swooped halfway down the body and little cap sleeves held together by demure black bows. It was dangerous and sweet at the same time, and she stroked a finger over the leather and imagined her breasts behind those laces. Caged, on display but trapped, desperate to spill free.

Just like she felt. "This one. I want this one."

The man behind the makeshift counter squinted as he eyed her. "It's handmade. Ain't cheap."

"I recognize quality craftsmanship." She recognized the look he was giving her too. Her borrowed clothes weren't expensive enough to be worth his consideration. She imagined Jasper's presence was the only thing keeping him from sneering. "You make clothes for Lex, don't you? The style's very similar."

He grunted in assent, his gaze flicking to Jasper. "You a friend of hers, girl?"

"I like to think so. I've been borrowing her clothes, but I need to purchase some of my own."

"We could make a deal, I bet. Cash or trade?"

Her moment of confidence wavered. With Jasper at her back, she'd felt safe enough to pretend he was just another merchant, but her knowledge of navigating expensive, sneering shops ended at the city walls. She didn't know the value of cash or how many crumpled bills compared to the intangible credits she no longer had access to.

The man stared at her as if every moment of silence cemented his original assessment, and she had to say *something*. "Cash."

Jasper laid a hand on her shoulder. "This is Noelle. She's the newest O'Kane."

Stuart cleared his throat and nodded. "Yeah, okay. No problem."

Amazing, how smoothly the transaction went after that. Stuart indicated a price that would have been a steal in credits, but Jasper's tiny headshake encouraged her to counter. Stuart accepted her offer without a murmur, and Noelle peeled the correct amount off the roll of bills in her pocket with mixed feelings.

She could believe that tangible cash held a higher value than credits, which could disappear with a flash of electricity. Less credible was the notion that Stuart would have accepted her counteroffer so willingly without Jasper looming behind her, his arms a walking advertisement for the O'Kanes.

Her independence was as dubious as the respect she'd been given in Eden as a councilman's daughter, a fabrication based on fear and someone else's power. But if she took O'Kane ink, those tattoos would curl around her wrists too. Still borrowed power, but power she'd earned by finding a place.

A shameful place, according to everything she'd ever learned. A degrading place. But something inside her hungered for the sin.

And now, watching men eye Jasper with wary concern and respect, she hungered for his power, too, even if it was only reflected on her. She'd have to give up everything to belong to him—her secrets, her body, her shame.

It might all be worth it if he could set her free.

6

A CE HAD FINISHED the outline already, and Jasper winced as soon as his friend turned away to switch out his equipment. "Are you off your game today? This hurts like hell."

"Is that the tattoo or your balls?"

"My balls are fine. Wanna check?"

Ace made an amused noise. "No, thanks. Unlike you, I was smart enough to get a ride or two last night."

"And who said I wasn't?" Noelle wasn't ready for it, not remotely—after spending the morning with her, he was more sure of that than ever—but she didn't have his dick on a chain, either.

"Dom." Ace swiped his shoulder and set the needle against skin. "He's talking shit to anyone who'll listen."

Dom was a mean motherfucker who had the brawn but not the brains to rise up as one of Dallas's more trusted men, and it ate at him like a cancer. "He talks a lot of shit about a lot of stuff." Jasper paused. "What's he saying?"

"That you've got a limp dick and no spine. Bastard's just pissed because the girls cut him off. Which is what happens if you don't bother to make sure they have a good time."

Limp dick, no spine—meaningless, unimaginative words, easy to brush aside. But while Dom posed no threat to Jasper, that didn't mean he wouldn't apply himself wholeheartedly to harassing Noelle. "If he has such a beef with me, we should hash it out in the cage."

Ace snorted. "Do it. Make everyone's night."

No. He wouldn't give the man the satisfaction of answering his cowardly challenge, but if Dom came at *him*, spoiling for a fight, he'd get one. "Everyone going to the warehouse tonight?"

"Probably, as long as nothing goes down with Sector Three. I'm hitting my stops early tonight." Ace moved the shader to a new spot.

Jasper clenched his jaw as fresh pain welled. He could handle getting punched in the head better than he could handle these damn needles sometimes. "You need backup?"

"Nah. Bren's coming with me."

"The two of you aren't likely to run into trouble." Jasper bared his teeth. "Unless you want to. We can take Dom along, settle things nice and uncivilized in an alley. Who'd miss him?"

Ace grinned. "Not even his mama."

Another time—and with a little more reason. Jasper glanced down at the red heart emerging on his chest. "Make it bloodier. Truth in advertising."

"Yeah, you and your bleeding heart." His friend sounded amused. "What's next? Gonna rescue some kittens?"

A foregone conclusion, apparently, that he'd mark Noelle. A done deal. "She was horrified last night. Would you saddle yourself with an old lady who's ashamed of fucking?"

Ace choked on a laugh. "Shame I'll give you, brother, but the only thing that girl's horrified by is how much she gets off on being a bad little girl. If you don't want her, I'll spank the *shame* right out of her." He paused for a moment. "Or maybe I'll watch Lex do it."

If Jasper could be sure that Noelle was only struggling with the novelty of exploring her sexuality, he'd mark her. "Maybe it's just new. We'll see. And I *do* plan to see."

"Is that your way of telling me to keep my dick out of her?"

"It's my way of saying tread lightly." Jasper lifted an eyebrow. "Some of 'em aren't quick fucks unless you push them, and she doesn't need to be pushed."

"Bleeding fucking heart," Ace muttered, returning his attention to the tattoo. "You know, her father's directly responsible for making our lives hell. Has it occurred to you that's the real reason Dallas is keeping her around? You might not want to get too attached."

For information, perhaps. Anything more sinister and Lex would kill him—and Dallas knew it. "Or it's all the more reason for me to look out for her."

The lights above them flickered, and Ace bit off a curse. "I think the back generator's acting up again. Need to get a grease monkey out here to look at it."

"That'll take forever. Have Rachel knock off her shift early and check it out."

"Rachel can't stand the sight of my face. Maybe you should ask."

Jasper sighed. "You wouldn't have this problem if you weren't such a fucking *jerk*."

Ace seemed unperturbed. "Could be worse. I could be

Dom."

"Barely worse."

"That's the blue balls talking."

"Shithead." Jasper stretched his neck, trying to ease a little of the trapped feeling he always got sitting in the chair too long. "Make sure you put healing gel on the tat. Maybe I'll go out with you and Bren tonight before the fights, after all. Clear my head."

"Hey, man, if you want to. We've got liquor deliveries to make to those dives west of the market district, and then we need to collect protection money from the brothel."

Work. A task that could consume his attention as well as anything else. "I'm in."

Ace swiped at Jasper's chest again and paused to consider the bleeding heart taking shape there. "I still have to fill in your princess's bar code. Think she's going to faint on me?"

Jasper remembered her skin heating under his hand the night before, how soaking wet her pussy had been after one smack on the ass. She'd liked having her hair pulled, liked the commands as much as the touches and tongues.

Did she get off on other kinds of pain too? Would having the needles thrust into her delicate skin over and over get her as hot? He could picture the black vinyl seat, slick and shiny with the evidence of her unbearable arousal. They'd have to strap her down to stop her squirming, but once they had, he could put his face between her thighs, fuck her with his tongue while Ace obliterated the bar code, her last link to the city that hadn't wanted her.

He wanted her.

"I'll bring her in," he muttered. Better he be there— just in case.

Three days outside Eden, and her old life seemed like a dream.

Noelle leaned against the bar and watched Rachel swirl alcohol into a shot glass, the other woman's movements practiced and effortless. The scent of liquor was amazing, sharp and heady. Every moment in the sectors was so *real*, gritty and hard, smashing into her numbed senses. She'd eaten at the most expensive restaurants in Eden, but nothing had tasted as rich as the charred grilled cheese sandwich the grumpy cook had shoved on her before the bar opened.

Three days, and she still hadn't grieved.

It had to be partly shock. The trauma of going from jail to the streets to drugged out of her mind. But when she tried to picture her bedroom at home, she didn't miss the luxuries. Showers with endless hot water, electricity that came from underground wires rather than loud, smoke-spitting generators. Instead she remembered the locks on her windows. The cameras that tracked her every movement. The guards. The rules. Her father's endless sermons.

Her father's endless rage.

Shivering, she banished his face from her memory and concentrated on Rachel's movements. "You came from Eden too, didn't you?"

"Yep. I doubt we ever ran in the same circles, though." The blonde smiled impishly. "I was solidly middle class."

Noelle tried to return the smile. "My acquaintances were limited mostly to the families of my father's political allies. We had bodyguards with us whenever we left the house—I always thought they were there to keep us from being exposed to dangerous ideas or people."

"Dallas has meat shields go everywhere with him

here, but it's mostly to keep people from blowing his head off. Your boy Jasper's one of them, you know."

Your boy. Another inexplicable discovery. Jasper had hardly said two words to her that weren't about sex, and she was infatuated with him. Or maybe she wanted to believe it was *him* and not the way he made her feel, dirty and fulfilled all at once.

And yet... "I don't think he's my boy. He won't even...you know."

Rachel dumped ice into another, larger glass. "Won't what? Fuck you?"

"Yeah." Noelle had expected it at Dallas's party. She'd wanted it, after he'd made her come. But he hadn't let her open his pants, not even to try Lex's tricks on him. And he'd left her after their shopping excursion with nothing more than a kiss. "I don't know, maybe he feels sorry for me because I almost passed out at his feet."

"Mm·hmm." Rachel held up another bottle. "Whiskey, our most popular. Never water it unless they ask you to—Dallas's orders."

"All right." She consigned that bit of information to memory and wondered what she'd have to forget to keep it there. "How do you remember all the recipes? Practice?"

"Mostly." Rachel set down the bottle and leaned her hip against the bar. "A good trick? If you don't know how to make something, tilt your head, smile, maybe laugh a little, and admit it. *Huge* tips."

"Really?" Noelle started to tilt her head and then caught herself. She'd seen Jasper's eyes narrow with tight hunger when she tilted her head and confessed ignorance about some sexual matter. "Oh. The men like us to be a little clueless, don't they?"

"They all like to be the first to plow some virgin soil, that's for sure." Rachel brushed her short blonde hair out of her eyes and stuck a cigarette between her lips. Noelle's worry that Jasper was taking pity on her vanished, replaced with the gnawing fear that he'd only find her interesting while she was mostly innocent.

So what? There were other men. She could be like Lex, free to touch whatever man she wanted. Or she could be like Rachel and earn her keep working the bar. "You weren't at the party last night. Do you not go to them?"

"Sometimes. I usually sit out the action, though. Have a drink and watch the show."

Noelle felt her cheeks warm. "You don't agree with Lex about having fun with the men?"

Rachel laughed. "Lex is Lex, though most of the women around here enjoy it too. I don't know—it's enough for me to know that I could, if that makes sense."

Why couldn't that be enough for her? Probably for the same reason she was here in the first place. Some twisted, broken need inside her that pushed her to risk everything. "Are you waiting for the right person?"

The woman chuckled and picked up the shot she'd poured. "Yeah, maybe I am."

Noelle gestured to it. "Can I try that?"

"Sure." Rachel handed it over.

It burned going down and brought tears to her eyes. Noelle wheezed out a breath and wondered if her throat was actually dissolving. "Okay, the alcohol I was arrested for drinking? Most definitely watered down." Her idea of *drunk* was probably as inadequate as her idea of *orgasm*.

The quiet amusement was back on Rachel's face, sparkling in her eyes. "Stick around. This place is like that—intense."

"Does it ever stop feeling...?" Noelle shook her head and set down the glass. "Feeling. That's it. I feel so much right now, I don't know what to do."

That sobered the blonde, who straightened with a

faint frown. "Why would you ever want to stop feeling?"

"No, I don't want to," she said quickly. "But *intense* is the right word. It's so intense, all the time, and I don't know if this is what life is, or if there's something wrong with me."

"Give it time," Rachel advised. "You'll figure it out soon enough."

As if it mattered either way. The Broken Circle held a seductive promise, with its dark corners and smoky scent. Sometimes she thought she was a little high just from being here, like she could close her eyes and float.

Or she could open them and make choices, the first of her pampered, silly life. "Will you show me how to make that other drink again?"

"Anything you want to see." Rachel began to gather the ingredients. "You going to the fights tonight? I was thinking about it, but I have a side job to get on. Maybe later?"

Fights. Violence was almost as taboo as sex in Eden. "Jasper mentioned that, but why are they fighting? Did something happen?"

"Yeah, they're breathing." The blonde rolled her eyes. "Why *don't* they fight? To settle scores, win respect, blow off steam. Make the chicks' panties fall off, that's a big one."

"I've never seen a fight. Is it really that compelling?"

"Depends. I'll admit, there's something to be said for sweaty, half-naked guys beating the shit out of each other. A certain..." Rachel's lips curved in a tiny smile. "Animal appeal?"

Noelle tried to imagine it. Jas, stripped to the waist, fighting. Raw, unchecked violence. Fists against flesh, all of that power realized. "I guess I can see that."

"I guess you can. Tonight, after closing. Main warehouse over on Sixth."

"If you want, I could cover the bar for a while so you

can do your other job." She'd probably fumble half the orders, but no one seemed to care once the girls started dancing. "Then we could go over to the warehouse together."

"Thanks, but it shouldn't take long." Rachel finished pouring the liquor and added a dash of bitters. "The generator over at the parlor's been acting wonky, so I told Ace I'd fix it up."

The name was naggingly familiar. "Ace... The one with all the tattoos?"

"That's him. He does good work." Rachel held up her wrist, where you could barely tell the cuff of ink obscured a city bar code. Then she turned and lifted her shirt, revealing two lotus flowers, one at the small of her back and the other between her shoulder blades, both connected by a tangle of vines.

As tempting as it was to reach out and trace one of the lifelike vines, Noelle kept her hands to herself. "That's gorgeous. But didn't it hurt?"

"At first. After a while, I don't even think I was conscious anymore."

"It hurt *that* much?"

Rachel laughed and took another drag from her cigarette. "No wonder Lex has taken to calling you baby girl."

Heat rose in Noelle's cheeks, bringing the first rush of humiliation with it. She didn't know which stung worse—knowing everyone thought she was stupid, or knowing they were right. "I must seem ridiculous to you."

"No." The woman slid an arm around her shoulders and squeezed. "You've got a lot of living to do, that's all. You want to come to the parlor with me? I'll be finished before you know it, and we can go watch Jas kick the shit out of someone. He never loses, you know."

Living. Most emphatically *not* what she'd been doing in Eden. Noelle reached for the remaining glass and knocked it back. It still burned its way down her throat and kicked in her stomach, but she liked the tingles that followed. She was warm. Loose.

She was living. "I'd like that."

 ace

"HERE'S YOUR PROBLEM." Rachel wiped her cheek with the back of her hand, leaving behind a black smudge. "Your voltage regulator's shot."

Ace knew he should be listening to the words coming out of her mouth, but damned if he'd ever been able to. Rachel Riley was a golden angel begging to be debauched, even in a pair of cheap overalls with grease on her face.

Fuck Jasper for sending her over here, anyway. And fuck Jasper for not fucking the new princess already. Noelle had come trailing in behind Rachel like a lost little duckling, and oh, she and Rachel made a picture. He'd carve out a kidney to see all that blonde and brunette hair tangled together—preferably while they fought over who got to suck his dick first.

For a man who'd had a hooker on him less than an

hour ago, he was damn hard up for some blighted satisfaction.

Rachel waved a wrench at him. "Are you even listening to me?"

Ace blinked away the image of hot, clumsy blowjobs
with a sigh. "Yeah, sweet thing. Something with a regulator is shot. Can you fix it?"

"Probably. I'll adjust the phase compensation, see if
that clears it up." She grinned. "What's it worth to you?"

"The whole ten inches?"

"Charming, but I prefer cash. Though I'm not above
bartering." She turned to Noelle and handed her the
wrench. "What do you think? Could I use another tattoo?"

Ace's dick went rock hard, and it had nothing to do
with how Jasper's princess pursed her lush lips as she
considered the question. Having Rachel in his chair was
torture. She didn't just get off on the adrenaline of the
needles—she went beyond herself. He'd seen women
flogged into that blissful state before, but she'd been the
first one to drift there while he laid ink.

It was the closest he'd ever come to fucking her.
"Princess doesn't know about tattoos, sweetheart. Jas is
bringing her back tomorrow to get her bar code filled."

"I know that, but she can still help me with aesthet-
ics."

Noelle was watching him like she was afraid he'd eat
her if he opened his mouth, which was pretty damn shy
for a girl who'd ridden Jasper's finger to ear-splitting
orgasm only a few feet away from him the previous night.

Maybe Jas was right. Maybe the girl was another
Rachel, not another Lex. Bottled up and repressed.
Didn't mean he wouldn't tease them both the same way.
"You saw her flowers, Noelle?"

The brunette nodded. "They're beautiful."

"Damn right they are." A woman lost in a sensual

haze in his chair always inspired him to impressive feats of artistry. "I could always extend them. Vines around her waist or down her arms. Flowers just above her cuffs."

"Around my hips, maybe." Rachel slid her hands from the small of her back all the way around to her upper thighs.

Christ, he'd have his face practically in her pussy. "What do you think, princess?"

"I think it sounds beautiful." Noelle narrowed her eyes, her tone stiff and prim. "And I'm not a princess."

"Oooh, feisty." Ace poked Rachel in the side. "You teaching her to use her teeth, Rae? And after Lex spent all that time teaching her *not* to use them."

"An angel and a devil," Rachel murmured. "One on each shoulder, huh?"

If he didn't know better, he'd think Rachel was sneaking a peek at his dick. Let her see how hard he got when he reached out to tangle a lock of her blonde hair around his finger. He tugged, not looking away from her face even as he addressed Noelle. "Rachel here is our good girl. But she'd be wasting her time whispering in your ear, princess. I think you already know you want to be very, very bad."

Rachel licked her lips. "Maybe every woman does if you can figure out what turns her on."

Even angels. Even her. "Fix my generator, Rachel, and you can have any tattoo you want."

She arched an eyebrow and held out her hand. "Deal."

Ace folded his hand around hers with an easy smile. Jasper and the other lumbering hulks could chase after the baby deer in the woods. There was no challenge in that hunt. No satisfaction.

He knew how to take his time.

7

DOM WENT DOWN with the second blow, and Jasper supposed it was too much to ask for him to stay there.

He didn't really want it anyway. His whole body was tight, jittery, and even the run out to Sector Three had provided no satisfaction. Quiet, uneventful, and now he had to sate his appetites on nothing more rewarding than Dom's face.

Jas had been in worse spots.

Dom spit blood as he staggered back to his feet, uglier for taking the hit. His insults hadn't gotten any more original, either. "You punch like a pussy."

"Hard enough to put you on the mat." Jas stretched his neck and circled, not bothering to guard with his fists and arms as he faced the other man. A matter of time, that was all, and he'd lunge in, desperate to land a punch on an unprotected area.

"Gave you that one," Dom lied, feinting left with a quick jab. "Figured I'd let you hit something, since you can't get it up for that that sweet city ass."

"Christ, is that your game? Bore me to death because you punch like a little boy?"

Dom rose to the bait, charging toward him with a bellow. His hook came slow, so slow the man wasn't just telegraphing his moves, he was sitting down to write them fucking love letters. Jas took the hit, using the distraction to drive a fist into Dom's midsection.

When he doubled over, wheezing, Jas grabbed Dom's hair and kneed him in the face. Bone cracked, and he hit the ground again, blood gushing from his broken nose.

Jas kicked him for good measure, a light tap to the ribs. "You're not even trying, man. Get up."

That brought the man to his feet again, snarling and rabid. He lunged forward and rammed Jasper against the side of the cage, and the watching crowd roared.

Still no match for straight-up brute strength. They grappled, and Jas lifted Dom off his feet and slammed him to the mat with a growl. Dom drove his knee into Jas's hip and tried to roll them, but he couldn't get the leverage.

Neither of them wore shirts, so Jas grabbed at Dom's hair again instead of sweat-slick skin. "You better tap out before I pound your fucking face in, shithead. I'm in a mood."

Dom tried to twist and then slapped his open palm on the mat with a snarl. "You fucking fucker."

Jas considered pressing a foot to the man's throat, just to teach him a lesson, but backed off. "You're welcome."

"Fuck off, Jas." Dom pressed a hand to his bleeding face and rolled to his knees. "Next time, I'm smearing you all over this mat."

"You're gonna try." A redhead—one of the dancers, maybe—opened the cage door and offered Jas a towel and a smile as he walked out. Noelle, on the other hand, stood at the fringes of the cheering crowd, a beer in one hand and a bewildered look on her face.

If that had been all, Jas would have kept walking. But a fire burned in those big eyes—admiration and even pride, but not fear.

He took the beer from her hand and drained it. "Like the show?"

"It was..." Her fingers hovered over his chest before brushing the spot where Dom's fist had abraded his skin. Worry creased her brow, along with something darker. An edge, possessive and angry. "You must have let him hit you. I saw how fast you can move."

He caught her hand, pressed it to his skin. "It doesn't hurt for long." Unlike the rest of him, which was throbbing thanks to her simple touch.

As if the words gave her permission, she smoothed her other palm up his side, fingers slicking over his bare chest, past his new tattoo and up to his shoulder. "You're so strong," she whispered, tracing his biceps with something damn close to reverence. "Powerful. Raw."

"Hungry." He didn't even look at the throngs of people milling around them. "You keep touching, and I'm bound to think you want to do more."

Her touch drifted lower. Over the curve of his elbow and along his forearm. "Like what?"

He slipped his hand into her hair. "Like try out some of the stuff Lex showed you."

She licked her lips like she could already taste him, and her sharp breath made it clear she wanted to. "Right here? In front of everyone?"

If he said no, she'd pout. If he said no, his own body would murder him in his sleep. Jas untied the top of the new leather corset she'd bought from Stuart and dropped to the nearest free couch. "Show me."

A few people turned to stare, but that didn't stop Noelle from kneeling between his legs, breathing so hard her tits were damn close to spilling out of her top entirely. She smoothed her palms up his thighs and rested her fingers on his belt. "Rachel said you never lose a fight."

"I never have." He caught her chin. "Is this my reward?"

She inhaled sharply. "Would it be a reward?"

"To come in your mouth?" Jas eased the top of her corset down a fraction of an inch, but it was far enough for one luscious pink nipple to spill out. "Hell yeah. Unless you want me to come somewhere else instead?"

"Where?" She fumbled with his belt buckle, her expression an endearing mixture of frustrated impatience and anticipation.

He tweaked her nipple with just a hint of pressure. "Your tits?" He moved his hand to her mouth, a lingering brush of his thumb over her lower lip. "All over this pretty face?"

Her movements stilled as she whispered against the pad of his thumb. "You'd like that?"

It was like the ink—no one would wonder who she belonged to, or what would happen if they tried to touch her. "It's sexy when a woman lets you come on her. Sexier when she likes it."

Without looking away from him, she wrapped her lips around his thumb and slipped his belt free from the buckle. Her fingertips ghosted lovingly over the leather strip, and she raised her head. "Do you know what the show was last night?"

"At the Broken Circle?" With the way she was fondling his belt, he didn't even have to ask. "Ace likes spanking before fucking. He takes it further than I would."

Her blush spread to her neck as she ducked her head

and tugged at his fly. "I wouldn't think being struck with a belt would be pleasurable."

"Me neither. But plenty of people get off on it." He lifted her face to his again. "Are you one of them? You liked it when I slapped your ass."

She swallowed hard and stared at his chin. "What would you do if I said yes?"

"Depends. Do you want it...or *need* it?"

"I don't even know if I like it," she said quickly, dragging down the zipper on his pants. "It's not important. I can't need something I've never had."

Those were the things people needed the hardest. "Noelle."

"I don't know." She left his pants hanging open and met his eyes. "I know I want to do this. I want to..." her voice faded to a husky whisper, "...suck your cock. I want to do things you like. Not things you don't."

Her hair was soft under his hand, and he twisted the strands in his fist. She seemed to enjoy that more than the pain—the *force* behind it. The domination. "Do it."

She was awkward at first. Her fingers trembled as she eased his cock free and stroked them up his shaft. She wet her lips first, then dragged her tongue around the crown with a humming noise of satisfaction.

Heat. Jas gritted his teeth and used the hand on her head to guide her. "Bold, honey. Don't think about it so much. Do what feels good."

Her licks got longer. She worked her way along his shaft until it glistened before taking him into her mouth. She gripped his belt and bobbed her head, eyes closed and face slack with a blissful sort of peace.

Because she liked it, or because she wanted to be his? The question ripped at him even as her touch tightened his skin and made his balls ache. It wasn't something he could answer, not here or now.

So he gave in.

"Deeper." He wanted to be *inside* her. Wanted her to take him.

She tried. She surged down, took him deeper with every moan until she was damn near choking herself because she didn't know how to deep throat.

It would have been scorching hot—if she'd meant to do it. Jas pulled her head up and wrapped her hand around his cock. "Look around, honey. What do you see?"

Her gaze drifted over the crowd as she stroked him. "Fighting. Fucking. No shame."

What she wanted to see. "It's a bunch of people who've never seen anything like you before. Not because you're from the city, or because you're damn near a virgin. Because you're *you*."

She turned back to him, confusion creasing her brow. "How can they know what that even means? I'm still trying to figure it out."

"Because they're not trying as hard as you are."

Her hand stilled on his cock. "What do you see?"

A woman who needed to let go. A woman who didn't know how. A woman he couldn't claim until she learned. "I don't know yet either, honey, because I'm trying just as hard as you."

She tested his grip in her hair by straining toward his lap again, but her eyes never left his. "We're not going to find out what I really am by being gentle."

"Or by making you do what I want." He released her and spread his arms wide on the back of the couch.

No mistaking the disappointment in her eyes—she tried to hide it, but every damn thing she felt played across her face. She worried her lower lip with her teeth and lifted her hands to finish unlacing her corset. "I'm in control?"

He was riveted to those hands, that soft, pale flesh, like a kid who'd never seen a woman naked before. "Complete, total control."

88

It took her forever to pull the last lace free. Her corset fell to the ground, and she returned both hands to his
cock. "I want you to come on me."

There it was, the same lust that had gripped him as
he'd watched her blow Dallas. She wasn't skilled or experienced, but when she set herself free, even just a little...

She wanted it. *Hungered* for it, and Jas would crawl
across the floor to taste that hunger.

This time, she closed her lips around his cock without hesitation. She drew him into the heat of her mouth
and sucked, tongue working in time with her hand.

A groan fought its way out of him, and he let his
head fall against the sofa. A bit of control could be a
heady thing, and something told him Noelle would get off
on it, if only because the inevitable would come, that
moment when she'd hand it back to him.

"Fuck, that's good." His voice had dropped to little
more than a rasp.

She hummed as she pushed lower, pushed until his
cock bumped the back of her throat, then retreated with
a frustrated noise.

Jas checked the command that rose automatically.
Instead, he let himself feel it, every press of her fingers
and flutter of her tongue, even the hesitation when she
tried to take him into her throat.

After another attempt, her head popped up. She
slicked her tongue around the crown again before exhal-
ing softly. "I'm going to ask Lex to teach me. I want to be
able to do what the girl with Ace is doing."

The woman wasn't part of the gang, but she came to
watch the fights all the time—and she'd do any goddamn
thing Ace told her to do. He had her on her knees, his
hands gripping her head as he fucked her face, hard and
deep. "Honey, there are seasoned pros who can't do that."

For the first time, Noelle flashed him a wicked little
smile instead of lowering her eyes bashfully. "So it'll take

89

time to learn. Am I really so bad at this that you don't want me to practice on you?"

"No." He covered her hand with his and stroked down the length of his cock.

She gave him big eyes and an innocent expression. "No, you don't want me to practice on you?"

"You're not bad at it, brat. When you let yourself like it."

Noelle ducked her head, but the heavy tumble of her hair couldn't hide her satisfied smile. The moment of teasing power had stripped away one layer of shyness, revealing mischief and heat.

The same heat wreathed her voice. "If I feel bad about it later, maybe I'll let Lex spank me."

The very idea tumbled Jas that much closer to desperation. Lex was safe, a willing, eager lover who wanted to get off without needing to hold on to either of them after the fact. "You like her?" He slipped his hand to the back of Noelle's head, resting gently without applying pressure. "She wouldn't just spank you. She'd fuck you."

"Then she'd have to spank me again." Her hands quickened under his guidance, moving up and down his shaft in hot, rough drags. Her gaze found his. "Or you could, right now. After I beg you to come on my face."

Denying her was denying himself, but the words rasped out of him anyway. "I'm not going to spank you."

"Oh." She stroked him faster, in time with the short breaths that made her breasts dance. "But you'd watch Lex spank me?"

"Right after I—" *Fuck.* His breath caught as a pulse of heat rocketed up his spine. "Right after I came on your tits and made her lick you clean."

Noelle moaned and arched her back, pushing her breasts toward him. "She'd have to spank me hard. I'd deserve it."

"No." He urged her head down, just far enough for

her parted lips to touch his cock. "But you want to."

A shiver. "Yes. God help me, yes."

A half-step from begging, and the image of her un-done, insensate with lust and need and a thousand other things, drove him over the edge. Jas jerked their hands over his shaft with a rough groan, riding the throb that centered on his dick but echoed through him.

He spurted on her face, the lush bow of her mouth and the pink flash of her tongue. She licked her lips as come dripped off her chin, and he milked his cock on her breasts, thrusting against the soft flesh and taut nipples.

Noelle swiped her fingertip over her chin and brought it to her mouth, lapping up the taste of him like she couldn't get enough.

His ears ringing, Jas pulled the towel from across his shoulder and held it out to her. "When I can stand up again, I'll walk you home. Keep your clever fingers out of your panties, though—no coming tonight."

She blinked at him, clearly torn between disap-pointment and fascination. "Why not?"

"Because tomorrow you get your cuffs. Your first ink," he explained. His gaze strayed past Noelle, over to where Ace had the fight groupie squirming on his lap, her hands tied behind her back. "Our resident tattoo artist has been dying to get you strapped in his chair. Dying to get his tongue in you too."

Noelle blushed as she clutched the towel and shifted, rubbing her thighs together like she was trying to relieve arousal. "That would make the tattooing difficult, I'd think."

"Your own reward," Jas said softly. "Get through both tats and we'll make it all better, honey. I promise."

She rubbed the towel over her breasts in silence, shivering every time the fabric rasped over her nipples. "All right," she whispered finally, casting the towel aside. She crawled up into Jasper's lap, straddling his hips and pressing her tits to his chest. Her face went to his neck, nuzzled trustingly against his throat. "Tomorrow."

"Tomorrow."

8

JASPER HADN'T BEEN exaggerating about the straps.

The odd chair had been adjusted to a mostly upright position with platforms stretched out on either side for her arms. As soon as she settled into place, Ace grinned and wrapped a thick leather strap over her elbow, tugging it tight before buckling it into place.

Restrained. She twisted a little, and Ace laughed and toyed with the second strap closer to her forearm. "What do you say, brother? Is she a squirmer?"

"You should know." Jasper leaned against the open archway separating the room from the area of storage and machinery in the back. "You had a front-row seat to the show at Dallas's party the other night."

A snort, and Ace winked at her and took his time buckling the second strap. "Too bad Lex isn't here to hold you down this time. You'll have to settle for leather and steel."

From the smug way he ogled her nipples as they poked against her thin top, it must have been obvious that the harsh bite of leather aroused her just fine. Noelle swallowed and tried to keep her voice casual. "I don't mind it."

"I bet you don't, princess." Ace dropped to a stool and jerked his head at Jasper. "Why don't you take care of her other arm while I check out her bar code?"

Jas crossed his arms over his chest. "Afraid she's gonna punch you in the head once you break out the needles?"

"Maybe." Ace leaned forward and lowered his voice. "Jas is a real stubborn jackass, you know. Can't tell him to do a damn thing without him deciding to do the opposite."

Because he was a man who took orders from no one—except for Dallas. Jasper's confidence was intoxicating in a world that seemed fluid, lawless. "I wouldn't know," she murmured, drinking in the sight of Jas with his muscular arms draped over his chest and his expression stern. "I don't give him orders."

He stepped forward and dragged his thumb down the inside of her elbow before beginning to buckle a strap. "Because you're smart, honey. Ace doesn't understand smart."

Ace's laughter drifted over her, but Noelle couldn't look away from Jasper as he fixed her elbow in place. Helplessness had been her constant companion since she'd stumbled through the gates of Eden, but this wasn't frightening. This was giving over control, putting herself in his hands, and it made helplessness her own choice.

She drew in a deep breath and wiggled against the seat. "What does Ace understand?"

"Sex. Simple control." Jas pulled the strap taut. "The moment, but not what comes after it. After everyone comes down."

Coming down had been the sweetest part of the previous night. Not that Jas had let her get off—she was still strung too tightly after no relief and a night of erotic dreams—but he'd stroked her and petted her as she eased away from the edge, turning the sharp scorch of frustration into a slow-burning promise.

Jasper moved to the second strap, and Ace swabbed something cool and wet over the inside of her wrist. She started to glance back at him, but a soft *buzz* filled the room as pain jabbed into her wrist.

It hurt. It hurt the same way as when her mother had pinched the inside of her arm in punishment for using unladylike words, vicious little twists that left her bruised under her prim, long-sleeved blouses. Noelle clenched her free hand into a fist and dug her teeth into her lower lip, remembering Jasper's words.

A reward. All she had to do was endure the pain.

Jas stroked her brow, trailed his fingertips over her temple and into her hair. "Filling in the bar code will probably hurt the worst." His voice was low, even. "But it's all you have to do today. If he finishes and you want to go for the full cuffs, that's okay. But you don't have to, not yet."

Slow breaths. She snuck a peek at Ace, but watching the needle stab into her skin made her woozy, so she turned back to Jasper, leaning into his touch. "Dallas is okay with me having the cuffs?" Surely it couldn't have been a week already, though the days and nights blurred together in a haze of liquor, smoke, and sex.

"He changed his mind about the wait." Jas smiled. "My guess? You were right, and Lex went to bat for you. He doesn't tell her no."

No, he didn't seem to. Noelle closed her eyes as the

spot where the needle pierced her wrist began to burn. "Tell me what they mean. What will happen if I take them."

"It's O'Kane ink. Once you have it, you *are* the gang. Anyone hurts you, they hurt all of us. They hassle you? They answer to everyone."

Ace swiped at her wrist again. The burning worsened, but the pain melted somehow between her arm and her brain. Her heart beat faster as he spoke, his words drifting over the hum of the needles. "You'd be one of us, princess. Everything you need taken care of, as long as you put the gang first."

"I can do that," she whispered, pressing her thighs together. God, being touched was supposed to be the reward. What would Jasper think if he pried her knees apart and found her aroused?

"You'll belong to Dallas, same as we all do." Jas stroked the inside of her unmarked wrist. "Then, when you're ready, you can belong to someone else in a different way."

She'd met a girl in the bar who wore ink like a collar around her throat. Anyone who looked at her knew she was taken. A more primal version of the wedding bands worn in Eden, but with the same significance. A woman belonged to her partner.

At least out here, the men seemed wary of pissing off their women.

Ace started another line, and Noelle sank her teeth into her lower lip as the pain intensified, and the pleasure along with it.

Jas gently freed her lip from the bite of her teeth and licked it. "Getting better?"

Every bit of warmth rushed to her center, as if his tongue had granted her permission to feel. She moaned and arched as much as she could, and the leather straps digging into her arms only made it more delicious. "Yes," she whimpered, finally understanding Rachel's words. This... This could be addictive.

Jas spoke, the words hot against her skin but not for her ears. "How much longer?"

"Another couple minutes." Ace chuckled. "You're a dirty girl, aren't you, princess? I can't tell what you like more, the leather or the needles."

Both and neither, because only one thing tied them all together. "Jasper. I like Jasper more."

"No whining," he murmured, then licked the corner of her mouth. "Barely even a whimper. You deserve your reward, honey."

"What'd you promise her, brother?"

"Your tongue, for starters." The back of Jas's hand brushed her nipple through her shirt. "I figured you'd be down with that."

She squirmed as Ace laughed, the sound dark and low. "Better tell me where I can and can't put it. Fingers too."

"Both, wherever it gets her off the hardest." A thread of steel wound through Jas's voice. "But keep your dick in your pants. This is about Noelle."

About her. All about her, and she was already melting at the thought of it. She twisted her head and tried to catch Jasper's mouth, but he held her back and licked her lips again. "When Ace has you fixed up, honey. Then I'm going to kiss you while he fucks you with his tongue."

She had to pant to get enough air to speak. "That's so dirty."

"Mmm." Jas reached down to grip her leg, his fingers curving along her sensitive inner thigh. "You can tell him not to touch you."

Did he want her to? Was this a test of loyalty? Tension started to curl around her, until she realized her answer was the same either way. "He can if you want him to."

Ace clucked his tongue. "If you'd ever had my face between your legs before, you'd sound more excited."

Noelle ignored him and stared into Jasper's eyes as the world floated around her. "Anything, if you think it'll make me feel good. I want to feel good."

Jas's fingernails dug into her skin, just a little. "You can't separate them, can you? Whatever *I* want will get you off." He bent low, spoke directly into her ear. "I want you to have other people, find out what you like. Get and give pleasure before you settle on me."

There was a message under the words, one she'd have to think hard about. Later. For now, she could only nod and ease her knees apart. "I like this." If he slid his hand up a few inches, under her skirt, he'd see how much.

Instead, his hand retreated. "Open your mouth."

She obeyed without hesitation.

He studied her, his gaze roving over her parted lips. Finally, he eased his thumb between them. "Suck."

It was like one of her dark fantasies come to life. Jasper, looming over her bound, helpless body, rasping dirty commands. Orders that absolved her of any complicity in her own defilement. Shuddering, she sealed her lips tight and sucked, and she'd almost forgotten about Ace until he hissed out a breath. "Fucking hell, Jasper."

"I know." He glided the pad of his thumb over her tongue. "She's beautiful."

Drunk on the look in his eyes, on the buzz trembling through her body, Noelle scraped her teeth over his thumb.

He pulled free of her mouth with a *pop* and smiled approvingly. "That's good, honey." The smile lingered as he tugged lightly at her silky shirt. "Is this Lex's too?"

"Yes. I didn't buy much yesterday." Mostly just the corset, the one he'd liked so much.

He drew something from his pocket, but she didn't

get a good look at it until it clicked and light glinted off the blade. A knife. He teased the tip under the already-plunging neckline and slit the fabric clean away from her skin.

Her breasts spilled free, unbound and heavy. She twisted so hard that Ace grabbed her forearm with a warning noise, but she *couldn't* sit still. Her pulse pounded in her ears and between her legs. She was painfully aware of her clitoris, of the way it seemed as hard and hungry as her nipples.

If he cut off her skirt, she might come from that alone.

But he folded the knife and put it away. "Stay still, honey. The longer it takes, the longer you wait."

"Jasper—"

Before he could say anything, Ace tweaked her nipple, pinching hard enough to force her breath out in a moan. "Jesus, she's hot for it," he murmured as he went back to the tattoo. "One more line, honey, and then we'll play with you."

"She'll want the cuffs too." Jas sounded certain.

"That so?" Ace drawled.

As if there was any question. Noelle felt as if every day stripped away a layer of numbness, a layer of respectability. The girl who'd stumbled out of Eden might have bowed beneath the hard work and endless rules of the commune.

The girl she wanted to become could only live here, in the darkness of the sector slums. "Yes. I want cuffs."

Ace hummed. "What do you say, Jasper? How much more can she take without someone working her off?"

He stroked the same nipple Ace had tweaked, a gentle touch instead of a rough one. "Not long. Finish blacking out the bar, and we'll give her a break, make her come. Then you can start on the rest."

Noelle groaned and rocked on the seat, so hungry she

didn't care if she looked shameless. "Have you two done this a lot? Tied a girl up and made her listen to you talk dirty about what you were going to do to her?"

"Oh, she's cute, Jas. She thinks we've been talking dirty."

"Ace isn't dirty," Jas observed conversationally as his hand drifted down, over the waistband of her skirt. "He's obscene."

Lower. *Lower.* If she thought it hard enough, maybe he'd slide his fingers over her wet panties and realize how close she was to shaking to pieces. "What's the difference?"

Ace finished the final line with a flourish and reached out to catch her chin, forcing her to look at him. "Dirty's saying I'm going to make you come. Obscene's saying I'm going to spread your pretty pink pussy lips open and spank your clit until you come all over my face."

Oh *God.*

Jas chuckled softly. "Obscene makes for quite a show, doesn't it, Noelle?"

Obscene made her clench tight in anticipation. Not even embarrassment could banish the entrancing image, though her imagination put Jasper between her knees. His hand opening her, his fingers delivering punishment and pleasure.

She wet her lips and closed her eyes. "I like it."

The hem of her skirt inched higher on her thighs. "How much?" Jas asked.

Saying it shouldn't be any worse than enjoying it, but she had to force the words out in a raspy, self-conscious whisper. "Enough to beg you to—to touch my pussy. Either of you. Both of you."

"Enough to trust us to take care of you, no matter what?"

"Yes. *Yes.*" And it wasn't a lie. Even Ace's irritating

princesses and crude flirting didn't bother her when Jasper so obviously ruled over his friend. And she trusted Jasper. With everything.

Jas's hand slid higher under her skirt, almost distracting her from the stab of discomfort as Ace smoothed some sort of gel over the inside of her wrist.

She felt like the surface of the family's garden fountain before the workers turned on the water in the morning. Still and dark, a smooth mirror that would erupt in endless waves with a single touch.

One touch. She could have arched her body off the chair and found his fingers. Instead, she let her eyes drift open and stared up at Jasper. Waiting. Needing.

He licked her lips and fused his mouth to hers.

It wasn't the right sort of touch, but she melted into it anyway, moaning against his lips as she strained toward him. She barely felt Ace's fingers stroking down her arms, because everything was Jas. His lips, his tongue, the scrape of his beard, the promise of everything he'd give her.

"Open," he whispered again, into her mouth, and she didn't know if he meant for him or for Ace, so she parted her lips and slid her knees wide.

It was Ace who shoved her skirt up, and Ace who groaned. "You've got to be shitting me. Who bought her the fucking white ruffled panties?"

She couldn't answer with Jasper's tongue in her mouth, but if it hadn't been there, she could only have managed pleas. Her clit pulsed, ached with a ferocity she hadn't imagined possible. If Ace would simply touch her...

But he didn't. He swept his fingers along the insides of her trembling thighs and laughed when she squirmed. "Should I rip 'em, Jas? Or do you want to cut these off too?"

Jas pulled away far enough to answer. "Neither.

Leave them around her ankles."

"Yeah, I'd want to keep them around too." Ace urged her hips up, and Noelle lifted her body as much as she could with her arms bound immobile.

The reminder of helplessness sharpened her need, and she whimpered and rubbed shamelessly against Jasper. "Please, Jas. Please make him touch me. I want to come—I need to."

Ace settled his hands on her knees and pressed them wide before tracing back to her sex. "Now, Jasper?"

"Now."

Noelle tensed, dizzy with anticipation, but Ace moved just his thumbs, stroking her folds before parting them. She was held open in every sense of the word, her arms flung wide, her knees forced apart, her most intimate places utterly on display.

It should have been humiliating. In the one second she had to think, she hated that it wasn't, hated herself for her deviance.

Ace's mouth closed over her clit, and he sucked so roughly she screamed at the shock of it with the last air she had before orgasm crashed into her, tearing everything else apart. She screamed and she shook, her entire body tensing and releasing with each wave, and distantly she heard Ace's groan of approval, felt his fingers twisting and stroking, landing on her clit in stinging little slaps that dragged her from the hollow of one wave to the peak of the next.

She must have begged for mercy. She *must* have, because the pleasure faded and she found herself limp and trembling, Ace grinning up at her—no, not her. He was grinning at Jasper. "Shit, man. I barely got started."

"Go easy." Jas dragged the backs of his fingers down the inside of her thigh. "Soft."

Ace chuckled and pushed her knees even wider, like he was holding her open for Jasper. "Your girl likes hard just fine, brother. Maybe too much."

"Not for long. She'll be finished." Jasper's hand trailed lower, fingertips brushing the drenched inner lips of her pussy. "She has to keep up for a while yet if you're doing her cuffs today."

Noelle shuddered and met Jasper's eyes. "Cuffs," she whispered, turning the words into a challenge. A reminder that he'd promised her freedom, for all that she was bound and helpless. "I want them today. Now. While you touch me."

"Today," he agreed, moving his fingers slowly. He stroked her, slicked through her wetness, and teased her with the promise of how much better it would feel when he pushed those fingers inside.

She was so fixated on Jasper's touch that she didn't realize Ace had moved until a drawer rattled behind her. "I bet she'd like these."

Jasper reached out, and Ace dropped two metal circles into his hand. No, not circles—rings with jeweled crossbars through them. Only when Jas pulled the bars apart and let them fly together with a metallic clack did she realize they must be magnetized.

As to their purpose... Her mind stumbled over the likeliest possibility. Memory supplied an image of the woman at Dallas's party, the one whose shamelessly bare breasts had been adorned by sparkling jewelry.

Imagining the sensitive tip of her nipple pinched between cool metal set Noelle to squirming again. "Is that...?"

Jas answered by bending his head and tonguing her nipple, drawing a gasp from her as her flesh puckered. "They go like this," he murmured, situating the first ring around her nipple.

The bars snapped tight, and she hissed as pain bloomed for a moment. Only a moment; the pinch wasn't strong enough to do more than ache in a way that made her heart pound. She forced her gaze to his and wet her lips. "The other, too? Please?"

"Told you," Ace muttered. "Such a bad girl."

"Maybe." Jasper pinched her other nipple before putting the ring in place, then slipped his fingers down to brush her clit. "What else do you want, sweetheart?" She wanted him. She wanted to come. She wanted to belong in this life, where the shame burned away and nothing but giddy pleasure remained. "I want my cuffs."

"You'll get them." He pushed one finger inside her and curled it, stroking over that sensitive spot that sparked a feeling too intense to be called pleasure. Pressure, maybe, and a desperate hunger for *more* that had her voice breaking on a plea.

Ace's voice rumbled close to her ear. "Maybe I'll give you your cuffs while you're riding Jasper's hand. Would you like that, princess? Do you want him to feel your pussy clench around his fingers? He'll know how hot the needles get you. He knows how hot this is getting you right now. I bet you're squeezing him so tight he's imagining you all hot and wet around his dick."

"She wouldn't be still," Jasper whispered. "She's fighting the restraints right now." He pulled his finger free only to return along with a second, thrusting deep.

Noelle let her head fall back as the stretch drove a moan from her. What a picture she must make—bound, spread wide, her clothing sliced away and her body writhing under the intoxicating mixture of pleasure and pain. Anyone could walk in and watch her work her hips up and down, and that pushed her tension to a dizzying peak.

It wasn't bad enough that she wanted to be defiled. She wanted people to watch. "I'm so bad," she whispered, voice slipping into a moan as she teetered on the edge of release. "I'm dirty."

Jasper shook his head, his jaw tight. "If it were

shameful, you think I'd do this to you?" He moved his hand faster, his fingers fucking in and out of her with firm strokes.

No. Ace would. Dallas might. But Jasper was so careful with her. So controlled, so deliberate, coaxing her forward one step at a time as he stripped away her defenses. She could trust that it wasn't disgraceful.

But trusting wasn't feeling. She struggled against the straps, panted at the bite of leather, and groaned at the pinch of steel. When his broad fingers slammed into her one last time and she came screaming, she felt *dirty*, crude and broken and so, so good. Humiliation and pleasure twisted together, fed on one another until the illicitness felt better than the physical release.

He stopped thrusting and curled his fingers, making firm little rhythmic motions inside her as Ace bumped his thumbs against the metal rings pinching her nipples in painful, beautiful counterpoint.

Jasper's voice rasped over her. "Again."

"I can't," she protested, a stupid thing to do when fluttery spasms were already driving her higher, but it couldn't be possible to feel so much, so fast. "I *can't*."

Ace's hand closed in her hair and twisted roughly. Another layer of confused sensation, and she whimpered as he flicked one of her nipples. "Sweet little liar. If I were you, brother, I'd make her come two more times for every lie."

"Just once." Jasper licked her jaw, her lower lip, and then nudged Ace's fingers aside to tease his tongue over her nipple.

It burned, and then she burned, propelled beyond herself for one exhilarating, wild moment. No shame, no guilt...no body. Just floating bliss and *him*, and she stopped fighting and rode the first of a dozen waves.

Up and up and no down, no end. Not until fingers stroked her cheek and a rumble shook her, and she realized she was wrapped in a blanket and cradled against his chest. Blinking, she let her head fall back and caught sight of Ace watching them with an oddly intense look, one she swore was jealousy.

It vanished a moment later as he smiled. "There you go, Jas. Your girl's drifting down."

"Beautiful." Jasper stroked her hair, brushing the tangled, damp strands away from her forehead.

The gentleness made her shiver. She turned her face toward his palm and closed her eyes. "I don't know what happened."

"Before or after we made you come?"

She laughed. "After. And maybe while."

"You took a little trip, sweetheart." Jasper kissed the spot just behind her ear. "Now Ace is going to ink your cuffs."

"But you took me out of the chair." And she felt no pressing desire to leave the warm cocoon of his embrace.

Ace snorted out a laugh. "Under the circumstances, I'll make do. For all I know it's going to send you flying again, and your big, dumb brute will rip my balls off if he can't pet and cuddle you."

Jasper kicked the footplate. "Less talk, more work."

They were situated so it was easy enough for Noelle to squirm her arm out of the blankets and lay it down for Ace. He winked at her before bending to his work, and Noelle looked away with the first prick of the needles.

It barely registered as pain, just a buzzing that vibrated through her, and she closed her eyes with a humming sigh. "What happens after this?"

"You get ready for tonight." Jasper smiled against her cheek. "Every time Ace lays O'Kane ink, we have a party."

"What kind of party?"

"Not like the one in Dallas's rooms. We drink, and we celebrate the fact that there's another one of us."

"Fun." She was floating again, floating on his voice and the warmth of his body and the sweet kiss of pain that was its own sort of claiming. Jasper was claiming her.

Dallas's mark and Ace's ink, but every jab of the needle plunging into her skin was Jas, binding her to the gang, binding her to him. "Don't let me go."

"I won't, Noelle."

dallas

O'KANE LIQUOR PROSPERED through hard work, and that work had to be done every day, even when Dallas's right-hand man was wandering around like a pussy-whipped fool. Not that an outsider would be likely to notice the change in Jasper's stony expression, but Dallas had known his friend too long. Noelle was a sweet little piece of ass, and Jasper was well and bloody hooked.

Even now a tiny smile played around the edges of the other man's mouth. At least Bren looked like his usual violent self. In five minutes, the door across the room would open, spilling out reluctant allies who could become enemies with damn near no provocation. Dallas had picked the meeting point this time, an abandoned bar on the border between the third and fourth sectors. Everyone was less twitchy in neutral territory, but violence had broken out before—and would again.

But hopefully not today. "So is your girl ready for her big welcome party, Jas?" Dallas asked.

"Yeah, bandaged wrists and all." Jasper arched an eyebrow. "Having second thoughts about letting her in so fast?"

He'd left second thoughts behind the day the girl had stumbled into Jasper. Tonight, he was having fifteenth thoughts. "Just counting the days until you mark her."

That straightened out the edges of the man's smile. "We'll see."

At least the bastard was glaring, and none too soon. Footsteps shuffled in the hallway, and Dallas nodded to Bren and Jas before relaxing into a deceptively casual sprawl that left his hand close to the gun strapped to his thigh. "Here we go."

Wilson Trent *always* glared, and today was no exception. He walked in, followed by four of his men, and surveyed the room before taking a seat. "O'Kane."

"Trent." The other leader had brought more than the customary two lieutenants for backup, but it was the tightness around his eyes that told Dallas they were treading close to a trap. Trent's glare seemed too forced, too fixed. Anticipation hung in the air, so thick Dallas could taste it.

Fuck. The bastard was going to play one of his games.

He confirmed the suspicion a heartbeat later. "I'm surprised you didn't just send your men tonight. Word in the sectors is you've got your hands full playing daddy over in Four."

Damn Jasper, and damn Lex too. They'd plucked a girl off the street like shining heroes, and everyone smelled weakness. "Never too busy for you, Trent," Dallas replied mildly, trusting Jasper to keep a leash on his temper for the words that followed. "But we can talk about the new girl if you want. Big eyes, tight little pussy. Ever defiled one of Eden's angels? They start out shocked, but if you break 'em in right, they'll beg for cock."

Trent shrugged one shoulder. "What new girl? I was talking about that dancer—" He turned to the muscle on his left. "What's her name, again?"

"Alexa," the man rumbled.

"That's the one."

Lies. They reeked of deception, but Dallas couldn't blink. Couldn't flinch, couldn't stir so much as an eyelash and give them the impression Lex meant a damn thing to him. He certainly couldn't cut out the man's tongue for daring to say her name.

Watching him bleed and cry would brighten up Dallas's shitty day, though.

He hadn't gotten this far without being as good at lying as he was at spotting liars, so he smiled. "Lex is a hell of a dancer. Not too easy to shock, though, if that's your thing."

Trent lifted one hand and signaled his men. "I brought her something. Figured you could deliver it for me."

It took everything in Dallas not to tense as the door opened again. A feminine growl of outrage preceded the unmistakable sound of an open palm cracking against skin, and he put it together with Trent's taunting question about Noelle—and it *had* been about her, before the bastard had wiggled the knife for a weak spot—and saw the shape of the trap.

So he wasn't surprised when one of Trent's men dragged a struggling brunette into the room. She was a sleek creature, curves over muscles and shapely legs shown off by a skimpy miniskirt. Her leather bra matched. So did the cuffs that trapped her wrists together and the collar around her throat. Her cheek bore a vivid handprint, but she seemed unsubdued. When the man dragging her jerked the chain connecting her collar to her cuffs, she snarled and spit on him.

"Charming," Dallas drawled, turning his attention back to Trent. "But Lex already has a new toy. If I give her two girls to play with in one month, she'll get spoiled."

"Slavery," Jasper spat. "It's dirty, even for you, Trent."

"Don't be such a snot. You might call it something different over here in Four, but pretty words don't change facts. You peddle more flesh than I'd know what to do with."

Dallas raised two fingers. "Enough." Trent's men would beat the shit out of the girl if they thought it would goad one of Dallas's men into a reaction, and Jas was just softhearted enough to walk into the trap.

He'd give him hell if they had to leave the kid to Trent's nonexistent mercies, though. Dallas gave her poor odds of surviving the night.

With an internal sigh, he tested the edges of the trap. "If she's such a prize, why are you getting rid of her?"

"Because she's—" Trent stopped short when Bren yawned, then shook his head. "She's not my type. I like blondes."

The brunette bared her teeth in a half-crazed grin. "And he couldn't stay on top of me."

It earned her another backhanded slap and a choking jerk on her collar, and Dallas hardened his heart against her involuntary tears of pain. Only a mewling excuse for a man had to beat a woman to keep her in her place, but this girl wasn't his responsibility. Every time he showed weakness, he endangered the women who already trusted him with their safety. He couldn't save them all.

Seeing the unfeigned hatred in her eyes, Dallas wondered if it might be worth it to save this one. There was intelligence there too—though it was difficult to see through the rage—and his gut told him she could be a useful source of information. Trent, in his idiocy, had always underestimated women.

Intimate association with Lex had long since taught Dallas better. "Bren, you like girls with fight in them. You want to break this one in?"

He inclined his head in a slow nod. "I can handle her."

"In your dreams," the girl snarled.

Dallas ignored her and quirked an eyebrow at Trent. "I'm not paying for her, if that's what you're hoping. I'm here to discuss our trade agreement."

"I know." Trent reached out and poked the girl in the hip. "Consider her a bonus, and our terms stay the same. I think that's more than fair."

The brunette opened her mouth again, and Dallas cut her off before she could say something that would stab at Trent's tiny ego and blow the whole thing up in their faces. "Gag her. I'm sick of the screeching."

"Yes, sir." Bren rose, unwinding a length of fabric from his wrist as he moved.

The girl fought when he touched her, thrashing with the blind instinct of an untrained street brawler. She knew how to land an elbow in a sensitive spot, but instinct couldn't compete with Bren, who stood impassive and unyielding as she battered at him. She even sank her teeth into his arm hard enough to draw blood, and he just stared down at her until she began to still. "You done?"

Hatred burned in her dark eyes, but Dallas caught another hint of animal cunning too. Maybe she recognized a rescue, because she did the smartest thing yet.

She kept her fucking mouth shut.

Dallas returned his attention to Trent. "What's her name?"

"Six." Trent leaned back in his chair. "You like?"

He shrugged as Bren gagged the girl with that same bland detachment. Jas was probably fuming inside, but Six would survive a little callous handling a lot easier than whatever Trent meted out to the women who pissed him off. "Like what? Her name? Her looks? Pussy in general?"

Trent laughed. "You're an odd man, O'Kane. Are we *square?*"

"We're square. Your usual shipment of grain for our usual shipment of liquor. And we won't sell to anyone else in Sector Three."

The man spread his hands wide. "Then everyone's leaving here happy. Tomorrow night, you know the place."

"I do." Dallas let Trent rise before grinning. "And, Trent?"

"Yeah?"

"Next time you feel generous, Lex likes redheads. Sweet ones with big tits."

"I'll remember that. Hell..." Trent shrugged. "Maybe I'll set my sights on figuring out what else she likes."

Real men. The thought of what Lex would do to a spineless, pathetic bastard like Trent was the only thing that kept Dallas smiling. That and the fact that the idiot was tipping his hand, poking and prodding for a weak spot.

Trouble was coming, and he needed to be ready. "See you tomorrow."

Trent slipped out the back door. His guards filed after him, one pausing for a long last look at Jasper, who bared his teeth in a snarl.

Dallas waited until he heard the rumble of engines outside. Bikes, because Trent's sector barely had roads and the cars Dallas kept running would be useless. Sighing, he pointed a finger at Six. "It's your lucky day, sweetheart. Play nice now, and gagging you's the worst we'll ever do."

She stood stiffly in Bren's grip, her mouth bisected by the gag, but it didn't take her long to nod once.

Smart girl. "Get her to the car, Bren."

"I don't like it," he murmured.

"I know. That's why you're taking her to the car instead of Jasper. Pat her down too, for Christ's sake."

"You got it." He urged the girl toward the other exit, leaving Dallas and Jasper alone.

Dallas allowed himself a sigh. "Odds are good she's a spy."

"Or worse." Jasper retrieved a crumpled pack of cigarettes from his pocket and lit one. "Trent seems pretty pleased with himself."

"Sure does." Dallas pulled out his own cigarettes and tapped the pack on the table. "Trent and I have always had a difference of opinion when it comes to women and their uses. Maybe he wised up and that girl's a trap. And maybe she's just a distraction, and the trap's going to get a whole lot of us really fucking dead tomorrow."

"There are ways to minimize losses."

"And we'll take them." Dragging smoke into his lungs, he rose. "Tomorrow. Tonight, we've got a party to get to. Don't get too wasted, eh? Leave that to the lady."

"Noelle will be all right." Jasper's gaze drifted to the door. "What about that one?"

"If she cooperates, she'll be all right too." Dallas clapped Jasper on the shoulder. "Cheer up, buddy. Even if she is a spy, Trent treats his women like something he scraped off his shoes. Any of our girls would spit on the best he has to offer. We make that clear enough, chances are she'll turn."

"Or else?" Jasper snorted. "Maybe we should have

said no. It's less of a risk."

"Call it a hunch." It was the only explanation Dallas intended to give, and for Jasper—for now—it would be enough. Most of his people knew to trust his instincts.

As they rolled out of the meeting place, Dallas's gut told him something else. Something in Jasper had shifted already, whether the man wanted to admit it or not. He'd come face-to-face with a legitimate damsel in some serious fucking distress, and he'd fixated on the risk she represented.

Jasper was thinking like a man who held lives in his hands. Maybe one life in particular. Dallas only wished his gut hadn't already warned him how much trouble Noelle Cunningham could be.

9

WHEN QUERIED ABOUT the dress code for a welcome party, Lex had told Noelle to wear clothes.

Seeing the O'Kane women turned out in costumes that ranged from scraps that barely qualified as underwear to elaborate dresses with several flavors of denim and leather besides, Noelle understood that the response hadn't been as sarcastic as it had seemed. The women simply wore what they wanted to wear, and no one gave a damn if they were half-naked or covered from head to toe.

Her own outfit fell somewhere in between. A pair of her new jeans hung low on her hips, and her shirt was close to transparent in the front, with two dozen tiny black straps crisscrossing her back. Revealing, especially since she wasn't wearing anything under it.

Lex had laughed herself silly when Noelle had asked

whether or not she needed a bra. Going without had been Noelle's bold choice, made with flaming cheeks in spite of Lex's mirth. She'd joined a sector gang—*the* sector gang—and if she wanted to go to a party in clothes so skimpy everyone could see her breasts, no one could stop her.

She was a little drunk on her own belligerence, and she hadn't even touched the liquor yet.

A small brunette with a tiny but intricate tattoo high on one cheekbone stood near the door, a plastic bottle of water in one hand. "You're Noelle, right?"

"I am." The woman had ink around her throat too, a collar of black, swirling vines thick with thorns. Noelle had seen other women with ink collars curling around their throats, but not this close. The delicate details were art, testimony to Ace's skill, if he'd been the one to create them.

The woman held out her hand. "I'm Amira. You took over my job at Circle."

"Oh, you're Flash's..." Noelle trailed off, awkwardly shaking Amira's hand as she cast about for the right word. Girlfriend? Woman? She didn't even know.

Amira just laughed. "Yeah, I'm Flash's. Or you could say he's mine. Both work."

Noelle winced. "I'm sorry. I don't think Lex told me what you call it. Or really what it means, except that the marks..." She touched her own bare throat. "They mean something."

"Yeah—everything." Amira mirrored the movement, tracing her fingertips over a whorl of ink without glancing down.

The dreamy expression in her eyes said more than words ever could. The ink circling Amira's slender throat was supposed to be a mark of ownership, but Amira didn't look owned. She looked happy, satisfied. She looked blissful.

Noelle envied that surety, a ridiculous thought with her newly healed wrists standing as proof of her new freedom. She didn't need a man's mark around her throat to protect her, not with O'Kane cuffs adorning her skin from the base of her hand to midway up her forearm.

She didn't need it, but that didn't stop her from wanting. She had to fight not to scan the crowd for Jasper's familiar form, keeping her attention on Amira instead. "Congratulations on the baby. You must be so pleased."

Amira's smile widened. "I am. When I was living in the city, I never dreamed I'd be able to have a baby."

"That's so wonderful." It took money, influence, or luck to obtain access to the fertility drugs that made conception possible, sometimes a combination of all three. And getting your hands on the medication didn't make a child legal, not within the city. Without an official—or forged—birth record and bar code, building a life inside the walls of Eden was all but impossible.

Self-consciously, Noelle tilted her wrist. Her bar code was only a shiny black square in the center of her wrist now, with delicate lines swirling out of it to wrap around her arm. No bar code meant no going back.

"You're staying with Lex, right?"

Noelle tucked her wrists where she couldn't stare at them, hooking her thumbs into the back pockets of her jeans. "Yes, I am. She's been really great. She and Rachel both, helping me get settled in."

"A couple people thought she might make a play for you. Not Rachel, of course. But you're kind of Lex's type." Amira hesitated, then shrugged. "Especially if you're also Dallas's type."

"You mean..." Noelle struggled to realign a world that had tilted slightly. A relationship with more than one person didn't seem so odd when the two people were Dallas and Lex. She could imagine how she'd fit into that equation all too easily...and she didn't think she'd ever be more than a buffer. "No, I don't think I'm Dallas's type," she said, then realized she'd just insulted her new leader. "I mean, not that I wouldn't want to be. Or be flattered."

Amira laid a hand on her shoulder. "Hey, don't sweat it. Maybe you're better off."

That sounded almost foreboding. "I am?"

"Yeah. That can be messy. You might not want to crawl in the middle of it without taking a man of your own along."

She wouldn't check for Jasper. She *wouldn't*. "I guess I have some time to find one now. It's just nice to have a choice."

That earned her a confused look. "I thought you and Jas were a thing. I'm so out of the loop, but I could've sworn Flash said something like that."

"Oh. We're...something. I mean, I want us to be, but I don't know—" Every word out of her mouth only made her feel more awkward, and she desperately wished she'd had a drink or two already. Liquor loosened her tongue, and she never cared as much if the words came out sounding stupid. She took a deep breath and tried again. "I don't want to read too much into things, you know? I don't know how things work here, not for sure."

"You have time." Amira nodded to the slowly filling room. "Feel it all out."

Noelle stared at the woman's marks again. "How did you know that you and Flash were a thing?"

"When it became about more than sex." She leaned closer. "Coming from the city, I didn't get it at first. Sex there is so taboo—so controlled—but it's so fucking *easy* here. The trick is understanding. Does that make sense?"

"I think so." Easier now that Ace had been between her thighs. His touch had been pleasurable, but he wasn't the one her gaze kept automatically seeking. Sex, but nothing else. Nothing more.

"Sex can mean nothing. That's simple. It can be curious or spiteful or friendly—a thousand other things that are mostly simple too. But it can get complicated fast."

"Just for us?" Noelle asked softly. "Or for the men too?"

"For everyone. Absolute freedom of choice, Noelle. You don't have to pick a very proper, appropriate man—or a man at all. Hell, you don't even have to choose only one person. It's...heady."

The words held an odd sort of intensity, almost as if Amira was trying to convince Noelle. Or maybe warn her.

"It is heady. It's overwhelming."

"Which makes time your friend, yes?"

She couldn't help but smile. "Jasper agrees with you, I think. Either that or I'm doing something really wrong."

"No, Jasper's a smart one." A hint of color rose in Amira's cheeks. "Though I can understand why you'd be eager to lock that down."

She made it sound like a competition, but when Noelle glanced over the crowd again, she saw far more men than women. Lex had told her outsiders wouldn't be allowed tonight, unlike the fights and some of Dallas's more extravagant parties. Tonight was only O'Kanes, and when Noelle realized that, she realized how many men were watching her.

Too many. Maybe the transparent shirt with her breasts on proud display had been more of an invitation than she needed. Amira was wrapped in a flowing gown that clung to her curves but covered her modestly enough.

Noelle tipped her head forward so her hair slid over her shoulders to mostly cover her flaming cheeks. "Are they watching me because I'm the new girl, or because Lex shouldn't have let me wear this?"

"Maybe they want to find out if they have a shot." Amira chuckled and stretched up to kiss Noelle's cheek.

"Welcome to the family."

Returning the kiss would probably bring more male attention, but Noelle brushed her lips over Amira's soft skin. "Thank you. And I'll be grateful forever if you tell me what I'm supposed to do tonight."

"You're supposed to drink, princess," a familiar voice drawled from behind her. Ace swooped down to lay a smacking kiss on Amira's lips before winking at Noelle. "Jasper and Dallas will be along in a few minutes, and then Noelle here can run the gauntlet."

"The gauntlet?" Noelle asked, sounding more alarmed than she'd intended.

"Part of the family, part of the business." Amira looped an arm around Ace's neck. "Tonight, you familiarize yourself with the O'Kane product line."

Ace tugged Noelle against his side. It didn't seem particularly sexual, no more than everything else Ace did. He tucked Amira under his other arm as if casual touches were to be expected, even when a woman belonged to another man.

There didn't seem to be any harm in it, so Noelle relaxed into the easy embrace as Ace grinned. "One shot of each, princess, and be glad you're a woman. For men it's two shots, though we have one sassy lady who ran the full line up and down and did it better than most of the brothers."

"Lex?" Noelle guessed.

"Rachel," Amira corrected. "Poor Ace. A woman who can drink him under the table. I think he lost his heart that day."

Ace huffed. "I think we all did, doll. O'Kane is liquor, and Rachel's our goddess."

"Then have a few for me tonight, huh?" Amira looked down at the swell of her belly, barely noticeable until she rubbed her hand across it.

Noelle expected another lewd comment, but Ace untangled himself from their embraces and crouched in front of Amira. Pulling the fabric taut across her belly, he leaned close. "Listen to your Uncle Ace, peanut. You come out gorgeous like your mama instead of ugly like your papa, all right?"

"Hate to interrupt a moment of Ace being adorable," Rachel said from behind them, her voice full of amusement. "But I've got to steal Noelle. Open bar time, honey."

"I'm always adorable," Ace retorted, and Noelle laughed as she turned to Rachel. Her gaze drifted over the crowd again, but Jasper still hadn't appeared.

It hurt. He'd stripped her bare that morning with Ace, not just her body but her *soul.* Nothing that intense could simply be sex, not when he'd held her and stroked her as she drifted in warm haze long past the point where Ace had finished and put away the needles.

Or maybe that was what Amira had been trying to tell her, that a girl from the city couldn't possibly understand the difference between *casual* and *more* after less than a week.

Wetting her lips, Noelle fell into step next to Rachel. "Ace said Dallas and Jasper were on their way. Should I wait?"

She shook her head. "They got hung up with work. They'll be along later."

The gang came first. That was the rule she'd tacitly accepted when she let Ace etch the O'Kane symbols into her skin, which meant facing the gathering group of too many smiling men with a stiff back and a raised chin. She would pretend she was Lex, unperturbed by their lecherous stares and the frank appreciation in their hungry gazes.

Hell, maybe she'd kiss one of them. Or more than one. She was a free woman now. She was an O'Kane. Her body belonged to her, and if Jasper wanted claim over it, he'd have to put his mark around her throat.

Jasper leaned against the wall and stared at the woman in the chair. She stared back, impassive, heedless of the heavy chains that bound her. "Is that necessary?" he asked. "We're smack in the center of Sector Four now. Where would she go?"

Bren mirrored Jasper's stance with a grin. "She wouldn't run. She would, however, bite your face off, given half a chance. Wouldn't you, sweetheart?"

"Why would I bite his face off when yours is right there?" Six bared her teeth and, judging by the focused fury in her eyes, her rage was for Bren alone.

Bren shrugged. "I don't know—variety?"

"Fuck variety." Her gaze slid to Jasper. "Are you here to hold me down while he fucks me? Or is that your job?"

Under the taunt lay a very real fear. Dismissing it would be cruel, but so would taunting her in return. Jasper settled for shaking his head.

His restraint didn't soothe her. Her hands fisted, and she jerked against the chains for the first time, like his unwillingness to abuse her frightened her more than the threat of violence could. "This is some sick shit. Why the hell are you—?"

"Enough," Dallas said from behind Jasper. "Lex?"

Lex's heels clicked on the floor as she walked to the center of the room. "Why bother? She's not going to believe me. Where she's from, there are plenty of women who'll sell each other out for a little security."

Dallas sighed. "Could you pretend for a fucking second that I'm the boss and *try?*"

"Words are just words. You can tell someone you're a saint while you're stabbing a kitten. Does saying it make it true?"

Six sneered at them, her lips twisted in disgust. "What, you haul some poor bitch in here to yell at you and I'm supposed to believe I'm in a fucking paradise because you don't beat her face in? Did you write all the lines for her, or does she come up with them on her own?"

"See?" Lex knelt and stared up at the new arrival. "They screwed her up so bad she doesn't know what to think."

"I'm not screwed up," Six snarled, but even Jasper could hear the desperation under the words. Her rough façade was cracking, and with it, her composure. "I'm one of the strong ones. I survived, and I don't need your pity."

"Oh, I don't pity you. I kinda think they shouldn't have brought you back here. You're trouble."

That brought the woman's teeth together with an audible clack. She studied Lex, as if trying to figure out how the words could be a trap. Next to Jasper, Dallas opened his mouth and then shut it again without saying a word, watching the two women instead.

After a long silence, Six tilted her head. "I can't tell if you're all damn good liars or just fucking crazy."

"See?" Bren straightened off the wall and walked around behind her. "Told you she was smart." The chain rattled as he unlocked it and then let it clatter to the floor.

Dallas tensed, and Jasper knew it was taking all of his self-control not to haul Lex away from potential danger. Six seemed to notice too. "He'd snap my neck if I laid a finger on you, wouldn't he?"

"Dallas? Probably." Lex smiled slowly. "Unless I got to you first."

Bren laid his hands on Six's shoulders. "You want to hurt Wilson Trent?"

She carefully untangled herself from the chains. "I want to hurt Wilson Trent. But I'm not going to spill my guts and trust you not to dump me in the river when I'm done."

Jasper couldn't fault her for that. "Fair enough. What do you know about the drop tomorrow? We figure Trent's got plans for us. Ugly ones."

She studied each of them before turning just enough to stare at Bren's hand resting on her shoulder. "I'll tell him."

Bren nodded slowly. "What do you say, Dallas?"

"We'll be in the hall," Dallas replied, inclining his head toward the door. "Talk fast, sweetheart. We're late to a party."

Jasper crossed his arms over his chest. "You sure you want to be alone with the face-biter, Bren?"

He made a dismissive noise and stroked the backs of his fingers absently down the length of Six's hair. "We're past that. If I piss her off, I think she'll at least give me a good warning punch first."

She jerked her head away from him. "Touch me again and I'll bite your fucking hand off."

"See? When she figures out I'm not going to maul her, we'll be fine."

Lex didn't move for a long moment, then rose. "Tread lightly, sweetheart. They're not going to hurt you unless they have to...but I'm not as nice as they are."

"That's enough, Lex," Dallas said, stepping forward to rest a hand on her hip. "You and Jasper go to the party. You shouldn't miss your girl's big moment."

She took a single step back, another, and then re-lented with an annoyed exhalation. "Yes, sir."

The door slammed behind her, and Jasper rubbed the bridge of his nose. "Her girl?"

Dallas snorted. "I was talking to both of you. If you plan on making any grand gestures, I suggest you get there before Lex does."

"She wouldn't." Not even someone with Lex's sexual

appetites would try to snatch up Noelle when her atten-tion was so obviously focused elsewhere.

"I give you five minutes, tops, before Noelle's drink-ing her shots straight from Lex's luscious lips."

That wouldn't do. Jasper headed for the door—and told himself he was rushing for Noelle's sake, not his own.

He didn't believe it either.

10

THE PROCESS, AS Rachel explained it, was simple—
drink a shot, then celebrate with the other O'Kanes
gathered around the makeshift bar. Eight shots, eight
passes around the cheering crowd.

The liquor ranged from the really cheap moonshine
apparently favored in the other sectors to an exquisite,
high-end single malt whiskey—which explained how
Dallas could afford to throw pre-Flare artwork at Lex
like it was nothing.

The whiskey burned smooth all the way down, worth
every penny Dallas charged, and Noelle barely had time
to lift the empty glass triumphantly above her head
before someone dragged her into the crowd. Lips landed
on her cheek. Someone else swept her into a hug. The
redheaded stranger from Dallas's party snatched her
away from Amira and planted a kiss right on her lips

before passing her on to the next person in the circle with a grin.

So it went, all the way around the circle. Kisses, hugs, a few pats on the shoulder and one or two on the hip, but all fond and good-natured instead of lascivious. Ace got her last and sent her back to Rachel with a swat on the ass.

Noelle still held the shot glass in one hand, so she slammed it on the table upside down and laughed. "Do I do that every time?"

"Do what?" Rachel asked innocently as she handed over another shot. "Vodka's up. Next is the tequila, so pace yourself."

Sound advice, but Noelle downed the vodka and dropped the shot glass this time before she was whisked away by the revelers. Her skin tingled more this time around, and she was laughing by the time she reached the table again.

The tequila made her cough, but she drank all of that, too, before spinning into the crowd with a triumphant noise that felt right. Ace grinned and claimed his kiss before passing her along. It took longer, the hugs lingering and the kisses coming in twos and threes.

She was only halfway around the circle when the dizzy warmth crept from her stomach up into her chest, which was right about when the latest man relinquished her quickly.

To Jasper.

He looked down at her with a half-smile and rubbed her bare upper arms. "Sorry I'm late."

The warmth of his hands shot straight to her core, though that could have been the tequila, too. Or the vodka. Maybe the whiskey, making its presence known with a slow burn that turned her smile wickedly bold. "You missed two kisses. I gave them to Ace instead."

"Hell yeah, she did," Ace called from the opposite

side of the circle. "You gonna come get them, brother?"

"Wouldn't be the first time." Jasper tilted her head back with his fingers under her chin. "Three shots. Still steady on your feet?"

"Steady enough," she lied, fidgeting under his unwavering gaze. He had a way of looking at her that made the rest of the room seem frozen, as if they couldn't possibly be interrupting anything because nothing important would dare happen while his attention was fixed on her.

"Good." He released her, but not before brushing his lips over hers. "Congratulations, sweetheart."

No, that warmth wasn't the liquor. It was all him, and it expanded to fill her as she leaned up to kiss him once more. "See you next time around," she whispered against his mouth, then laughed and spun into the arms of the grinning man next to him.

She *wasn't* steady on her feet by the time she came back around to Ace. He whirled her like a dancer, and the room kept on moving, dipping dizzily to the side before righting itself. She stumbled back toward Rachel and crashed into Jasper.

Again.

Blinking, Noelle pulled back to peer up at him. "Did you come to get your kisses from Ace?"

Jasper didn't answer. Instead, he picked up the next shot Rachel had poured and tipped it back. Then he slipped an arm around Noelle's waist, dragged her close, and bent his head to hers.

Liquor spilled across her tongue. Not the whole shot, not even most of it, but enough to give her the taste of it. His lips crushed against hers, hot and a little rough, the sensation a thousand times more intense with the entire gang forming a cheering, catcalling wall around them. She couldn't forget that everyone was watching as he chased the booze with his tongue, and then she couldn't care because he knew how to kiss her knees weak.

Lex's voice cut through the cheers, close and wry. "That's real subtle, Jas."

Jas released Noelle, and she swung around to face Rachel. "That has to be cheating."

"Not exactly," she hedged. "Technically, you don't have to *finish* every shot. Not by yourself, anyway."

"Jasper just hung a big 'no trespassing' sign on you." Lex wound her arm around Noelle's shoulders. "Good thing I like to live dangerously."

Jasper glared, and it was hotter than it should have been. His furrowed brow and his tight expression, all of him poised as if he'd snatch her out of Lex's grip at a moment's notice.

Smiling slowly, Noelle leaned in to the other woman. "He didn't ask me if I wanted you to trespass."

"Do you?" A whisper, and Lex's breath stirred the hair curling against the side of Noelle's neck.

Noelle wasn't sure what made the decision for her. The vodka, maybe, or the tequila. Some bit of wildness buried deep inside her, only uncovered when liquor had burned everything else away.

The way Jasper's gaze all but dared her to do it.

She only had to turn her head a little bit, and then Lex's mouth was pressed against hers. Soft lips, more yielding than Jasper's, and gentler. It seemed that way, at least, in the moment where Noelle could only kiss the other woman awkwardly, terrified it might be a mistake after all.

Lex licked her mouth and tilted her head to part Noelle's lips with her tongue. Still soft, but no less demanding than Jasper's kiss, especially when she eased Noelle down to sit on the edge of the table and inched a hand under her shirt to stroke her belly.

Then Lex broke the kiss with a slow smile and reached for the next shot on the table. "Gin," she whispered huskily, pressing the glass into Jasper's hand.

He growled. "You like to play with fire." But he drained the shot, jerked Noelle's head back by her hair, and fused his mouth to hers. Moaning, Noelle tangled her fingers in his shirt, clinging to him to try to keep her balance.

Even that wasn't enough when Lex pressed parted lips to her throat, teeth closing lightly on her pulse as Jasper licked the taste of gin onto her tongue. This time, Noelle really had forgotten about everyone else until Ace shouted, "Fuck, Jasper, let her breathe!"

But breathing was overrated, and doubly so when Jasper nudged Lex out of the way to lick Noelle's throat, soothing the ravaged skin. She grasped at his hair, tangling her fingers in the short strands as much as they'd allow as her heart beat its way toward her throat. "Aren't you supposed to let everyone else congratulate me after each shot?"

"You eager to get up?" he asked, nudging Lex's hips harder into the open vee of Noelle's legs.

"Not really," she managed in a shaky voice. It took another deep breath to strengthen her tone. "But I want to do it right. I want to belong."

"That's a done deal, baby girl." Lex lifted Noelle's hand and nodded to the fresh ink encircling her wrist and forearm. "You belong. You always will."

The words hit her in a place the alcohol couldn't, and she tilted her head back to stare up at Jasper. "Three more."

Three more shots and three more kisses, each one dirtier than the last. By the time Jasper let her taste the abrasive, fiery moonshine from his mouth, Noelle had to wrap her legs around Lex's thighs just to keep the room from spinning.

Lex laughed and reached around Noelle to brace her hands on the table, the movement rocking their hips together. "You've *got* to be drunk. It'd be wrong to put my hand in your pants now, wouldn't it?"

Noelle didn't care if Lex stripped her out of her pants entirely, as long as someone kept rocking against her. She stroked Lex's cheek, contrasting the silky softness of the other woman's skin to the alluring scratch of Jasper's beard. "I hear music. Is there going to be dancing?"

"Do you want there to be?"

Noelle almost missed the question when Jasper shifted his hands from her waist to her breasts, his palms crushing the gauzy fabric of her shirt against her tightened nipples. Moaning, she tipped her head back. "Dance. I want to dance. Not like they do in the city, though."

Lex hummed and tugged her off the table, out onto the floor. "I think I know what you want."

Between one thumping bass beat and the next, Noelle found herself pressed against Lex, with Jasper close at her back. He dropped his hands to her hips, holding her steady as he ground against her.

Free. Sinful. Noelle swayed with the music, wrapping one arm around Lex and lifting the other to curl her hand around the back of Jasper's neck. "I'm tingly."

"Wasted's what you are." He laughed, his shirt brushing the skin left bare by the scant back of her blouse.

She had to be. Everything was far away, at a dreamlike distance, as if time bent around her. But touch—oh, touch was *good*. Jasper, hard at her back, and Lex, so soft, rubbing against her chest. Words didn't need to stop at Noelle's brain before tumbling past her lips. "This would be better if we were all naked."

Dallas's laugh rumbled over her as he loomed out of the darkness behind Lex. "I'll say. Sorry I missed your big debut, kitten, but it looks like you're well in hand."

Lex sucked in a soft breath, one Noelle wouldn't have

noticed if they hadn't been dancing so close. "The girl wants to move a little," she whispered, tipping her head back on Dallas's shoulder. "Surely Jas and I can handle that."

Dallas dropped an absent kiss to the top of Lex's head and gripped her hips, mirroring the hold Jasper had on Noelle. The moment twisted easily to encompass their leader, and Noelle's imagination conjured the four of them naked and moving together. Not so different from that first party, when she'd had her mouth around Dallas's cock.

Cock. She was even thinking like an O'Kane now, foul in the silence of her own mind. She watched, still lost in that dreamy haze, as one of her hands drifted up all on its own. Over Lex's neck and down, trailing across her breast. "You're beautiful."

"Look at you. So bold." Lex shivered and circled her hips, grinding higher on Noelle's thigh. "You want to climb on top of me sometime, you be my guest."

Jasper groaned. "But not tonight."

Noelle wiggled her ass against his hard erection. "You can't stop me."

"Don't have to." His thumb slipped under the top of her pants to brush her hipbone. "Tell her, Lex."

"Hmm?" Lex arched into Noelle's touch instead.

She couldn't help but laugh. Lex wouldn't pay attention to anything or anyone with Dallas grinding up against her, and the man knew it. He grinned at Noelle over Lex's head, his dangerous eyes dark with amusement. "If you weren't liable to pass out soon, kitten, I'd invite both of you back to my rooms for all of those wicked games you're imagining. Some other time, hmm?"

Her good sense was still disconnected from her mouth. "I played a wicked game this morning," she retorted, and the memory of Ace's odd little nipple rings clamping tight gave her inspiration. The next time Lex arched into her touch, Noelle caught her nipple and pinched it.

The response was instantaneous. Lex gasped, her nipple hardening to a stiff point, but she twisted away from Noelle. "Better sleep it off, baby girl. Soon, you'll get that wish I see dancing behind those big blue eyes."

Dallas filled the empty space in front of Noelle and caught her chin. For a moment, she was frozen in place, trapped between Jasper's unyielding bulk and Dallas's dangerous strength.

The gang leader rubbed his thumb over her lower lip with a smile that seemed more warning than anything else. "Don't be a brat, kitten. Jasper's not going to let you do anything you might regret, no matter how hard you push him. But pushing him won't get you what you want either. You get me?"

Lying was beyond her. "Not really."

He snorted and leaned in to kiss her soundly. "You will. Welcome to the family, sweetheart."

Jasper spoke, his voice low in her ear. "Time to say good night, Noelle."

She watched Dallas melt into the darkness before looking around. Plenty of people were dancing and drinking, and some were doing far dirtier things than that. "The night's barely started," she protested, turning to face Jasper. "I don't want to be the soft city girl who couldn't drink her shots and couldn't stay at her own party."

"Is that really what you're worried about?"

Of course he couldn't understand. He was a rock. Unmoving, unmovable...strong and secure in his place. Noelle slid her hands up his chest with a sigh. "Maybe I just want to have fun. Why does everyone care if I'm wasted? I let you do worse stuff to me when I'm not."

He stiffened, his brows snapping together in a frown. "Worse? That's still what you think, isn't it?"

"No, I don't mean it like that." Fear swept up out of nowhere, spurred on by the hard set of his jaw and the darkness in his eyes. "I know it's not bad, because I trust you. And I don't care. I like it. I want it."

He looked around and exhaled roughly. "You know, you're right. It's your party. You should hang out for a while."

She hadn't fixed it. The words she'd blurted without thinking had damaged something, and she didn't know how to get him back, the fond Jasper with the possessive glint in his eyes. She hovered, torn between storming away in a fit of newly claimed independence and buckling under in pleading submission.

Neither appealed to her.

The stern set of Jasper's jaw softened, but he shook his head. "I'll see you tomorrow." He took a step back, another, then turned and made his way through the crowd.

He left her alone, swaying for reasons that had nothing to do with music. The room swirled around her, heat and music and warm bodies, but Lex had vanished and Rachel was just as absent, and no amount of alcohol made seeking sanctuary in Ace's arms seem like a safe option. She was stranded in a crowd of strangers who were supposed to be her family.

And Jasper had left her alone. To her horror, tears stung her eyes. She whirled to follow him, ready to beg for forgiveness if she had to, and slammed into a solid chest instead.

Brendan caught her before she pitched over. "Chin up," he murmured, "and dance with me. Jas is mad at himself, not you."

Hearing so many words from the usually quiet man shocked her into compliance, and she had both hands around his neck before she knew it. She didn't think he'd said two words to her before tonight, but he and Jasper seemed friendly. "Are you sure?"

"Positive."

"I didn't help much." She dropped her forehead to Brendan's shoulder with a groan. "I *am* too drunk. I keep saying things that aren't a good idea."

He patted her back. "All the more reason to take the night slow."

Brendan was solid like Jasper. She supposed he was attractive, too—not handsome like Ace, but appealing in a raw, starkly masculine sort of way. Her body appreciated being pressed up against his every bit as much as it had approved of Lex, even though his touch was friendly, not seductive. Noelle sighed shakily. "He's the one who started all the fondling. It seems unfair now."

A crooked grin curved Bren's lips. "Life, Noelle. I heard it's like that."

She made a face at him. "Who would ever believe I'd have more luck getting sex in Eden than I have in the heart of O'Kane territory?"

"Well, you're looking at it backwards." He spun her slowly under one upraised arm before drawing her close again. "You can go anywhere and get fucked. You come here to get it good."

This time, pressed against him, she shivered. "You O'Kane men are all very confident."

"That sounded almost like a complaint."

The words came without warning, bubbling up and out in a tangled jumble. "He wants me to figure out what I want but he won't give it to me and something tells me he won't be any happier if I get it from someone else."

Bren brushed his thumb over her lower lip and nodded. "Now you're starting to catch on."

She licked the pad of his thumb. "Maybe I'll just decide not to care if he likes it or not."

"If you figure out how to stop giving a shit whenever you want, let me know how, huh?"

Time to be bold. Time to be a fearless member of the O'Kane gang instead of a sheltered fool from the city. She bit the tip of his thumb and gave him what she hoped was a sultry look. "I could start by having sex like everyone else."

He shook his head, a genuine look of regret painting his features. "Nah, you don't want me. I'm convenient, that's all. But I appreciate the offer."

"You're more than convenient," she protested, because it was the only thing to do other than sink into the floor and die of mortification.

"Are you always this apologetic?"

Noelle hesitated. Considered. "I suppose...yes."

"Why?"

"Because that's what I was raised to be." She dropped her cheek to his shoulder and closed her eyes. "I was supposed to marry an important man and entertain his important friends. I was supposed to be invisible except for when I was supposed to be decorative, and capable enough to keep everything running smoothly. If anyone was dissatisfied with anything, it meant I wasn't doing my job."

Bren pressed his lips to her temple. "But you're not in Eden anymore."

His touch was almost tender, and Noelle melted against him. "I thought you were supposed to be scary, but you're sweet."

"I'm both, darling. Most everyone here is." He paused. "Remember that."

 lex

S HE DUCKED INTO the closest room with a door that locked. The storeroom was packed high with boxes, but it also held an extra corner booth from the Broken Circle, its table stripped away, leaving only a semicircle of plush black leather.

She didn't have to wait long.

Dallas closed the door and twisted the lock. "Your little pet's growing up fast."

"Isn't she?" Lex backed up to the wall beside the leather seat. "It's enough to give a woman ideas."

"Why am I not surprised?" He slid onto the leather and stretched his arms across the back of the booth. "The boys are stroking their dicks half raw imagining what you do to her every night when you close your bedroom door."

She eased onto the seat beside him. "You don't have to imagine. You could watch."

He arched an eyebrow. "Is that an invitation to start something, or confirmation that you're corrupting her when the lights go out?"

It was hard to tell which answer he preferred. "It could be an invitation," she murmured. "If Jas doesn't mark her soon, you could step in. No one would fault you for it."

"No one except Jas." Dallas continued to study her. "I can't tell if you want me to fuck Noelle or collar her, but I'm sure as hell not doing the latter."

"Don't you like her?"

"She's not my type, love. If Jas handles her right, he'll have a sweet little sub to pet and cuddle. That's fun for a night or two, but it's not for me."

And yet Lex could have sworn that was exactly what Dallas wanted—a woman who would gladly, happily be owned. "I think it might be—under the right circumstances."

His dark gaze didn't shift from her face. "And what are those?"

Always so intense, and it was that intensity that drew her closer even as she felt locked into place. Ensnared.

Lex straddled his leg and settled with her hand resting lightly on his fly. "I know what you were thinking the other night. What you wanted to see while she was sucking your dick."

His expression remained bland, but his dick hardened. "What did I want to see?"

She leaned in, putting her mouth close to his. "My head between those pretty, pale thighs, for starters."

"Your head between anyone's thighs is a hot sight." He stroked her cheek and then brushed his thumb over her lips. "You've never been under me. You don't know what I do with the women in my bed."

The lack of personal experience was irrelevant. "I know what you like, Dallas. What gets you off. I pay attention."

He nodded once. "And when you bring Noelle to my bed? What do you imagine we'll do with her? It *would* be both of us, wouldn't it?"

"Nothing so inflexible." Lex grinned and tugged at his pants until the button and zipper both opened under her fingers. "Did you like watching her touch me?"

Dallas growled. "What do you think, Lex?"

His cock jumped in her hand, rigid and hot. "You liked it. Maybe..." She fought to steady her breathing and stroked him slowly. "Maybe you're more interested in watching *her* eat *my* pussy. You'd have to teach her how."

"I think we're into your fantasies now." He sank a hand into her hair. "Not that I wouldn't enjoy the hell out of watching her lick you with her shy little tongue. It'd take her forever, but that's part of the fun, isn't it?"

"Part of it." The rest was the thought of control, both seizing and relinquishing it.

Maybe it showed on her face, or maybe he just knew her that well. "She'd do anything I told her to. I don't think you'd be as obedient."

"You don't want me to be." Lex leaned over and let her hair trail over his dick.

He jerked the hair he held twisted around his hand and hauled her head up. "When I want your obedience, I'll get it."

He seemed so sure of that, as sure as he was of everything else, and the realization both terrified and comforted her. There was no mountain Dallas O'Kane couldn't climb. No woman, either.

She swallowed hard. "Noelle would mind herself, kneel at your feet and await your command. So would that new girl—Six."

"Probably," he agreed mildly. "Noelle doesn't know any better, and Six has been beaten down."

"Not me." An unpleasant possibility drew Lex up short, and she stared at him. "Is it a problem?"

"Now what part of what I just said made it sound like a problem, Lexie? You think I want you to be clueless?" His hand relaxed, cupping the back of her neck as he smoothed his thumb over her throat. "You think I want you beaten?"

"No," she whispered. "But I'm starting to think you don't want me to be the way that I am."

Dallas sighed and closed his eyes. "There's what's good for the gang, what's good for business, and what's good for you. What I want doesn't rate on the list most days."

She couldn't let him own her, but it still hurt to watch him like this. "Is this about Trent?"

"It's about you being exposed." Dallas released her and refastened his pants. "I like you just the way you are, Lex. I don't want to put you on a leash. But you stand out, and that's not safe for you."

She barely heard the words, all her attention focused on his hands. He was getting good at that, at pulling away when she wanted to bring him closer. At one time, her touch had melted his resistance, and it had been enough. But now...

Distance. She could feel it, a chasm yawning between them, and a blowjob wouldn't fix it. She'd been so damn *careful* not to challenge him outright, never to compromise his authority.

Somehow, she'd failed.

Lex couldn't stop the words that tumbled out. "You don't want me on a leash, but that's what they'd like to see, isn't it? It's what they understand." She caught his wrist. "Collar me. Give them the show they need."

Dallas hauled her down into his lap. "Say that again?"

It sounded like a request, except for the intense thread of command in his voice. "A collar," she repeated softly. "Not for real, I mean. We'll know the truth."

"A collar. For show." A low laugh shook his chest. "Don't lie to yourself, Lex. You're smarter than that. You and I can't share a bed for show."

He'd have her on her knees every night, screaming herself hoarse. "I'm not talking about fucking." She held his gaze. "I'm talking about control. Enough to satisfy anyone who thinks I'm stringing you along by your dick."

He gave her a too-serious look, ruined only by the twitch of his lips. "Aren't you?"

She didn't bother to be careful where she put her knees as she climbed off his lap. "Go ahead and laugh at me, Dallas. Like I give a shit."

He uncoiled like a spring, shooting half off the couch to drag her against him. This time, he closed his hands around her arms and trapped her, her back to his chest. "This is all my fault. I let you get away with shit none of the others would dare, and you're so used to it you don't even realize."

She struggled, her own fury rising. "Then don't do me any more fucking favors. Treat me like everyone else."

"I'd turn anyone else over my damn knee right about now. Settle the hell down."

Lex stilled, forcing herself to slowly breathe in and out. "Can I go now?"

"No." His grip eased, caging her without crushing her. "We haven't discussed the collar yet. It's a good idea, if we can do it without killing each other."

"It's not the only solution." She craned her neck to look back at him. "I can find someone else. You didn't want me, simple as that."

"I think we both know that's bullshit."

Which part? "Then you're stuck with me, Declan."

"Mmm." He rubbed his thumbs over the backs of her arms, stroking in slow, lazy circles. "The collar might be for show, but I'm not a noble man. You know you can't fuck anyone else while you're wearing it."

She shivered. "It wouldn't be very convincing if I did. Unless you were with me."

"And I will be." Dallas pressed his mouth to her ear. "Put yourself in my hands, Lexie. Just a little. Let me keep you safe, and I'll make it worth anything you have to give up."

You had to have something in order to give it up, and what did she have? Desire, a longing so primal it felt as if it had always been a part of her. His lips grazed her ear again, and Lex released a shaky breath. "How will you do that?"

"You'll see, love. Soon enough, you'll see."

11

J ASPER WAS HALFWAY into a bottle when someone
pounded on his door. Noelle's voice followed, low and
intent. "Please let me in. I forgot to put on pants."

Of course. Groaning, he rubbed a hand over his face
and opened the door. "What the fuck are you doing with
no pants on?"

"Bren put me to bed." She ducked under his arm
without waiting for an invitation, padding into his room
on bare feet. "I got up after he was gone, but I've never
been to your room before. I knocked on three wrong
doors."

Jesus Christ, she *was* in her underwear, tiny black
panties that bared more than half of her ass. "Well, here
you are. What do you want?"

She wandered over to his punching bag and traced
her fingers over the leather. "This is the first time we've

been alone together. In private, I mean. You never touch me when we're alone together, only in front of other people."

He'd thought it the most expedient way to cut through the inexperience she sometimes wore like armor. "You don't like it?"

"I like it when you touch me in front of other people." She wandered around the punching bag, dragging her hand across it until she'd made a full circle and was facing him. She was still drunk, sleepy-eyed and loose-tongued, and she kept talking, raw truth tumbling past her lips. "I like it more than I feel like I should. Sometimes I wish you'd just *tell me* I'm bad. Take me over your knee and spank me and let me pretend I'm atoning for my sins instead of committing a new one by wanting your hand on my ass until it's all I can think about."

Maybe it wasn't a hurdle to get past, an obstacle to surmount. Maybe Ace was right, and the punishment was part of her pleasure. "Bend over the table."

Her breathing hitched. "Don't tease me."

He swept his arm across the table, shoving his keys, wallet, and books to the floor. "Now, Noelle."

Wide-eyed, she crossed the room and bent forward until her elbows rested on the table. Her scant tank top slid up her spine, revealing the generous curve of her hips and how skimpy her panties really were.

He took another swig of whiskey and set the bottle aside. "Is this what you want?" he asked, teasing his fingertips above the top edge of her panties. "For me to spank your ass until you can't sit down, tell you how naughty you are for wanting it?"

"Yes," she whispered. "Only you don't want me to feel dirty. I can't even do this right."

"I don't want you to believe everything those bastards in the city told you. But if you like it..." He scratched her skin lightly and dragged her panties down.

"If you *really* like it, Noelle, I'll punish you."

She shifted her weight uncertainly. "I don't know why I want it. I don't know how to find out without *doing* it."

He stared down at her pale skin, but he didn't touch her again until he hit her, his palm smacking hard against her flesh. Noelle gasped, sucking in air before releasing it in a hungry, helpless little noise.

Instead of slapping her this time, he wound his other hand in her hair and pulled her head back. "What do you like about it? Tell me."

"I don't know," she whispered, scraping her nails over the table. "It hurts, but not really. And I don't—" She bit her lip.

He slid his hand around to the front of her throat. "You don't what?"

She swallowed. "I don't have to feel guilty for liking the shame, because that's the point."

All twisted up, and he'd been a fool to think he could unravel it. "Why can't you just like it?"

Noelle let out a frustrated noise and arched up on her toes, practically wiggling her ass at him. "Maybe I could if you'd *do it.*"

And he'd do it...if she just liked it. He'd had lovers who got off on pain before, but never one who used it as an excuse. "I didn't say you could move."

Noelle scoffed, no trace of the shy, demure little city girl left in her eyes as she glared back at him. She was drunk enough to throw caution to the wind and she did, taunting him. "What are you going to do? Spank me?"

He leaned over her, frustration twining with anger. "You'd like that, wouldn't you? Is that your plan? Push me until I'm *really* pissed? Until I lose control?"

Her spine stiffened. She tore her gaze from his, fixing it on the wall instead. "No. I don't want you mad at me."

Jasper laid his hand on her ass and squeezed the reddened skin.

She trembled in reaction, but she didn't look at him. "Do you have to be angry to want this?"

"To really want to punish you, yes. Otherwise, it's just another thing that gets you off." He slapped her ass again. "If you like it, I'll do it." Another blow. "I'll do anything. But I want to know why."

"I don't know," she panted and squirmed. She spread her arms wide, palms flat on the table, as if she needed to balance herself to stay standing. "It should be punishment, but it's not. That's the part I like."

"What does that mean to you? That you're dirty, Noelle? That there's something wrong with you?" If he slid his hand down, he knew he'd find her thighs slick, her pussy swollen. "That there's something wrong with *me*?"

"Not with you." The words were too fiercely protective to be anything but the truth. But the fight went out of her in the next moment, and she dropped her cheek to the table. "But maybe there *is* something wrong with me. I don't like things even though they feel shameful. I like them *more* because of it."

So close. "Why, sweetheart?"

She barely whispered the answer. "Because it feels good."

"Would it feel as good if you weren't ashamed?"

"How can I tell?"

The question was so earnest that it left him with only one answer. "I don't know."

Sighing, she rocked up on her toes again. "Help me find out? Please?"

He couldn't, not if he had a hope in hell of keeping his own head on straight during all of it. "If you trust me, I have an idea."

She whimpered. "Does your idea mean I have to go back to my own bed all—all wet and aching and *frustrat-*

ed?"

"No." He kissed her shoulder and backed away. "Turn around and sit on the table."

"I trust you." She kicked free of her panties before sliding onto the table with her knees tucked primly together. "I don't need the other stuff. If you don't like it, if you don't want it, it's okay—"

"Open your legs."

Her teeth snapped together and her cheeks flushed, but she spread her legs wide. "Should I take off my shirt too?"

Jasper had to drag his gaze up to her face. "That depends. If you were alone in your room, would you take it off? Play with your pretty little nipples?"

"No," she said after a moment's hesitation. "If I started doing that in Lex's room, I don't think I'd be alone for long."

He couldn't help his bark of laughter. "No, I guess you wouldn't." Her nipples were hard under the thin fabric. "Leave it on. Touch yourself."

"What?" She sounded shocked—scandalized—but her hand was already drifting toward her breast. "You mean...touch my nipples?"

Her bewildered shock tightened his balls, made them ache. "For starters. Then we'll move on to everything else."

After another breathless moment, she obeyed, closing her thumb and her middle finger around one bud. Her gaze stayed fixed on his as she pinched and tugged until a moan escaped her.

"You like it hard," he murmured. "I remember."

She nodded and brought her other hand into play, mirroring the movements of the first. "I thought of asking Ace if I could keep those little magnetic rings, but I didn't think I'd be able to survive the teasing."

"That's the whole point." Jasper nodded to her

spread legs. "Lower, Noelle. Show me how you touch your pussy too."

"I've never touched it like you do," she admitted, sliding her hand down. She brushed her fingers over the dark curls there before inching the very tip of her middle finger over the hood of her clit in a tiny circle. Her eyelids drooped as she repeated the caress. "Just like this."

He felt an answering tug, a tingle at the base of his spine. "Do it again."

She caught her plump lower lip between her teeth and obeyed. It was a light, shy touch, one that barely counted, but this time she didn't stop. She edged her fingers lower, parting her swollen folds as she explored tentatively. "I liked your fingers inside me."

"Gonna try yours now?"

She did, leaning back to brace her weight on one hand as she pushed two fingers inside. A slow, wicked smile curved her lips. "Not as good. Too small. Too short."

Jasper caught his breath. "You have more fingers."

"Show me." She worked a third finger into her pussy in spite of the words, moaning when she thrust them deep. "Why won't you touch me? Don't you want me when we're alone?"

He dropped into a chair to keep from crossing to the table. "You're drunk, sweetheart, and I have my rules."

"I don't understand them. I'm doing everything you tell me to. My hands might as well be yours, except they're not as good."

Maybe she was right. He nodded to the bedroom. "Bed's through there. I'll take the couch."

Shock painted her features, followed swiftly by mortification. She stumbled off the table and snatched up her panties, and by the time she dragged them up her legs she was shaking.

Her next stop would be the door. Jasper shot across the space between them and grasped her upper arms. "If you don't see the difference between me touching you and what was happening, that means there *is* no difference. I shouldn't have been doing it."

"Why is it always so easy for you to *stop?*" The question tore free, ragged and edged with honest pain. "I must want you so much more than you want me. I'm like one of Ace's groupies, needy and pathetic."

He wanted to shake her. "Because I don't get to lose control. If I lose control, people die. Things go wrong." Her hair brushed the back of his hand, and he couldn't resist running his fingers through it. "You'd get hurt."

He saw the moment the words penetrated, the moment she not only understood but believed. Her eyes widened, and she pressed both hands to his bare chest, fingers splayed wide. "Don't you get tired of it? Having to be in control, having to protect me?"

"Yes *and* no." He tugged at her hair, then indulged himself by stroking his fingers over her cheek. "In the long run, it's worth it."

She absorbed that in silence as she turned her face into his palm. Her lips tickled the heel of his thumb in a ghost of a kiss. "Don't make me sleep alone. I won't try to do anything, just...hold me? Please?"

"Noelle..."

Something wet brushed his palm. Tears. "I don't understand the rules here. I'm trying. I swear I'm trying."

She was crying. *Fuck.* Jasper folded her in his arms. "Stay. I want you to. I can keep my hands to myself."

"I'm sorry. I'm sorry, I didn't mean to—" She swiped at her cheeks angrily, dashing away tears. "I should go. I don't want to stay like this."

"This is why you *should* stay," he argued. "Not sex, not like this. But being here is okay."

She shivered and leaned closer, rested her forehead against his shoulder. "When I was ten, one of my tutors gave me a kitten. I only had her for a few hours before my father came home, but I fell in love with her. She would nuzzle my cheek and climb all over me... I had something to cuddle."

Jasper hooked his arm under her legs and picked her up. "Your dad made you get rid of her?"

"My father got rid of her, and then he got rid of the tutor, too. They told me at dinner, and when I cried, my mother slapped me so hard she split my lip. She said decent ladies don't cry, because tears are how wicked women make righteous men doubt their convictions."

A heartbreaking moment, and the saddest part was that it had to have been one of many, a string of confusion and shame. "I'm sorry, sweetheart."

She rubbed her cheek against his chest with a sigh. "I don't want to manipulate you. I just don't want to be alone, and I don't want to be with anyone else."

"Shh. Right now, it's time to sleep it off." He eased his bedroom door open with his foot.

Noelle huffed. "I wish you were drunk. Then you'd tell me things about you."

Oh, if only she realized. "I *am* a little drunk." He eased her onto his bed and tumbled after her. "What do you want to know?"

She seemed to consider the question with adorable gravity as she wiggled into a comfortable position with her cheek resting on his arm and her hand over his heart. "Where are you from?" she asked finally. "Eden, or the sectors?"

"Neither. I grew up on a farm east of here."

"In the communes?"

Nothing so sterile or acceptable. "A private operation. We grew corn for the distilleries, along with some other things."

"Oh, one of the illegal farms," she murmured sleepily. "We're not supposed to know about those. In Eden they tell us that nothing can live outside the communes, that the land can't support people. But I heard my father arguing with a partner once about whether or not to send the military police to shut one down. I think some of the councilmen pay to support private farms so they won't have to worry about rationing during the lean harvest years."

If they did, they relied on outfits more reputable than the one Jasper had worked. "My parents dropped me off when I was ten," he told her. "An apprenticeship, they all called it, but the only thing I learned was how to survive. I guess that's a trade all by itself these days, though."

Noelle lifted up onto her elbow and peered down at him. "They left you when you were ten?"

He couldn't meet her gaze. "Had to get to work."

She laid her palm over his cheek, her skin soft and warm above his beard. "That must have been so hard. And terrifying."

The farm had housed kids even younger, children who couldn't handle the backbreaking work. "I'd still be there if Robbins—the man who ran the place—hadn't traded me to Dallas to settle a debt."

"How old were you then?"

"Twenty-two." And Dallas had been in the beginning stages of building an empire.

The curling ends of Noelle's hair tickled his throat as she kissed his temple. "I'm glad he took you. You're worth more than any debt."

"That's what he thought, I guess. He still made me work it off, though—one year." After that, he'd been free to go, but where? Sector Four was as good a place as any, even before he'd proven himself loyal to the O'Kanes.

She settled close to his side but kept her fingers pressed to his cheek, absently stroking his beard. "You're all so strong. You've been through terrible things and you still *live*. I don't think I ever realized how numb I was until they threw me away. Like I was a shadow of a person."

She felt good cuddled against him, so good it dulled the razor's edge of the lust. "Sometimes...you have to hit bottom before you can figure out where to go."

"I've been slipping for a while. Ever since—" She broke off, tensing. When she continued, her words were lower. More intense. "My father had started negotiations for me to marry. After that, nothing mattered. I didn't care if I was ruined. I thought my father would cover it up to save face but all of the important men would know, and no one would have me after that."

"There are worse things than being alone on your own terms." Though maybe not in the city.

"I thought so, too. I knew my father would restrict me to the house for a few years to keep me from harming the family's reputation, but I didn't mind that. I'd have had access to a desk and the city's library. But then something else happened."

Jasper's stomach clenched. "What?"

As if she felt his tension, she made a soothing noise and stroked his chest. "Somewhere between deciding to let that boy touch me and getting arrested for fornication, I woke up. Even if my father had kept me in the city, I wouldn't have been happy locked up alone with my books anymore. I know I'm all tangled up inside, and I know it bothers you...but I'm sure about one thing. I'm not made to be untouched and alone."

Nobody was, least of all a woman as filled with life and curiosity and *desire* as Noelle. "I know what you mean." He kissed the top of her head. "Sleep. You're gonna feel like shit in the morning."

"Don't care." With a sigh of satisfaction, she squirmed closer. "At least I'll feel."

He waited until her breathing began to slow to whisper, "Me too."

12

NOELLE WOKE UP dying.

Her skull pounded. Her mouth tasted like she'd swallowed cotton, and the roiling in her stomach reminded her she'd swallowed something far, far worse. Even shifting to her side made the room tilt and the churning increase until she whimpered.

"Don't move. It makes it worse."

"Lex?" The pillow smelled like Jasper, and the bed didn't feel like the pull-out couch. It couldn't be Lex's bed, either—the sheets weren't nice enough. "Where am I?"

"Jasper's place. He had to go." Lex rattled a small bottle. "Head hurt?"

"Not so loud, please." Noelle pressed her palm to her temple and tried to keep her head from throbbing so hard it split open. "I don't think I can eat or drink anything right now."

Lex touched her cheek. "You've got to. Water and as-pirin, honey, that's all that's going to fix this."

Groaning, Noelle eased carefully onto her back and squinted up at Lex. "Where did Jasper go?"

"Business. Well, trouble," she amended. "Something's going down tonight. Got to prepare."

Noelle choked down the aspirin with as small a sip of water as she could manage and studied Lex's face. There was no hint of subterfuge, no sign that Jasper had dumped Noelle on Lex to get away from her.

That would be more comfort if Noelle's memories of the previous evening were clearer—or less embarrassing. "I think I was very drunk."

Lex grinned. "Does that mean you don't remember making out with me? I'm crushed."

It surfaced in a rush, a vivid memory of Lex's tongue swiping through her mouth before Noelle ended up sprawled on the table. She groaned again and covered her eyes with one hand. "I remember. I guess it's a good thing Jasper drank half my shots."

"Relax. As far as those parties go, it was damn tame." Lex stretched out beside her. "Bren said he got you back to my room, but I figured you must have dragged your drunk ass down here to have it out with Jasper."

She remembered that, too, far more clearly than she wanted to. "I changed my mind. Maybe I wasn't drunk enough."

Lex laughed. "Being passed out cold has its upsides."

"It probably keeps you in bed where you belong." No-elle eased onto her side and smiled at Lex. "I think it ended up all right, though. We talked."

"Good. He seemed square this morning, anyway."

That gave her hope. Between the humiliation of beg-ging for something Jasper wasn't ready to give and the mortification of breaking down into tears, the evening should have been a disaster. But the moments she re-called most vividly were those spent cuddled against his side.

She couldn't remember how long they'd talked before she'd drifted to sleep, but the low rumble of his voice had chased her into dreams, a whisper that made her feel safe and cherished.

Moving slowly to avoid upsetting her body's precari-ous truce, she curled her hand around Lex's. "I'm glad I'm an O'Kane."

"Me too, honey." Lex propped her head on her other hand and looked down at Noelle. "I know what you want from him, and I need to explain something to you about the way things work here."

A different sort of queasiness stirred Noelle's gut. "Did he tell you what happened?"

"Jasper? He doesn't talk, not about that. But he doesn't have to." Lex tapped her temple. "I see the hun-ger, Noelle."

"How can you even tell what's what? I'm starving for everything."

"No, you only *want* some things. The others... Yeah, you're starving for those."

"What am I starving for?" No, that wasn't the real question. In her heart she knew, and so did Jasper. The question he wanted answered was the one she couldn't begin to unravel. "And *why?*"

Lex shrugged one shoulder. "I don't worry about why. *Why* doesn't matter. It won't change what you need."

"It matters to Jasper."

"Not even slightly." Lex leaned closer, held Noelle pinned with her dark gaze. "Jasper doesn't want to go too far because he's worried about what happens after. If you think it's all fucked up and wrong, eventually you'll hate yourself *and* him. You'll hate your life."

159

"Oh." Put that way, Noelle understood his fear. And as much as she wanted to brush it away, she couldn't. Not honestly. "I can't help it. I want to believe it's not wrong. I think I'm starting to, but I don't know."

"So take your time and enjoy the ride."

It couldn't be that easy. "What did you want to explain to me?"

Lex's brow furrowed. "The things you've been offering him—and what you've been asking for in return—it's fast. Even for an O'Kane. So don't be surprised if he hesitates, okay?"

Noelle closed her eyes as her stomach churned with more than the aftereffects of the liquor. "So the things I'm starving for aren't the things I'm supposed to want."

"Don't put words in my mouth, baby girl," Lex said, gentle but firm. "Fast, not wrong."

Except wanting them fast must be wrong, or at least naïve. "Help me understand. What makes it different from all the other things people do?"

"You really don't get it, do you?" Lex sat up then, her spine stiff and her dark eyes clouded. "You don't *need* him, Noelle. You don't need anyone, not anymore. You have the gang, and you have yourself. You can do whatever the hell you want."

Lex sounded as confused as Noelle, and she felt laughter bubbling up. Of course Lex couldn't understand her question. She lived in a world where all the lines were drawn, where her body and her mind were her own to give. Where giving had some meaning, because she knew how to hold back.

"I was trying to do what I wanted," Noelle confessed, safe behind the shield of her hands. "But no one can tell, can they? Jasper doesn't know if I can say no. None of us do, not even me."

"I think that's the heart of it," Lex admitted in a whisper. "*Can* you say it? You have to find out, for your sake and Jasper's."

It wasn't likely to happen while he was handling her so carefully, but a darker part of Noelle acknowledged that it might be harder to know when he stopped handling her gently. "To him? I don't know." She brushed her fingers over Lex's hip. "Maybe not you, either. I don't *want* to say no."

"Uh-huh." Lex twined her fingers with Noelle's. "Is that why you're hitting on me in Jasper's bed?"

This time she did laugh, even if the sound made her temples throb. "Only by mistake. The room isn't spinning anymore, but my head still is. How long until this goes away?"

"An hour or two? Could be *all day.*"

Noelle fought a whimper at Lex's gleeful tone. "Nothing makes it better?"

"Not drinking until you pass out is a start." She urged Noelle over and pulled her close to her chest, one arm curled around her. "Go back to sleep. I'll stay."

Lex's warmth against her back made it easy to relax. That was the seductive lure of strength—you could close your eyes and drift, content to trust your safety to someone else's hands. "I'll get stronger."

"I know."

As long as Lex believed it, Noelle would, too.

Jasper carefully stripped the red plastic from the wire between his fingers. "Want to let me know why we're not just yanking the blasting caps and hauling ass out of here?"

"Because." Bren didn't sound nervous. No, he seemed perfectly at ease with a pair of wire cutters in his hand and a fifty-pound stack of plastic explosives in front of him. "If Trent has his goons check the device before tonight, we want it to look operational."

Dallas loomed over them, chewing absently on a toothpick as he watched them work. "Guess the girl wasn't playing you after all, Bren."

"Told you she wasn't."

Jasper hadn't been so sure. Still wasn't, truth be told. "How do we know this wasn't the plan? We get down here early to defuse Trent's little surprise, only the *real* surprise is when he blows it up in our faces?"

"We don't know," Dallas replied. "Losing your nerve in your old age, son?"

"That tends to happen pretty fast with my balls parked this close to a shit ton of RDX."

Bren grinned. "He needs those balls for pretty little Noelle."

"I thought your kitten already had 'em tucked in her pocket." Dallas laughed and shook his head. "She was showing her claws last night."

"We worked it out," Jasper muttered. "I *am* pissed at you, though. You could have warned me you were serious about Lex maybe wanting to keep Noelle all to herself."

"The warning *was* your warning. Lex takes what she wants."

And Dallas didn't sound happy about that. Jasper swiped the back of his wrist over his forehead and listened to the trickle of water in the corner of the small, dank basement. "And if they pair off?"

Dallas clenched his teeth around his toothpick. "Then they pair off," he ground out. "And since they both like dick, some lucky bastard can crawl all up in the middle of it."

Bren snipped a wire and frowned. "I don't get why the both of you don't just head it off. If you've shared a woman before, what's the big deal in making it two?"

Noelle was the big deal. Noelle, who—for all her sensuality and hunger—could still barely wrap her head around the idea of sex, casual or otherwise, with a single partner. The idea of any permanent arrangement with not one but *three* other people could send her screaming.

Unless she liked the idea.

Jasper shook his head. "Three possessive assholes in a bed is a few too many, especially when you're only talking about four people total."

Dallas chuckled. "Says you. To me, it sounds like a party."

It would be mind-blowing—for a night or two. "Long-term?"

"Maybe. Hell, long-term ain't the sort of thing you decide without a trial run or ten. And probably not while you're sitting on a bomb."

Bren flipped the wire cutters in his hand and held them out to Dallas. "Which we're not anymore."

Dallas didn't ask if he was sure, just took the cutters with a nod. "I want you up high tonight. No matter what goes down, Trent doesn't walk away from this pretty little trap."

"You got it."

Jasper rose. "I'll send Flash after the explosives later. It's hard to get your hands on this much of it. Makes you wonder how Trent managed."

"Someone backed him," Dallas agreed. "The real question is whether it came from the sectors or straight out of Eden. A couple of those bastard councilmen are clever enough to set us up to kill each other." His eyes tightened as he met Jasper's gaze. "Noelle's father, for starters."

The hair on the back of Jasper's neck prickled. "Even if that's true, it has nothing to do with her."

"Probably not." Dallas waved the wire cutters at the bomb. "This? This wasn't a couple days of planning. Even if it *is* daddy dearest, it has nothing to do with her—but that doesn't mean it never will. I knew that when I took her in, but if you care a damn about keeping her safe, you'll stop falling asleep every time I bring up city politics."

Burn it all down. Jasper's blithe, easy answer to the political machinations, the careful dance of offense and defense Dallas lived with every breath. But if it put Noelle in danger...

"I can learn," Jasper said, hefting the bag of tools they'd brought over his shoulder.

That earned him a searching look, Dallas's eyebrows drawing together as he flipped the wire cutters over and over in his hand. "Just like that, huh?"

"No, but I'm not stupid. I know what the right answer is."

Dallas snorted. "It's always been the right answer. Hasn't stopped you from telling me to go fuck myself before tonight."

"Maybe it's just time."

"Maybe it is." Dallas glanced at Bren. "You need time to scope out a good spot, or are we ready to roll?"

He checked his watch. "Fifteen minutes. I'll be ready."

"Good. Don't let that bastard shoot me."

"Jas won't let that happen." He picked up his bag and headed away from the door, deeper into the recesses of the darkened basement, out of sight.

Dallas shook his head. "Someday I'm going to teach that bastard to have a sense of humor."

"He has one, it's just massively fucked up and approaching inhuman." Jasper reached for the wire cutters, shoved them into the tool bag, and stowed the whole thing behind a crate in the corner.

They were almost to the stairs when Dallas stopped him with a hand on his arm. "I wasn't joking about the blowback we could get if word gets around Eden that Cunningham's youngest daughter is wearing O'Kane ink.

Personally, I'd get some sick satisfaction over watching them devour that self-righteous ass...but he could decide to make the embarrassment go away."

The growl escaped before Jasper could stop it, a surge of rage at the possibility that Noelle could have lost everything and it still wouldn't be enough for her father. That he might want to ensure her silence. "I'd kill him first. Is that political enough for you?"

Dallas barked out a laugh as he started up the steps. "It's a start. She's safe enough for now. After we deal with the current mess, we'll see about making sure she's safe for good."

She already was. His or not, Jasper would make sure she never had to worry about her safety again.

Wilson Trent was a terrible liar. He couldn't stop the corners of his mouth from tipping up, and Jasper fought not to roll his eyes. The man couldn't have been any more transparent if he had a blinking sign above his head: *I planted a bomb in the basement.*

Dallas was a hell of a lot better at deception. Jasper could have almost believed his impatience and irritation as he checked his watch. "You sure you gave your driver the right address?"

"He'll be here," Trent assured him. "Probably had to circle around because of a blocked street."

"He'd best hurry his ass. I've got plans tonight that don't include dancing with the military police."

"I don't think you have to worry about that, O'Kane."

The big, blinking sign might as well have come with a klaxon horn. Jasper shifted his weight and crossed his arms over his chest. "You could head on back, Dallas. I'll stay to make the trade."

Dallas checked his watch again and sighed. "Maybe

I'll do that. You and Flash can handle the shipment."

For a moment, Jasper thought Trent might break. Instead, he slammed his hand down on the table. "I don't send my men to do business for me, and I expect the same courtesy from you."

Dallas didn't even crack a smile, just arched one eyebrow and gave Trent the opening he was dying for. "If it's that fucking important to you, go do your damn business and find out where the truck is."

The man blinked, though it only took him a second to recover. "Yeah. Yeah, I should do that." He turned to the two men who'd accompanied him, brand-new faces Jasper had never seen before. "You boys stay here as a show of good faith. I'll be back in a minute."

It was forced and overplayed, ridiculous in a dozen ways, not the least of which was that in the three years of their alliance, Jasper had never seen Trent take so much as a casual suggestion from Dallas without turning it into a pissing contest.

Dallas held his annoyed expression. "Fine," he muttered, turning to study the two men Trent clearly intended to sacrifice. "Make it fast."

Trent hesitated, as if fixing the scene of his triumph in his mind, then smiled. "Sure thing." He headed for the door, a shade too fast to be convincingly casual.

The heavy steel slammed behind him with a clang, and Jasper counted off the seconds. One, two, three, with the fourth count splintered by the crack of a rifle shot.

Dallas drew his handgun and leveled it at the man on the left. "That was your boss's head blowing out. Time to ask yourself whether he's worth dying over."

The other man looked like he was going to make a move, so Jasper bared his teeth as he pulled his own pistols free of their holsters. "Don't."

For a second, he thought it really would be that easy. But Trent's men only shared his lack of brains, not his lack of loyalty. The taller of the two kicked a chair to-ward Dallas and dove out of the way of his first bullet, drawing his gun as he moved. The shorter twisted his hand, and a knife flashed.

The blade zipped through the air. Jasper spun and deflected the knife with his arm, wincing as the sharp edge glanced off skin with a shallow, wicked slice. The man already had another knife ready to throw, so Jasper put two shots in his chest and a third in his head.

When he turned, Dallas was putting the man's part-ner down. The final shot echoed through the room, and Dallas glanced toward the door. "Think anyone else will come running? Or are the rest of them holed up some-where, wondering why this place hasn't gone up yet?"

"I'd go with the latter." Jasper put his pistols away and looked down at his arm. A steady stream of blood trickled from the cut, but it was slow enough not to worry him. "Think Trent was smart enough to have a backup plan?"

"Not fucking likely, judging by how he played the rest of it." Dallas holstered his gun and nodded to Jas-per's arm. "Do we need to bandage that?"

"I'll get some gel on it. It'll be fine."

"Let Noelle patch you up." Dallas grinned, and it held a feral edge. "I bet she'll kiss it all better."

She'd been eager to suck his cock after a cage match. What would she be eager to do after a *real* fight? Jasper pushed through the door. "Should have let you get banged up a little, then."

"I'll tell Lex I almost let some bastard shoot me. She'll beat me up *and* kiss it bet—" Dallas stopped cold at the sight of Bren—and Wilson Trent, bound and gagged on the cracked sidewalk. "What the fuck?"

The man was only half-conscious, bleeding from one knee. From the livid marks around his throat, Bren had throttled him pretty good.

The blond man blinked at Dallas now, then gestured to Trent. "Thought I'd take him back with us. He's someone else's kill."

Dallas's confusion melted into narrow-eyed disbelief. "The girl?"

Bren slipped a hunting knife from the sheath on his leg and dragged Trent's head back by his hair. "If it's a problem—"

"No." Dallas waved the offer away. "Fuck, she earned it, if she wants it. If not, you clean up."

Right on schedule, Flash pulled to a stop at the corner and climbed from behind the wheel of the truck. Three dead men, and a messy plot foiled. By the end of the night, word would spread through all eight sectors— Trent had tried to fuck Dallas, and now he was dead.

Whether that would spell the end or the very beginning of their troubles was anyone's guess.

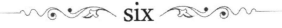 six

T HE LAST TIME Six had seen Wilson Trent, she'd been bound and gagged, bruised and bloodied, her pride stripped away and her future in jeopardy.

This moment had a certain symmetry, which was the first thing she'd found amusing in over a year. She lifted her gaze from the half-dead body to the man who'd brought him. Brendan Donnelly was solidly built, with just enough flesh over hard muscle to hide how much of it there was until he flexed, or wrestled you into submission, or dumped a six-foot man at your feet.

He watched her, waiting for a reaction with an air of anticipation that had her shivering. "I don't understand. Does Dallas want me to kill him as a test of loyalty or something?" If so, it was a damn shitty one. Most of Trent's men would have stabbed him in the back for fun.

The corner of Bren's mouth quirked up. "That'd be

stupid. Dallas isn't stupid." He held out a knife, his fingers light on the blade and the handle pointing toward her. "I figure this one's yours, that's all."

She could snatch it from his hand and sink it between his ribs. In her fantasies, at least—and maybe his, too, judging from the way he watched her sometimes, as if he liked the idea of her being as dangerous as he was.

Fantasies were the only place she was dangerous. He'd stop her before she grazed the blade across his skin, but apparently he'd let her take that same knife and sink it into Wilson Trent's traitorous excuse for a heart.

Still, she didn't reach for it. "No tricks?"

"No tricks."

Six nudged Trent's leg with her boot. "Untie him."

Bren didn't move, only waved the knife at her. "You do it."

She curled her fingers around the hilt. It was heavier than she'd expected, the blade itself nearly half a foot long. Trent choked out a muffled protest and squirmed back, and Six felt the first stirrings of satisfaction as she sliced through the ropes.

Fear before death was too good for him. He'd taught her that there were worse things than fear. Things like hope. "Get up."

"Fuck you," he rasped.

She planted a boot in his side. "Get up, bastard. Get up and fight. I thought you liked hitting me."

He lunged up on one knee and grabbed for the knife. Fast, but not fast enough. She slammed her knee into his face, reveling in the crunch of bone as his nose broke. "Take this," she snarled at Bren, thrusting the knife at him.

"You sure?" But he was already reaching for the blade.

"I'm sure."

When Trent rocked up, she smashed her fist into his

jaw. Pain splintered through her hand and up her arm, and she relished it. Relished the faint hope in Trent's eyes, as stupid and reckless as it was. He'd fixate on the fact that she was unarmed, see her as the victim he'd made her, and somewhere in his sick fucking skull, he'd think he had a chance.

She'd beat the hope right back out of him, like he'd done to her, and *then* he could die.

13

H ER HEART IN her throat, Noelle shoved through the door to Dallas's bedroom and nearly moaned her relief at seeing Jasper on his feet, more or less whole. *Bring the med kit to my room* was all Dallas had told her before wheeling off in search of Lex, and the five minutes it had taken her to collect the first aid supplies and traverse the maze of corridors to the large suite had been among the longest in recent memory.

But she was here now, and he was *alive.* "Jasper? Are you hurt?"

He held up his arm. "It's nothing. Just a scratch."

An odd piece of furniture sat a few feet in front of her, one that looked like two padded leather benches connected back-to-back, so they faced in opposite directions. She set the med kit down on the shared back and lifted the cover. "Sit and let me look at it. I'm not very good, but I know how to use gel and bandages."

Instead, he slipped his hand into her hair and yanked her down for a rough kiss. The pounding of her heart shifted from fear to exhilaration as she slapped one hand on his shoulder to keep her balance.

Even that didn't help when he dragged her into his lap and pressed the slim tube of healing gel into her hand. "This and you. That's what I need."

She had to catch her breath as she twisted the top off the tube. "How did this happen?"

Jasper growled. "Some bastard got this bright idea to blow Dallas up. We stopped him. Had a little bit of a fight, though."

Her hand trembled, and it took another breath to steady it enough to apply the healing gel to the long, shallow cut. Blood had dried on his skin, bisecting the flesh left bare of ink, in some places looking like artwork of its own.

"You all could have died," she whispered as the truth of that fact hit her hard in the gut. The cage fights, those were manufactured danger, violence in controlled form. Tonight had been real.

"We smelled the trap," Jasper countered. "We had it, solid. No reason for you to worry."

She frowned. "You're bleeding."

"That happens more often than you'd think out here."

"Then I get to worry if I want to." She dropped the gel back into the kit and found a precut bandage. His muscles were so large that it only wrapped around his arm twice, and she stripped away the protective panel from the adhesive at the end and sealed it in place with a kiss to the coarse fabric. "I don't like it when you bleed."

He smiled, slow and hot. "Liar."

It wasn't the blood that stirred her, but the fact that

he was whole. Hard against her, so vital, so alive... "I don't like it when you bleed," she repeated, kissing the warm skin above the bandage. "I like it when you win."

"*That* I believe." He slipped his arms around her and kissed her again. Slow and warm and wet, his tongue working past her lips to stroke the inside of her mouth, each deep caress tugging at things low in her body.

In minutes, she was squirming in his lap. "We could go back to your room," she offered against his lips. "I can like more of you."

"We could do that." Jasper trailed his mouth to her jaw, then to the spot below her ear. "Or we could stay here. Dallas went to find Lex."

Memory rose, a fractured piece with no beginning or end, just the feeling of Jasper at her back and Lex crushed against her chest, and Dallas smiling as he gripped Lex's hips. All of them moving together, grinding, swaying...

She shuddered and tilted her head back. "You don't mind?"

"No." He nipped at the front of her throat and soothed the bite with his tongue. "You want me, but you want them too. Tonight's the night we find out how much. How far."

Not a night for saying *no*, then. Hopefully not a night where he'd want her to. But she could draw one line. "I have a condition."

His hands traced up her back. "What?"

She sank both hands into his hair and adopted the firmest, fiercest look she could manage. She was an O'Kane woman. She could say these words. "I want you to fuck me tonight."

Jasper shifted beneath her, his arousal as evident from his heated gaze as from the growing hardness of his cock. "Say it again."

"I want you to fuck me." She rocked against him,

wishing she'd worn a skirt instead of her jeans. Some-thing easy to jerk out of the way, because she'd spent too many nights going to bed frustrated, and she thought she might be able to chase her pleasure just like this...if he let her. "Promise you will."

"I'll fuck you," he whispered. "I promise, Noelle."

"No cheating. No *technically*. You have to really do it." She released his hair and gripped her shirt instead, tearing it over her head, leaving her hair a disheveled mess. Her bra was the only one she actually owned, the only one not borrowed from Lex, a clever bit of lace and wire that pressed her breasts together and up, and the way Jasper's gaze lingered made it worth every credit. "You promise?" she asked again, while she had his atten-tion and the advantage.

He dragged her arms behind her back, pinning them above the swell of her ass. "I'll fuck you," he answered in a rough murmur.

Maybe Lex had been right. The more she demanded, the more he gave her exactly what she'd wanted all along. She wiggled a little, enough to trigger that deli-cious sense of helplessness without the risk that he might mistake her squirming for actual struggles.

Trapped. *Finally*. Noelle wet her lips and summoned another challenging glare. "Tell me how. Tell me the dirty details. The obscene ones."

"No." He hefted her against his chest and rose.

Her heart skipped, slamming against her rib cage as her breath caught. "Tell me," she snarled—or tried to snarl, only without air it came out as a gasp, a begging plea that used up all the oxygen she had left.

He didn't answer. He dropped her on her knees on one side of that odd, two-sided bench and bent her over the center section of it. He pulled at her jeans, drawing the button and zipper free in one hard yank. Her heart started pounding, her pulse throbbing *everywhere*. She could hear the blood rushing in her ears, could feel it between her legs, an ache that wouldn't go unanswered this time.

She tilted her head to toss her hair from her face and blinked at the wide metal rings affixed to the opposite side of the bench. They were clever, nearly invisible unless you knew to look for them, but once she did she found more on the sides. "What is this thing?"

Jasper's nails scratched her skin as he pushed her jeans and her panties down. "Ask Dallas. He'll show you."

Oh God, this was familiar, too. The bite of the bench against her stomach, the scrape of fabric over her thighs, that heady mixture of anticipation and helplessness that came from being exposed. Last time she'd wanted too much—or too fast—and it had twisted into disappointment.

Not a mistake she wanted to repeat, so she tried to shove away anticipation and focus on his words. "Dallas isn't here. Can you show me?"

"Sure he can." Lex closed the door behind her and smiled at Noelle. "I know where the cuffs and chains are."

Cuffs and chains.

Yes.

She was drunker now than she'd been last night, drunk on the possibility of having everything she wanted at her fingertips. Smiling, she spread her arms wide across the back of the bench, her fingertips inches from the rings. "Then maybe *you* should show me."

Lex dragged two leather cuffs and a thick length of chain from the bedside table drawer and walked over. She leaned in to kiss Jasper with a pink flash of tongue, then unhooked Noelle's bra. "We don't want to rip this."

Dazed by the sudden tangle of emotions, Noelle let Lex coax the fabric down her arms. Seeing another woman kissing Jasper should have made her jealous. Maybe it had, a little, but only a dull niggle that tasted as much of what she *should* have felt as what she really did. Arousal. Belonging. She wanted them to kiss. Kiss each other, kiss her—one got her as hot as the other, because no one would be left on the outside and wanting. Not this time.

Lex tossed aside the bra and stood there, her hands on the bench, and she didn't move them until Jasper said, "Touch her before you put on the cuffs." Then she lifted her hands to Noelle's face as Jasper slid his lower, drawing the denim all the way down.

Noelle shivered and met Lex's eyes. "Kiss me?"

Lex tipped her head back and drew her thumb across Noelle's bottom lip before licking it. The sensual shock lasted only a moment before a greater one overtook it— Jasper's tongue across the small of her back.

"That's right," Lex murmured and kissed her, her mouth open and seeking. Wet warmth and the tang of liquor, and Noelle moaned into the other woman's mouth as Jasper slipped off her shoes and her jeans and spread her legs wide.

He molded his hand to her pussy, cupping her before easing one finger over her clit.

She cried out against Lex's lips as the jolt of pleasure jerked her entire body. It was too much, too fast, the kind of overwhelming sensation that had her using the leverage of the bench to squirm her hips up and away from such direct contact.

Jasper pushed her back down with a firm hand on her hips. "Chain her."

Lex broke the kiss and buckled the first cuff around Noelle's wrist. "What made you pick the bench?" she asked softly.

"It was the closest—" She yanked against the chain as Jasper's finger brushed her clit again. The sound was breathtaking, the rattle of iron and the kiss of it sliding over leather. Noelle whimpered and uselessly tried to twitch her hips out of Jasper's grip. "I didn't pick it on purpose."

Lex fastened the second cuff and ran her thumb over it. "If you like this, you'll be glad. So glad." She took a step back and started unbuttoning her shirt.

It wasn't a show, not like when Lex danced on the stage, but Noelle couldn't tear her eyes away as fabric teased apart, baring tawny skin stretched over sleek muscle and intriguing curves.

She wasn't wearing a bra. Naked from the waist up, she moved closer, until one nipple hovered near Noelle's mouth. Jasper reached out, curled his fingers in the top of Lex's skirt, and dragged her across the remaining space.

Not a verbal order, but a command nonetheless. Noelle swiped her tongue experimentally across Lex's peaked nipple. It hardened under her touch, even more when she closed her lips around it and sucked hard.

Jasper slipped his fingers away from Noelle's clit to thrust two inside her. Wide and stretching but shallow, only to the first knuckle. "Show me your tongue. I want to watch you lick her."

She was having too much fun listening to Lex make satisfied little noises, and she liked the way Jasper growled when she challenged him. Ignoring the aching demands of her body, she paused only long enough to say, "I'm busy," before catching Lex's nipple again, this time with a wicked smile.

"Lex?"

She shivered and moaned, even arched her back before meeting Jasper's gaze. When she did, she twisted her hand in Noelle's hair and jerked her head to one side, forcing her mouth open.

It hurt, hurt in the good way that started as pain and dissolved somewhere between her brain and the juncture of her thighs, where her inner muscles squeezed tight on Jasper's fingers as her entire body seized for one long shudder.

Someday she'd ask if it was meant to be a reward, part of the game and something they enjoyed as much as she did. Someday when she wasn't floating on the illicit thrill of closing her eyes and parting her lips in newly earned obedience.

"You like that, don't you?" Lex's voice was thick with desire.

A rhetorical question. It had to be, because the words hadn't yet died in the air when Jasper drove his fingers deep into Noelle, all the way in, and rocked them inside her.

This time there was nothing to muffle the sound, not of her cries and not of metal slapping against leather as she tried to rear up. Lex hadn't left much slack in the chains, and Jasper's hand at her lower back kept her hips pinned.

No retreat, no leverage, nothing to do but twitch as his blunt fingertips massaged inside her, moving in a seeking pattern that made little sense until he brushed something that brought her thighs together as she whimpered and fought to rock away.

Noelle hadn't heard the door open, but Dallas's low chuckle drifted over her. "You got her over the bench and didn't bother tying her legs? Lexie love, get me the rope. The silk one."

"I don't know where it is," she said lazily.

"Liar." His reply was every bit as easy, but the hand he wove in Lex's hair made her grip on Noelle seem gentle by comparison. He fisted the strands and hauled her up from the bench with a roughness that made Noelle's heart pound as Lex's eyes clenched shut. Dallas licked the shell of her ear. "The silk rope, Lex. And maybe the pearls, too. You know which ones."

After an eternity, she nodded. "I know."

He released her hair and swatted her hip. "Go." Then he turned to Jasper—and Noelle. Her cheeks warmed under his amused, appreciative gaze, especially when he stepped forward to brush a fingertip down her jaw. "Do you like pearls, kitten?"

There had to be more to the question, unless Dallas's enjoyment of buying Lex jewelry extended to draping her in it while they had sex. But trying to determine what that *more* might be was impossible with Jasper's fingers so deep inside that she could barely draw breath. Her thighs ached from clenching together, but she couldn't make her body relax, not when every instinct conspired to protect her from the agonizing pleasure she craved.

Jasper whispered against the naked curve of her hip. "Settle down, honey, and answer him."

She shuddered and nodded. "Yes. I like pearls."

"Good." Dallas circled the bench and smoothed one work-roughened hand over her hip and down to the back of her thigh. "Can you get her knees apart, Jas? Or do you need a little help coaxing her to open up?"

"She'll open for me." Jasper eased his fingers free of her body to urge her legs wide again, and apparently he could do what she couldn't—demand her body's obedience.

Lex came back with strands of pearls and two lengths of silk rope. She wound the rope loosely around Dallas's neck and nuzzled his temple. "Are the pearls for her or me?"

"Maybe both." Dallas winked and tossed one of the ropes to Jasper before wrapping the other around Noelle's thigh. She shivered as much at the touch of his hands as the rope sliding over her skin. He looped it carefully around her leg, just above the knee, and threaded it through one of the iron rings. "Tell her what's special about the pearls, Lex."

She teased the end of one strand over Noelle's bare back. "If she tells me what Jasper did with his fingers that nearly flipped her off this bench."

Noelle didn't know how to describe it, didn't know the words, though they had to exist. Something that powerful must have a name, a name spoken in hoarse whispers and broken pleas. "He—he touched me. Some-place inside me."

"Your G-spot." Lex sounded sure as she rubbed a few of the pearls over Noelle's skin in rhythmic circles. "If he can do that with his fingers, imagine what he could do with these."

"In—inside—" Instinct tried to pull her legs together again, but the ropes held snug, tied firmly to the base of the bench. She truly was helpless this time, her body spread wide and primed to explode, and all she could manage was a throaty, hungry moan.

Jasper leaned over her, his chest bare now and pressed to her back. "You want it, sweetheart?"

It would drive her beyond herself, fracture her world. She panted for breath, every gasp chafing her nipples against the supple leather, but before she could form a reply, Dallas stepped into view again and smiled. "Hard-ly a fair question when she can barely imagine what you're offering." Dallas lifted a second strand of pearls from Lex's grasp, letting it trail down to reveal several feet of round, shiny beads strung tightly together. "Why don't we show her, Lex?"

She toyed with the short hem of her skirt. "Right here?" She sat sideways on the unoccupied side of the bench. It left Noelle hovering over her, and Lex tilted her head back, rubbed her cheek against the leather.

Dallas laughed. "Naked. You want to give her a good view, don't you?" He didn't wait for an answer—Noelle was starting to notice that he never really seemed to expect one, as if he couldn't imagine a world where he wasn't obeyed—and tugged at her skirt as he winked at Noelle. "I heard you were watching pre-Flare porn before you got booted from the city. Do you like to watch people fuck, kitten?"

Like was the perfect word for how she'd felt about those scratchy videos. Like. A pale, numb word for the sorts of pale, numb feelings she'd had in Eden. Safe feelings, without the ability to cut as deep as her passion for Jasper, but likewise unable to evoke a fraction of the tangled, wild sensations twisting her into knots.

"I liked the porn," she told him, wiggling to feel the ropes dig into her flesh. Sharp, raw...so good. "I think I could love watching *people* fuck."

Lex laughed, low and a little drunk, just like Noelle felt. "Dallas isn't going to fuck me, baby girl. Not the way you think of it."

"Lots of ways to fuck," Dallas countered. He caught Lex's hips and tipped her back on the wide seat, her hair spilling off the end as he hooked his fingers into the waistband of her skirt. In the next moment, he slid her skirt and panties both down her legs, a smooth motion that left Lex sprawled naked—and Noelle wondering how much practice it took to get that good at stripping women to their skin.

Lex caught her breath and gripped the chain that bound Noelle, rattling it in the rings that anchored it. "There are those wide eyes again, Jas."

He chuckled, his breath blowing across the back of Noelle's neck. "I think that's what you like most, Lex."

Dallas made a rumbling sound, a laugh that didn't quite form but lingered in his chest instead. One broad hand closed around Lex's ankle, the one closest to the bench, and he dragged her leg up until Noelle could have craned her head and kissed the other woman's shin.

That didn't seem to be his intention, though. He checked where Lex's thigh brushed Noelle's arm and adjusted the angle a little before nodding to Jasper. "Right about here will give our girl a nice view."

Jasper wrapped one huge hand around Lex's calf, his thumb stroking over her skin, and dropped his other hand to Noelle's hip. "Watch," he whispered.

She barely had a choice, but that wasn't what drew her gaze to Dallas's hand as he tracked his fingers down Lex's leg to her pussy. He used the blunt tip of his middle finger to part her folds, teasing his way up to brush around her clit before working his way lower and deeper. As Lex arched off the bench with a shaky moan, Dallas spread her other thigh wide and buried his finger in her body with a satisfied growl. "She's already so fucking wet. You two get her running hot."

Lex opened her eyes and met Noelle's gaze. Then she jerked the chain harder and smiled. "She'll find out soon enough, won't she?"

"Why wait?" Dallas fixed his hypnotic stare on No- elle, and she felt as trapped by his eyes as she was by the chains and rope, by the bulk of Jasper's body pressing down on her.

Out of the corner of her eye she saw him raising his hand, but she couldn't tear her gaze from his until he lifted his slick finger to her lips with a growled command. "Suck it."

Noelle almost hated herself for how quickly, how ea- gerly, she obeyed. Then again, all she did was part her lips and Dallas was there, plunging his finger deep, working it back and forth between her lips with an ob- scene thrusting rhythm that her hips tried to match. Her inner muscles clenched around nothing, intensifying the ache of being so empty.

She licked the oddly addictive taste of Lex off his fin- ger with quick, obedient strokes, each one a silent plea he ignored, except to growl again. "If you're half this enthusiastic with a cock in your mouth, it's a fucking miracle Jas ever puts his pants on."

Jasper bit the back of her shoulder. "Tell him about the last time you sucked my dick."

The last time had been the first time, the only time, and it was only natural that the realization led to the fantasy of Jasper circling the bench to thrust his cock into her mouth, into her throat, though she still hadn't learned how to take him that deep without choking and *God*, right now she wouldn't care.

Dallas slid his finger free with a soft *pop* and caught her chin. "What happened last time you sucked him off?"

It was getting easier to say the things she never could have imagined before, even if her voice wavered and cracked at the most embarrassing moments. "He came on my face. And my neck. And my—my breasts."

Laughing, Dallas released her and reached for the string of beads. "I guess that's another way to get a pearl necklace. These look gorgeous wrapped around Lex's throat and tits, but not as good as they're about to."

He echoed Lex's earlier movements, rubbing a few of the smooth spheres against the woman's skin, low on her abdomen. She trembled under his touch and locked her fingers around his arm, her nails digging into his skin. "Please, Dallas."

Quiet but needy, close to begging.

Noelle knew how she felt.

But Lex's torment was nearly at an end. Dallas used one hand to part her folds—*No*, corrected Ace's voice, mocking even in Noelle's imagination, *her pussy lips*— and used one finger to nudge a long loop of pearls inside her body, the soft click of the beads knocking together undercut by Lex's harsh groan.

She twisted, thrusting her hips toward him. "More."

Noelle held her breath as he repeated the process again and again, pumping his finger in and bringing another few inches of the long strand with him each time. "This is what we'll do, Noelle," he said in a hoarse voice, speaking over Lex's whimpers. "Everything Jasper wants to do to you, I'll do to Lex first. And if you want it, you wrap your tongue around the dirty words and you beg him to give it to you."

Noelle whimpered, too, shifting her hips as much as she could. "I want it. I want that."

"Uh-uh." Dallas rocked two fingers into Lex and flexed his wrist, doing something to the pearls inside her that made her entire body jerk. "Tell her you want the details, Jas."

Jasper straightened and moved his hand from her hip. For the longest moment, he didn't touch her at all— and then his hand fell heavy around the front of her throat. "Say it, sweetheart."

Before Noelle could speak, Lex sucked in a breath and released it with a curse. "Fuck. *Fuck.*" The chain rattled again as she dug her teeth into her lower lip and struggled against both men's restraining hands.

Lex's pleasure turned her own arousal sharp enough to cut. Noelle squeezed her eyes shut and forced out the words, each one slicing through her self-consciousness until the plea tumbled from her lips. "I want the pearls in my pussy. Please, Jas, please let me have them, please let me come."

Instead, his touch vanished again.

Noelle bit off a panicked moan as her heart slammed into her throat. He'd lied, he'd lied and he was going to leave her like this, begging and wanting and always empty, always starving—

Dallas caught her chin and lifted her head. "Easy, love. He went to get something. We've got you."

Jasper stared at her as he walked back to the bench, a small bottle in one hand. "She doesn't trust me yet," he muttered.

"I do," Noelle protested weakly, but Dallas pressed

his thumb over her lips before she could say anything else. "Don't lie," he told her softly. "It's not just something you do, it's something we earn. Let us earn it tonight, kitten." He used his grip on her chin to turn her face toward Jasper. "Look at him. Look him square in the eyes. Don't think about forever, think about tonight. Can you trust him to take care of you tonight?"

Still ashamed by her weakness, she nonetheless lifted her gaze to Jasper's. His eyes were dark, endless, and there was a wariness there alongside the hunger. Even lashed to a bench, physically helpless, she had the power to hurt him. Not only with words, but with something as visceral and silent as a moment of fear.

"I'm sorry," she whispered. The next words were harder, because she had to say them knowing that a wrong one might end the night, like it had before. She had to take the step over the edge of the cliff, blind and willing to shatter if he stepped away and let her fall. "I promise to trust you."

The words rolled over him, relaxing a little of the tightness in his eyes. "Maybe you shouldn't yet, since I'm not giving you what you asked for." When he stepped behind her, his slippery fingers skated over her pussy but didn't linger. He touched her ass instead, probing between her cheeks. "Not exactly."

His fingertip pressed against her back passage, stretching the tight ring of muscle with a painfully pleasurable jolt that startled a cry out of her. Her gaze found Lex's, and she whimpered a question she hoped the other woman could understand.

Her leg was still propped high against the middle of the bench. She lowered it a little, reached up and brushed the back of her hand over Noelle's jaw. "Relax, baby girl. He'll make you feel good. All you have to do is let it happen."

Noelle panted as his finger pushed harder, and this *was* pain, the kind she wasn't supposed to like but couldn't stop craving. Her clit pulsed with every slow twist of his finger, and she caught herself rocking mindlessly against the leather padding, reveling in the friction against her nipples.

There was only one thing to say. One thing to beg for. "More."

Her name melted into a pleased rumble as Jasper gathered the second strand of pearls and drew them up the inside of her thigh. "I'm going to put them in your ass, darling. Should we let Dallas decide what I put in your pussy?"

She was so distracted by the sensation that the truth tumbled free, the naïve, silly truth. "I never knew there were so many possibilities."

"Everything you ever wanted," Lex whispered, slipping her fingers into Noelle's hair just as Jasper pressed the first of the pearls into her ass.

It was impossible to define the feeling of intrusion, impossible to narrow it to only one feeling at all. She seesawed between the giddy burn of the tight muscles resisting to the heady relief each time he pushed the widest part deep enough for her body to do the rest.

She lost count after three. It could have been only a few more or a hundred, she only knew that she felt full and empty at the same time, and when the next little sphere popped into her body, she moaned and tugged against Lex's grip in her hair. "Tell him what to put in my pussy," she whispered, not even stumbling over the word. "Anything, anything, please, just *something...*"

"Like what, kitten?" Dallas bent and licked the corner of her mouth with a teasing laugh. "Do you like steel? Something long and hard? Or do you like the way those little round pearls feel pushing inside you? I have a second set of big brass balls, you know. Lex screams when I fill her up with those."

"You're an impossible bastard," Lex rasped as she re-leased Noelle's hair and scratched her nails over Dallas's chest.

"Mmm." Dallas caught her hand and bit the inside of her wrist. He trailed his other hand between her legs and ground a doubled-over string of pearls back and forth over her clit.

Lex cried out, shocked and sudden. Her skin flushed, and her hips jerked up with every rough caress. Noelle had never been this close to a woman in the first grip of orgasm. It looked agonizing—Lex's entire body tensed, muscles taut and face fixed in an openmouthed grimace. It could have been mistaken for pain if Dallas hadn't driven another round of cries from her throat with a twist of his wrist.

"You like watching her." Jasper's breath tickled No-elle's ear as he parted her pussy wide and slipped two fingers teasingly over her entrance. "You could make her come that hard."

Noelle squeezed her eyes shut and tried to chase his hand with her hips. The rope around her thighs had no give, but spreading her knees wider gave her enough slack to rub against his fingers with a pleading noise. It didn't embarrass her anymore, not when need had burned away everything else. "I need to come, please let me. Please."

Those two fingers pushed just inside her and rubbed in a slow circle. "You don't have to beg, sweetheart. Not for this." A little deeper, but before she had time to focus on the delicious stretch, Jasper tugged on the string of pearls.

She squealed when the first popped out, triggering a shudder of pleasure that swept up her spine and was still rocking her when the second slipped free and sent her spinning into release. Her toes curled and she jerked at the chains, desperate for something to cling to as her inner muscles spasmed around his fingers in short, sharp clenches, each one releasing a wave of liquid heat that flooded her limbs.

He slid his free hand down her back. "Shh. Just ride it, Noelle."

Somehow, Lex was on her knees now, her lips pressed close to Noelle's ear as Dallas stroked her back with the same soothing possessiveness alive in every touch of Jasper's fingers.

There was no choice for Noelle but to ride it, to tremble as the waves gentled to rolling swells, and the spasms came farther and farther apart. Her head drooped, but Dallas wrapped his hand in her hair and tugged gently, guiding her chin up until her neck was arched under Lex's lips. "She's ready," he murmured, looking past her to Jasper.

She wet her lips. "Ready for wha—?"

He growled and moved his fingers again, pumping them in slow, sure strokes. "For this."

Pleasure, which had been a lazy, sleeping thing, roared up, dragging her right back to the edge. Dallas tightened his grip in her hair. "Does Lex have permission to leave marks?"

Lex made a soft noise and nipped at Noelle's earlobe. "If Jas doesn't want me to, he'll have to stop me."

Jasper groaned and thrust his fingers home—hard and fast. "Do it."

Noelle didn't have time to ask what they meant. Dallas guided Lex's mouth to her throat with a rumbled, "Bite her," and Lex's teeth closed tight on her skin as Jasper twisted his fingers deep in her pussy. Pain and pleasure crossed paths somewhere in between and melted into hollow, blind need.

She had time to anticipate it, time for her muscles to tense. Time for her body to teeter on the brink as she

strained and panted and scratched her fingernails helplessly on the leather bench. *Please* was the only word she
remembered, and it didn't matter if Jasper expected her
to beg.

She couldn't stop chanting the word, not until he
eased another finger into her pussy and curled all three
against her G-spot as he began to slowly pull the rest of
the pearls out of her ass.

If she could have gotten free she would have
squirmed away after the first stroke. It was still too
intense, more jolting sensation than pure pleasure. But
every touch built on the last, and he had a sadistic sense
of timing. Stroke. Tug.

Stroke. Tug.

Stroke—

She cried out when the third pearl jerked free, cried
out as her entire body drew taut in the prelude to something massive. She closed her eyes and strained toward
it, strained until she was stretched in all directions,
trembling with a tension that would kill her if it didn't
snap.

Jasper pulled the finals pearls free, one after another, and she catapulted past bliss into oblivion.

Lex lit a cigarette and watched Jasper as he stroked
Noelle's hair. "Is this how she was with you and Ace
when she got her tattoos?"

"Close." So close, but even that couldn't compare to
the open way she'd embraced ecstasy this time. Jasper
had felt the difference, the absence of any sort of walls or
space between them. "She's perfect."

"Mmm." Lex took a deep drag from the cigarette and
passed it to Dallas. "If I'd known, I would have tried to
fuck her already."

Dallas leaned against his massive mahogany head-board and eyed Jasper with a shake of his head. "You're a dumbass if you still doubt whether she's into it."

"I never doubted that." It just wasn't that simple.

"If you say so." Dallas dragged Lex up against his bare chest and offered her the cigarette again as Noelle murmured something and rubbed her cheek against Jasper's shoulder.

Dallas's grin widened. "You coming back to us, kitten? You came so hard you passed out."

Noelle made a grumpy noise and nuzzled her face against Jasper's neck. "I'm not a kitten. Or a princess."

Lex nudged her with one bare foot. "Or a baby girl, huh?"

Noelle huffed, but Jasper felt her smile against his collarbone. Whatever else, she liked the teasing, and the genuine fondness Lex obviously felt for her stirred his banked desire. Noelle had made passes at Lex while she was drunk or craving touch, but how deep did that attraction go?

Lex caught his look and grinned. "Watch it, Jas. She needs to pace herself."

"Pace myself at what?" Noelle twisted in his lap.

Jasper drew the tip of his finger around her nipple. "Too much, too fast. You need a break, or you really will be finished...and I haven't kept my promise yet."

She shivered, her nipple tightening under his touch, but she reached down, her fingers splaying across his cock. "What about you? Do you need to pace yourself?"

Yes. The word tripped up on his tongue, and he guided her hand over his cock, a firm pressure that left him thrusting against her touch.

Noelle smiled and peeked at Lex from beneath the tousled fall of her hair. "Can we have another lesson?"

Lex's gaze was dark as she studied both of them. "If we both suck Jasper's cock, he might not be *able* to fuck you later. You gonna let Dallas do it instead?"

Jasper growled and opened his pants. "I'm not a kid, Alexa, and I'm not Dallas. I won't blow just because you put your tongue on me."

Dallas leaned over to snuff out his cigarette. "I don't know which one of you to spank."

Jasper freed his cock, stroked it slowly, and watched Noelle. "What do *you* think?"

She twisted to straddle his knees, flushed and beautifully naked and, for once, seemingly oblivious to it. She wrapped both hands around his shaft and studied it with adorable seriousness. "If you come now, will it be hard to...to get hard again?"

Just that bare touch made his balls tighten. "Right now? Hell, no."

Her fingers trembled as she traced them up to the crown, then circled her thumb around the head. "How do I take him deep, Lex? How do I take all of him?"

"I'd show you..." Lex leaned over and slipped her thumb into Noelle's mouth before slicking it over the head of his cock. "But I don't think he has a healthy appreciation of my talents."

Jasper ignored the pleasure skating up his spine and wound his hand in Lex's hair. "Behave yourself, and you might end the night with a healthy appreciation of mine and Noelle's talents."

"Don't waste your time, Jas." Dallas slapped Lex's hip. "She doesn't behave. Do you, love?"

"For nobody but you." She stretched out on all fours, her ass high in the air. Dallas smoothed a hand over it and smiled at Jasper, looking pleased with himself and the world in general.

Noelle seemed pleased by Lex's proximity too. She left one hand wrapped around Jasper's cock, but the other touched Lex's cheek as Noelle leaned in to kiss her. "Teach me," she murmured against the other woman's lips. "I want to make him come."

Lex's dark gaze went soft. She wouldn't do it for any-one but Noelle, and the thought of that link aroused Jasper. The three of them could fuck without Noelle, but it wouldn't be the same as coming together to teach her, to show her the pleasure to be had under the right hands and mouths.

"Suck me," he whispered, slipping his fingers from Lex's lips to Noelle's.

Lex licked Noelle's mouth, all the while guiding her down toward the head of his dick. "Put your tongue on him first." Lex demonstrated with a long, slow draw of wet, pink tongue up the underside of his shaft.

Jasper's breath caught, and he held it as he waited.

Noelle's gaze flicked to his, and she smiled softly and licked the other side of his cock without tearing her eyes from his.

He gritted his teeth as they ran their tongues over his rigid flesh, sometimes tangling together in an open-mouthed kiss, but never stopping. When his cock glistened, wet and slick, Lex wrapped her hand around the base of his shaft and pushed Noelle's head down.

Noelle didn't hesitate. She slid her lips around the head and suckled a moment, her eyes glinting with mis-chief, before she pushed lower, taking another two inches.

Even in the hot grip of her mouth, Jasper found him-self distracted by the sway of her ass in the air. Lex caught the direction of his stare, smiled slowly, and spanked Noelle hard enough to drive his dick deeper into her mouth.

Oh, hell yes.

Vibrations from her helpless moan fluttered her tongue against him. She flailed for a moment, hands groping wildly for something to cling to before finding his forearms.

"Mmm." Lex laid her cheek on the back of Noelle's shoulder. "She likes that."

Dallas rolled from the bed and padded toward the bulky mahogany cabinet pushed against the wall. "You gonna let Lex spank her?" he asked, glancing back at Jasper as he tugged open the doors. Inside lay his extensive collection of leather straps, whips and other toys, all expensive and most custom designed by crafters in the sectors.

If Jasper said no, Noelle was liable to bite him. He opened his mouth, but all that came out was a groan, and he had to nod his assent.

Chuckling, Dallas took down a leather crop with a square tip graced with a heart-shaped cutout and tossed it onto the bed. "Get started, Lex. I'm going to consider my options."

She slipped the leather strap around her wrist. "Options for what?"

"What you're going to do to her. And what I'm going to do to you."

"Good." She traced the end of the crop over Noelle's ass, then wound a hand in her hair and pulled her head up gently. "Jasper's never hit you with anything but his hand, has he?"

Noelle peeked at him as she answered. "No." She rubbed her lower lip against the underside of his cock and smiled. "His hand was impressive enough."

Lex rolled her eyes with a grin, a tease meant for Jasper alone. "We'll have to get him one of these. Unless you'd like a paddle better..." The crop zipped through the air and landed on Noelle's skin with a smack.

She jerked, her fingernails digging into his forearms as her lips formed a silent *O* of surprise. He'd seen the expression on her face before, knew that the excitement that accompanied her shock would have her pussy wet and clenching.

He could draw her into his lap and fuck her, have Lex spank her ass in time with every deep thrust. Or he could let Dallas call the shots, exert enough power and dominance to get Lex off just as hard as Noelle.

Dallas made the decision for him, sliding onto the bed near Jasper's feet to deliver a swat of his own to Noelle's ass. "Take his cock back into your mouth, kitten. Suck him deep." Dallas twisted his hand in Lex's hair and grinned at Jasper. "And Lex will do whatever Jasper tells her to. Won't you, love?"

Lex muttered something, but her retort was lost to the roaring in Jasper's ears as Noelle obeyed Dallas's order, enclosing him in the willing heat of her mouth only to sink down until she bumped the back of her throat.

"Jesus." He touched her head but didn't dare sink his fingers into her hair. He'd hold her there without even meaning to, and he knew it.

"They make a picture, don't they?" Dallas's voice was raspy, his gaze intense as he clutched Lex's hair and stroked her bare hip. "Hit her again, Lex."

She bucked against his touch. "I thought you said Jas was—"

Jasper cut her off. "Do it."

Lex practically hissed at him, but she straightened and brought the crop down on Noelle's ass—a different spot than before, and Jasper watched, spellbound, as the pale flesh reddened. Her ass wiggled as she squirmed, but her moans were muffled this time. Even with her body trembling, she kept working his cock, driving down far enough to gag herself before easing back.

"Such a good girl," Dallas murmured, stroking up to tweak one of Lex's nipples. "Do you like that, kitten? Like how his cock feels, shoving so deep you can't breathe? Lex loves it when I fuck her face until she chokes on my dick."

"You're lucky, Declan." Lex swung the crop once

more, twice. "Any other man who tried it would lose some precious parts."

Noelle moaned, her entire body rocking as she panted. "I like it," she gasped, raising her gaze to Jasper's. Her lips were swollen, her eyes glazed. Tangled strands of her hair stuck to her face, but she made no move to push them aside.

She just stared at him, open and hungry and so clearly willing to take any pleasure—or pain—he offered.

He could give her this.

"Turn around," he rumbled, reaching for the leather crop. "It's Lex's turn. Dallas will show you what to do."

Noelle eased around on wobbly knees to face Lex, who knelt near the foot of the bed. Dallas crawled onto the mattress behind her and clasped her inner thighs, pulling them wide as he lifted her to straddle his own spread knees.

Lex laughed as she reached up and wrapped her hand around the back of Dallas's neck. "He's been waiting for this, baby girl." She licked her lips. "So have I."

When Noelle hovered uncertainly, Dallas winked over Lex's shoulder and slid his hands up her thighs to stroke her pussy. "Crawl on over here, honey, but keep your ass in the air for Jasper."

Noelle obeyed, going to her elbows in front of Dallas and Lex. Her ass was already reddened, except for the tiny heart-shaped spots of pale flesh left untouched by the paddle's cutout.

Jasper rolled the long, thin handle up over the bowed curve of Noelle's back. Her pussy was wet, the swollen lips pouting for his touch, and he indulged himself by stroking one hand down the length of his erection before speaking. "You want me to spank you?"

Her shiver made her entire body sway for him. "Yes."

Dallas met his eyes and nodded once, silently giving him control of the moment. A rare concession, a true gesture of trust—especially since it was Lex in his lap, Lex he was turning over to whatever happened next.

Jasper released a breath. "Lex left some beautiful marks back here. She deserves a reward, I think." He flicked the crop against the side of Noelle's hip. "Lick her cunt. Make her come and I'll fuck you."

No hesitation. Noelle rocked forward with an eager sound as Dallas used his fingers to spread Lex wide. "That's it," he rumbled, his gaze fixed to where Noelle's tongue darted out in quick, nervous licks. "Lick her all up and down. But if you want to hear her squeal, suck on her clit."

Lex choked on a moan and lifted her hips. "Slow and a little rough."

Noelle obeyed as effortlessly as always, licking where Dallas told her to lick and sucking Lex's clit hard enough to set the woman thrashing in Dallas's iron grip.

Jasper swatted Noelle every time Lex cried out, leaving red marks on her thigh, hip, and ass. "Dallas?"

"Your girl's got a clever tongue no matter where she puts it." Dallas licked the side of Lex's throat with a rough laugh. "Tell him, Lex. Tell him how close you are."

She whimpered instead, and Jasper caught only a glimpse of her glazed eyes as she turned to catch Dallas's mouth in a bruising kiss. But he'd seen her balanced on the edge of orgasm before, her restless movements and flushed skin, and she was close.

Damn close.

Jasper dragged the crop down Noelle's back and leaned away just far enough to slap the flared leather end hard against her pussy.

Her reaction was everything he hoped for. Trembling thighs and a breathless moan, the wildest of her noises muffled as she—judging by Lex's indrawn breath— redoubled her efforts.

Dallas broke their kiss with a rough laugh and

curled his hand around the front of Lex's throat. "Look at those big eyes, Lex. She's got her face buried in your pussy and she's loving it. Maybe if you're good, Jasper will let you get your fingers in hers."

"I'm always—" The strained words cut off in a violent curse and then a wail as her head slammed against Dallas's shoulder. She gripped the back of Noelle's head and shuddered, her chest heaving.

Noelle hummed her encouragement, the same as she had with her lips locked around Jasper's dick, but her knees edged apart and her hips lifted, a silent, desperate invitation for him to spank her again.

But he only leaned over her, his own body aching. "I promised," he whispered, then grasped her thighs and drove into her pussy.

She was so tight. Hot and tight, her body gripping him hard and giving way with reluctance. Her head snapped back, lips parted on a silent cry that melted into a moan. "Oh...oh *God.*"

Jasper was vaguely aware of movement, of Dallas and Lex shifting on the bed, but his world had narrowed to Noelle. He dragged himself under control and rocked against her. "Yes?"

"Not empty." Her elbows slid to the side, unfolding as she spread her arms wide and pressed her cheek to the sheets. With her eyes closed and her lips parted, her profile seemed reverent. "You make me so full."

"Gorgeous." He could fill her up even more, try out all the toys in Dallas's room. One by one, until he found the ones that made her scream.

She shifted her hips restlessly, easing away and then back with a hiss. "Are you all the way in?"

Christ. "Not yet, sweetheart." He rocked a little harder and she sucked in a breath, her fingers curling in the sheets as her pussy clenched, impossibly tight around him.

"I want it all." She freed one hand and reached for him, her fingertips digging into his hip as if she planned to pull him into her by force. "Does that make me shameless?"

"That makes you hungry." One more hard thrust buried his cock all the way inside her. "It makes you mine."

"Yours." When she wrapped her lips around the word, it sounded like a prayer. The words that followed, though, were innocence corrupted. "I love having your cock in my pussy."

He stilled with another groan. "So fuck it."

Noelle peered back at him, her brow furrowing as she blinked her glazed, hungry eyes. "Fuck...fuck what?"

Innocence wasn't his thing, but the way she combined it with a sincere and abiding *lust* intoxicated him. Jasper rubbed the back of his hand over her hip. "Move, sweetheart. You want me? Fuck me."

Her eyes brightened with unfettered glee. She shifted her weight to her elbows again and rocked experimentally, only a few inches at first, but she still moaned as she shoved back, taking him deep. "I can fuck you," she whispered, repeating the movement. Her pussy gripped his cock, and she slammed her hips back, driving him roughly into her body.

"Someone's finding her power." The words drifted through Jasper's haze. Lex, amused as always, but with an edge of something biting. Envy.

Jasper glanced at the other side of the bed. Dallas had sprawled on his back with Lex on top of him, straddling his head and facing his feet—and his dick. Clearly displeased at her lack of focus, he slapped her hip and buried his face in her pussy.

Lex almost wrenched away before relaxing with a whimper, and she stroked Dallas's cock as it nestled between her breasts. "I was paying attention," she vowed.

Noelle twisted to study Jasper, her cheeks flushed. "Can we try that next time?"

"If you're good." A threat and a promise, all at once.

She shuddered and dropped her head, her hair tumbling forward as she lost herself in fucking onto his cock. "Like this? Is this being good?"

With her neck bared, Jasper couldn't resist. He slid his fingers under her throat, firm on her delicate skin. "Dirty. And so, so good."

Her moan vibrated under his fingers, and her pussy clenched. "You like it when I'm dirty?"

He tightened his hand and met her next movement with a hard thrust. She choked on a breathless noise and faltered, her steady rock turning into hungry little jerks, each one grinding back against him in search of something more, though he'd bet she wasn't even sure what.

The sound of palm cracking against flesh filled the room before Dallas spilled Lex to the bed next to Noelle. "Do you want to keep her to yourself the first time? Or do you want to share?"

The question from any other man might have sparked jealousy, but Jas felt only curiosity and certainty. Curiosity that Dallas would fuck a woman he hadn't collared—something he rarely did—and certainty that of course he would make an exception here, now. For Noelle, who was so beautiful, so responsive. So hungry.

"She's mine right now," Jasper muttered. "Next time, if she wants."

Dallas smoothed a hand down Lex's spine. "I wasn't asking for me. But if you're worried your cock can't compete with her tongue..."

A quick shift of his hips, and Jasper hauled Noelle up against his chest, careful to keep most of the pressure from his arm on her shoulder, not his hand on her throat. The position left the front of her body bare—and, with her knees on either side of his, open. "Like this?"

Dallas leaned over Lex, still half-clothed, grinding against her bare ass as he brushed his lips over her ear. "Look at her. All stretched wide and waiting for you. Do you wanna play with her?"

"Don't you?" Lex reached out.

Jasper couldn't see what she did, but he felt Noelle's reaction—a sharp jerk as her breath hissed out. Her hands flew to his hips, clutching for balance, and the movement arched her back and thrust out her breasts.

Grinning, Dallas rolled from the bed. "What do you want, kitten?"

Noelle's throat worked beneath Jasper's hand. "Everything."

"Uh-uh," Dallas chided. "Not good enough. Be a dirty girl and beg for what you want. I know you want something, I can see it in your eyes."

Pleasure pulsed up Jasper's spine as she squirmed before craning her neck to meet his eyes. Her cheeks were pink, her gaze adorably uncertain.

He kissed her softly. "We can't read your mind, sweetheart. But if you tell us what you want, we can give it to you."

The tip of her tongue darted out, wetting her lips in a nervous gesture. "How do I know if it's a bad thing to ask for?"

Time to find out how much she liked the spankings. He met Dallas's gaze over her head. "If it's bad, all the better. If it's *too* bad, we'll have to punish you."

"Oh yeah, we will." Dallas waited until Noelle looked at him again before turning to retrieve a simple pair of leather cuffs with a short length of chain between them. He tossed them on the bed between Jasper's knees. A bottle of lube followed, and two shining steel butt plugs with jeweled ends. "Lex, tell her how we punish bad girls."

Lex licked her lips, her attention riveted to the jeweled plugs. "You make them scream."

Shuddering, Noelle dropped her head back and rocked her hips restlessly. "I want her to do to me what I did to her. To—to lick my clit. Even though you're inside me..."

"Mmm." Lex bent her head, touched her tongue to the soft inside of Noelle's knee, and then blazed a wet path up her thigh. "I could get you both off like this."

She licked the base of Jasper's cock first, slow and firm, and he couldn't stop his hips from flexing in a short thrust as her tongue disappeared, traveled upwards, and Noelle groaned, lifting both hands to Lex's head as she pushed closer to her mouth.

Dallas grinned at Jasper, wound a hand in Lex's hair, and jerked her head back so her tongue hovered just shy of Noelle's body. "Ask again. And none of that bullshit about how he's inside you. Tell Jasper you want him to slam his cock into your tight little pussy. Tell Lex you want her to suck your clit until you come on her face."

Noelle whimpered and reached for Dallas's wrist, trying to pull Lex back. He held firm, and she sucked in another pleading breath.

Jasper could hear her voice wrapped around the words already—the lilting, embarrassed hesitation over *cock* and *pussy*—and he had no idea how he'd last if she actually *said* them out loud. But even if it hurtled him over the dizzy edge into orgasm, it didn't matter. Lex was there, Dallas, and either of them could fall on Noelle, lick and stroke her until she came just as hard as he had.

So he released her throat and gathered her arms behind her back. "Lex could suck me instead. And we could hold you right here, like this. Waiting."

"Lick me," she choked out, twisting desperately in his grip. "Please, please."

Dallas laughed and rubbed his fingers between Lex's legs, working her pussy while Noelle watched in tortured frustration. "You can do better than that, kitten."

Noelle sucked in a breath and slammed her head back against Jasper's shoulder, her entire body convulsing as the words burst out of her in a ragged cry. "Fuck my pussy, fuck it with your cock, I want it, I want to be fucked and—and sucked and *please*—"

He gave her one slow thrust as Dallas let go of Lex. "I go first," the woman whispered huskily before lowering her mouth again.

Every exploring, teasing lick made Noelle jerk against Jasper's chest. He held her still, and by the time Lex finally moaned and focused her attentions, Noelle had started rocking her hips, obviously desperate for a more intense touch, a specific sensation.

More.

Dallas swept up the lube and trickled it onto Lex's ass without warning her. "Don't be greedy, love. Give Jasper a turn."

She kissed her way up the center of Noelle's body, pausing to swirl her tongue around one hard, puckered nipple. "I *am* greedy." Then she dropped her hands to grip Noelle's hips and kissed her, driving her tongue past her lips.

Noelle whimpered, straining against Jasper's grasp to get closer. When her head tilted, their lips slipped apart enough to show Jasper a flash of tangled tongues, Noelle chasing Lex back into her mouth with an aggression that would have been impossible to imagine a few short days ago.

He gritted his teeth, locked one arm around Noelle, and resumed his rocking motions. Deep but not easy, angling his hips with every thrust and grunting as her body clasped his, slick and hot.

The bed dipped as Dallas knelt behind Lex. He gathered her wrists, coaxing them from Noelle's body. She broke the kiss, tilting her head to his as he cuffed her hands behind her back.

A laugh, heady and drunk, as Lex rubbed her cheek against Dallas's. "I lied. *Now* it's my turn."

"Maybe it's mine," he rumbled, slicking his hand down to tease her clit. "Everyone's had someone's face in their lap but me."

"You get cranky when you're horny." She closed her eyes and circled her hips under his hand.

With his other hand, Dallas reached out to pinch one of Noelle's nipples, tugging at it until she cried out and jerked in Jasper's arms. "Why don't we let them fuck, then, and see what we can do about it?"

In minutes, the two of them would be too wrapped up to notice anything. Jasper pulled free of Noelle's body and eased her to the bed, coaxing her onto her back. "Look at me."

She blinked twice before her gaze focused on his, already reaching for him. She clutched at his shoulders and tugged, trying to draw him closer. "I don't want it to be over."

The night had to end. "We'll just start again," he promised, sliding into the cradle of her hips.

Her brow furrowed and her lips pursed as she lifted her hips, grinding her pussy against his cock. "You're not inside me," she protested. "Are you going to make me beg?"

As much as she seemed to like the idea, he shook his head. "I can't right now." He reached down and held her still as he drove into her again.

Noelle cried out. Her legs tangled around his hips, her fingers curled around his shoulders, even her lips wrapped around his name as her pussy tightened, her pleasure driving his. He hooked his arms under her legs, pushing her knees toward her chest, and began to ride her.

The first time he hit her G-spot she sobbed his name, her nails pricking his shoulders, and started begging. Not as coherent as the words Dallas might have demanded, but plenty filthy. She pled for his cock, begged him to drive it deep, to take her, fuck her, and each time he slammed home the words broke a little more, until she was making choked noises as she teetered on the edge.

His entire body pulsed with need, the kind that prickled over his skin and narrowed his world to *Noelle*. Jasper cupped her shoulders and moved faster, harder, ignoring the Siren call of release as he commanded her to come. "Now."

"I can't—" The protest died with his next thrust. Her eyes squeezed shut and she twisted, digging her head back into the bed as the first tremors of orgasm began with her clenching pussy.

One more thrust and she came, screaming.

A fucking earthquake couldn't have kept him from following her in a rush of heat that scalded him from the inside out, stripped away the last of his defenses. He shuddered above her, *in* her, spilling as she contracted around him, milking his cock.

She kept shuddering even after he stilled, whimpering every time an aftershock shivered through her. Her lips moved, mumbling the same hoarse sounds over and over. "Oh, God...oh my *God*."

Jasper let her legs down and rolled so that Noelle was on top of him. Her hair spilled across his shoulders as she panted openmouthed against his chest, every breath out accompanied by a twitch of her hips. "Jasper..."

"Shh." Words were for other things, things that didn't matter just yet. Right here, right now, they didn't need anything else.

14

"RACHEL!"

Dallas's roar was so out of place in the after‑ noon emptiness of the Broken Circle that Noelle nearly dropped the glass she was wiping clean.

Next to her, Rachel sighed and slung her towel over her shoulder. "How can I help you, Dallas?"

Scowling, he dumped one of the most outdated com‑ puting tablets Noelle had ever seen onto the scuffed bar. The LCD screen was cracked at one edge, but Dallas's ire seemed directed at the screen itself, which had locked down into the sterile *Insufficient Access* placeholder.

Dallas jabbed one wide finger at the tablet with a snarl. "You're the fucking mechanical genius. How do I keep this thing connected?"

"Do we have to go over this again?" Rachel picked up the tablet. "Mechanical. Machines. I'm as shitty with tech as you are."

"Smartass." Dallas glanced at Noelle, and the tiny quirk of his lips was all it took to bring color rushing to her cheeks. He'd been long gone by the time she'd woken up in his bed that morning, but she wasn't sure she'd *ever* be able to look at him without blushing again.

From the smug look in his eyes, he knew it. He liked it. That pricked her growing pride just enough to bring up her chin. "Can I look at it?"

Rachel passed it over. "It's better off in anyone's hands but mine."

Noelle flipped the tablet over and squinted at the model number before sliding her fingers along the edge to find the nearly invisible latch that released the back. "This is an older version that's mostly been replaced by new tablets with better wireless integrity. The signal's not really supposed to be broadcast outside of Eden, though, so I'm surprised it's been working at all."

She eased off the back panel and glanced at Dallas, who was staring at her with narrow-eyed assessment. "It only works about half the time."

"Because it's set to access the broadcast tower nearest to whoever officially registered it before it was sold on the black market." It only took a little wiggle to pop the power supply free. She unplugged the battery and waited for the tablet to reset. "Wireless is restricted by neighborhood, partly to keep the best equipment for the richest families, but mostly because they can't do much better than that without satellites. And those were all destroyed by the storms."

Dallas was staring at her like she'd started speaking gibberish. Rachel heaved another sigh, poured a glass of whiskey, and slid it across the bar until it bumped his hand.

Ignoring his disbelief, Noelle reconnected the power and reassembled the tablet before flipping it over. "You just need to know how to fool the tablet into giving you administrative access. They fixed this workaround in the newer models..."

She pulled up the settings screen and inputted the code every rich kid in Eden learned by the time they were twelve. Most wealthy families had old tech piled up in storage rooms or junk closets, and having a backup tablet meant the difference between privacy and constant parental monitoring. Of course, most of the other kids she knew had hacked tablets to gain access to restricted video games or pre-Flare entertainment programs. She'd craved unfettered access to Eden's digital library—and she'd gotten it.

Once she bypassed security, it only took a minute to set the tablet up to connect to the nearest signal tower. "There. That should work in any sector, as long as you're within a half mile or so of the city walls. Beyond that, I don't know."

Dallas accepted the tablet and stared at it in perplexed silence.

Rachel leaned over the bar to look at the screen, then burst out laughing and punched him in the arm. "You got schooled, son."

"Bite me, Rachel." He dropped the tablet and leveled a threatening finger at Noelle. "You've been holding out on me, sweetheart. Would've been nice to know I had some kind of hacker under my roof—unless you don't want to use those skills to help the family for some reason."

Stung past caution by the unfairness of the accusation, Noelle retorted, "In my peer group, I'm considered barely proficient. I didn't think it was relevant."

Dallas tipped back the shot Rachel had poured him and shook his head. "Women. You're all impossible."

The blonde refilled his glass. "Don't be a dick. It's unbecoming."

He grumbled something Noelle was glad she couldn't understand and drained the shot glass again before sighing. "Fine. I should have figured they'd be dumping tech in your cradle."

They had, but not out of any desire to see her excel at it. The mandatory classes on raising healthy, moral children all stressed the necessity of minimizing a child's dependence on tactile affection, even in the form of toys or stuffed animals. Tech could enrich the mind without weakening the body...or so the theory went. Her parents had been particularly zealous adherents, for all the good it had done them.

Dallas was still watching her, so she shrugged and went back to polishing glasses. The patrons weren't likely to care if there was dirt or grime as long as the liquor was pure, but some of those perfect hostess lessons had stuck harder than others. "I'm also good at planning dinner parties," she said tartly. "I know the names, positions, and politics of every powerful man in the city, along with their food allergies. I'm filled with useless knowledge."

"Nothing useless about knowing a man's weakness," he drawled.

"I said allergies, not—" She snapped her teeth together, and Dallas grinned. Not the sexy, knowing smile from before, but a cold, ruthless one that curled his lips but left his eyes frozen and empty.

Rolling around naked in Dallas O'Kane's bed might have stripped away a level of intimidation, but she'd do well to remember that he was still a cold-blooded criminal, a man who killed to protect his business interests as quickly as he killed to protect himself.

He slid his shot glass back to Rachel before sweeping up the tablet. "Breathe, kitten. I'm not going to turn you into a culinary assassin. Not this week, anyway. But someday soon, we may have a talk about what else is rattling around behind your big eyes, hmm?"

She couldn't gather enough wits to answer, but Dallas didn't seem to think it was necessary, anyway. He winked at Rachel and departed with the tablet clutched in one big hand. It wouldn't occur to him to wait for Noelle to make up her mind, because she'd made a promise when Ace wrapped the ink around her wrists.

O'Kane above all else. The gang came first.

This time, Rachel refilled the glass and pressed it into Noelle's hand. "Don't let him get to you. If you were still someone off the street, maybe he'd really be pissed. But you're an O'Kane now. He might be irritated, but it'll blow over."

Her fingers trembled a little as she lifted the glass. The whiskey still burned on its way down, but she didn't choke like she had the first time she'd tried it, and the warmth that seeped into her limbs helped her breathe easier. "I didn't realize," she admitted. "I just assumed everyone in Eden..." Too late, she bit back the thoughtless words. Rachel was from Eden too. "I'm sorry."

"Forget it. He has no problem assuming *I* know everything about technology because I'm from the city. If he wasn't a bastard who couldn't see past your tits, he could have bothered to think the same about you."

Noelle reached for the whiskey bottle with a laugh that felt like Rachel's tone—edged with bitterness. "I don't think it has anything to do with my tits. I think Dallas knows exactly what I was raised to be—decorative and helpless. Useless outside of Eden. I'm as surprised as he is to find out I'm not."

"Hey, don't." Rachel grabbed Noelle's shoulder and turned her around. "Knock it off. You're not helpless. I never thought you were."

That seemed impossible. If she hadn't been helpless, she'd never have stumbled across Jasper to begin with. "I feel like I am."

"You're not." Rachel's dark eyes hardened. "Damn Dallas, and damn Jasper too. They'd let you keep thinking it if they had their way, I bet."

Defensiveness stirred, but not for herself or Dallas. "Jasper's not like that. Why would he want me to be useless and needy?"

Rachel relented with a shake of her head. "He wouldn't. I'm sorry. I'm just being an asshole."

"No, you're not." Noelle caught Rachel's hands. "There are men who would. Jasper... He's not one of them. Right?"

"No, it's Dallas," she muttered. "He pisses me off sometimes."

Because he looked at Noelle and only saw her tits? Or because he looked at Rachel and didn't seem to see hers at all? Noelle would guess the latter—there was a decidedly asexual affection in the way Dallas treated Rachel, although *asexual* wasn't a word she'd ever thought to associate with Dallas O'Kane.

Smoothing her thumbs over Rachel's hands, she lowered her voice to a whisper. "He's a powerful man. Powerful men can be incredibly blind, and incredibly stupid. Even the smart ones."

"Yeah." Rachel squared her shoulders and smiled ruefully. "They can also be incredibly not worth the drama. Lex can have him."

Lex *would* have him—of that, Noelle was certain. Whether the two would survive the experience was another question. "I don't envy her that challenge."

"Neither do I." Rachel paused. "Not anymore."

But she had, and Noelle couldn't blame her. Dallas could be hypnotic. There had been times the previous night where she'd felt guilty over how strongly she responded to his laughing commands, shamed that she could find him so arousing. He was a force of nature, overpowering and irresistible.

And distant. Noelle's attraction to Jasper was already melting into a delicious blend of craving and affection, a need that couldn't be filled by sex alone, no matter how obscene. She was starting to want his company as much as his touch, the quiet moments where he smiled and teased her, where he held her.

Noelle squeezed Rachel's hands in understanding. "It's different here, isn't it? Different than it is in Eden, yes...but different from how it was before the Flares, too. The way people come together. What you give and what you're supposed to hold back."

"I don't know." Rachel pulled free and lifted another rack of glasses onto the bar. "I try not to overthink it. Like...if I just sit back and let whatever happens *happen*, then it'll make sense."

"Does it work?"

She met Noelle's gaze with another almost sheepish smile. "If you have to ask, I think you already know the answer."

No. No, it couldn't possibly work. Not in a place like this, where intimacy between lovers could be withheld as surely as it was in Eden. The O'Kanes gave their bodies freely enough, their affection. You could be family or fucking or both, but wasn't that what Lex had tried to explain to her? That thing she wanted too fast, the thing she offered along with her body.

She didn't have a word for it, but she knew what it was. Too much trust. A yearning for possession that went both ways. Hope that what you had would never change.

Maybe it was love.

The unsettled feeling from that afternoon hadn't gone away.

Noelle stared unseeing at her own reflection, only

vaguely aware of the rote movements as she dragged a brush through her hair. Lex's vanity was another oddity in a room filled with oddities, beautifully restored and covered with silver-backed hairbrushes and expensive glass bottles that wouldn't have been out of place in Eden. Some had undoubtedly been gifts from Dallas, but Noelle had yet to see Lex touch any of it. She kept her makeup, lotions, and perfumes in utilitarian containers cluttering up her bathroom sink, out of sight behind the closed door.

The vanity was a stage. A scene as carefully set as the vast bed and its lush pillows—the romanticized version of a woman's private domain, with the messy reality tucked away.

The fact that Noelle felt more at home in the polished, empty fantasy than she did anywhere else wasn't flattering or reassuring. If she unfocused her eyes a little and let her mind drift, she could be back in her own bedroom, a room filled with empty tokens and an empty girl being groomed as Eden's flawless, unrealistic version of a woman.

Decorative and hollow.

What a horrible, hateful ideal.

Lex lay with her head pillowed on her arms, watching. Finally, she made a sleepy noise of amusement. "One hundred strokes before bedtime. Do they teach you that in Eden too?"

"Yes." Blinking, Noelle shifted her gaze to Lex's reflection in the mirror. "Do they teach you that in the sectors?"

"Mmm, Sector Two. That's where I'm from." She closed her eyes. "'It's all in the presentation, Alexa. A woman must never be herself.'"

The words could have come from her mother's lips. "So it's not so different from Eden, there."

"In some ways." Lex sat up and reached for a cigarette. "My mentor at the training house was stone cold. Makes Dallas look like a fucking saint."

"Training house?" She wanted to snatch the words back the moment they left her mouth, because of course there was only one thing they could be training Lex to do in the sectors, and it didn't have anything to do with hosting dinner parties.

"You haven't heard what they do out in Two?" Lex took a deep drag off her cigarette. "They buy up pretty little things, train 'em just right. Sell 'em to all the rich old men looking to corrupt some innocent darling who isn't too innocent to suck their balls on occasion."

Noelle clenched the brush until she could feel each individual swirl of the handle's carvings digging into her skin. "I'm sorry. That's—" Horrifying. Degrading. And the fact that she could recognize that and understand it only made her craving for corruption and a little degradation at Jasper's hands that much more twisted. "I'm sorry."

"For what? I didn't stick around for that shit. I ran away."

"Good." Noelle said it forcefully, trying to hide her confusion from Lex. She set down the brush and dragged her hair over her shoulder to braid it, watching her fingers so she wouldn't have to meet Lex's eyes. "Is that what men really want? Someone they can corrupt?"

"Depends on the guy." Lex crushed her cigarette, slipped from the bed, and walked into the bathroom. The water cut on a moment later, and she ducked back out, her toothbrush in her hand. "In Sector Two, the rich men buy girls as companions—gay or straight, whether they want one or not. They have to if they want to fit in."

Noelle had almost grown accustomed to Lex's casual nudity, but it was different tonight. Different because she'd had her face between Lex's thighs, because she'd felt pleasure at her touch. It was impossible to figure out the boundaries now, which was why she was still seated at the vanity, fiddling with her hair. Would it be a rejection to climb onto the couch after she'd slept tangled between Jasper and Lex? Or an invitation she didn't understand to crawl into the vast comfort of Lex's own bed?

She did the cowardly thing and stayed put, carefully smoothing each strand of hair into its place in her braid as she rested her gaze safely on her own hands. "I knew the sectors were all different, but I hadn't realized how different. Are they all like that? Each its own little world?"

"Kind of. Three's not so different from us, and Six and Seven are a lot alike."

"It's so much to learn." With the end of her hair tied off, Noelle had no choice but to look up. "I'm still trying to understand the rules here."

One corner of Lex's mouth quirked up. "Is that why you've been sitting at my vanity for way too long, looking nervous as hell? You don't know if you're supposed to sleep with me?"

Yes, trying to hide things from Lex was pointless. Noelle flushed but refused to look away. "Mostly, yes."

Lex gestured to the bed. "Are you unsure about whether or not you're invited, or concerned that I might try to fuck you?"

"Try?" Noelle wrinkled her nose. "You'd succeed. I just...don't know the rules. You know, with Jasper? With me? If he expects..." She was afraid to finish the sentence, afraid to see sympathy in Lex's eyes. For all Noelle knew, Jasper was in bed with another woman right now. It didn't feel like something he'd do...but he hadn't come to Lex's room, wondering where she was, either.

"If he expects...?" Lex asked leadingly, then stuck the toothbrush in her mouth.

She didn't know if Lex honestly didn't understand, or

was forcing her to say it. "If he expects me to be...faithful." That made her sound like a loyal pet, but she didn't know a better word. Surely *monogamous* couldn't apply, not when most of their sexual encounters had involved other people. "He's said some things, but not exactly about that."

Lex rinsed her mouth and then the toothbrush. "What'd he do, tell you not to mess around with anyone else?"

"Not exactly," she repeated, remembering the night of the fight. He'd come on her face and she'd been so wet she ached when he told her to keep her fingers out of her panties. She'd spent half the night pressing her thighs together and listening to Lex's breathing, as turned on by the command and denial as she had been by touching him.

It wasn't explanation enough. Lex was still watching her, so Noelle clutched at the hem of her T-shirt. "The night before I got my cuffs, he told me not to touch myself."

Lex's brows drew together in a stormy frown that slowly smoothed into an expression of understanding. "Oh—not without him." She wrinkled her nose again, this time with a laugh. "Damn, that's hot. I'm impressed."

A little of the tension knotting Noelle faded, even as her cheeks burned. "It was hotter than I expected it to be. And then the next day..." She shivered. "That was the most I'd ever felt, until last night."

"I didn't know he had it in him." Lex flipped off the bathroom light, climbed back into bed, and patted the mattress beside her. "No wonder you're spinning."

Switching off the vanity light plunged the room into darkness, but just enough light snuck under the door to the hall for Noelle to navigate to the bed. Lex's features were a vague outline mostly in shadow, and knowing hers would be similarly shadowed made it easier to talk. "Sometimes he talks like he wants to own me. And that shouldn't be okay. I shouldn't like it, because that's what they wanted to do in Eden. Own me."

"Does it feel the same?"

"No. But does that matter? Isn't it still being trapped, in the end?"

"Maybe." Lex traced a gentle fingertip over the ink encircling Noelle's wrist. "You're an O'Kane now, for good or bad. Does that make you feel sad and stifled?"

"No. A little nervous, maybe." She told Lex what had happened with Dallas at the bar, and admitted what she hadn't told Rachel. "The more I thought about it, the more I realized how much I *do* know. Things my mother taught me so I'd be able to help my father and my future husband, things that could hurt the important men in Eden. Not just allergies, but secrets. Scandals. Dreams that they'll compromise for, and weaknesses in their families that a smart woman could exploit."

"Or a smart man, like Dallas."

"Or a smart man." Noelle caught Lex's hand and twined their fingers together. "They're not all corrupt. One or two of the councilmen try, and even the bad ones... Their wives and children are as helpless as I was. I don't want to hurt people unless it means protecting us."

"Oh, honey. I know." Her fingers tightened around Noelle's. "At some point, he's going to ask, though. It's bound to happen."

She swallowed and closed her eyes. "I'll have to tell him, won't I? I made a promise."

"You wouldn't want to try to lie," Lex agreed quietly. "Especially if he came to you for information like that, because he wouldn't do it unless he had no other choice."

"I don't want to lie. I want to trust him." And that was the crux of it, the part that felt foolish and hopelessly ingenuous. "I want to tell him everything and believe he wouldn't hurt anyone who didn't deserve it, not unless he had no other choice. Does that make me stupid?"

"Not stupid. An optimist." Lex nestled closer, curling up behind Noelle. "You don't know yet. How hard Dallas has to work to keep life around here the way it is."

As comforting as Lex's warm body was, Noelle missed the heavy press of Jasper's arm. Both nights she'd slept with him, he'd tossed it over her body, pinning her in place with an unconscious sort of possessiveness. She didn't have to be pressed tightly to his side to wallow in his warmth because he exuded heat.

She hadn't seen him since that morning, and she missed him. "I guess the men work hard. The women too, I mean...but the guys seem to be gone a lot."

"They're around more than you think." Lex laughed and nuzzled the back of Noelle's neck. "You don't have to wait for him to come to you, you know. If you want him, go get him."

Noelle bit her lower lip. "What if there's someone else in his bed?"

"Do you suspect there is, or do you want me to tell you if that's how Jasper operates?"

"Is it?"

"No."

Noelle exhaled and clung to Lex's hand. "Go get him? Just like that?"

"Just like that."

It could work. Maybe it would even help. All the questions about her ability to say *no* might matter less to Jasper if she was busily, aggressively saying *yes*.

First she had to figure out how. "Lex?"

Lex rubbed Noelle's arm. "Yeah?"

"Will you teach me to dance?"

"Sure, if you want. You don't like hauling drinks?"

Noelle laughed. "I don't mind it. And I don't know if

I'll be any good at dancing, but I want to learn how to be like you. Sexy and strong and seductive. Proud of it."

But Lex only snorted. "It's all in the presentation, remember?"

"Then you can help me with that too." Lex wouldn't see her flushed cheeks and smile, but she could probably hear the amusement and embarrassment in Noelle's voice. "I apparently have a lot to learn about where jewelry goes."

"Short answer? Wherever you want to put it."

"Lex!"

"What?" She laughed. "It's true."

Tomorrow, Noelle would find some jewelry. Maybe she'd even let Lex show her how to wear each piece—or where. If Jasper had a problem with that, he'd have to do something about it.

Like claim her for good.

15

J ASPER KNEW IT was damn near the end of the world—again—when Dallas rounded up everyone for a meeting. He usually preferred to deal with his men in small groups, but right now time was of the essence, and they all needed to be informed.

Dallas lit a cigarette before sliding the pack over to Bren. "Everyone's heard what went down with Wilson Trent. Our immediate problem is that we're short one supplier, and we need to fill the gap fast if we're not going to slow production. Big picture's even uglier. No way could Trent have gotten his hands on those explosives on his own. Someone's backing him—someone with money or power or both. And we need to find out who."

"City black market would be the likeliest source," Bren said. "Military police. I have a friend on the inside I can contact. Have him look into things."

"Do it," Dallas told him without hesitation. "What about Trent? Did he say anything interesting before he died?"

"He mostly screamed."

Even Dallas lifted his eyebrows at that. "Do I need to worry about who that girl's gonna want to kill next?"

Bren matched his expression. "Probably not until her hands heal."

At the other end of the table, Flash laughed. "What, that tiny piece of tail beat Trent to death bare-knuckled?"

"I guess so." Dallas shook his head. "Don't get any ideas, Flash. No women in the cage fights. I don't want Lex twisting your dicks off if you win, and I sure as hell don't want to listen to you cry if you don't."

Already, in Dallas's mind, Lex was the one who took care of the women, his own counterpart in leadership. It made Wilson Trent's taunts about her all the more chilling. "Couldn't hurt to consider *why* this happened," Jasper observed. "Whether Trent approached someone for help getting rid of you, or it started out the other way around."

Dallas drummed his fingers on the table. "Trent was stupid, but he knew how to suck up to power. And if he wanted something we had badly enough..."

"He'd start dumbass negotiations with someone who hated you in a heartbeat," Jasper finished.

"Isn't hard to find people who hate me. Someone who would trust that bastard not to fuck it up? That's harder."

Bren drained his drink and set the glass down with a thump. "Unless it didn't matter because Trent was a very expendable test shot, and the real shit has yet to go down."

"Pretty damn likely." Dallas let his gaze drift around the table, taking the time to meet every man's eyes, from Jasper and Bren on either side of him straight down to where Dom glowered at the far end of the table. "We've been top dogs in Four long enough to get a little lazy. That has to stop, because we're playing in the big leagues now, whether we want to or not. We're making too much damn money for everyone else to ignore. And that means we need to get better at *information*. Cultivate some more reliable contacts in all the sectors. We need to get smart."

Jasper pulled out a chair, turned it around, and dropped onto it. "Flash and I are friendly with fighters in all the sectors. Ace has the women covered. A girl in damn near every brothel, right?"

Ace flipped him off, but not without a grin. "They like tattoos, I like blowjobs. It's good math."

Bren looked skeptical. "He's not going to start liking information as much as he likes his dick. No way."

"He will if I tell him to," Dallas rumbled, smashing out his cigarette in the nearest ashtray. "Jasper, have you still got contacts in the countryside? We're going to need more grain, fast."

One of his friends from the farm was managing his own now. "I can handle the corn, but I'll have to make inquiries about the barley."

"Good. Bren, work with the girl. See if you can get anything else out of her about Trent's organization. Especially the people likely to take over now."

"Maybe it should be us," Dom muttered.

"Edge into another sector?" Dallas's fingers stilled. "We're spread thin enough as it is. I don't want more territory, I just want their contacts. However we have to get them."

"And maybe the next guy won't be an idiot like Wilson Trent. Then you've got bigger troubles."

"We've got bigger troubles either way, which is why we're going to dig in and protect what we have, not get greedy and sloppy." Dallas jabbed a finger at him. "If

you're so hot to expand, work on finding new recruits—
loyal ones who can earn their place the hard way. No
shortcuts."

Dom lowered his gaze, his beefy arms still crossed
over his chest in a posture that screamed defensiveness.
Dallas ignored him and scanned the table again. "Trent
said a few other things I didn't like, particularly about
the ladies. I don't want the women out unaccompanied
until we know what we're dealing with."

Jasper rubbed a hand over his face. "I thought you
didn't want Lex twisting off any dicks."

Dallas pinned him with a cold look. "I'll handle Lex.
I'll handle all the other girls who aren't marked or collared, too. Those of you who have women, keep them
close."

A taunt wrapped in admonishment. For all his posi-
tives, sometimes Dallas could be a prick as well as a
hypocrite. "Message received," Jasper drawled.

"We'll see, won't we?" Dallas straightened and raised
his voice. "Hit your rounds. It's early last call at the club,
and the girls'll want you to clean up pretty and party
with them. Get laid good tonight, because we're all going
to be busting ass for the next couple weeks."

The men started to file out, but Jasper lingered.
"Should we more than double up if we have to go into
Sector Three, or let those stops slide for now?"

Dallas gestured for Bren to hang back and waited for
the other men to close the door before speaking. "Anything outside of Four, I want the two of you on it
together. I trust your guts and your heads. You'll know if
shit's too hot, but you won't get twitchy and start a territory war."

Bren shoved his hands in his pockets. "You think a
war is what Dom's after? He's bucking for you to send
someone to take over Three, and he sure the hell wants it
to be him."

"I think Dom wants to get out from under my boot."
Dallas reached for his cigarettes again with a sigh. "He's
a bastard, and more of one every fucking week. Violence
should be a tool, not the only way you get off. Not sure he
knows that anymore, if he ever did."

They could let him try to take over Three, but even if
Trent's remaining men sent Dom back in a box, the other
sector leaders would see it as an outright declaration of
aggression on Dallas's part. "We can't let him try it.
Nobody would believe he'd acted on his own."

"No, I'm going to keep him on a short leash. Pair him
up with Maddox." Dallas's grin bordered on sadistic.
"Dom's not smart enough to know he's too stupid to fool
Maddox."

Because Mad was an evil genius, the only man in
Sector Four more brutally efficient than Bren and more
charming than Ace. "I didn't know he was back."

"He's not—yet. But he should be rolling in tonight
before the end of the party."

For all the joking Jasper and Ace had done, it
seemed Dom might end up dead, after all. "If anyone will
know how to handle it, it's Mad."

Dallas nodded. "Now, on the topic of information...
Bren, get what you can from Six. Make her life a little
more comfortable. I don't want her running unsupervised
through the compound yet, but once we're sure she's not
playing a long game..."

"I'll make sure she's happy."

"*Without* giving her any more people to beat to
death."

Bren nodded blandly. "I've got it covered."

Dallas swung to face Jasper. "As for you and Miss
Cunningham, I think she knows more about the people
running the city than I gave her credit for. Find out how
much. No need to interrogate her, but I think she'll take
it a hell of a lot better if you ask than if I have to."

So that was his endgame. "Do you want me to squeeze her for information or collar her? Because they might wind up being mutually exclusive options."

Dallas rocked back in his chair and lit his cigarette before eyeing Jasper over the smoke. "You think it would hurt her?"

"Noelle's father is a powerful man," Jasper reminded him. "Yeah, I think she'll mind if we have to crush a few just like him. Not for their sakes, but for the collateral damage."

"And if it comes down to them or us?"

"She's not weak, and she's not stupid."

Dallas took a long drag and stared up at the ceiling. "I've got a little time. You make your decision about her, and then I'll make mine."

Jasper had made his choice, and the rest was up to her. No way could Dallas say the same. "She's still new."

"She's one of us." Dallas's flat tone invited no argument. "If you can't keep her and question her at the same time, I'll respect that. But it means I'll be the one asking the questions, and hoping she's as strong and smart as you think she is."

"Understood."

"Yes. Yes, it is."

Dallas seemed just as upset by the conversation as Jasper was, and that quelled a little of his irritation. "Cheer up. Like you said—Noelle's one of us."

"Mmm." Dallas exhaled again, blowing smoke into the air and watching it disperse. "I suppose I couldn't have you all to myself forever. Get out of here and get some work done."

Not in the mood to talk about it, then. "Fights tonight?"

"Damn straight. Bet we'll see a big crowd, too. They always come sniffing around when there's blood on the concrete."

"The spectators are even more bloodthirsty than the fighters." Jasper held up his fist.

"Always." After only a moment's hesitation, Dallas left the cigarette between his lips and bumped his own fist against Jasper's. It was silent acknowledgment, an apology and forgiveness in one gesture.

"Tonight." The only promise he could offer. He'd get things straight between himself and Noelle. The rest of it was between her and Dallas.

Noelle didn't need to ask Lex for advice on her wardrobe anymore. She'd chosen tonight's ensemble on her own, everything from the short leather skirt to the matching halter that wrapped around her throat and ended just above her belly button, baring pale skin and the curve of her hips. She had new boots, too, custom-crafted ones that somehow managed to mix tough practicality with a sleek sort of sensuality.

Dressed in leather and ink and her newly blossoming pride, she looked like an O'Kane. It was exhilarating.

The noise of the celebration hit her the moment one of the bouncers hauled open the door for her. Screams and cheers, drowning out the faint hint of music coming from the far side of the room. The warehouse had stark lighting, bare bulbs that looked like they'd been scavenged from before the storms. They cast their brash but uncertain light everywhere but where the action was—the cage.

A fight was winding down, judging by the shouts and whistles. Noelle ducked past two groupies and started for the far side of the room, where the O'Kanes usually claimed the best tables and couches. More than one unfamiliar fighter grinned at her, and all made slow appraisals of her body that invariably stopped at the tattoos on her wrists. The smiles melted away a little faster than the men, but every one disappeared into the crowd before he could get caught ogling an O'Kane woman.

God, power felt good.

Lex lounged on a low sofa near the bar, a drink in one hand. "You look nice, baby girl."

"Baby girl? You're Noelle?" A young woman in tattered jeans and a tight pink tank top perched on the arm of the couch gave Noelle's outfit a once-over before groaning. "God damn, Lex. She's barely been out of the city a week. Where do I get one of your makeovers?"

"You're not dirty enough, Nessa." Lex softened the words by stroking the woman's arm. "It just wouldn't work for you."

Nessa. Rachel had mentioned the name more than once as the brains behind some of the O'Kanes' biggest breakthroughs in liquor production, but Noelle had pictured someone older. Nessa looked to be near Noelle's age, though her slender body and heart-shaped face made her look younger. Sweeter.

Until she scowled. "I'll be plenty dirty when I'm good and ready," she retorted, swinging her legs out of the way to make room for Noelle to sit. When she did, the girl thrust out her hand. "Nice to finally meet you. Dallas keeps me chained up in the distillery, and not with the sexy chains, either."

Judging by the knowing grin on her face, it was another tease, like Ace's. Noelle accepted the ribbing as inevitable and shook the offered hand with a smile. "Well, I'm glad he let you out for the night."

"He wouldn't have let you miss this." Lex sat straighter and nodded to the cage. "Here he goes."

Bren had just climbed inside the cage, stripped to the waist, his feet bare. He stood on one side, near the bars, his head bent, stretching his shoulders.

"Oh my God, Bren's fighting?" Nessa's eyes widened under her spiky, bleached-white bangs. "Oh man, oh *man*. We're all gonna feel a little dirty tonight."

Baffled, Noelle glanced at Lex. "I'm missing something, aren't I?"

"Nope." Lex finished her drink and motioned to Rachel, who stood at the end of the bar. "You're missing *everything*."

A stranger climbed into the cage with Bren, a bulky man with ink, but not O'Kane markings. The tattoos were distorted by his bulging muscles, which the man flexed repeatedly to earn squeals from some of the groupies on the opposite side of the crowd.

Next to him, Bren looked...average. Strong but compact, and outweighed by enough to stir real worry in Noelle's chest. "Is he going to be okay?"

Rachel chuckled as she walked up with a tray cluttered with overflowing shot glasses. "He'll be dandy after he gets the crap beat out of him."

"And they throw a chick in there," Nessa added. "Dallas should start auctioning off the privilege. He'd make more on that than he does the booze."

Noelle prodded Lex with her elbow. "Is she serious?"

"About which part?"

It was answer enough. Noelle snapped her gaze to the cage as the stranger took his first swing. Bren blocked it, but his opponent came back with an even harder blow to the ribs. Bren took it and staggered against the bars.

Rachel shook her head. "This guy's a tank. Fifty bucks says Bren ends it early because his dick hurts."

Nessa thrust out her hand. "I'll bet a hundred that he plays with the guy for a while, but doesn't bother dragging the girl out of the cage before he fucks her."

Lex slapped her palm. "If he's *that* hot for it tonight, I might be the one jumping in there with him."

Their voices slid past Noelle as she watched the cage, transfixed by the sheer violence contained within the bars. The huge stranger looked furious, his face red and his veins bulging. He came at Bren again and again, roaring curses and swinging with meaty fists. Sometimes Bren dodged or blocked with a lazy ease that made it even more confusing when a blow he should have avoided smashed into him.

She'd watched Jasper fight with focused intensity and unwavering attention. She'd seen Flash dominate an opponent with his huge fists and sheer size. This was something else entirely, a completely unbalanced fight— because Bren didn't seem to be trying.

Another rough hit slammed him against the cage bars, and Noelle winced. "He's not going to fight back?"

"Sure, he will." Rachel grinned and passed her a shot. "When he's had enough."

Their scattered comments coalesced, formed a cohe‐ sive whole, but Noelle still couldn't quite believe what they were saying. "He likes getting beat up?"

Nessa snorted. "Like? Try gets off on in a major, se‐ riously hot way."

"She means that he's a masochist." Amira dropped to the couch with a sigh and draped her legs across Lex's lap. "He derives sexual pleasure from pain. Intense pleasure, apparently."

Noelle's cheeks flamed. She very carefully didn't look at Lex, and didn't blurt out *there's a word for it?* either. She did rub her thumb across the inside of her wrist, remembering the tiny stabs of pain as the needle pierced her skin, each one an irritation on its own, but all of them together burning through her into something hot and hungry. "Oh."

"*Oh*, she says." Rachel tugged at a lock of Noelle's hair. "Bren's a special case. Most of the people I've met who like pain are subs, but not him. By all accounts, he's damn bossy while you're whipping him."

A roar went up from the crowd, dragging Noelle's attention to the cage just in time to catch Bren twisting his opponent's arm high behind his back. "So he really is playing with the other guy? He could win whenever he wants to?"

"You don't know?" Amira cracked open a fresh bottle of water. "He was on the military police force in Eden. Special Tasks. He could snap that guy's neck without breaking a sweat."

Belatedly, Noelle drained the shot Rachel had handed her. She needed it as she studied Bren again. Within Eden, people barely admitted that Special Tasks agents existed. The city of the future should have no need for men trained to stalk and kill...but of course they did.

"That explains a lot," she said faintly. "About how he can fight so well, I mean. I don't know what to think about the rest of it."

Lex raised an eyebrow. "You plan on fucking him?"

Noelle made a face, remembering how gently he'd rejected her the night of her party. "Even if I were, I don't think he's interested."

"Then why do you have to think anything about it?" Lex slipped out from under Amira's legs and walked off, into the crowd.

Rachel watched her go. "Jesus help us all. She's in a mood."

Apparently so. Lex had already disappeared into the mass of bodies, and Noelle didn't think she'd appreciate being followed. "It's not something I said?"

"Maybe," Nessa told her, patting her shoulder awkwardly. "Or not. You'll never know. That's the beauty of Lex."

But Amira shook her head. "It's Dallas. Has to be."

"Ah, yeah." Nessa blew her bangs out of her eyes and gave Noelle a speculative look that left her squirming.

"You were with them the other night..."

She trailed off, as if inviting Noelle to fill her in on all the gritty details. Maybe that was common—sex and gossiping about it. Or maybe Nessa was nosy and Lex wanted her privacy.

Not that Noelle had anything useful to contribute. She'd spent the night so wrapped up in Jasper that Lex and Dallas could have had a fight a foot from her head without her noticing. "They seemed fine then. Though Dallas did come around this afternoon to tell us we can't leave the compound alone."

"That could be it," Rachel observed. "She doesn't respond well to orders. Which means half the time, she's giving Dallas the finger..."

"And the other half, *he's* giving it to *her*," Amira finished, holding up her hand.

Nessa slapped her palm. "And his thumb too, when she's lucky—oh Lord, have mercy and look out. Bren's had enough."

The man in the cage swung, and Bren caught his opponent's fist in one hand. Another swing, with the same result. When he held both of the man's hands trapped in his, Bren grinned ferally and headbutted him. Once, twice. The man swayed, dazed, as Bren released him.

Then he dropped to the floor, unmoving.

The crowd cheered, and even Nessa bounced up off the couch with a triumphant shout. Caught up in the excitement, Noelle raised her voice, too. She'd never cheered before, but it turned out to be the most natural thing in the world. Her shouts rose to meld with the other voices, made her as much a part of the group as Nessa's arm around her shoulders.

Dallas was the one who hauled open the cage door and gestured for someone to drag away the fallen man. Noelle watched his lips move, though she couldn't hear what he said over the din in the large room. Bren answered with a curt nod, and a scuffle broke out between several of the women standing near the cage.

Amira made a disgusted noise. "Girl, look at that pushing and shoving. No pride whatsoever. Bren's hot, but you don't make a fool of yourself over a man who isn't yours."

Bren seemed to have come to the same conclusion. He stared at the women surrounding the cage door for a moment, then stepped out and stomped past them, his chest still heaving.

Was that how she looked to Jasper? Desperate? Worry gnawed in Noelle's gut until she remembered she'd been in the warehouse for at least twenty minutes without scanning the faces in the crowd for him, much less throwing herself at his feet like the pouting girls in front of the cage.

Of course, the thought of him forced her gaze through the throng until she spotted his familiar profile in the far corner. He was standing next to a man Noelle had never seen, one with O'Kane tattoos winding up his bronzed arms. Coal black hair fell rakishly over his eyes, and he smiled when he caught her staring, an expression as wicked as any Ace had ever offered her.

Noelle looked away before Jasper could follow the man's gaze and find her mooning over him. "Who's the man with Jas?"

"That's Maddox." Rachel tipped back another shot. "Just got back from a trip south of the city."

"Ace will be disappointed," Nessa said, reaching for a drink of her own. "Mad's just as charming, but he's got these eyes... Oh, you could drown in them. I mean, if you weren't already drowning in Jasper."

"You should meet..." Amira trailed off and winced. "Oh, yeah. They're fighting."

Noelle followed her gaze and saw Lex headed for the back exit with two rough-looking men trailing behind her. They were dressed almost like Nessa—ripped jeans, big boots, and lots of silver jewelry flashing under the bare lights—but the tattoos covering every bit of available flesh were even rougher. Gawkish. Nothing like the breathtakingly detailed work Ace did, so maybe he had earned a little bit of his ego.

Nessa groaned and drained her shot. "Lord save me. Dallas is going to be unlivable for the next week, and I have to deal with him."

"He doesn't *own* her," Rachel said firmly. "If he wanted to lock that down, he could. We all know it."

"You mean with the marks?" Noelle asked, glancing at Amira's throat. What would it be like to have Jasper's ink wrapped around her neck? To feel the needle and know each stab of pain said *mine* and *forever*? Her body tingled at the thought of it.

"He could start off with a collar." At Noelle's confused look, Amira explained, "It's a less permanent option."

"But otherwise it's pretty much like being marked," Nessa added. "Totally at the guy's mercy. Man, I don't even know. Dallas is hot enough to melt a girl's panties, but we're all pretty much at his mercy already. Can you imagine how much more intense it'd be if he collared you?" She shook her head. "Maybe he knows better. Lex would try to kill him, and that wouldn't end well."

Noelle wasn't so sure. She'd seen the give and take between Dallas and Lex...but she'd seen Lex give in, too. Seen her melt for Dallas—all of her, not just her panties. "Maybe she'd feel differently if he offered instead of acting like he owns her already."

Amira smiled. "Looks like you've got Lex figured out. Maybe you should clue Dallas in."

Laughter came easier than Noelle expected, and it wasn't because of the whiskey humming in her blood. She was as sober as she'd ever been, though maybe high on the feeling of belonging. "I'm not getting in the middle of that. I don't want Lex to stab *me*!"

"That," Rachel declared, "would never happen. She has a real soft spot for you, one she doesn't even have for Dallas."

"Because you're sweet," Nessa said. "And loyal. I've only given you about a hundred chances to dish all the dirty details about Dallas's bedroom and what he gets up to in it."

Noelle flushed. "I don't—"

"Nah," Nessa cut in. "It's okay. I should go easy on you because you're new, but I can't help myself. I'm a compulsive gossip. Ask Amira."

The tiny brunette nodded. "It's true. She's horrible."

At least they wouldn't be upset if she refused to betray Lex's trust. Noelle rubbed her hands over her thighs and shook her head. "It's not that I'm not used to gossip. That's all the women are allowed to do in Eden. I'm just not used to women talking about sex so openly. Or...well, at all, really."

"No harm, no foul." Rachel straightened and rose, her eyes on the crowd. "I'm gonna go dance with Ace. I might actually let him touch me tonight."

Nessa whooped her approval before slugging Rachel on the shoulder. "Make him work for it. Begging's good for him."

Rachel turned and tilted her head. "You know it."

Noelle watched her thread her way into the crowd as another fight started between two men who weren't O'Kanes. Ace was grinding between two blondes whose adoring expressions vanished when Ace abandoned them to wrap an arm around Rachel's waist.

"Why doesn't Dallas let more women into the gang?" she asked Nessa and Amira as the two groupies sulked toward the cage. "They all seem willing enough."

"Yeah, willing enough to get laid and paid," Amira

said. "You think those two give a shit about Ace? I doubt they even know his name."

Nessa nodded in sharp agreement. "You can tell the ones who care. Like Trix." She gestured to the bar, where a pretty redhead in jeans and a tightly cinched corset poured drinks for the people watching the fight. "She started by coming to the fights, but she got to know the guys *and* the girls. Got a job and made herself useful. I think if she wanted to go for ink, Dallas would consider it."

Presumably it was a much rarer occurrence than Noelle had realized, which said a lot about her own easy acceptance—or maybe more about Lex's influence. Dallas had made it pretty damn clear he hadn't expected Noelle to be of any use at all, which left Lex as her savior.

Lex...and Jasper. Noelle sought him out again and found him still deep in conversation with Maddox. "I guess there must be a lot of gossip about me, then. And how fast he let me in."

Nessa actually turned a little pink. "Uh..."

Amira slid her arm around Noelle. "I think you've already figured out what everyone's been saying, haven't you? Lex and Jasper wanted you here, and that's enough for Dallas."

"Yeah, mostly that." Nessa slid to the couch and mirrored Amira's gesture. "We all love Jas, okay? And you make him happy. Growly and confused like a big dumb oaf, but that's just because he's a man. Men need to get used to being happy. Amira can tell you—no one did growly and confused like *her* big dumb oaf."

She covered her face with her hands and laughed. "Flash was *terrible*. It was all this pushing and pulling, like he didn't know what the hell he wanted."

A weight Noelle hadn't realized was there lifted, and she clutched at the words. "So that's normal? Wanting more and then less, or speeding up and slowing down?

Lex told me I should just go for him, but I don't know what he wants."

"In my experience? It's totally possible he doesn't know, either."

That part was less reassuring. Noelle had to fight to keep a plaintive note out of her voice. "So what do I do?"

"Whatever you can," Amira murmured sympathetically. "Whatever you want. That's all there is. It falls into place, or it doesn't."

So, in the end, Lex was right. There were no guarantees, no easy ways. She could float through this, too, like she'd floated through life, floated through rebellion. Jasper might take her. If he didn't, someone else could. She could be kept, marked, trapped in all the ways Eden had made her.

Maybe the secret was to make a choice.

Leaning over, she pressed a kiss to Amira's cheek. "Thank you. I mean it."

"Don't thank me," she demurred. "It's all you. Remember that."

"Remember what?" a deep voice rumbled behind them. Flash bent down to kiss Amira before resting his hip against the arm of the couch. His hand fell to the back of her neck, a protective gesture he barely seemed aware of. "You girls up to no good, I hope?"

"Hardly. Just some hot and heavy gossip." Amira wrapped her arm around his thigh, as absentminded and possessive as his hand on her neck.

"A guy can dream." He dragged his fingers through her hair. "I've got a little bit before my fight's up, baby. Came to check on you."

She rolled her eyes and swatted at his hand. "I'm the same as I was twenty minutes ago. I've been sitting on a couch, for Christ's sake."

"That's our cue." Nessa hopped up and dragged Noelle after her. "He'll just get more and more annoying until we move so he can cuddle her."

Flash's glare was so growly, so *grumpy*, that Noelle broke out laughing. That earned her a glower of her own, but Flash circled the couch to claim their spot, and it was impossible not to melt when he eased Amira into his lap and wrapped both arms around her. One of his hands dropped to the curve of her belly, and his surliness evaporated.

Staying felt like intruding, so Noelle smiled. "I'm going to dance. I'll be back later."

Amira didn't look up. "Bye."

Nessa giggled and pulled Noelle out onto the floor. Rachel caught sight of them and tipped her head. "Over here."

Ace swung his arms wide to pull the three of them into a laughing, hip-grinding tangle of limbs. "Who's the luckiest bastard in Sector Four? I got all the hot O'Kane girls to myself."

"Not all of them." Rachel shifted closer, sliding one hand into his hair, and licked the corner of his mouth.

For the first time since Noelle had met him, Ace seemed at a loss for words. The easy rhythm of his hips faltered, and she was close enough to hear his groan, low and hungry, the realest sound she'd ever caught slipping past his lips.

Amazingly, with that one little touch, Rachel had damn near brought him to his knees.

Lex was definitely right. Noelle had to make her choice and make her move.

Soon.

 dallas

HE'D BEEN ALL of nine years old the day his mother had taught him the lesson that would define his life.

Life on the farm had been hard. The world his mother had known had been dead for a decade, but she'd never curled in on herself like so many of the weak and the terrified. Nineteen years old when the lights went out, she'd given birth to him six months later and had held on to her little scrap of Texas at the point of a shotgun, more than willing to kill to defend her son and the people who relied on her wits and strength.

She could be cold-blooded, his mother, but she didn't believe in waste. Rage could give a body the strength to survive in a world gone mad, but not if it was unleashed without care. So the afternoon she'd caught him in a hair-pulling brawl with a boy half again his size, she hadn't taken the other boy to task. No, she'd dragged Dallas to the nearest trough by the scruff of his neck, dunked him in the water until he sputtered, and hauled him to the barn to take out his fury on the woodpile.

Get angry, she'd told him, on that afternoon and a dozen times after it. *Get angry, and then make something out of it. Don't fight unless you have no choice, and even then you don't waste time. You end it quick.*

So he had. Every day of his adult life, it seemed, he'd gotten angry. And he'd turned that anger into a business, and then a gang, and then a whole fucking sector that he ruled over as absolutely as his mother had over her little ranch. She'd never held as many lives in her hands as he did, but her advice still fit. It worked.

Most of the time.

She'd never known him as an adult. She'd never known Lex, a woman who could make him so damn furious it was amazing he hadn't taken over *all* the sectors by now. He'd watched her waltz out of the warehouse with two hulking cage fighters. Rubbing them in his face.

You don't own me. She might as well have screamed it. And he couldn't so much as blink a fucking eye, because he didn't own her. Dallas fucking O'Kane couldn't be seen wanting something he couldn't have, because Dallas O'Kane could have anything he wanted.

"Make something out of it," he grumbled, kicking open the door to the workshop. Salvaged lumber lined one wall in towering stacks, mismatched boards from demolished buildings. Someone had pounded out the nails and cut them into manageable pieces, all stacked, waiting to be burned with the O'Kane logo and turned into crates for packing bottles of moonshine.

On the other side of the room, Bren was already bent over the wide worktable. Dallas supposed he should have expected that, too. "Bren."

"Sir." He tucked a pencil behind one ear before looking up. "Ready to get to work?"

"You bet." Dallas closed the door and strode to the table. "Might as well knock out enough crates for the next shipment, eh?"

Bren made a wordless noise of agreement and reached for the measured stack of boards. He fired up the band saw, its whir even louder than the jumble of thoughts racing around in Dallas's brain.

Not that it kept the damn things from racing. Sometimes Bren's silence was a blessing, but right now Dallas would take any distraction from the image of Lex dragging her new playthings out of the warehouse.

He couldn't give her the satisfaction of knowing she'd gotten to him, or she'd do it all the damn time. And *that* thought had him driving the first nail into wood hard enough to split the board. "Fuck."

Bren shut down the saw and tossed the last of the cut pieces of wood onto the table. "Question."

Thank God. "Yeah?"

"If it bothers you, why let it go on?"

If Bren found the situation perplexing enough to bring it up, shit really had gotten out of control. If it had been anyone else, Dallas would have brushed it off, but Bren was closer to him than anyone but Jasper—and Jasper wouldn't have had to ask the question. He already understood the answer on a gut level.

Bren needed to learn it. "If I start treating women like Wilson Trent does, what the fuck hope do they have with the rest of you?"

"No, I mean—" Bren barked out a laugh, more self-deprecation than humor. "I guess there really aren't many ways to handle it."

"For you, there might be. For me..." Dallas shrugged and reached for a new board. "It's not always good to be king."

"I see." Bren busied himself with fitting four cut

pieces together to form the bottom of a crate.

Sometimes it was hard to tell if the man was biting his tongue or had moved on. "If you've got something to say..."

Bren smiled faintly. "Is that my position? Court jester? I get to safely say whatever the hell I want because someone has to speak truth to the king?"

"Trusted lieutenant," Dallas corrected softly. "You and Jas both. He won't let me get too hard, and you can't let me get too stupid."

The man braced both fists on the table and stared down at its cluttered surface. "Never known you to be scared of anything, that's all."

He could sidestep the words easily by claiming he wasn't scared of Lex, and it was true. Lex herself didn't frighten him. The thought of how quickly she could come to hate him, though... "Not scared. Cautious."

"Caution is smart. Admirable."

"Could you sound a little less convinced?"

"Probably not, though I could try."

Dallas sighed and drove a nail into the side of the crate. "You're a lousy jester. All of the truth, none of the jokes."

Bren shrugged. "I have no sense of humor—isn't that what everyone says?"

Everyone except Jas, who never failed to comment on Bren's twisted idea of what was funny. Dallas had always thought it was a lot simpler. "You haven't had much to laugh about of late."

"No one has, right?" Bren reached out and plucked the hammer from Dallas's hand. "I tried to collar Lex once. Did she ever tell you?"

Dallas's fist clenched around empty air, and Bren was too clever by half. Not that Dallas would have swung a hammer at one of his own men—probably—but the impulse alone was enough to give him pause. "No, she never mentioned it."

"I'm not surprised."

Dallas fought to keep his voice even. "So. You tried."

"I was still new," Bren explained with a shrug. "I didn't know yet."

A leading sort of statement. Its own trap, the kind meant to make him ask, *Know what?* As if the answer wasn't hanging in the air—everyone thought Lex was as good as his, and Dallas didn't bother to correct them. Neither did she, God bless her.

Most of the time, anyway.

With the thought of Lex's two suitors threatening to rear its head again, Dallas forced the conversation in a new direction. "How's the girl doing? Six? She getting her head around trusting us yet?"

"Nah." Bren held out the hammer. "It's a little soon for that, I think. She's still half convinced we're going for the long con. Maximum mental anguish."

Dallas raised an eyebrow. "Is that what Trent did to her?"

"Yeah. Maybe the worst thing he did."

It was sophisticated for someone like Trent, a vicious game that required patience and an ability to lie that Dallas had assumed was beyond the bastard. Or maybe it had never been a lie for him—maybe he'd just been that fucking childish. A kid who cherished his favorite toy until he got bored, then shattered it so no one else could play with it.

There was probably a lesson in there, an intensely personal one that Dallas didn't want to ponder too close-ly. "She must trust you, at least a little."

"Getting there." Bren flipped the crate over and laid strips of wood across the bottom.

Dallas abandoned the pretense of building and moved to the far wall, where Bren had already stoked the fire they kept banked in the massive hearth. Maddox had spent a year perfecting an electric heating element for the O'Kane branding irons, but Dallas preferred the old-fashioned way. The electricity they leached from Eden's power grid was far more reliable now than it had been in earlier years, but there were still failures and blackouts. Work had to go on, even when the lights were out.

He selected the two largest irons and set them into the flames. "Let me know when you think it's safe to loosen the girl's leash. I'm not ready to give her free run of the place, but she doesn't need to stay locked up all the time."

Bren hammered the last nail into place. "I'll let you know when I think you can turn her over to Lex."

He couldn't hold back his snort. "I don't think Lex is looking for another playmate. She's pretty well enamored of Noelle."

Bren pulled up short and eyed Dallas with a shake of his head, then returned to the task at hand with an unintelligible mutter. This time, Dallas didn't feel like poking for an answer he didn't want to hear. He knew what it would be.

Turn her over to Lex.

Like Lex was his damned queen. Like she wasn't off screwing a couple of street brawlers just to remind him that he could own her allegiance, but he could never own her body. The harder he closed his hands around her, the more she'd slip away...and the thought of losing her for good made him want to wrap her in chains.

Maybe he should. He could use the excuse of Trent to slap that collar around her throat and show her how good it would be.

If she'd take it. If it would be enough.

No, no use pretending, even to himself. It would never be enough. Not a collar, not a mark. He wouldn't be satisfied with anything less than all of her—mind, body and soul—and Lex would never give up that much control. They'd destroy each other. He'd destroy *her*, and that was the one thing he couldn't bear. Better to take what he could get and leave them both whole.

Mostly.

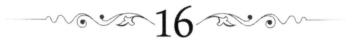

16

I N NOELLE'S IMAGINATION, her seduction of Jasper had started differently.

For one thing, in her imagination she'd had time to
prepare. To take a bath, to pick the perfect outfit. The
perfect underwear. The perfect jewelry, all wonderfully
illicit, turning her on before she even reached his door.

Her fantasy hadn't included a sick waitress, a club
full of rowdy drunks, and Dallas deciding they would
damn well stay open until the idiots stopped throwing
around fistfuls of money. By the time the bouncer rolled
the last one out the door, Noelle was frazzled, a little
disheveled, and caught in some jittery place between
exhausted and so hyped up she could barely sit still.

She almost decided to forgo the entire thing in favor
of a quiet hour unwinding in Lex's tub and a night of
sleep. But as she found herself in the long hallway that

led to Jasper's rooms, then at his door, the truth was stark and undeniable.

He was how she wanted to unwind, even if it meant nothing more than the chance to kiss him before she went to bed without him. So when his door swung open in response to her knock she did exactly that, ignoring all of her careful plans in favor of rising up on her toes to seal her lips to his.

He lifted her in his arms, his mouth still on hers as the door slammed shut behind her. His tongue traced her lips, then eased between them, a lazy exploration he didn't end until her back hit the wall. "Long night?"

"Endless." Amazing how promptly her aching feet recovered once they were hovering three inches above the ground. She wrapped a leg around his and smiled. "Dallas wouldn't close the doors until he'd emptied everyone's pockets. But the drunker they got, the better they tipped."

"That's a good thing, right?"

Noelle dug in her pocket and pulled out the thick wad of tightly rolled bills. She'd counted each one before adding it to the stack, stunned by how quickly they added up, and how freeing it was to realize they were *hers*. "As long as you promise to take me to the market soon. I promised Dallas I'd wait for you."

"He's coming down like that on everyone, not just you." Jasper stuffed her money back in her pocket and started for the bathroom. "We're all on restriction, for obvious reasons."

"I know. Lex is in a mood about it." Which was the politest way to describe her temper. Everyone had tiptoed around her today—except for Dallas. He'd acted like nothing was wrong, and that had only pissed Lex off worse.

Jasper set Noelle down and cut on the shower. "Dallas has his asshole moments, but this isn't about some sexist bullshit. I think there's something else going on with them."

Noelle couldn't argue with that, but she didn't want to discuss it, either. Lex's pain was too real—too *raw*—to make gossiping about it anything other than cruel. "Are we taking a shower?" she asked instead, watching as he fiddled with the knobs. Sex against the tiles would be delicious, she imagined, hard and slippery and quick, no time for the slow torment Jasper loved so much.

He made a noncommittal noise and stripped his shirt over his head before turning his attention to the hooks on her corset. Each gave way with a soft click, her breasts spilling free as he unhooked the final fastening and let the structured leather slide to the floor.

God, she loved the way he looked at her. He traced the very tips of his fingers across her shoulders and down the slopes of her breasts, stopping just shy of her nipples. "Want me in there with you?"

"Yes." She arched her back, pressing up into his touch as she reached for his belt. "You're all I want to-night. Just...you. Wherever, however."

"However?" His hands dropped to her ass, and he dragged her closer.

The movement left her hands pinned between their bodies, her fingers crushed against the solid heat of his abdomen. His skin was so close to her mouth that she couldn't stop herself from kissing him, parting her lips against his shoulder before stealing a taste.

She had to be honest. She had to say *yes*, before he even asked the question. "Maybe fucking, if you want."

"Mm-hmm." He released her and backed away. "Clothes, Noelle. Take them off."

She started with her cutoff shorts, dragging the zip-per open before wiggling the denim off her hips with enough gyrating to make Lex proud, though with a frac-tion of the other woman's grace.

At least Jasper didn't laugh at her.

She had to bend down to unfasten her shoes, pre-senting Jasper with an unobstructed view of her ass covered only by her favorite ruffled panties. That part of the fantasy matched her imagination, and she peeked up at him as she worked at the second buckle. "Should I take yours off next?"

He shook his head and unbuckled his belt. "Get un-der the water."

His voice held an implacable edge. It was an order, for all the easiness of the words, and she slipped out of her underwear and obeyed.

He stood at the open shower door and watched her as he took off his pants. "I like the way the water drips off of you. The way your skin looks when it's wet."

Noelle shivered under his gaze, though the water was so hot steam drifted up around her. "I like the way you watch me. It makes me wetter."

The shower stall seemed roomy—until Jasper stepped into it. He loomed over her, pressing her against the tile. "How wet?"

Words froze in her throat because it was hard to breathe with him stealing all the air from the tiny space. She wanted him so much that she started to reach for him, then hesitated and lifted her arms above her head instead. "You could touch me and find out."

His erect cock nudged her hip as he closed the scant space between them and rested one arm against the tile. He slid his other hand down, over the crest of one breast and farther. To her upper thighs. "Open."

She inched her legs apart without looking away from him. "That word makes me wetter, too. It used to be such an innocent word, but now..."

Jasper arched an eyebrow but didn't move his hand. "Now that you know all the delicious ways you can be opened?"

"No," she whispered, spreading her legs wider. "Now that I know all the ways I can open for you."

"You don't know them all." His fingers slipped over her folds, parting them, wet from the water *and* her arousal. "Not yet. But you will."

This was heaven and hell in one. The slow glide of his fingers working against her, sparking pleasure from the touch and kindling a deeper anticipation. Her nipples tightened into aching points, and she dropped one hand to soothe that need, stroking herself with a sigh. "I'll do anything with you."

He moved fast, jerking her hand back over her head. "Leave them there."

Her pulse pounded in her ears, and she stretched her arms up until her hands brushed the shower fixture. She curled her fingers around it as her rasping breaths echoed in the shower stall.

She couldn't move, but she could speak. It was good practice for the next time Dallas decided to hold her release hostage to her willingness to say obscene things. "My nipples ache. I want you to touch them."

Jasper ran his hand down her body again, avoiding the tips of her breasts. "I'll get around to it."

Impossible not to whimper at that, and she twisted a little, rubbing her hip against his cock with a groan. "Did you bring me in here to tease me?"

He closed his eyes, but only for a moment. When he opened them again, they were blazing. "This is what it means to belong to me—that you trust me to give you what you need. Can you handle it?"

She did trust him. She trusted him all the more *because* he was teasing her, because it twisted her up and made her wild, and he knew how to make it exactly what she needed. He knew how to turn her inside out.

His eyes were so dark. So intense. She wet her lips and nodded once. "I can handle it. I trust you. Just because I beg for something else, that doesn't mean I want you to give it to me. Sometimes I like it more when you tell me no."

"Do you think I need to be told that?"

No, he knew. He'd known all along, while she had struggled to make sense of the shame and the need. She tightened her grip on the fixture and shook her head. "No."

"Then hush." He drew his thumb over her lower lip. "Stop telling me that you trust me and show me instead."

He didn't wait for a response before dipping his hand between her thighs. Two of his fingers eased inside her. He began to move them in rhythmic motions, rubbing against her inner walls and pushing deeper with every stroke. Pleasure built, brick by brick, each stroke almost inconsequential on its own but part of a slow-rising tension that had her squirming, fighting the urge to rise on her toes to steal a moment's respite or rock against his hand to hurry his pace.

Trust. She had to show it, even if her entire body ached now, hungry for harder and faster and *more*.

His touch slowed. He slipped his fingers free of her body, teased them over her clit, and lightly caressed her inner thighs.

Then he started all over again.

Noelle whimpered, unable to control the desperate twist of her hips as she chased his retreating touch.

Jasper pressed his lips to her cheek. "No matter what you say, what *I* say, this is undeniable. You, moving your body. Fucking my fingers. That's what I pay attention to."

His beard scraped her skin, but she rubbed her face against his, hungry for any chance to touch him. "Do you want me to fuck your fingers?"

"Not consciously. I don't want you to decide to." He trailed his lips over to her ear. "That's why I didn't ask. I made it happen."

Hot breath tickled over damp skin, sending tingles shivering through her until she squirmed again. There was something dangerously seductive in his words, a promise that he'd been watching her, learning her, that he understood all the dark twists and turns that made up her desire and wouldn't hesitate to follow them.

She could have anything she wanted—everything—but only if she trusted him to give it to her. Only if she waited. Not passively, because there was nothing passive in the restraint it took not to reach for him, not to dig her nails into his shoulders and beg, but that was the sweetest part of the game. Her fingers would be numb from clutching at the fixture, and she didn't care. The discomfort was part of the pleasure, just like the anticipation. The mystery of wondering when she'd snap, and what he'd do to drive her there...

And the reward. Oh God, the reward would be sweet.

"Yes." He worked a third finger into her pussy, stretching her as he watched her face. It was intense, considering the size of his hands, filling her until she hissed in a breath and inched up on her toes in an attempt to slow his advance.

He gave her no respite. Instead, he followed, thrusting his fingers deeper.

Yes. She couldn't stop panting long enough to say the word, but surely he could read it in her eyes as she forced her feet back to the ground. The slick tiles and the steam and the hot water became secondary sensations, fading into the background as every squirm of her hips elicited more pleasure *and* discomfort, a heady mix that only made her hotter.

"You want it to stop," he whispered, "you tell me *no.* Anything else, and I'll keep going."

She nodded to show her understanding, then sucked in a deep breath and begged. "Don't stop, please don't stop."

He urged her hands from the showerhead and turned her around to the opposite side of the stall. His wide shoulders blocked the spray, and he pushed her arms above her head again as water trickled out of her hair. Bending his head, he caught a drop as it gathered on her nipple. Pleasure jolted through her, bringing her up on her toes as she pressed greedily toward his mouth.

The rasp of his tongue was so sweet it melted away what was left of the stretching pain of his fingers. She shifted her hips in tiny movements, shocked by how quickly *too much* had become *not enough*.

Jasper surged up and kissed her, his teeth scraping her bottom lip as he rocked his hand. Away, slowly, but when the hard press of his fingers returned, the stretch was harsher, almost unbearable.

Four fingers. It had to be. Nothing else would feel so commanding, so beautifully overwhelming, and hard on the heels of the realization came that *moment*, the one where surprise twisted into helpless arousal. Shame should have followed, the dizzying tangle of emotions, good and bad, that always sent her flying.

Not this time. Oh, she was flying, but not because of some empty inhibition that would leave her drowning in guilt and regret. She was high on being filthy, on choos‐ing sin and loving it, on being wanted for loving it.

As long as they both wanted it, nothing Jasper did to her would ever shame her.

Noelle pressed her open mouth to Jasper's cheek as she shuddered. "I love your fingers."

"I know." He bit her ear, sharp and rough. "What should I put inside you next?"

The words forced a groan from her. If he stroked her clit, she'd come like this, riding too many of his fingers in the haze where pain meant pleasure. But she didn't ask for it, didn't beg.

He knew.

"Anything," she rasped instead, trembling against the slick tiles. "Anything you want. Because I'm dirty." *And you like me that way.*

"Indecent," he agreed. His thumb rubbed slow circles over the outer and then inner lips of her pussy, venturing closer and closer to her clit. "Vulgar. Wicked." She couldn't focus on his words, only the path of his thumb. She held her breath every time it started another upward arc, straining, praying he'd edge just a little higher, only to voice her protest with a whimpered moan when his touch receded again. Her fingernails dug into her palms as she struggled not to reach for him, not to reach for *herself* and seize her own release with a quick, rough touch.

Her pussy clenched hard around his intruding fingers. So close. So damn *close*—

He shifted his hand, and the teasing promise of his thumb on her clit vanished. Instead, he curled his fingers inside her and thrust his hips close to hers, and the length of his cock, steely but soft, glided over her clit. Not enough friction, not nearly enough, though that stopped mattering as soon as he ground against her with a delicious groan.

She came without warning, without realizing the tension had snapped until she heard her own voice bouncing off the stall walls, wordless, moaning cries that crested with every violent shudder.

Jasper didn't stop. He pressed her against the tile, his hips still moving, his cock caught between his hand and her pussy. Her knees melted, and she clutched at his shoulders as the grinding pressure of his shaft set off another wave, little pulses of pleasure that peaked as her inner muscles gripped his fingers.

"Oh God." Her voice, raspy and pleading, and she thumped her head back against the tile when he kept grinding, kept fucking them both, until she was so wet and hot that even four fingers didn't hurt anymore, and she told him so in broken, sobbing gasps, begging him to shove them deeper, to give her everything, to make her feel it, to *own* her.

He bit her again, this time hard enough to bruise, his teeth sharp on the soft underside of her jaw. His groans intensified along with his thrusts, built until his fingers jerked and his body tensed, straining. He came, semen splashing hot on her hip as he pulsed against her.

"Jas..." She shivered and let her head fall forward, burying her face against his throat. Even that tiny movement shifted her body on his fingers, and she whimpered as the friction abraded hypersensitive nerves.

He distracted her with a kiss as he eased his fingers free of her body, his chest heaving. "Okay?"

Her nod rubbed her cheek over his shoulder, but she realized that might not be enough. She needed to find a verbal reassurance, but her tongue tripped over even simple words. "Better'n okay. Good. So good."

"Mmm." He guided her under the warm spray again and picked up the soap. In moments, she was soapy and slick, wallowing in the sensual glide of his hands over her skin.

She closed her eyes and tilted her head back, tipping her hair under the water before smoothing the heavy, wet strands away from her face. "Was that one of the delicious ways I can be opened?"

Jasper smiled. "One of them—though I didn't take it as far as I could have."

He'd taken it as far as she'd been able to handle, and Noelle doubted it was an accident. More like a carefully calculated advance, because she'd felt his single-minded focus as he pushed her past the boundaries of her experience.

What would it be like to follow him step by trembling

step past every line she'd ever drawn and some she couldn't imagine existing?

Beautiful.

Liberating.

She returned his smile and pressed a kiss to his chest. "Maybe next time you can take it further."

His low laugh echoed off the tile, warming the scant space between them. "If you're good."

17

INSTEAD OF MANDATING the buddy system for leaving the compound, Dallas should have brought the whole damn market to them.

Jasper wrapped his fingers around the pile of money Rachel had handed him and peered down at her list. "Why don't you come with us?" he asked.

"Insert myself into your quality alone time?" Rachel shook her head. "No, thanks. If the list is a problem—"

"It's not," he interjected.

"Well...okay, then." She grinned and pulled the dish towel off her shoulder as she backed toward the bar. "Quit complaining and pick up my shit."

"Smartass."

Noelle arrived a moment later, pushing through the employee door in jeans and a tank top that showed off her tits and her ink. She was clutching a list of her own, which she waved at him with a smile. "Nessa asked me to pick up a few things for her."

He held up the list in his hand. "Rachel's."

She reached his side and rose on her toes to brush a lingering kiss over his lips. "Hopefully we can carry it all back."

Jasper caught her around the waist and held her, his mouth hovering close to hers as he drank in the sensation of her soft curves against his body. "If not, fuck 'em."

With a teasing wiggle of her hips, she laughed at him. "That sounds fun too."

"More fun than shopping, anyway," Lex drawled from the doorway.

Noelle glanced over her shoulder without pulling away from Jasper. "Hey, Lex. I was looking for you earlier. Everything okay?"

"Peachy. Heard you were headed down to the market."

"Right now," Jasper confirmed. Rachel might have had qualms about intruding on their walk, but Lex wouldn't.

She proved it with her next words. "Can I come along? Dallas has had me locked up tight."

"Sure, that's fine." Noelle met his eyes, resigned but pleading. "Right?"

She looked so hesitant that he blew out a breath and smiled. "Orders are orders, right?"

Smiling, she kissed him again and eased away. Her fingers trailed down his arm to twine with his. "You can help us carry all of Rachel and Nessa's requests back."

Lex wrinkled her nose, but Jasper turned for the door, his hand at the small of Noelle's back.

It was still early, and the sun hadn't quite had time to burn the chill off the air. He shrugged out of his jacket and draped it around Noelle's shoulders.

"Thanks." She pulled the jacket tight and kicked an

empty liquor bottle off the sidewalk. Her gaze jumped to Lex, then back to Jasper. "Do you know how long Dallas wants us going out in groups?"

Damned if he'd tell her they still didn't know who'd bankrolled Trent's attack—or what it meant. "Until further notice, sweetheart."

"Just curious." She bumped her hip against his. "I don't mind the company, and I still get turned around in all these back streets. Though it would be fun to get a chance to test my cuffs."

At the moment, the O'Kane ink could be more of a bull's-eye target than a warning. Jasper opened his mouth, but Lex cut him off.

"Hey." She stopped Noelle with a hand on her shoulder. "Testing your ink is a shit idea right now. Dallas is a prick, but he's not stupid. If he's restricting our movements, it's about safety."

Noelle studied Lex's face as she rubbed her thumb over the sleeve of Jasper's jacket. "Should I have covered it up?"

She shook her head. "If things were that dire, we wouldn't even be allowed out with Jasper."

Relief filled Noelle's features as the tension in her posture eased. "Okay. I don't want to do anything dangerous, but..." She shrugged. "I like showing it off."

Jasper cupped a hand under her elbow. "I get it. We don't hide our ink, Noelle. But smart is smart. Someone's gunning for Dallas right now."

And hurting Lex would be a prime way to kick him in the gut. Judging from the look on her face, she knew it. She crossed her arms over her chest, her gaze darting back and forth as they walked. Watching, assessing the potential danger.

Noelle seemed to realize it, too. Her worried gaze followed Lex as they rounded a corner, and her hand snuck out from under his jacket to find his. "I'm all for smart."

So was he. The few people going about their business in the alley seemed interested in their movements, but most were faces Jasper recognized. Faces that bore no hint of deception or guilt. Still, by the time they cleared the end of the alley, he was ready to call off the trip. Anything that left him feeling this uneasy wasn't worth it.

The problem was the marketplace. Though it was early in the day, the place would be throbbing with people, crowded and loud, and any asshole with a sharp knife would only need a second of distraction to do his job. In and out in the confusion, gone before Jasper ever realized someone was bleeding.

He rounded on Lex. "This is a bad—"

A loud crack. The dirty brick in front of him chipped, drawing his gaze even as tiny shards flew back to bite into his cheek. *Shots.* He reacted on instinct, drawing Noelle and Lex in front of him as he hustled them around the side of the building, into the alley.

"Stay down." Jasper whirled, already drawing his pistol. No one on the street, which meant eyes up high. He scanned the broken windows on the opposite building, looking for the telltale flash in the morning sunlight. *Come on, where are you, you bastard—*

Another shot.

A cry of pain. *Noelle's* voice, shocked and cut off as she clamped her teeth together. He turned in time to see her slap a hand to her arm.

Jasper's gut clenched. "Lex."

"I got it." She shielded Noelle's body with her own and tugged at the jacket. "Let me see, honey."

"I don't think it's bad," she whispered, sliding her hand away. Pain bracketed her eyes, but she held it together as Lex ripped away the hem of her faded T-shirt and wrapped it around Noelle's arm.

Jasper locked down his panic, shut it away behind

the cold wall that would allow him to function, and kept looking for the sniper. "Get her back inside before he takes another shot. Hurry."

She dragged Noelle up, her uninjured arm draped over Lex's shoulders. "Let's go, baby girl."

A third sharp crack almost drowned out the last word, and Jasper felt a surge of satisfaction as he finally spotted the rifle barrel in a fourth-story window, along with the vague outline of the shooter behind it. He fired off three shots in quick succession, and the rifle slid out of the window and tumbled to the ground as the shooter vanished.

"Jasper!" Noelle's voice again, but not pained this time. Panicked. He whirled to find her kneeling next to Lex, both hands pressed to Lex's side as blood welled between her fingers. "I don't know what to do!"

Fuck. He holstered his gun and glared at the handful of people clustered at the other end of the alley. "Go get help. *Now.*"

One man rushed off, and Jasper dropped to the cracked asphalt beside Noelle. "How bad does it look? Can we move her?"

"I don't know." Her hands trembled. "I've never dealt with anything you couldn't fix with med-gel. Should I move my hands? What if the bullet went through—?" Her voice broke. "Lex, can you hear me?"

She didn't stir, so Jasper smacked her on the cheek. "*Lex.*" She struck out, swinging one fist, but only clipped him on the shoulder. "I'm going to pick you up, get you inside where it's safe."

Boots pounded on the concrete behind him, followed by Ace's swift, vicious curse. "Jesus *Christ*," he muttered, dropping to the opposite side of Lex's body. "Someone flagged me down and—fuck, it doesn't matter. Should I carry or cover?"

"Cover." Jasper's self-control was starting to fray

around the edges, and he avoided looking at Noelle as he gathered Lex in his arms and rose. "I think I hit the bastard, and he dropped his rifle. Might be able to trace it."

"I'll send Bren." Ace drew his gun and pulled Noelle to her feet. "Stay close, sweetheart. Between me and Jas, okay? You with me?"

Noelle said something that was lost under the scuffle of Ace's boots, but it must have reassured him because he lifted his voice. "Got your back, brother, and hers. Let's roll."

It took an eternity to reach the door. Rachel had it open and waiting, her face peaked and worried. "I heard the shots, but I didn't know they were so close." She turned to Trix. "Fetch Dallas."

There wasn't a good place to put Lex, so Jasper laid her out on the edge of the stage and shoved her already-torn shirt higher. "Left side. Probably missed her liver."

"Still plenty of things it could have hit. Spleen, for one." Rachel helped him ease her up onto her right side to check her back. "Exit wound. We need that doc—the surgeon."

"I'll get him," Ace said from behind them. "And then I'll find Bren and take him back to the alley."

The front door slammed shut behind him, and Noelle appeared at Jasper's side with the Broken Circle's heavy med kit in one hand. "What does she need? What can I do? Clean towels or bandages..."

All they could do was try to staunch the flow of blood and wait, hope the wound was superficial and she wasn't bleeding even worse on the inside. "Towels. Rachel—"

But she was already on it. She unfolded and refolded the terrycloth, pressed it tight to the holes on either side of Lex's body.

Jasper was left with nothing to occupy his shaking hands, and he found himself reaching for Noelle. "Your arm."

"I'm all right." But the words trembled, and she shivered uncontrollably as she stared at Lex with huge, terrified eyes.

"Hey." He caught her chin and forced her to meet his eyes. "Don't lose it. Quick help—that's all we can do." After an endless moment, she blinked and focused on him. She drew in a deep breath, another, and nodded. "I think my arm needs some gel."

He shook his head and peeled the makeshift bandage away just enough to catch a glimpse of ravaged, bleeding skin. "Looks like a flesh wound," he muttered through the rage. "It'll hold until we take care of Lex."

"Okay." She grabbed his hand. "Are you okay? Did you get—?"

"What the *hell* is going on?" Dallas's roar made Noelle start, her fingers clenching convulsively around Jasper's. Dallas shoved through the door from the back hallway, a frantic Trix half-running to keep up with him.

He took two steps into the room and caught sight of Lex. The rage and worry slipped from his face, leaving behind the blank, cold mask that scared the living hell out of Jasper.

He stepped between Dallas and the stage. "Sniper. Ace went for the doctor."

Dallas's head turned toward him first, followed belatedly by his impassive gaze. The effect was chilling. "Who's going after the sniper?"

"If he hasn't bugged out already, Bren will round him up."

"Good. Now get the fuck out of my way."

"I'm sorry," Jasper rasped. "We were headed back—"

Dallas punched him, snapping his head to one side, then strode past him without another word. Noelle pressed close to his side and lifted her good arm to touch his jaw. "Are you all right?"

A sniper, and Lex bleeding on the Broken Circle stage. Jasper swallowed a mirthless laugh. All things considered, he was damn lucky to only get smacked in the face. "I'm fine."

Dallas spoke from the stage, where he was bent over Lex, stroking her hair. "If you're fine, go meet up with Bren. Find the bastard who did this."

Noelle's fingers tightened at the words, but Jasper peeled them away from his arm. "You'll be all right." he murmured. "Doc can take a look at your arm too, okay?"

She opened her mouth, but Dallas cut off any chance of a reply. "*Now*, Jas. I'll take care of your woman."

The way you should have taken care of mine. He didn't say it, but he didn't have to. The words echoed in Jasper's head, followed him all the way out into the sunlight.

He skirted the spot where Lex had bled on the dirty asphalt. Bren was standing at the end of the alley, the offending rifle in one hand, his gaze riveted to the building that had served as the sniper's perch.

He turned at the sound of Jasper's footsteps. "Fourth floor?"

"Yeah—that window right there." He pointed. Already, his hands were steadier. The immediate danger was past, Noelle was fine, and Lex would be too—she *would* be, damn it. For now...he could occupy himself with work.

Bren hefted the rifle. "Top of the line. I've never seen one outside of Eden before."

That drew Jasper up short. "You think this was a city hit?"

"Not just. Military police. They use these Mark 30s on the guard towers out at the wind farms. They're fast, they're accurate—" He met Jasper's gaze, cold and calculating. "They're traceable."

"To users?"

"Uh-huh." He tilted the rifle and slid his thumb over a shiny square panel at the base of the stock. The panel flashed red, and some mechanism inside the rifle clicked. "Modified at issue for maximum ergonomic efficiency and encoded with biometrics. I've already got Cruz tracking down the serial number on this one. As long as we have a thumb, we'll know we found our guy."

"We need answers." An MP sniper on a hit in the sectors was certainly something one of Eden's powerful councilmen could have ordered. "We need him alive."

Bren snorted. "Fuck answers. Do you know anyone stupid enough to end the guy before Dallas gets his pound of flesh?"

No. Jasper knew he was one of Dallas's most trusted men, but he was still lucky to walk away from the whole clusterfuck with no broken bones—and he hadn't even been the one shooting the place up. "I think I winged him when I fired back, but it could have been a more solid shot. We should do a sweep."

"Nah." Bren pointed to the broken window. "We can check that room, see if you killed him. If not, he's in the wind. But we'll get him back."

He seemed so damn *sure* of both points that Jasper didn't argue. "You know Eden politics. Do you think Noelle's father is cleaning up loose ends?"

"Couldn't tell you." Bren shrugged and started backing away. "I'm out here because I was particularly *bad* at Eden politics, remember?"

18

W HEN DALLAS GOT angry, Dallas spent money.
Braced against the bed's massive headboard,
Noelle ran her fingertips over the smooth new flesh on
her upper arm. Regen technology was ridiculously expen‐
sive in Eden, and supposedly impossible to obtain in the
sectors.

Apparently nothing was impossible to obtain when
Lex had been shot in the gut. Within an hour of the
doctor's arrival, Ace had returned with a thin, silent
woman shadowed by two bodyguards who made Flash
look tiny. Her black case had contained all the equipment
necessary for accelerated regeneration, and Dallas hadn't
stopped with healing Lex, though that alone must have
cost a fortune. He'd stampeded over Noelle's protests and
paid to patch up her wound, as well, though the doctor
had declared it would heal on its own in a few weeks.

Lex was stretched out beside her, sleeping off the sedative she'd been given for the procedure. From time to time, Noelle stroked her hair, sifting her fingers through the smooth strands. Her panic had been quieted by a sedative—a much smaller dose than Lex had received, though enough to fuzz out the world for a few hours—but the ensuing sleepiness faded as afternoon stretched toward evening, and worry took its place.

She wanted Jasper to come back. She wanted Lex to wake up.

She wanted to believe that the bullet that had torn through her friend's body hadn't been meant for her.

Lex stirred. "You and Dallas both have a thing for my hair, don't you?"

Dallas had seemed so intent on stroking it that Noelle assumed Lex found it soothing, but maybe he'd been soothing himself. "It's pretty hair. Welcome back."

After slowly blinking, Lex carefully shifted upright. "How's your arm?"

"Like new." Noelle reached out to steady Lex and twisted so she could see the pink, slightly puckered skin. "I tried to tell Dallas it would heal fine on its own, but he told me to shut the fuck up. He's not as charming when he's worried."

"I'm shocked as hell that you think he's *ever* charming." Lex pressed a testing hand to her side and bent a little. "Regeneration, huh? I'm glad he sprung for yours too. I would've pinched his dick off if he made you suffer."

The mental image was enough to make Noelle wince. "No, he wasn't really in a listening mood. More like a killing mood."

"He gets that way when shit goes down."

"He was worried about you. Really worried."

"Of course he was." Lex closed her eyes, the dark circles beneath them standing out in stark relief against her pale skin. "He'll get over it."

Noelle tried to coax her back to the mattress. "Rest for a bit. You're not supposed to move much tonight."

Lex shook her off. "I'm not moving. I'm sitting. Still, as a matter of fact."

And if she wanted to move, Noelle didn't have the will to stop her, not with guilt churning in her gut. "Sorry. I was worried too."

"Don't." The corner of Lex's mouth curved up. "I'm tough. They have to work a lot harder if they want to kill me."

Relieved by the ghost of a smile, Noelle wrapped her arms carefully around Lex. Maybe she *had* been the intended target. Lex was the one who mattered to Dallas, the one who was a danger in her own right. The only person in the world who could be angry with Noelle, personally, was her father, and even he couldn't want her dead.

Probably.

Lex coaxed Noelle's head down to her shoulder and patted her back. "Did they catch the guy yet? Was it one of Trent's men?"

"I don't know," she admitted. "Dallas sent Jasper and Bren after him and then parked me in here with you and told me not to move. One of the men is guarding the door—Maddox, I think."

"Sounds serious."

She was making fun of Dallas, and Noelle felt a disloyal stab of sympathy for him. "You were bleeding all over us. It seemed pretty damn serious."

Lex sobered immediately. "I know. I'm sorry."

"Just don't get shot again, okay?" Noelle dragged in a breath and lifted her head to offer Lex a lopsided smile. "If you don't act like *that* part doesn't matter, I'll gladly get mad with you over the rest of it. Because I'm going a little crazy being stuck here with no idea what's going on."

"Yeah? Welcome to my life," Lex muttered.

Noelle laughed. "I haven't met Maddox. Can we talk him into letting us out?"

"Mad? Hell, no. We'd be better off crawling out a window or blasting through the wall."

"Well, I should at least tell him you're awake. Dallas will want to know." She hesitated. "Unless you don't want me to just yet?"

Lex shook her head. "It's okay. I had my reprieve. Though if I know Mad..."

Noelle didn't have time to ask. Footsteps sounded in the hallway, and she realized Mad must have heard them talking. A moment later, Dallas proved her right by shouldering through the door and slamming it behind him.

This was bound to be an intense, personal moment, so Noelle inched toward the edge of the bed only to freeze when Dallas pointed at her. "Stay put. The doc told you to sleep off that shit he gave you."

The doctor had told her she could be up and about when she felt able, but with Dallas's eyes blazing, Noelle didn't dare argue with him.

"Don't yell at her." Lex snorted in disgust. "You can't stand it, can you? Sometimes shit happens, and it's not anyone's fault, and *you can't stop it.*"

Dallas glared at her. "Glad to see you're perking up, love."

"Why wouldn't I be? Seems like someone blew a shit ton of money putting me back together."

"Gee, honey. Don't sound so happy about it."

"Oh, I'm ecstatic." Lex shrugged. "You maintain what's yours, right? Have to keep it all in working order."

Noelle was starting to wish she'd slipped off the bed anyway, anything to get away from the anger filling the space between Dallas and Lex.

Especially when he took a menacing step forward.

"You think it's bad now? You just wait, Alexa Parrino. You don't *know* what it's like to belong to me, but mark my words, girl—"

"You insufferable—"

He continued as if she hadn't broken in. "You are going to find out."

"Asshole." Lex threw a pillow at him, then another. She was reaching for a third when she had to stop and clutch her side with a grimace. "Ow, *fuck*."

"Lex—" Noelle wrapped her arms around her and glared at Dallas, any hint of fear lost in a growing surge of rage. "What's wrong with you?" she snapped at him. "Is this how you take care of people? I'm not allowed to move but you'll drive her into the ground?"

Lex touched Noelle's arm, the fight already melting out of her. "He's just being Dallas. This is my own stupid fault for throwing shit."

Dallas glared at Noelle. She flinched under the weight of his blazing stare, but refused to buckle, and he shoved a hand through his hair with a growl. "Don't practice sharpening your claws on me, kitten." No affection curled around the nickname this time—just a cool warning. "You're not ready to hunt big game."

"*Dallas.*" Lex's voice was hard, chiding, but after an interminably tense moment, she held out a hand to him.

He approached the bed, his expression still blank, but some of the tension around his eyes softened as he eased down beside her and pulled her close. "No more throwing shit. You hear me?"

"Can you knock off the bossy act for five minutes?"

"Maybe." He tucked her head under his chin, settled against the headboard with her curled against his left side, and lifted his right arm. "Come here, Noelle. I won't bite."

Noelle hesitated, even less willing to interject herself into a tender moment than she had been an angry one.

"If you need a minute, I could go check with Mad. Lex should eat..."

"I can't think of anything I would *less* rather do." Lex beckoned. "Come. Sit with us."

In the end she did, sliding across the mattress until Dallas hooked his forearm around her waist and dragged her the rest of the way. He smoothed a hand down her arm to her hip as he kissed the top of her head. "I promised Jas I'd take care of you until he got back."

"All right." Noelle slipped her hand over Lex's where it rested on Dallas's chest. Maybe this was what family was supposed to be. Anger and rage, but never lingering when someone needed comfort. "We'll all be okay."

"Dallas is still a jerk." Lex rubbed her cheek against his shoulder before tilting her face up to kiss his jaw.

Dallas chuckled, his chest rumbling under Noelle's ear. "I love you too, smartass." It was a joke. Easy words that were safe because everyone knew he didn't mean them.

Except Noelle was pretty sure he did.

Someone pounding on the door interrupted the moment, and Lex sighed. "What?"

The door opened a crack, and Bren stuck his head through. "Heads up, Dallas. My friend is on his way. He has something I think you want."

Dallas's arms tightened. "ETA?"

"Should be rolling up any minute." Bren hesitated. "He had to burn himself over this. We gonna make that right?"

"If he brings me the bastard who pulled the trigger, he can name his price."

"Okay." Bren ducked back out, closing the door quietly behind him.

Lex struggled upright and grimaced down at her skimpy tank top. "I need some clothes."

"Lex." Dallas gripped her shoulders. "I need something from you, honey. One thing. I need you to stay here."

She flashed him a look of disbelief. "Oh, you're kidding me."

His jaw clenched, and Noelle held her breath as Dallas leaned closer. "I'm asking." Asking, not ordering, and even she knew how rare a thing that was.

Lex must have realized it too. Still, it seemed like forever until she lifted a trembling hand to his face. "Okay. But only because you've had a really bad day."

Dallas caught her hand and pressed a kiss to her palm. "It's looking up. I'll be back soon."

"Don't lose your temper," she warned him softly. "Information first."

"I know." He grinned, the expression so predatory, so full of anticipation, that Noelle shivered. The look in his eyes meant death, and his smile said he'd enjoy it. Not just enjoy—revel in it.

It was hard to tell what scared Noelle more—Dallas's thirst for violence, or the realization that she shared it. Lust wasn't the only vice the sectors taught, and it was time for her first lesson in revenge.

Jasper didn't know what Alistair Martel looked like, and that bothered him more than it should have.

Oh, he knew the face that came up onscreen when they scanned Martel's bar code, and he knew the man's thumb reactivated the rifle used to hurt Noelle and Lex. He had no doubt about the man's identity, no qualms about the beatdown Dallas was currently administering.

No, what rankled was the way the man's swollen eyes and broken, bloody nose obscured his true features. Jasper would never be able to haul the man up by his collar, threaten him, and watch the fear gradually shadow his face. Too late for quiet, violent promises, the kind the man deserved.

Far too late, especially since Dallas seemed intent on beating the truth out of him as slowly as possible. Jasper had seen Dallas work an adversary with nothing but terror and the mere whisper of violence until words spilled free unchecked, but such a light touch seemed beyond him today. He smashed his fist into Martel's gut with a snarl, doubling the man over and leaving no breath to answer a question.

Not that Dallas had asked one.

He needed to, though, so Jasper did it for him. "Who do you work for?"

Martel spat blood on the concrete floor. "Eden. I work for Eden."

Jasper fought to keep his face impassive, but a growl escaped him. "If he's not talking, we should get this over with. Bren's friend probably has the intel we need."

Martel's eyes widened in panic, but Dallas was already turning toward the table to retrieve his brass knuckles. "Good point. Bren and Cruz can tell us everything we need to know about what went—"

"Gareth Woods," Martel said, his voice edged with panic. "I work for Gareth Woods."

Dallas turned and slipped the heavy brass knuckles over his fingers. "The councilman?"

Martel nodded jerkily.

There was only one reason another of Eden's councilmen could have wanted Noelle dead. "This was a fucking frame job?" Jasper demanded.

Another jerky nod. "Nothing personal, man. Just had to take the girl down with a city weapon. None of your people were supposed to get in the way."

Rage boiled up. Jasper reached out, and he had to take a hasty step back before his hands closed on the man's hair. "Nothing personal?"

Dallas backhanded Martel, whipping the man's head to one side. "Noelle's one of my people." He didn't give Martel a chance to respond before hitting him again. "Why frame Cunningham? What did your boss have to gain?"

"I don't know." Martel recoiled when Dallas lifted his hand again, jerking against the chains that bound him. "I fucking well don't. I shoot whoever I'm told to shoot. That's my job. That's all I ever know."

Jasper believed him, which meant the man was stupid on top of everything else. It was one bit of wisdom Bren had passed along—assassins didn't ask, didn't often care about the reasoning behind their jobs. But they always, *always* knew why, because they couldn't afford not to.

"This is useless," Jasper muttered, more to himself than to Dallas. Martel was a dead man already, and only information could delay his execution. If he didn't have that, he was out of time.

Dallas watched their captive, icy rage gathering behind the blank expression he'd worn since he'd first seen Lex, unconscious and bleeding. "I agree," he said. "Unless you want to take a couple swings for Noelle, why don't you go see if Bren's friend is any smarter than this sorry bastard?"

Jasper shook his head and turned. Even if he had the stomach for it, it wasn't his style. "Martel's yours." He tossed the words back over his shoulder.

"Damn right he is," came Dallas's reply, a claim reinforced by the sound of a fist hitting flesh, along with Martel's pained grunt.

The cries rose into screams, and Jasper closed the door behind him to shut them out. Bren's friend, Lorenzo Cruz, sat at the square table in the center of the room, his shirt stripped away. Rachel perched beside him, swabbing antiseptic on his shoulder.

Jasper watched as she set the gauze aside and reached for a wickedly sharp scalpel instead. One cut, shallow and slow—and Cruz didn't blink, showed no sign whatsoever that he felt the incision.

Ace winced at another muffled scream from behind the door. "I don't know what's creepier. That guy's screaming, or the fact that Rachel's cutting a tracker out of this motherfucker's flesh *without drugs*, and he's not even twitching."

"I have a delicate touch," she murmured, then flashed Cruz a reassuring look. "It's okay, right?"

"It's fine." Cruz shared a tight smile with Bren. "I've been through worse."

"He's being modest." Bren tapped the table. "We were running an undercover op once. Dipshit here got shot in the leg and still managed to con his way through a sector checkpoint without blowing it."

"You do what you gotta do to get the job done." Cruz met Jasper's gaze. "When it's a job you can live with. Fewer and fewer of those coming down from on high these days."

"Or you've worked your way too far up the food chain to keep your conscience clean." Jasper dragged out an empty chair and sat. "Can you connect this guy to Gareth Woods?"

Cruz nodded. "No doubt. Martel's been tasked to Woods's security detail for the last six months."

"Why would Woods want Noelle dead? How did he even know where she was?"

Both of Cruz's eyebrows swept upwards. "You must not have access to the vid network out here."

Ace answered with a frown. "Not without patching in, which is usually more trouble than it's worth. Why, has Noelle been in the vids?"

"Nonstop for the last couple days," Cruz replied. "Someone leaked a video of her serving drinks at that

club of yours, and now everyone in Eden thinks her father's doing dirty business with Dallas O'Kane."

It made killing her the perfect way to discredit Cunningham. Everyone in Eden would assume he'd done it to
cover up his dealings with Dallas. "How many others
would jump at this chance?" Jasper asked. "Even if we
deal with Woods, is she still in danger?"

Cruz blinked and glanced at Bren. "Is this guy for
real? He's just going to *deal with* a councilman?"

"Him? No." Bren inclined his head toward the door.
"But Dallas? Yeah."

Jasper bit his tongue, but not even that could hold
back his vicious curse. "Fuck that. I'm not passing *everything* off to Dallas, not this time."

"You can't waltz into Eden and double tap the guy
with a forty-five, either. Hitting Woods is going to take
money, planning, and a hell of a lot of favors." Bren lit a
cigarette. "Dallas is the only one who can get it done, no
matter how much you want to be the one protecting
Noelle."

"Shit." Cruz's face shuttered. "As long as she's in the
sectors, she's a liability for her father, which means she's
a target for any of his enemies. Cunningham knows that.
This morning he put out a press release talking about
how he was going to rescue her."

Jasper bit off a curse. "So the only way to stop the at-
tempts is either to scare the shit out of anyone who even
thinks about trying it...or to send her back to her family."

Ace interrupted for the first time. "She's inked. Will
they even take her back? How much juice does her pop
have?"

"He has plenty," Rachel answered. "At least, he did
when I lived there. I'm sure he'll spin it like she's gone
nuts, but he couldn't leave her out here, so he brought
her home to recover."

"The trauma of the sectors," Cruz drawled. "She

could strip naked and walk down the streets of Eden, and people would eat up the scandal. If her father managed to bury the original charges, he could play the martyr. The loving father struggling to save his daughter's eternal soul. Of course, he'd have to ruin the men who originally arrested her..." He glanced at Bren. "But most of the councilmen aren't above framing good men for their own gain."

"It's been known to happen," Bren agreed mildly.

"There." Rachel dropped something tiny into a metal bowl with a *clink*, then smoothed down the edges of a small, square bandage on Cruz's arm. "No more tracker."

"Thanks." Cruz flexed slightly, testing his shoulder. "I guess there's no going back for me. The Cunningham girl is lucky the rules don't apply to her."

"Yeah." But something told Jasper that Noelle wouldn't agree.

The door to the back room crashed open, and Dallas stepped through, wiping his bloody hands on a rag. Through the doorway, Jasper could just make out the still, unmoving form of Alistair Martel.

Bren rose. "It's done?"

Dallas nodded shortly and met Cruz's eyes. "I know what you gave up to bring us Martel. I'll make sure we're square." Dallas shifted his attention to Rachel. "You and Ace take our new friend out front. Get him something to eat, and anything else he needs."

They hustled the man out of the room, leaving Jasper staring at Dallas and Bren. "Tell me this isn't as fucked up as it seems."

Dallas listened in silence as Bren relayed everything Cruz had told them, and shook his head when the man finished. "This is what I've been trying to tell you all along, Jas. Politics in Eden are like a vicious, bloody game of chess." He sighed. "I'd bet my boots a story about the attempt on her life is about to hit the vid network, if it hasn't already. Noelle's on the board now, and the game doesn't end until she's either back in Eden or dead."

All that mattered to Jasper was her safety. "I'm going to see what Mad can set up. We need to monitor the situation in Eden."

"Bren can do that." Dallas gestured. "Go now. I need to talk to Jasper."

Jasper wasn't remotely in the mood, and he told Dallas so before the door even snapped shut. "The pep talk's gonna have to wait, coach."

"This isn't a pep talk." Dallas braced both hands on the table. "What are you going to do if her father shows up to rescue her? If he offers her a free pass, all sins forgiven, right back to her cushy, safe little life? What are you going to do when she looks to *you* to help her decide?"

He'd tell her that it wasn't his decision, that she was the only one who truly knew what to do—except he knew it was a lie. He'd do everything he had to do to keep her out of danger. "I'll tell her she needs to go," he snarled.

Dallas didn't look surprised. He didn't look happy, either. "Can you live with that?"

"I don't exactly have a choice."

"You have two choices, and they're both shit."

Let her go, or keep her and maybe get her killed. "They're both shit," Jasper echoed. "But they're all I've got, unless you're cooking something up in that head of yours."

"I have a few ideas," Dallas said, but held up his hand before Jasper could say anything. "But nothing that'll make her any safer than she is now. Hell, for all I know, we're headed into a territory war. I'll protect Noelle like she's one of us—but you know what war means."

First Trent's bomb, and now a sniper from Eden. Things were going to shit all over the place, just like the days when they'd had to scrounge and fight like hell for every scrap of peace that came their way. If they were smart, they'd take precautions.

Some of the men hadn't hesitated to take women then, even knowing they might not come home to them at the end of the night, but Jasper had never been one of them. "I won't keep a woman I can't protect. That hasn't changed."

Dallas sighed. "Can't say I fault your logic, Jas. Maybe we're both looking at cold, lonely lives."

"There are worse things." Like more gunshots, and Noelle's eyes blank and unseeing instead of snapping with life.

"All right." Dallas straightened and rubbed a hand over his hair. "I'll reach out to Cunningham and let him know I'm open to talking. Maybe you won't have to make the choice at all."

"He'll want her back." Jasper took a deep breath. "What do we do with Martel's body? Make it disappear, or make sure they find it?"

Dallas stared at the wall and flexed his hands thoughtfully. "Put him on ice," he said finally. "Let me hear what Cunningham has to say, and then we'll decide."

"Speaking of ice, get some on your hands," Jasper advised.

"Yeah." Dallas stared down at his bruised knuckles. "I need to go tell Lex it's over before she crawls out of bed and hurts herself again."

It was his job to check on Lex, to make sure she was recovering and safe. It was Jasper's equal responsibility to do the same for Noelle, but he needed distance. He needed to let go. "Will you...?"

"I'll take care of her," Dallas replied quietly. "You go find Bren and Mad. It's going to be a long night."

That it was.

19

J ASPER WAS AVOIDING her.

At first, she thought it was her imagination. Dallas had returned late and grumpy, and Noelle had been too wrung out to traverse the warren of hallways back to Lex's empty bed. But sleep had been fleeting and restless, interrupted whenever she slipped her hand into the vacant space to her left. Every time she woke, she forced her eyes shut again by promising herself that the next time she flung her arm wide it would slam into the unforgiving wall of Jasper's chest.

It never did.

She'd edged out of the huge bed at dawn, fleeing a loneliness that was more cutting in Dallas and Lex's presence than it could have possibly been alone. Dallas had cracked open one eye to squint at her as she pulled on her clothing, but after admonishing her not to leave the compound, he tucked Lex's sleeping form more firmly against his side and closed his eyes again.

He'd probably assumed she was going to find Jasper, but she hadn't. She'd already felt it then—something beyond sneaking suspicion. The certainty that Jasper wasn't simply not present, but absent. Deliberately *not there*.

It wasn't until she was huddled in a cooling bath in Lex's quarters that she understood the conviction. Her hands trembled as she scrubbed a washcloth over her newly healed skin, and she needed him. She needed to see him, touch him, know he was safe. She needed to curl up in his arms and know *she* was safe.

She needed him, and he was supposed to know that. He *had* to know that. If he didn't, how could she trust him to know everything else she needed? And if he did know but was ignoring her...

No. It was too soon for such thoughts, especially with all the danger. Dallas had admitted to sending Jasper out on some unspecified errand. Maybe it had taken most of the night. Maybe he'd fallen into his bed not long before she'd crawled out of Dallas's, and if she went to him now he'd open his arms and fold them around her—

She didn't. She told herself it was because he needed rest, and because it didn't matter anyway. She drained the tub and dressed for the day, braided her hair in a crown around her head and picked out a short-sleeved T-shirt that left her arms—and her tattoos—bare. Paired with heeled boots and jeans and one of Lex's studded leather belts, it felt like armor.

She was an O'Kane. One night of uncertainty wouldn't change that. *Nothing* could change that. That was the promise tattooed into her skin—her loyalty in exchange for their protection. Forever.

Besides, she wasn't entirely helpless anymore. She didn't need Jasper or Lex to hold her hand and give her something to do. The stage had been cleaned of Lex's blood, but the club still needed tending. Trix would be there to open the doors by noon, ready to serve the truly dedicated drinkers and sell individual bottles of liquor to anyone unable to strike a special deal with Dallas.

Life had to go on.

Noelle had swept the floor and taken down the chairs by the time Trix arrived, trailing a quiet bouncer named Zan. Zan nodded to her and positioned himself just outside the door, a solid wall of muscle that could—and would—turn deadly at the slightest hint of danger.

Noelle had traded her broom for a cloth to wipe down the scarred wooden tables when the door swung open again, admitting two men almost as large as Zan—and tragically familiar.

Her father's bodyguards.

She barely had time to wrap her brain around that— *her father's bodyguards*—before he followed them inside, blinking against the darkness and skirting tables with a wide berth, as if merely touching them would contaminate him.

Her father. *Here.*

Noelle clenched her fingers around the cloth until the nubby fabric dug painfully into her skin. Her father looked impossibly older, as if months or even years had passed instead of weeks and days. The grooves carved around his steely eyes were deeper, the furrows that formed when his brows drew together more intense. He seemed tired, stressed, and she knew with a certainty borne of painful experience that her absence couldn't possibly account for either state. Not on its own, anyway.

He looked at her—no, *past* her, his gaze gliding by without a glimmer of recognition before snapping back to her face. His brow crinkled, and he straightened the hem of his jacket. "Noelle. I didn't recognize you."

She didn't know what to call him. *Sir* was an honor

she wouldn't give him, not anymore, but she'd never called him anything more familiar. She'd never been permitted to.

No greeting, then. Squaring her shoulders, she faced him with only her deathly grip on the dishtowel to betray her fear. "I wouldn't have expected to see you here."

"I've been looking for you."

Not very hard, obviously. "I've been here since the day I was banished."

His jaw tightened. "I didn't know where *here* was."

"Fine." It wasn't worth arguing about, so she changed the subject. "Why do you care?"

The question seemed to take him aback. "Because I'm here to take you home. Your mother and I—we want you to come home."

It was so unexpected, so *impossible*, that for a moment Noelle could do nothing but stare at him. He stared back, the perfect picture of polite surprise—and even here, in the sector slums, he might as well have been playing for the vids.

Anger took root, and she gave it voice for the first time in her life. "Why? I'm ruined. Damaged beyond repair. You'll never find a man in Eden who would agree to marry me."

He looked away. "Your citizenship will be reinstated, and you'll be free to live in Eden again. Isn't that enough?"

An answer that wasn't an answer at all. "Why?"

Edwin—she could barely think of him as her father anymore—huffed out a disgusted noise. "Why is *why* a question, Noelle? What's the alternative? You can't stay here."

She wanted more than anything to throw the word at him again, to taunt and prod at him, but that was the impulse of a child, not a woman. "I can stay right where I am," she said instead, keeping her voice as even as possible. "And I intend to."

He held out his hand, and one of the guards pressed a tablet into it. "Even if Mr. O'Kane contacted me about your presence here?"

"He wouldn't," she said without thinking, but the words were ash on her tongue before the sound died. Last night's guilt roared back to life, and she knew she'd been right. The bullets had been meant for her. Her father knew it, Dallas knew it... Jasper probably knew it.

He'd never come to find her. Maybe he hadn't wanted to say goodbye.

"It would serve everyone's purposes." Edwin's voice gentled. "Come home, Noelle. Your mother misses you."

Home. Her empty room with its endless trinkets, physical luxury and unending leisure. Hot showers and baths that never cooled, no matter how long you lingered. Soft lighting from every surface. Sheets changed every morning by silent servants.

Never being touched. Never feeling. No pain, no pleasure, just the anesthesia of safety.

Her lips were numb already. "Let me see," she whispered. "Let me see what he said."

Edwin passed her the tablet, and she looked down at the white screen with its sparse black type. *I'm willing to discuss arrangements.*

The words could mean anything. That Dallas wanted her gone, that he was willing to barter her for Lex's safety. And he would, if it came down to it—Noelle didn't question that for a moment—but Lex would never forgive him. She wouldn't have agreed to pack Noelle off to the city.

Of course, the words really *could* mean anything. Maybe she wasn't giving Dallas enough credit. She wore his ink now, and loyalty went both ways.

And Edwin had always told lies with the truth.

Fixing her expression, she handed the tablet back to him. "Doesn't say anything about me."

Instead of arguing, he nodded. "I thought you might take some convincing. Will you at least think about it?"

"About coming back?" She tossed the towel on the nearest table and spread her arms wide, showing off the black tattoos circling each wrist and forearm. "I'm an O'Kane, ink and all, and I like it here. What can you offer me?"

"Safety," he said immediately. "You won't be getting shot at anymore. Neither will..." He consulted the tablet again. "Jasper McCray?"

Fear twisted in her gut, but it was the look in his eyes that made her blood run cold. He knew. She shouldn't have been surprised—Dallas O'Kane's right-hand man and Edwin Cunningham's daughter together made for good gossip no matter which side of the city walls you called home—but she still felt exposed, as if he'd peeled back her carefully donned armor to find her weakest spot.

"You're a cold-blooded bastard," she told him, her thrill of defiance weakened by how hard her hands shook. She shoved them in her pockets to hide it and lifted her voice. "Get out."

"Noelle..."

"*Get out.*"

The door opened, and Zan stuck his head inside. "Everything all right, Noelle?"

"It's fine," she said, not taking her gaze from her father's. She wouldn't let him see her flinch. "He's just leaving."

No, she wouldn't let him see her fear.

"All right." Zan pushed the door all the way open, very deliberately bumping it into one of the bodyguards. "Sorry, man."

Her father was still watching her, and all Noelle

wanted was to get rid of him. "I'll think about it, but only if you leave now."

He relented, but not without a pointed look. "I'll be in touch. Soon."

Zan closed the door behind the bodyguards, and Noelle groped for the nearest chair. Her knees wobbled as she collapsed more than sat, the air rushing from her lungs with an explosive sigh.

Trix appeared at her elbow with a shot glass, her green eyes sympathetic. "Here. It's the good stuff." The redhead set the glass on the table and squeezed Noelle's shoulder. "Sounded like you might need it."

"I do, thanks."

"No problem." Trix retreated, and Noelle lifted the glass and stared at the richly colored liquid. The whiskey was the blood of the O'Kanes, their first and best product. Nessa had promised to show her how it was made, to explain the process in as much detail as Noelle wanted, but she hadn't made the time yet.

Maybe she'd never get the chance, now.

"You should think about it."

Jasper's voice, and her heart still thrilled at the rumbling tone though the full meaning of his words destroyed her calm. "So you were listening."

He stepped out of the shadows by the stage, his arms crossed over his chest. "I heard part of his pitch."

He'd listened in silence, in hiding, while her father twisted a verbal knife in search of a weak spot. Worse, he'd listened...and he *agreed*.

Even at her lowest moments this morning, she hadn't imagined anything could hurt as much as those words. *You should think about it.*

She drained the shot glass and slammed it down on the table. "You want me to go back to Eden?"

"It doesn't have anything to do with what I want," he whispered. "It has to do with what's true. What's right."

The front door clicked open. She turned in time to see Trix duck outside with Zan, leaving the bar as empty of distractions as it was witnesses. No one would save her from this moment, from the words she didn't want to hear.

Still staring at the front door, she cleared her throat. "Is Dallas getting rid of me because I got Lex shot?"

"*No.*" Jasper lifted her arm, sweeping his thumb over her wrist. "He wouldn't do that."

The ink. The promise. Dark laughter spilled free of her as she shook her head. "Yes, he would. Because it's Lex."

"Because it's Lex." Jasper released her with a sigh. "Everything is dangerous out here. That's just life in the sectors."

"Then why?" Noelle asked, rubbing at her wrist to banish the tingles from his touch. It wasn't fair that he could stir her body now, when his words chilled her. "If Dallas isn't trying to get rid of me, why are you?"

He took a step back. Away. "We tracked down the guy who shot you. Alistair Martel. Bren's friend brought him back last night. You knew that, right?"

She nodded.

"Dallas killed him. Not fast, just so he wouldn't be a danger. Slow." Jasper swallowed hard. "He beat him to death with a pair of brass knuckles. Caved the motherfucker's face in. I don't know how many busted bones he had, but he felt like a bag full of broken glass when Bren and I went to move him."

Her stomach lurched. Not only at the mental image, which was unsettling enough, but at the dizzy vertigo of trying to reconcile that brutality with the man who'd collapsed into bed with them last night and stroked Lex's hair until she slept.

Swallowing, she fixed her gaze on the table. "You already said it—that's life in the sectors. I'll get used to it."

"Except that you're not like everyone else, Noelle. You're not stuck here. You don't have to get used to it."

She forced herself to meet his eyes. "You're here." The admission stripped her raw. He wasn't fighting for her, so she couldn't add the rest. *You're worth it.*

It was the wrong thing to say. His eyes shuttered, and he shook his head. "This shit with Trent... We're going to war, sweetheart. I've never left a woman alone at home, wondering if she'd ever see me in one piece again, and I can't start now. Not with you."

"Not with me," she echoed. Soft words to let her down easy. *You're special,* they lied, blunting the truth. The heartbreaking, horrifying truth.

You're special...but not enough.

Her eyes burned, but she knew how to hide tears, how to swallow around the lump in her throat until her voice came out smooth and even, empty like Eden. "All right."

"All right." His voice was as dark as hers was light. As full and heavy as hers was blank. "You'll be safer this way. When you stop thinking I'm an asshole, you'll see. You'll—" He broke off with another step back. "You'll see."

Then he turned and stomped through the back exit.

A scream built in Noelle's chest, the need to give voice to her pain so intense that she dug her nails into her wrist until the prick of broken skin dispersed some of the pressure.

He'd walked away. He'd made his choice.

Noelle dropped both hands to the table and stared at the crescent-shaped cuts on her wrist. Blood and ink, black and red. She'd bisected one of the swooping vines encircling the O'Kane logo, and it seemed fitting some-how.

Maybe ink wasn't permanent after all.

 lex

S HE WATCHED, ALMOST shaking with rage, as Noelle shoved another stack of shirts into a cardboard box. "Tell me you know Jasper's an idiot," she demanded. "I mean, you're not actually *packing* your shit, are you?"

"Jasper's not an idiot." Noelle picked up a pair of jeans and smoothed out the wrinkles. "He's an asshole."

"Exactly. That's why you can't listen to a damn word he says."

"I know." She wet her lips and finally met Lex's eyes. "I don't know how to say this. I don't want you to take it the wrong way, because I appreciate everything you've done for me. You've helped me so much."

Oh Christ, she *was* leaving. "Uh-uh. You are too strong to puss out on me now, baby girl."

"I'm not." Once the jeans were folded and placed in

the box, Noelle smiled. "I told Dallas that if I'm a full member and not just Jasper's stray pet, I deserve my own quarters. He agreed."

"Oh." Lex wrapped an arm around one bedpost and sank to the mattress. "Why would that offend me?"

Noelle's smile twitched wider. "If I stay here, I'll feel like *your* stray pet. I need to be on my own for a little while, I think. I need to know what it's like."

"I get that." Crawling into Lex's bed every night was the last thing that would help Noelle stand on her own feet. "I'm bossy, but you don't have to let me be. You can go your own way."

"I like it when you're bossy. I think that's the hard part." Noelle returned to the closet for two of the leather skirts Lex had helped her choose at the market. "You were right. I have to get better at saying *no* before *yes* means anything. Maybe if I'd tried it out on Jasper earlier..." She shrugged and looked back to the closet. "It probably wouldn't have mattered."

The pain was a tangible thing, stabbing at Lex until she wanted to stab it back. She stepped up behind Noelle and slipped her arms around her. "It doesn't always work out the way we thought, but the fact that we're able to fuck up in the first place... You're free. It's not nothing."

"I'm free." The words sounded thick, but the ones that followed were tiny and hurt, a vulnerable whisper from a heartbroken woman. "He didn't fight for me. Not even a little."

Lex was pissed as hell at Jasper, and the last thing she wanted to do was defend his sorry ass. *And yet.* "Maybe he thought he was," she ventured quietly.

Noelle stiffened. "By sending me back there?"

"Come on, honey. We got *shot.* I know Dallas lost his shit, and he's not even—" Lex sucked in a breath and turned Noelle to face her. "That kind of situation can make people crazy. It doesn't mean Jasper was right, or that his dumbass behavior isn't beyond-the-pale stupid. But it does mean you have to try to look at it from his point of view, if only to understand."

"We got shot," Noelle agreed, her voice as numb as her eyes. "You got shot, and it was my fault. That's why I almost went back."

"That's ridiculous, and if you say it again, I'll spank your ass," Lex told her fiercely. "Someone could be gunning for me every time I walk out that door. Why do you think Dallas wants to lock me up all the time? It's a fucking jungle wasteland out there—and I wouldn't give it up for anything."

Noelle blew out a breath, and some of the chilling emptiness in her eyes filled in with wry, sad humor. "That's what Dallas said. Mostly."

"Which part? The locking me up or the danger?"

"Both." She wrinkled her nose. "I told him I was worried about putting you in danger again. He said you'd never forgive either of us if I made that my reason, and he wasn't going to let me hurt you like that."

"Score one for Dallas." And for the tentative peace they'd forged.

"He was...blunt." Noelle tossed the skirts she was holding onto the bed and shrugged one shoulder. "Edwin—my father—offered to help him deal with the man who hired the sniper, but only if Dallas sent me back. I made the choice."

"Hopefully it was to tell your father to fuck off and give Dallas all the damning details *you* know about Gareth Woods."

"More or less. I think it'll be easier to do now that Woods tried to have me killed."

"It always is." An inescapable fact of life in the sectors. Lex picked up another shirt and began to fold it. "Fuck Jasper. I know you want him like burning, honey, but you don't *need* him. You've got your job, your ink.

Your family."

"You." Noelle caught her up in a hug, clinging desperately. "God, Lex. I need my own space, but I still need you."

Even more heartbreaking than the palpable pain was the way tears thickened Noelle's voice. "You have me. I'm right here, whatever you need. I'm not going anywhere."

"Okay. I'm okay." A lie, and when Noelle lifted her head, the tears spilled over, tracking down her cheeks as quickly as she could wipe them away. "It's good that it hurts, right? That I can feel."

"Yeah." Lex smoothed the hair back from Noelle's damp face. "I know it's not a lot of comfort right now, but the bad reminds you just how good everything else is. You've got to have both."

Noelle nodded. "I can. I will. He's not the only man out there, right?"

She spoke the words, the right ones, but she didn't believe them, and Lex bit her lip against all the empty reassurances. Hell, she'd offer Dallas if only it would ease Noelle's pain, melt that lonely look in her eyes. "Plenty of men, and plenty of time."

"And I've got lots to do to keep busy." Noelle scooped up one of Lex's shoes, a towering five-inch heel she wore on stage. "You're still going to teach me, right?"

"To dance?" A sudden thought occurred to Lex—an utterly wrong, plain old *evil* thought. "Actually...I'll go you one better, honey."

Both of Noelle's eyebrows swept up, and *finally* something replaced the pain and sadness in her eyes—curiosity. "Better?"

"Better." Lex grinned slowly. "I'm gonna make you a fucking star."

20

A T LEAST NOELLE had the night off.
Jasper threw back another whiskey and banged his glass on the table. "You're slow with the refills to-night, Mad."

"You're quick with the drinking." Maddox tossed his hair out of his eyes and paused to flash a rakish grin at the next table over. The women—groupies Jasper had seen a dozen times before—giggled and ducked their heads together, whispering behind their hands. Satisfied, Mad slopped whiskey into Jasper's glass and topped off the others as well. "Pace yourself, or you'll be drooling drunk before Ace is."

Ace made a crude gesture. "Bite me."

"I'm not looking to get that drunk," Jasper groused. It might be easy, but it was also weak. There wasn't a damn thing about his situation that wasn't of his own making, and he didn't deserve to run from it.

She'd stayed. The damn woman had stood in this very room, looked at him and said, "Okay." Okay to the end of them, okay to going back to the safety of Eden. Okay.

And then she'd stayed.

If that wasn't a giant *fuck you*, he didn't know what was.

Ace planted his elbow none too gently in Jasper's side. "Brother, if you glare at the table any harder, it's gonna piss itself."

Jasper elbowed him back. "I'd be happy to glare at you instead."

"At least it'd be progress." Ace sighed. "Come *on*, man, you've got to do something. Live life. Get in a fight. Find some fucking pussy."

Jasper drained half the liquor in his glass. "Not all of us run at full-bore manwhore all the time like you. We work and sleep sometimes too."

"Whoring was only one of the options," Ace muttered. "But fuck it. Whatever, keep brooding."

Mad took a swig directly from the whiskey bottle. "You've got shit for tact, Ace."

The stage was still dark, and Jasper eyed it moodily. "Who's dancing tonight? I could try my luck with that." It couldn't go worse than his fling with Noelle.

Ace shot him an amused look, his earlier irritation forgotten as only Ace could manage. "Doubtful. I'm pretty sure Lex took someone's shift."

Well, fuck. Even if Jasper had felt like braving that minefield, he couldn't close his eyes and picture Lex naked anymore without also picturing Noelle kneeling between her thighs, eating her pussy.

"Yeah," Ace said, as if Jasper had spoken. "I thought so."

"Dallas doesn't feel much like sharing lately," Jasper

mumbled, then finished his drink.

Giggles drifted up from the table beside theirs, and Mad tilted his head. "Uncomplicated is easy to come by, if that's what you're in the mood for. There's only two of them, but I'll share."

A damn generous offer, when you got right down to it. Every one of the O'Kanes knew Jasper was nursing a bruised heart, so everyone around was bending over backwards, going out of the way to cheer him up.

Well...almost everyone.

He shook it off. "It is what it is, right? This too shall pass? Got any platitudes to add?"

Mad shook his head. "You're handling the clichés just fine on your own."

The house lights dimmed, and soft music began to play. It was so unlike the usual tracks chosen by the dancers that Jasper blinked. "This doesn't sound like Lex's sort of thing."

"No, it doesn't—" Ace started. A single light flared on the stage, and his eyes widened. "Oh, sweet mother of Christ."

Lex was sitting in a chair, dressed in demure white lace and silk. It was completely different from her usual act—until the music deepened into a rhythmic throb, and another woman, this one dressed in red, slithered onto the stage.

Jasper's heart kicked into high gear, his body reacting before his brain caught up.

Noelle.

Everything about her was sin to Lex's sweet. A blood-red corset hugged her torso, topped with low black ruffles that barely hid her nipples. The ruffles at the bottom didn't hide black lace panties or her smooth thighs, the pale skin bare and lush in the soft light.

She came to a stop behind Lex and pressed both hands to the other woman's shoulders, pausing for a moment to let the men drink in the sight of both of them. Her hips swayed, a gentle roll with the music more than an actual dance, and she caught one of the ribbons hold-ing Lex's virginal white top together...and tugged.

It was a dirty, dirty game, and Jasper couldn't look away.

The ribbons yielded one at a time, baring Lex's skin in the slowest tease the stage had ever seen. Ace shifted in his chair, muttering something too low to be under-stood. Mad just stared, unblinking, as Noelle wrapped her hand around the front of Lex's throat.

With the stage lit and the floor dark, there was no way Noelle could see him in the crowd, but her gaze still swept straight to him as she bent low and closed her teeth on Lex's earlobe.

Lex gasped, and Jasper felt an answering tug in his gut as his balls tightened. The perfect show, a role rever-sal. Innocent little Noelle playing the seductress, while Lex submitted with astonishingly convincing wonder.

Not that Noelle looked innocent now. She teased Lex's gown open far enough to bare her breasts, and Ace bit off a curse as Noelle licked her thumb before teasing one of Lex's nipples to a hard point. "Fucking hell, Jas. You tried to send *her* back to Eden? You're brain dead."

"Shut up, Ace. I mean it." Oh, she was teaching him a lesson now, all right. Showing him all the ways she'd never fit in back in Eden, not anymore.

And it only got worse. Noelle stroked Lex. Teased her. She stripped lace and silk from skin with lingering touches, ground against the other woman's body, and left no possible room to doubt that she loved it.

"Holy shit." Bren yanked out the fourth chair be-tween Ace and Mad. "I heard, but I didn't believe."

"Watch it," Ace warned. "Jas'll punch your face in if you comment on the beautiful thing happening on that stage."

"Like that'll stop me." Bren tilted his head as Noelle straddled Lex's thighs and rolled her hips. "Those two have no mercy, do they? A match made in heaven *and* hell."

"She's taunting Jas," Mad murmured. "That's one hard-ass lady. Lex's influence, I presume?"

"Or Jas just pissed her off that much," Ace said. "That's usually my job."

Jasper found himself nodding in agreement, so he stilled his head. "The whole damn thing is probably as much for Dallas's eyes as it is for mine."

Mad's laugh was mean. "Yeah, except he gets to curl up in between them if he wants."

"He'd be the only one anyway," Jasper rationalized. "He's always been possessive of Lex, and that shit's just getting more and more out of control lately."

"Coming to a head," Ace agreed. "Sooner rather than—oh *hell*, tell me Noelle's not going to—"

But she was. She slid to her knees in front of the chair, the stage lights gilding the perfect curves of her ass beneath her corset. Lex shuddered as Noelle slipped one questing hand up her inner thigh, closely followed by her tongue.

The whistles and calls from the audience almost drowned out Lex's cry as she arched her back and lifted her hips. She buried one hand in Noelle's hair, holding her in place, and raised the other to her own breast to pinch and tug at her nipple.

Ace forgot decorum—and the threat of Jasper's fists—and hooted along with the rest of the crowd. Jasper didn't care. He was riveted, locked on to the sight not only of Noelle but of Lex too. The abandoned, honest *pleasure*.

This was a message, all right, but it wasn't a *fuck you*, or even a *look at what you lost, dumbass*. It was a declaration, of independence and self-possession. Noelle's power, the spark of will that had always lurked inside her, in flames on the stage.

And she was beautiful.

Distraction was a bitch. A painful, bleeding bitch.

Jasper shook his hand and flexed his fingers. Smashing his knuckles into the engine block the first time had been stupid but understandable. But not paying enough attention to the engine block in front of him meant not only a second smash, but also lacerated, raw knuckles.

"You should be more careful," Rachel admonished. "A bike like that'll bite you."

Jasper choked back an instinctive, foul retort and released a deep breath. "Thanks. I'll bear that in mind."

"If you're going to do more harm than good, stick to watching." Dallas wiped his hands on a rag before digging through his toolbox. "These bikes are the only perk we got out of that bullshit with Trent."

"And they're classically neglected." Rachel didn't bother to hide her disgust. "Spit shined and perfect, but running like hell. They could all use tune-ups, that one needs a new carburetor. It's ridiculous."

Everything Trent touched was like that—only the show had seemed to matter to him, not the foundation beneath. "The man ran his bikes the way he ran his sector," Jasper muttered.

Dallas grunted. "Pretty on the outside. Dom's still pushing to take over his organization, but the more Bren finds out from Six, the more I think Trent pulled this stunt out of desperation rather than ambition. His business was collapsing under him."

"What better reason to go up against the O'Kanes?" Jasper sat back and studied his bleeding knuckles. "He had nothing to lose."

"He was alive," Dallas replied flatly. "As long as you're drawing breath, there's always something to lose."

Rachel dropped the wrench she was holding and wiped the back of her hand across her forehead. "Well, obviously that wasn't enough for Trent. Not sure it'd be enough for me, either, though not remotely for the same reasons."

Dallas smiled at her, though the expression didn't reach his eyes. "You gonna get all wise on us, angel?"

She matched his expression, right down to the way it didn't seem happy at all. "Wisdom would be lost on you two knuckleheads."

"Ah, hell. Not you too, Rachel." Dallas abandoned the bike and crossed the garage to retrieve a beer. "Which of us are you planning to chew on?"

"You both deserve it." She rose, hopped up to sit on a workbench, and pointed at Jasper. "You need to stop thinking you get to decide what's right for someone else. Noelle has a whole life that you haven't lived, you know, so you can't make *her* decisions. Just yours."

Jesus Christ, now he had to defend himself to her, too. "Not that it's any of your business, but that's what I did."

"Yeah?" She arched one blonde brow. "I hope that's not true. I was assuming you were a dickhead, not a coward."

Dallas damn near choked on his beer. "What has gotten into the women in this place? You're slicing us all to hell and back."

"Uh-uh, don't talk to me. You're no better. You might even be worse." She shook her head. "At least Jasper's thing makes sense, in a twisted sort of way. But you're just a big mess."

"Do tell, angel. Don't hold back now."

She rolled her eyes at his flat, indifferent tone. "Dallas O'Kane, the only man I ever met who'd drop ten grand on pretty presents when a fucking kiss would do."

Dallas didn't flinch, didn't even blink. "And Jasper's sin?"

"The opposite. Not making any grand gestures at all, even empty ones."

The words cut, drove Jasper to his feet. "Look—"

"But." Rachel silenced him with one upheld hand. "The good news for both of you is that some women are stubborn. Even if they know when to give up, they can't quite seem to do it. So there's hope for you yet."

"Oh, there is, is there?" Dallas set his beer aside and returned to the dismantled bike. "It's good to see you have us both all figured out."

"Of course I do. You're not me."

He barked out a laugh. "Yeah. Easy from the outside, huh? Talk about nothing to lose."

"I never said I wasn't a hypocrite." She slid off the bench and bumped Jasper with her hip until he wrapped an arm around her shoulders. "Find me a prince, boys, and I'll be too blissfully happy to bust your balls."

"Ace is as princely as he's getting, doll."

Merciless teasing, and Rachel blushed so deeply that Jasper almost felt sorry for her.

Almost. He kissed the top of her head. "You had that coming."

"I know," she grumbled.

Rachel could be hotheaded, but she was also a damn good judge of people. And if she was willing to stake that judgment on the fact that, whatever else, Noelle might not hate him...

And Jasper's sin?

The hollow ache in his chest throbbed and expanded. The past week had been a miserable haze of work and not much else, a bleak snapshot of how barren the rest of his life could be.

Not making any grand gestures at all.

If he had a shot, he had to try. And if Noelle Cun-ningham wanted a grand gesture, she'd get the grandest fucking gesture he could find.

21

F OR THE FIRST time in her life, Noelle had a space of her own, and she took great satisfaction in turning it into a glorious, cluttered mess.

Dallas had offered her the run of the dusty storage room, which had proved to be packed to the ceiling with furniture undoubtedly acquired through dubious means. Some of it was as elegantly understated as anything in Lex's rooms, and Noelle had avoided every piece that could have possibly belonged in Eden.

Instead, she chose the outrageous and the downright outdated, pairing a massive four-poster bed with a sleekly modern couch and a delicately carved vanity from a previous century. The colors clashed even more when she buried the furniture in mismatched pillows and threw her clothes over every surface with rebellious glee.

It wasn't a stage set for seduction. It wasn't anything

approaching stylish. But it was *hers*, from top to bottom, and the ability to close the world away on the other side of that door was a revelation.

Of course, the mess made receiving visitors awkward. She'd just finished braiding her hair when the door rattled under an abrupt knock, and she had to yell, "Give me a minute!" before gathering up an armful of new lingerie and shoving it into the closet.

Breathless, she wrenched open the door to find Jasper standing there, a paper-wrapped parcel under one arm. "Hi."

Just that. Just *hi*, and even after two weeks apart, his voice hit her in the gut and left shivers in its wake. It made her own voice husky. "Jasper. Hi."

His gaze traced her face, and he swallowed hard. "Can I come in?"

Only Lex had been past the threshold of her new domain, but if she denied Jasper access, she'd feel craven. Stepping aside, she held the door open. "It's a little messy. I had a late night..."

"Working. I know." He walked in and paused in the middle of the room to look around. "It's nice."

"Thank you." She didn't want his approval. Didn't want to believe it was sincere, and didn't want the warmth it kindled in her belly. And if she told herself that enough times, maybe it would become true.

"It looks like you," he murmured, then looked down at the package in his hands. "I brought you something, because we need to talk."

"All right." Once she'd shut the door, she shoved aside a stack of clothing on the couch, clearing a space for him. "You can sit, if you want."

He stopped her with a hand on her arm. "No, I'm okay."

The weakness inside her threatened to crack open and swallow her whole. She wanted to melt into his touch, melt into *him*, and God, it was supposed to get better. She eased her arm away and turned to the side table. "Do you want a drink, then? I have whiskey and rum."

"I was wrong," Jasper blurted. "Rachel's right—I'm a dickhead."

Noelle froze. "I'm sorry?"

"I shouldn't have tried to make you go back to Eden." His brows drew together in a stormy frown. "You were miserable there. Why the hell would you ever want to go through that again?"

She was so surprised by his words that she responded with the truth. "I wouldn't. I didn't."

"No shit." He held out the parcel. "Take it. I got it for you."

She closed her fingers around the package out of reflex, the brown paper crumpling in her grip. "Jasper, you don't need to do this..."

"I want you to give me a chance," he said firmly.

Her heart lurched painfully. "A chance at what? What do you want?"

His fingers tangled in her hair, but relaxed and slipped away without closing. "I want you."

How many times had she heard those words in her dreams, memories mixed with a yearning fantasy that left her empty and wanting? "You had me," she whispered, clutching the package. "And you didn't just let me go. You shoved me away."

Jasper nodded. "I did. I'm sorry. I think..." He looked away. "I didn't believe you were mine."

"I was." She watched his profile, drinking in the sight of his face when she knew her next words might drive him away. "But I'm not anymore. I belong to myself, and I'm not going to give that up casually again."

"I know. I don't expect you to. That's what the..." He gestured to the square package. "I got that."

Since he was watching her expectantly, she had no choice but to edge a finger under the wrapping and tear it open. Inside was a framed painting every bit as intricate as the one hanging in Lex's spare room, if half the size. Staring at the swooping brushstrokes, it was impossible for Noelle not to think about Lex, stashing gift after gift in a room full of baubles because Dallas kept trying to buy her affection.

The painting must have cost a fortune, but money was easy to come by as an O'Kane. A couple weeks of dancing had taught her that. "It's beautiful," she began, rubbing her thumb along the beveled edge of the frame, "but I don't need—"

"It's for Ace," Jasper cut in. "But you need to have it. Hang on to it 'til you're ready for us to make the trade. *If* you get ready."

Her confusion only deepened, though suspicion stirred in her gut, the first whisper of anticipation. Surely he didn't mean— "Trade for what?"

All his attention was focused on her mouth, and he stepped closer. "He won't take money for that ink," Jasper murmured, lifting his thumb to her throat. "Not for marks."

Marks. *Jasper's* marks. She shivered, and this time her nipples tightened, along with the rest of her body. Arousal sizzled both at the touch of his skin *and* the thought of a claim as permanent as the one wound around her wrists. Dallas had shown her the strength of that claim. Not many things were sacred in the sectors, but ink was a promise.

A promise Jasper was offering.

"You want to mark me?" She had to ask the question because she had to hear the words from his lips, blunt and unmistakable.

"I want to mark you." He drove his fingers into her hair again, and this time he nearly crushed the painting between them as he bent his head and captured her lips in a blistering kiss.

It was everything she'd been missing and more. The strength in his grip, the hot slide of his tongue, the way he worked her mouth open with strokes that demanded with steely gentleness. She wanted to give in, to bend to his unspoken command and glory in the bliss of submission.

She might have, too, if she hadn't felt the familiar flicker of shame. If she buckled now, the doubt would always be there, the knowledge that she'd betrayed herself out of fear and insecurity. She needed time, and she needed him to want her enough to fight for her.

Or wait for her.

It took every scrap of self-control to pull away. "I need to think," she gasped, which wasn't the most graceful way to say it, but if she didn't get the words out, she'd kiss him again and be lost.

He chased after her and licked her bottom lip. "Think. Yeah, all right."

She hadn't realized she'd been braced for frustration or anger until he gave her neither. "You're sure? You—you'll wait?"

He was panting, heavy breaths falling warm on her cheek. "All things considered, it only seems fair." Then he smiled. "I'd wait even if it wasn't."

The wicked curve of his lips rocketed her heart into her throat. So much promise. So much beautiful, filthy promise, and she couldn't stop herself from asking. "And if I say yes? How far will you take me?"

"As far as you want to go," he whispered. "No, all the way. I'm finished with limits."

It was her turn to stare at his mouth. She wanted to claim his lips, to kiss him again, just once, and if she did, she'd never stop. "I'll think," she said, stepping back before she could do something reckless. "I promise."

Jasper took a deep breath. "Think. Then come talk to me."

Holding the painting against her chest as a shield, she nodded. "I will. But you should go now."

"Because you don't trust me to keep my hands to myself?"

He was teasing her, and that was the part she'd missed most of all. Her lips twitched, and she had to fight to press them into a stern line. "Of course you will. You may not have noticed, but I've learned how to say *no*. Thanks to Lex, I'm getting pretty good at it."

"I've noticed." He rubbed his knuckles over her collarbone.

Noelle batted his hand away. "I'm saying it now. No, Jasper. I need time *and* space." Mostly because without the space, she'd never make herself take the time—but she wouldn't give him the satisfaction of admitting it. O'Kane men were already universally overconfident.

His discontented rumble melted into a sigh, and he held up both hands. "I'm going. You know where to find me."

She nodded, clamping down on the surge of panic that threatened. Watching him walk away would hurt, but she needed him to go. She needed to trust that he would come back. "I'll see you around."

He paused at the door, his hand on the knob, and smiled at her. "We're bound to run into each other, Noelle."

It was dangerous to tease, but she couldn't resist. "Especially if you keep showing up for my acts."

"It makes for a damn nice view, I've got to give you that." Jasper pulled open the door but paused just over the threshold. "Sweet dreams."

Noelle smiled in return, but when the door closed behind him, she collapsed onto the bed, cradling the painting in both hands as his words echoed through her mind in an endless refrain.

I'm finished with limits.

Oh, she'd have dreams all right, but *sweet* wouldn't begin to describe them, and he knew it.

She'd wanted him to fight for her. What she should have realized was that Jasper would fight dirty. *I want to mark you.* Not a fling. Not an affair, or even a collar. She'd wanted commitment, and he'd upped the ante. Everything, forever, if she could trust him.

If she could let herself trust him.

Two days of thinking brought no clarity, though Noelle had endured what felt like a month's worth of restless nights, drifting in and out of heated dreams in between long hours watching candlelight flicker across the ceiling. More than once, she'd almost rolled from the bed in search of Lex, but Lex...

God, it was disloyal to even think it, but Lex couldn't help her. Not with this.

One person could, which was why Noelle waited until Flash left to run an errand before knocking on the door of the suite he shared with Amira.

The petite brunette opened the door while stifling a yawn, and she waved Noelle inside. "I was wondering if you'd come around to see me."

"Does everyone know?" Not long ago, the thought would have made Noelle self-conscious, but now it only seemed...inevitable.

Amira shook her head as she waddled over to the couch, the curve of her belly more pronounced now than it had been just a few weeks earlier. "Secrets in a place like this? Never happen."

Noelle hovered until Amira was settled comfortably, then dropped beside her with a sigh. "I tried thinking on my own, but there's so much I still don't understand. And usually I'd just ask Lex, but..."

"But if she had it all figured out, she and Dallas wouldn't be at each other's throats half the time?"

"Lex has a lot of things figured out," Noelle replied, fighting the twinge of guilt. "I don't think surrender is one of them."

Amira waved that away. "Eh, goes both ways. It can't be on one person's shoulders. Give and take—that's what it's all about."

Noelle gestured to the ink swirling across Amira's throat. "Is that how you knew? The give and take worked?"

She seemed to consider that for a moment. "No, not really. I barely knew Flash was interested in me and suddenly, there he was, asking me to be his. All I really knew was that he'd do everything he could to make it work. I figured if I did the same, we'd be all right."

No clarity to be found there. Noelle sighed and slumped lower on the couch. "I've always wanted to give Jasper everything. The only thing that's changed is the reason why I'm afraid."

"So why *are* you afraid?"

Even admitting it made her chest ache. "He hurt me."

"Oh, Noelle." Amira's voice was filled with sympathy but tinged with wry humor. "He was a jerk, and he made a mistake. That's going to happen."

Her gut clenched as she thought of Dallas, pushing Lex until she lashed out and hurt herself. "All the time?"

"Of course not," Amira assured her. "But no one can hurt you more than someone you love. So I guess you have to ask yourself if it's worth the risk."

Noelle rubbed the heel of her hand over her breast-bone, as if that would soothe the pain that lingered in her chest. "Does it make us weak to forgive them?"

"No. Real forgiveness is damn hard, and you have to be strong to do it." Squinting, Amira tilted her head. "It's different from bowing down and taking shit from someone who treats you like crap."

"I was good at that. It's all I've ever been good at." She studied Amira for a moment, but her gaze was drawn inexorably to the ink, the mark around her throat that said she belonged to Flash, and Flash belonged to her. "He wants to mark me," she whispered. "He brought me this painting... Something Ace would want, I guess. He said he'd wait for me to decide."

"Okay. What do *you* want?"

"I want him. But I want to be sure that..." Trailing off, she reached for Amira's hand. "There's a middle ground, right? Between taking shit and turning into Lex and Dallas?"

Amira hesitated and then shook her head. "You lost me. I can't put those two things on a spectrum because I don't see the connection."

"The way they argue—" Noelle dug her teeth into her lip and tried to give voice to the uncertainty inside her. "Sometimes, watching Lex... She never stops pushing back against him. It makes me wonder if I'm weak for not wanting to fight all the time."

"Oh, sweetie. That's just Dallas and Lex. Maybe they'll get better when they figure out their shit, and maybe they'll always be that way." Amira shrugged. "Maybe they love it, who knows? You and Jasper aren't *them*."

No, they weren't. Lex had helped drag Noelle out of the numbness of her old self, but that didn't mean Noelle had to walk the same path. Even Lex might not want her to—that was what this newly acquired freedom was, after all. A chance for Noelle to decide who she wanted to be.

Which stripped away one set of worries, but left the

same nagging hurt, the one she could bury in words and excuses and rationalizations and never drown.

Jasper had hurt her. Whether through good intentions or carelessness, it didn't matter. He'd crushed something fragile, and while doing it had damaged her trust. She couldn't close her eyes and believe that he'd always know what she needed, that he'd always be there, giving it to her, no questions asked.

But maybe it had been the wrong sort of trust. Open, passive trust, the kind that was reckless to give and easy to shatter. The girl who'd been thrown through the gates of Eden had trusted blindly because she hadn't had any other choice. That kind of trust meant as little as one more *yes* from someone who never said *no.*

This time would be harder. She'd have to trust Jasper, knowing he was human. Knowing he could hurt her, even when he didn't mean to. She'd have to trust that he'd do his best, and make amends when his best wasn't enough.

She'd have to trust herself to tell him when she needed something he couldn't possibly know to give.

"You're right," she whispered, squeezing Amira's hand. "Forgiveness is hard. And scary."

"Hell yeah, it is. But what's the alternative?"

"Being without them, I guess."

"Yeah." Amira dropped her head to the back of the couch and grinned. "And that's definitely not worth it."

Noelle laughed. "No, they have their appeal. Even when they're grumpy. Maybe especially when they're grumpy."

"Mmm, that they are."

"So. Speaking of worth it..." She flashed Amira a smile. "The fighting is awful. How's the making-up part?"

Amira shifted onto her side and wrapped one hand around her belly. "I'm three miles wide and look like I'm smuggling basketballs, and you're asking me this question?"

"You look beautiful. You look *happy*." Noelle pressed a hand to Amira's. "That's why you're the one to ask."

It made the other woman blush. "I haven't figured out any grand, cosmic secrets, Noelle. I love Flash. This is where I want to be, that's all."

It might not sound profound to her, but to Noelle it was a simple, beautiful truth. All that mattered was where she wanted to be—in the sectors, with the O'Kanes.

With Jasper.

He wasn't the only one who had to be willing to fight for it.

22

T HIS TIME, SHE'D had an afternoon's leisure to plan
her seduction, and in the end she discarded seduction altogether. Drowning their pain in sex might be the
least awkward way to smooth the tensions between
them, but this was too important. This would be the
foundation, the way they learned to deal with inevitable
fights. Words needed to come first. If they were the right
ones, sex would happen on its own, whether she was
dressed in lacy panties or a burlap sack.

Not that she went that far. But she felt just as sexy
in a tight tank top and vintage, pre-Flare jeans as she
ever had in the skimpy little dress she'd borrowed from
Lex for that first party. It was the ink, she thought as
she paused outside of Jasper's door, her hand raised to
knock. Staring at the O'Kane logo and the intricate framing was a reminder of what she could be. Sexual.

Powerful.

Brave enough to forgive. Dragging in a breath, she knocked.

"Ow, shit." Jasper's voice drifted through the door. "Come in."

Frowning, Noelle pushed open the door only to stop dead at the sight of Jasper with a kitten perched on his shoulder, its tiny claws latched into his beard. Judging by the scratches on his cheek, it wasn't the first time.

He winced as he detached the mewling kitten from his face. "I called in a favor from the farm. It got here yesterday, and I think it hates me."

"I don't know, it seems to like you." Belatedly, she entered the room and closed the door behind her. The kitten proved her point by trying to claw its way back up to the crook of Jasper's neck. "Maybe it likes your beard."

"Fuck." He pulled its tiny claws free again and curled the kitten up in both hands. "That means it likes me? What the hell would it do if it didn't?"

"I'm not sure. Maybe pee on you?" She crossed to where he stood and stroked her finger over the kitten's head. "Is it a boy or a girl? Do you know?"

Jasper's ears turned red. "I told them to send you a good mouser."

That constant ache in her chest bloomed, expanding until she had to swallow around a lump in her throat. "It's for me?"

"Yeah." His glower softened. "I was going to give it to you with the painting, but there was a delay, and I couldn't wait on the other thing."

The kitten was an adorable bundle of orange fur with a squished little face and tiny teeth that closed on the tip of Noelle's finger in a playful bite. Her heart lurched again, and she pretended it was because she'd fallen in love with a little fuzzy ball of fluff. "Can I hold it?"

"Let's say it's a he." He gently shifted the kitten over

to her hands. "I haven't done the best job of this, have I?" Delicate claws scraped her palms as the kitten meowed and twisted. Noelle lifted him higher, nuzzled the soft little head with a cooing noise. "You got me a kitten."

"An apology," he whispered, watching her. "I'm sorry I tried to make you go back to the city."

Swallowing, she cuddled the kitten closer. "Explain it to me. Tell me why."

"You got shot, sweetheart. I wasn't thinking about anything else. I wanted to put you someplace where it wouldn't happen again." He rubbed his hands over his face and dropped to the sofa. "The whole damn thing made me a little nuts."

The wrong thing for the right reasons, then, and in her gut she'd known it all along. Jasper wanted to protect her, he just didn't know what scared her more than death.

So she told him. "I'd rather be shot. I'd rather be shot a dozen times. Maybe for someone else, someone with a less important family, Eden isn't all bad. My body would be safe there, but my soul would die. And I'm still learning what it's like to be alive."

"I know." He gestured helplessly to the cat. "I thought about all the things you'd told me about your life there, and I realized how idiotic I'd been."

The kitten bumped his head against her chin, and Noelle gave in to the smile fighting to form. "I should have told you. I guess I...wanted you to know. I wanted you to know what I needed, but maybe you couldn't understand that what I needed was you."

Jasper held her gaze, his eyes blazing. Intense. "Do you need me?"

She wet her lips. "I can survive without you, but it's only that. Surviving. I want to live."

He released a breath, sudden and relieved, and held out one hand. "Get over here."

"So demanding." Noelle cradled the kitten to her chest as she slid into Jasper's lap. "I think this little guy likes me. Or he's worn out from doing battle with you."

Jasper wrapped his arms around her. "You're a better person than I am. Animals are supposed to be able to sense shit like that, right?"

"I think you're pretty okay." With a final nuzzle, she set the kitten down on the couch. He spent a brief, adorable moment being distracted by his own tail before burrowing half under a battered pillow. Laughing, Noelle pressed her lips to Jasper's scratched cheek. "Talk to me next time. If things get intense, promise you'll talk, and I promise I'll listen."

He stroked his thumb over her cheek, the corner of her mouth. "Is this you, saying yes?"

"If you promise." She kissed his thumb. "I'll trust you with everything, Jasper. But if I'm going to be that vulnerable, you have to promise you'll always be there. No walking away and leaving me naked. Literally or metaphorically."

His voice was raw. "I promise."

"Okay." The word floated from her lips, and she felt light. "Okay. Yes."

She barely heard his low growl as he dragged her mouth to his. She *felt* it, felt his chest vibrating when he edged her lips apart with his tongue. No mercy, no hesitation, just him, inside her in not nearly enough ways. Groaning, she tangled her fingers into his hair and bit the tip of his tongue.

Jasper bit her back as the kitten wiggled between them. He broke the kiss and swept up the tiny animal. "Put him in the bathroom. I have something else for you."

It took her a few tries to detach the kitten from her shirt, but his yowling protests cut off abruptly when she set him down in front of the small bowl of food in the bathroom.

She eased the door shut to avoid distracting him, and turned to find Jasper holding two strips of leather padded with velvet.

Her heart damn near kicked its way out of her chest. Anticipation tickled up her spine, and she took two steps toward him. "Those are for me?"

"Mmm." He shook them, rattling the buckles. "Know what they are?"

"I think I can guess." She stroked the soft velvet and smiled, imagining how it would feel against her wrists...or ankles. "Cuffs?"

Jasper trailed each section of leather between his finger and thumb as he explained. "This longer one buckles around your upper thighs. The shorter one around your wrists."

"Oh..." Even imagining it tightened her body. Bound, helpless. Open to him. Trust, again, and she offered it by smiling as she toyed with her shirt, edging it up just far enough to flash skin at him. "Are you going to teach me about make-up sex?"

He shook his head. "I'm going to show you what it means to be mine, with nothing held back."

His. No shame, just anticipation and a thrilling tremor of something almost like nerves. Not fear, just the understanding that Jasper would push her beyond herself, beyond anything she'd known.

And she'd love it.

Noelle closed the distance between them and rose on her toes to kiss him. "Do I get to be bad?"

He licked her lip and wove a hand in her hair. "If you're willing to pay the price for it."

Even that was sweet heat, the softness of his mouth and the roughness of his hand a beautiful contrast. "What's the price?"

Velvet and leather brushed the back of her hand, and he drew the open cuffs up her arm. "Say yes and find out."

"Yes." She pressed closer, rubbed her tight nipples against his chest, and groaned her assent. "*Yes.*"

Jasper dropped the cuffs on the bed and kissed her, already moving his hands over her clothes. Pushing up her shirt to meet her waiting hands, and then moving on to the button on her jeans. They had to pull apart to get her tank top over her head, but her lips found his again as she twisted her arms behind her back to open her bra.

He shoved her jeans and panties down, and for a giddy moment Noelle imagined hard, fast sex, Jasper slamming her into the wall and plowing into her, but she should have known better.

Jasper always took his time.

Her back hit the bed, and he leaned over to strip off her shoes. "Second thoughts?"

"Maybe I'm wishing I'd brought my new jewelry..."

He yanked off her jeans and panties and dropped them on the floor. "You don't need it. I want you just like this. Ink and leather."

She inched up the bed, squirming when he loomed over her. He blocked out the room when he did, his broad shoulders filling her vision. "So is that what you want me to wear to Dallas's next party? Cuffs and ink?"

"We'll see." He buckled a band of leather around one thigh, then the other, and waited for her to hold out her wrists.

So serious. Biting her lower lip to hide her smile, Noelle moved her arms into place, savoring the soft slide of velvet as he buckled the cuffs.

"Now you're stuck." Jasper teased the tip of one finger over her hipbone before twining his fingers with hers and lifting her arms up and out. With those cuffs tethered to the ones on her thighs, the movement drew her legs apart. Wide open.

She drew in a ragged breath, tensing in spite of herself as his gaze drifted over her. That first thrill still hit her, the vulnerability of being bared to him, the illicitness and the pleasure. "I don't mind."

Her thighs trembled under his touch, even more when he bent his head, his beard tickling as he dropped openmouthed kisses to her skin. Slow, hot, the heat of his tongue and the scratch of his beard. She tried to press her thighs together and growled when the short chains snapped tight. "Jas..."

He ignored the plea as he licked his way to the top of her thigh. "You're wet."

"Of course I am." His breath ghosted over her, and she choked on another moan. Maybe if she begged with all the dirty words, he'd forget whatever torment he had planned and *touch* her already. "I'm so wet. Please, can I have your—your tongue in my pussy?"

"No." He spread her wide and circled the tip of his tongue lightly around her clit instead. Pleasure jolted up her spine, lifting her hips even as she cried out.

"That's a start," he whispered, then began to explore her pussy, tracing every fold, slow and firm. She was panting in minutes, tugging restlessly against the leather cuffs as he coaxed her body to painful, trembling arousal.

But not over the edge. Noelle raised her head and lost herself in the sight of him, bent over her, so intense, his fingers parting her, opening her for the lash of his tongue.

Erotic overload. Groaning, she dug her head back against the bed. "I'm never going to get to pay the price if you won't let me be bad."

Jasper laughed and turned his head. Bit her thigh. "This *is* the price. On the edge, Noelle, for as long as I damn well please."

She tried to close her legs and only managed to crush her knees against his shoulders. "Oh, God."

Again, deeper this time, his tongue thrusting inside her before dipping back out to flick her clit. She might have come then, if he'd kept up the pressure, but he retreated as she started to tense, easing back only to begin the slow exploration again.

And again.

The third time his tongue darted away from her clit just before release broke over her, she lost control of her tongue. With pleasure a throbbing, frustrating ache, the words barely registered as they tripped from her lips, begging and hoarse. "Let me come, please... I'll do anything, anything if you just—just—"

He flipped her onto her stomach, her cheek pressed against the blanket as the click of a buckle and the slither of leather broke through the fevered haze of blood pounding in her ears. One breath, two, and then his belt cracked against her skin, drowning pleasure in a momentary sting of pain.

Her body reeled at the sudden shock. It hurt more than his hand or the crop had, and Noelle sucked in a confused breath only to lose it in a groan as the belt hit her again, burning a stripe of fire across her ass. It was like the tattoos, sharp pain that built into something else, something hotter that left her squirming.

The third stroke drew everything tight. The fourth made her cry out. One more agonizing slap of leather and the throbbing of her blood in her ears expanded. She was throbbing everywhere, pulsing and tensing, *clenching*, and it had built so inexorably that she could do nothing but groan as heat burst through her, the sweet relief of an orgasm so intense she tried to muffle her screams against the blankets.

The sting faded into a warmth that unfurled slowly, an afterburn both soothed and urged on by Jasper's hands rubbing over her back and ass. He bent low, his now-naked chest pressed against her skin as he nudged her hair aside with his nose and murmured into her ear. "Beautiful."

She shivered and rubbed her cheek against his, still floating. "You like me like this?"

His teeth scraped her earlobe. "I love you like this."

Love.

Drunk on the word, she laughed. "Would you love me with my lips around your cock?"

"Yes." Jasper rose and pulled her upright to sit on the edge of the bed. He shed his jeans and gripped his cock. "Want it? Take it."

She started to reach for him and laughed again when her wrists snapped to a halt, tethered by chains she'd almost forgotten. He watched her, one large hand wrapped around his shaft, and at another time it might be beautiful to watch him stroke himself to release.

Today—today it was *her* turn to torment.

Flicking her gaze up to his, she leaned forward and extended her tongue, touching only the tip of it to the flared crown. A slow lick brought the taste of him into her, salty and musky and intense. "Like this?"

He urged her mouth wide with his thumb on her jaw. "Open up, sweetheart."

She obeyed—but not without a teasing retort. "You love to tell me that."

"Hell yeah." Gripping her hair, he teased the head of his cock past her lips, over her tongue...then deeper. Over and over, pausing to let her lick his cock as he groaned.

His next advance drove him against the back of her throat, and his fingers tightened on her skull, gentle but unyielding steel holding her in place as she struggled to relax, to ignore her body's instinctive response and savor the darker one, the should-be-shameful pleasure to be had in submitting to his whims.

She choked—*gagged*—and he eased back with a shudder. "Again," he commanded, but he didn't thrust forward. He waited for her to come to him, cupping her head as she took him as deep as she could.

Not all the way, not this time. And as if she'd proved her willingness by coming to him, his fingers tightened. She only had the chance to make an encouraging noise before he was pushing forward once more, choking her with his cock as her pussy clenched around aching emptiness.

Two heartbeats. Three. Jasper drew back, gliding his fist over his slick shaft. "Do you want me to fuck you?"

She wanted so much. She wanted everything, and for the first time she truly believed that was exactly what she'd get. Everything she craved, everything she needed. Heart pounding, she watched him stroke his cock with his broad fingers and gave him raw truth. "I want you inside me, any way I can have you."

He lifted her against him and spun, pressing her to the wall. "When I mark you—" The shaking words cut off as he drove into her with one long, hard thrust. "I want more than your throat. I want the ink all the way across your shoulders." With his hips pinning her in place, he lifted one hand to trace a meandering line across her collarbone and down to her upper arm.

With her legs wrapped around his body, the chains had just enough give to allow her to touch his sides. She scraped her nails along his skin, marking him in her own way as her body pulsed around the unforgiving steel of his erection. "You might need to get Ace another painting."

Jasper's eyes went dark, his pupils dilating as he ground deeper. "I'll think of something." His fingers slipped around to tease at the back of her neck. "Down your spine?"

The thought made her groan. "Only if you want to fuck me right there in Ace's chair."

He cupped her ass and lifted her higher. "Maybe

we'll take turns."

She wanted to reply, but the new angle was too sharp, driving his cock up into her with an intensity that scrambled her thoughts. Pleasure was building again, the kind that would wipe everything else away but the driving need to shatter that tension, and she was utterly helpless. Pinned between him and the wall, caught in his grip, her hands trapped. She couldn't even get the leverage to *move*, only to squirm.

"That's right." He rocked his hips in a short thrust, then backed away from the wall, kept moving until his legs hit the bed. He sat down and then lay back with Noelle on top of him. "This is what you were trying to do—ride my cock."

Still gasping for breath, she dug her fingernails into her own thighs and shifted experimentally. It might have been easier if she could have braced her hands against his chest, but there was something more intoxicating about having control—almost. The velvet and leather shackled her, a constant reminder of his power even as she claimed her own, lifting her hips only to drive down, taking him deep and hard, just how she wanted him.

Jasper met the next desperate rock with a rough noise. Instead of guiding her hips, urging her on, he slipped his fingers up her thigh, past the leather, to center on her clit. "Come on me."

Her hips jerked. Her rhythm faltered. It shouldn't have been so easy to haul her back up to that edge, but he had a way of touching her, the calloused tips of his fingers circling rough and fast, building up friction that rocketed through her in jolts that came closer and closer together.

In moments she'd lost her thrusts entirely, settling into a grinding rock that did more to rub her clit against his fingers. "Jas," fell from her lips, again and again, each time more breathless, but as the tension twisted tighter his name twisted, turned to *yes, yes, yes*—

When her body seized, throwing her into the bliss of release, even that word was beyond her. She cried out—groaned, moaned, *screamed*—coming so hard the blood throbbed in her ears and she could barely hear her own voice.

He took over then, gripping her hips and pounding into her. It kept her up when she might have floated down, twisted her straight into another orgasm so fierce and powerful it ached. His short fingernails dug into her skin, quick flashes of pain that traveled to her lower back, higher, his hands scrabbling as if he could draw her closer.

"*Noelle.*" A curse and a prayer. Jasper arched, his muscles rigid as he shuddered beneath her, pumping his release.

She slumped forward when he stilled, and he caught her and lowered her to his chest with more gentleness than she would have managed. With her ear pressed to his skin she could hear the racing of his heart, as quick and frantic as her own, and she closed her eyes and drifted on the peace of being his.

After long moments of silence broken by nothing but their ragged breathing, Jasper's chest heaved under her cheek in a sigh. "I meant it, you know."

Her thoughts were so scattered that it took a moment to understand. But only a moment. It had been there all along, seething underneath her skin, the truth that had made everything that much more intense, that much brighter.

I love you like this.

I love you...

Turning her head, she pressed an openmouthed kiss to the skin above his heart. "I don't know anything about love. But I've never felt..." She trailed off and lifted her head. "I've never *felt*. Not until you."

"Then I have a lot to show you, don't I?"

She tried to lean up to reach his lips, but her arms were still trapped, and she found herself oddly reluctant to do anything that might change that. Instead she nuzzled his throat. "If love is trust and need and always feeling better when I'm with you...I love you."

"Good," he said gruffly. Then he kissed her, soft and lingering. "How long do you want to wait to get your marks?"

"Until my knees aren't so wobbly?"

Jasper laughed. "It takes a little longer than that, sweetheart. First, we have to ask Dallas."

That made her frown, though she doubted he would protest. "He gets a say?"

"This is Sector Four," Jasper reminded her gently.

Of course. Apparently Dallas got a say in everything that happened, from sweeping political grandstanding to the quiet moments between two people. Though maybe she shouldn't begrudge him that, when he clearly took the responsibility seriously. "All right. So we ask Dallas. And then what?"

"Then we go see Ace, get your marks. And when they're all done and healed up, we show them off to the rest of the gang."

"A party?"

"Mmm. Let everyone know we belong to each other." Jasper tilted her head up and studied her. "Do you want me marked too?"

Her ink on his skin. Her mark, as permanent and undeniable as the one he'd place on her. "Yes. Even if I have to pay Ace for it myself."

A grin. "Nah. In this case, I think he'll kick it in for free."

"Maybe, if he's hoping for another show. Or a chance to play." She rested her chin on his chest and watched his face. "I don't care either way, you know. Whether you let other people touch me, or don't, it was never about them. Ace, Dallas... It doesn't matter who's touching me. It's hot because of you."

"I know." He stroked the delicate skin at the base of her throat. "I always knew."

She couldn't help but smile. "That doesn't mean I don't still like how...illicit it feels. Maybe I should be ashamed of that, but I don't think I am. You like me this way."

He arched an eyebrow and tightened his hand ever so slightly around her neck.

Blood singing, Noelle closed her eyes and savored the gentle steel grip, savored its warning and its promise. A lifetime without shame, because of the words that tripped from her lips, the truth he'd demanded.

The only truth that mattered now. "You love me this way."

ABOUT KIT

Kit Rocha is actually two people—Bree & Donna, best friends who are living the dream. They get paid to work in their pajamas, talk on the phone, and write down all the stories they used to make up in their heads.

Beyond Shame is their first dystopian erotic romance. They also write paranormal romance as Moira Rogers.

ACKNOWLEDGMENTS

Without certain key people—and there are many—this book never could have existed. We owe a round to the following:

Vivian Arend, Alisha Rai, Edie Harris, Ann Aguirre, and Lillie Applegarth, who all read this book in its various stages.

Sharon Muha, for having the sharpest eyes we've ever seen.

Sasha Knight and Anne Scott, the best editors we've ever had.

Courtney Milan, for being brilliant and fixing our cover.

Eliza Gayle, for sharing so much of her knowledge.

Keith Melton, because he's awesome.

And the LTSNBN, for being the best sekrit organization a couple of girls could hope to claim they don't belong to.

Turn the page
for a sneak peek at

1

T HE NIGHT WAS on fire. Lex could smell it, wood smoke and plastic burning in barrels and trash heaps. Gas, coal—anything that would take flame and light up the darkness.

A shatter of glass accompanied by victorious shouts echoed close by, maybe only three or four narrow streets over, and Lex lifted a hand instinctively to the pistol nestled under her jacket. It was the worst thing about these nights, the crime that swept through like a plague when the sectors went dark. People stole without thought or discrimination. Being disgusted by that might have made her a hypocrite, except that she never did either.

There was nothing *elegant* about looting.

The marketplace had been stripped of its wares, and the stalls stood like skeletons in the moonlight as she wound her way through the narrow street. Smart of the vendors to take their goods home with them, because boards and locks wouldn't keep out prying hands, not on a night like this.

Lex ducked into the alley behind Walt Misham's shop, sidestepped a pile of rotting trash, and knocked on the dented metal door.

Chains rattled on the other side before a rough voice challenged her. "Whoever it is, you should know I'm armed."

"I should hope so, Walt," she shot back. "Let me in."

The door creaked open an inch. "Lex? What the hell are you doing out on a night like this?"

"Business," she answered. He peered at her, one rheumy blue eye appearing out of the darkness, and she tilted her head to meet his gaze. "I finally got my hands on something you've been looking for."

"Let me see it."

Lex shoved her hands in her jacket pockets and squinted at him. "You know better. Mad's bringing it. He's on his way."

Walt's bark of laughter turned into a wracking cough as he pulled open the door far enough for Lex to slip inside. She had to ease carefully past a six-foot stack of crates in one corner, and a jagged wooden edge still snagged her hair.

She yanked it loose and followed Walt deeper into the back room of the shop. "You'll be glad to get out of here, I bet."

"Past time, to be sure." His breathing was raspy, and he led her toward a candlelit table before lowering himself heavily to his chair. "If these blackouts don't kill me first."

"The solar converter will help." She sat across from him and studied his face, which was heavily lined and shadowed in the dim light. "I tested it this afternoon, so it should be fully charged. You can try it out tonight."

His lips twitched. "If I meet your asking price, of course. You'd best give me a good deal, girl, if you want me around to buy your stolen goods."

"You're not my only customer," Lex drawled. "Still, it'd be a shame not to have you screeching at people in the market."

"Don't tease an old man, Lex." He grunted as he lift-ed a lockbox onto the table. "Name your price—unless you'd like to trade."

"Ten." A few grand less than she could get elsewhere, maybe, but Walt had cut her plenty of deals in the past based on her association with Dallas. Besides, it seemed wrong to play hardball over something like this. A pretty bauble, sure, but not a legitimate medical need.

Walt groused—he always groused—but fumbled with the lock on the box. "You want cash or clean credits?"

"Half and half. And bust the credits up onto a couple of different sticks."

A hollow knock sounded on the front door as Walt pried open the box. "Drag your young body over there and let your friend in, if that's him. I'll load up your creds."

"Cranky ass." But Lex crossed the room and peeked out the dirty window. "It's him."

It took a solid minute to disengage all the locks and chains, but Mad didn't seem impatient. He smiled as if the night weren't alive with the threat of violence and held up a crinkled brown paper bag. "Old man willing to deal?"

"I'm very persuasive." She opened the door far enough to admit him, then glanced around the square outside before securing the locks again. "Show the man what he's bought, Mad."

"The finest tech money can't buy." Maddox was near-ly twice Lex's size, but he moved with deceptive grace, claiming a chair across from Walt. "I'll have you know, old timer, that these aren't available to private owners. City-issue, strictly reserved for councilmen and military police. I still don't know how Lex managed to find one, but it's a thing of beauty."

"Never you mind how I found it." *Stole it,* she corrected silently. Not that it mattered.

Walt's gnarled hands shook as he reached for his breathing device. "Flex those clever fingers, girl, and help me hook it up. If it works, the money's yours."

Walt's assisted breathing device delivered oxygen through a simple set of nasal tubes. The complicated part was the apparatus itself, a small black box that worked as a conductive purifier. The small intake drew air in, filtered it, and both isolated and concentrated the oxygen content. It worked without power, but barely any more efficiently than simply breathing.

Lex slipped one of the small rechargeable battery cells from the solar converter and fit it into the slot Walt indicated. A tiny light on the side of the purifier flashed blue and then a solid green, and an almost imperceptible hiss filled the room as Lex helped Walt loop the tubes over his ears and fit the points into his nostrils.

Walt closed his eyes and inhaled deeply. Mad watched them both, a tiny smile curving his lips. "See, old man? Tech so smooth it's almost magic."

"Hush," Walt grumbled in between more of those deep, relieved breaths. "This one, Lex—he has no trouble getting air, and he wastes it on so many words. Does he ever stop talking?"

"Nope." Mad talked all the time—and mostly, Lex suspected, to convince people he was simple. Shallow. "Don't let it fool you though, Walt. He's sharp."

Walt huffed. "The whole lot of you O'Kanes are sharp."

"That we are," she teased.

The old man squinted at her. "I heard Dallas had himself some trouble, though. Should I be worried about moving out to the edge of the sector? Is the place coming down around our ears?"

"No more so than usual." Lex gathered the cash and

credit sticks in one hand. "Anything else you're on the lookout for? Just in case I stumble across it?"

"I've got a new customer, a collector. He'll pay top credit for pre-Flare videos. Westerns, he wants. Cowboys and outlaws." Walt showed his disdain for that preference with a loud sniff. "Fools with more money than sense. But fools make my living, don't they?"

"We've all got our something." Some people wanted porn, others wanted priceless art. And others wanted vintage Clint Eastwood. "I might be able to scrounge up a few. Keep in touch."

Walt followed them back through the labyrinth of crates and boxes to the back door, and Lex lingered outside long enough to hear the click and scrape of every lock and chain. "Got plans?" she asked Mad, her hands in her pockets.

"That's what I was about to ask you." He nodded to her jacket. "I saw you got credits."

She still had her fingers wrapped around the paper and plastic in her pocket. She pulled out the handful and shoved it at him. "You and Doc can split it up. You know the drill."

"Doc's got a girl who can use some of this tonight," he murmured, folding the bills before dumping the credit chips into his pocket. "Pregnant. She almost drowned in the river trying to get out of Two before—"

Lex closed her eyes, as if doing so would shut out the words, as well. "It's better if I don't know, Mad."

"You're doing good work, honey, helping people who need it. Why don't you ever want to hear that?"

Because it wasn't her job. Because it wasn't enough. Because Dallas would make her stop—or worse, try to throw in with her and do more. "This is the way I want it."

"Ah, Lex. All right." Mad threw a friendly arm around her shoulders and tugged her to his side for a brief hug. "You gonna let me walk you back to the compound?"

"That wouldn't be very sneaky," she demurred. "I've got to slip by Dallas somehow. I'm not supposed to be out after dark."

"Well, be good and sneaky, then." He squeezed her shoulders. "I know you can take care of yourself, girl, but have some pity on the rest of us. Dallas roars around like a lion with a thorn in his paw when he thinks you've been putting yourself in harm's way."

She'd planned to wait until morning to run her errand. She'd tried, even, but in the end she just couldn't. "Was I supposed to let a sick man huff and puff all night just to keep Dallas from flipping his shit?"

"You snarl and snap all you want, Lex. I know your dirty secret." Mad laughed and poked her in the chest. "You have a heart."

Now *that* she couldn't let stand. She grabbed his finger and bent it back until he winced. "What I have is money, along with a tiny bit of a conscience. That's not the same thing."

"We live in the slums of paradise, dollface." Mad looked down at the O'Kane logo tattooed around her wrist—the same logo inked around both of his. "Do you know what the street value is on a *tiny* bit of conscience? Don't undersell it."

"I only have it because I can afford to." She hated the almost frantic edge that tinged the words. "If I couldn't, you'd better believe it'd be gone."

"You can afford it." His words were intent, a quiet answer to the desperation she wanted to hide. "You're an O'Kane. Hell, you're the next best thing to *the* O'Kane."

"Don't let him hear you say that." Lex took a step back, then another. "If Dallas finds out we were out tonight, do me a favor, huh? Don't tell him anything."

"You asking me to lie to the king of Sector Four?"

"Hell, no. Just keep some shit to yourself." She flashed Mad her most irreverent smile. "Buck up. I've been doing it for years, and I'm still kicking."

If Dallas O'Kane had an ounce less self-control, he'd have found a way to plant a tracker on Lex to preserve his peace of mind. The tech existed, though most people would have to give up eating for months to get their hands on it. In the four decades since the solar storms had obliterated life as humanity had known it, technology had become a luxury enjoyed by the privileged and the powerful—or those willing to cater to vices the powerful were privileged enough to be allowed to enjoy.

Dallas had gotten rich off other men's vices, for all that he allowed himself only a few. The fantasy of track-ing Lex was one of them. Eden was the morally righteous city of the future—they must have come up with a hun-dred ways to keep tabs on the many sins of their citizens.

Not that they needed to trouble themselves with cov-ert surveillance. The Council tracked their sheep right out in the open, like any self-respecting theocratic oligar-chy. No one dared to breathe a word of protest, even when the councilmen parked their intrusive little spy drones right up some poor bastard's ass.

Sometimes Dallas envied them the bliss of blind obe-dience. Sometimes.

Liar, whispered a taunting inner voice. Dallas ig-nored it and dropped the butt of his cigarette to the cracked pavement, grinding it under the heel of his boot. He was all but invisible in the shadow of the garage, but from here he had a good vantage point of the side gate. If Lex was going to sneak back into the O'Kane compound, this was the likeliest place.

Blind obedience would never be a problem for Dallas as long as Lex was around, so any tracking mechanism he planted on her would *have* to be covert. Something unobtrusive that could be sewn into her favorite leather jacket or those shit-kicking boots with the heels that made her legs go on forever.

If she found out, he'd be the one getting kicked, and the fantasy of Lex coming at him with violence and passion all twisted up was a vice he didn't have time to indulge.

But fuck, it was a hot fantasy.

The scuff of boots interrupted his reverie, and Jasper's face flared out of the darkness as he lit a cigarette. "Last shipment's on its way. We had to siphon one of the trucks for enough diesel to run the club's generators, but we managed to keep the lights on 'til closing."

"Good work." Keeping the club open on blackout nights was worth the hassle. Anyone who wasn't out looting or had finished lining their pockets showed up to watch the girls dance, or to pickle their livers on the lifeblood of Sector Four—O'Kane liquor. "How's your lady handling her first night without lights?"

"Noelle's all right. She doesn't love it, but hey. The sectors are already darker than Eden, right?"

"Damn near every day." Dallas reached into his vest for his battered cigarette case as he studied Jasper. His right-hand man had the easy smugness of a guy getting laid well and often, a fact Dallas might have resented more if Jasper and Noelle hadn't been willing, even eager, to include him in their sexual adventures.

But he wasn't the only one they included. And if Lex had drifted back into the compound through the main doors, Jasper's girl was the one most likely to know where she was. "Don't suppose Noelle's seen Lex?"

Jas shook his head. "Nah, not tonight. But I can let you know if she shows up at our place."

Dallas paused with his lighter open but unstruck. "Does that happen a lot?"

"Often enough." The corner of Jasper's mouth

quirked up. "Had to get a bigger bed."

There was a mental image to give any man a raging hard-on. Sleek, hungry Lex climbing into bed with dreamy-eyed Noelle. A sexy, gorgeous sector woman and a soft, curvy princess out of Eden, tangled together. Naked.

And Jasper, the lucky bastard, getting to have them both in his damn bed. "What a hardship," Dallas drawled. "Must be rough."

A creak interrupted his reply. "You bragging again, Jas?" Lex closed the side gate and fixed the man with a challenging look. "Whatever happened to not kissing and telling?"

"Guess I'm not as well-mannered as you thought." He grinned at Dallas as he turned back toward the garage. "Good night. To both of you."

Dallas took his time lighting his cigarette, waiting until the door shut behind Jasper to click his lighter closed. "I'm surprised you're not curled around Noelle right now. You know city folk don't like the dark."

"She has Jasper." Lex was dressed in head-to-toe black and zipped up all the way to her chin. "Besides, I was busy."

"Mmm, busy." Even though his eyes had adjusted to the dark, she was barely more than a shadow. He couldn't see her face or judge her expression, which would have been a disadvantage with anyone else. With Lex, it never mattered. She'd been trained from the cradle to show the world only what she wanted it to see. "We're not under lockdown anymore, love, but you picked a hell of a night to go for a stroll."

"I know. But I brought you something." She stepped into the center of the courtyard and held out her hand. Moonlight glinted off her hair and the small glass jar in her palm. "It's strawberry."

"Jam?" Something that cost more than liquor or tech. Fresh produce was always at a premium in the sectors, since it had to be lovingly cultivated in dry, scorched earth or shipped in from the rustic communes far beyond the city. "Where in hell did you find this?"

"I have my methods." She wiggled the jar teasingly. "Well, do you want it or not?"

Dallas caught the jar and her hand along with it, folding her fingers under his. "Tell me you had backup, Lex."

"I'm not dense, Dallas."

Dallas, not his given name. Not *Declan*, the two syllables he only heard from her. Tenderness and rage brought them forth, and it was no wonder he had a hard time separating the two. At least now he knew she wasn't completely pissed. Yet.

He could fix that. "Good. Then I won't take you over my knee for sneaking out."

She stiffened, and a rueful, almost mocking smile curved her lips. "I almost forgot. Property of Dallas O'Kane, whether I like it or not."

Yes. Not a civilized thought, but this wasn't a civilized world, and he'd never pretended to be a civilized man. Letting his cigarette fall to the ground, he snatched the jar out of her hand and twisted her wrist until the moonlight spilled over her tattoo cuffs with the O'Kane logo. "Damn straight, honey. You and everyone else."

"Me and everyone else," she echoed flatly.

He ran his thumb over the skull etched into her skin. "You regretting taking ink, love?"

"No." She hesitated. "But would it matter if I said yes?"

His blood chilled. "O'Kane for life, isn't that the promise?"

"From the day I first darkened your door." Lex tugged at her hand. "I'm tired. I want to go to bed."

Resisting the urge to ask whose bed, Dallas released her and took a step back. Personal space, it turned out, wasn't optional when it came to Lex and his self-control.